were missing. The doll had lost part of its hair as well, revealing neat rows of holes over its scalp. The remaining tangled mess of hair was dark. There was nothing sweet or cuddly about it.

'Whose is she?' Rósa was the first to break the silence.

'No one's. Not any more.' Frikki was transfixed by the hideous vision at his feet. 'Perhaps it belonged to some little girl, a long time ago.'

'What was she doing in the sea?' Rósa was still young enough to believe that grown-ups had all the answers. She would soon be disillusioned.

'Maybe the girl who owned it was on a boat and dropped it overboard. Or perhaps she dropped it off the quay and the current carried it here. The line must have dislodged it from the seabed earlier and then it floated into the net.' Frikki was rising to the occasion pretty well, in Dísa's opinion. There was no need for her to intervene.

'Oh. Poor girl.' Rósa face was a picture of sadness and sympathy. 'And poor doll.'

Frikki bent down and made as if to put his hand in his sleeve before touching the doll. But then he changed his mind, no doubt keen to avoid coming across as a wimp. When he picked the doll up, streams of seawater began to pour out of its hip joints. 'I reckon we should throw it back.'

'No!' Rósa cried out. 'I want her.'

Dísa made a face again. 'It's a bit grim, Rósa. Look at all the horrible muck on it. Some of it's bound to be alive.'

But now that the fishing trip had produced a result, Rósa proved uncharacteristically stubborn. 'I want her anyway.'

Frikki's embarrassment made him suddenly revert to his familiar office persona. He glanced from Rósa to Dísa, racking his brain for a compromise. His suggestion, when it finally came, was feeble. 'I could put it in a bag?' It sounded like a question.

Before Dísa could refuse his offer, Rósa forestalled her: 'Yes. Put her in a bag. I can wash her when we get home.' She looked up at her mother with a hopeful smile. 'Maybe we can find the girl she used to belong to.'

Judging by the ecosystem that had made its home on the doll, it must have been at the bottom of the sea for years. 'I'm sure the little girl who owned it will have grown out of toys by now,' Dísa reasoned. 'She's probably forgotten all about it.'

'She might have belonged to a boy. You can't be sure it was a girl.' Not for the first time, Rósa proved more broad-minded and modern than her mother. 'And I'm sure the owner is still sad about losing her. I would be. Even if I was a hundred.'

Dísa didn't doubt it for a minute. Rósa wasn't the only child who thought of her toys as alive. Dísa herself still had several boxes of teddy bears and dolls in her parents' basement that she didn't have the heart to throw out.

Mother and daughter argued while Frikki stood by awkwardly. In the end, Rósa got her way and was allowed to keep the doll. Frikki's relief was palpable. He clapped his hands and suggested they eat their picnic.

But when they sat down to their packed lunches, it turned out that none of them felt like Dísa's flatcakes or the cheap, shop-bought sponge cake. Although the doll was now hidden away in a bag, they couldn't forget the gruesome sight, which would have been enough to rob anyone of their appetite. Even the gulls had disappeared.

When Frikki suggested they call it a day, neither mother

nor daughter raised any objections, so he put about and headed for shore.

In the end, Rósa's interest didn't last much beyond taking the doll out of the bag – wearing rubber gloves, at her mother's insistence – and putting it in the bath, where she quickly forgot about it. Her enthusiasm didn't extend to washing it or scrubbing off the barnacles. So there the doll sat, staring at Dísa out of its single eye when she went to the loo and, later, when she brushed her teeth before bed. Instead of replacing the plastic bag over the hideous object, Dísa took a photo and posted it on Facebook.

It wasn't often that she had anything unusual to report.

Her laptop was still busy alerting her to comments and likes when she put it down on the coffee table without bothering to close the lid and went to bed.

Dísa awoke with a jerk. As she sat up, she registered through her disorientation that she'd been disturbed by a strange noise, a loud crash that was totally out of keeping with the quiet of their home at night. Sleepily, she pushed back the duvet and got up to see what was going on.

As her head cleared, Dísa remembered the empty tins she had piled up behind the curtain on the windowsill in the little dining area that she rarely used. The window faced onto the back garden. The Greater Reykjavík area had recently suffered a spate of burglaries and Dísa had thought this the most likely place for thieves to try to get in. The noise of the falling tins was supposed to frighten them away – to some other house.

If the news was to be believed, the crime wave was over,

but Dísa had left the tins there, though she didn't always check any more that the window was closed. Had it been open when she went to bed? She couldn't remember, and her suspicion now grew that the noise had come from the tins. What else could it have been? She paused, frozen in her bedroom doorway, trying to come up with a less alarming explanation than a burglary. *A cat had got in. A glass vase had fallen on the floor in the neighbours' flat upstairs. There had been a collision in the street outside the house. A large bird had flown into the windowpane. The TV had switched itself on of its own accord. There had been an earthquake.* There were any number of harmless possibilities.

Dísa relaxed a little. As she did so, she realised she was desperate for a pee.

She decided to buy herself a little time by going to the loo first to relieve her bladder. She wasn't exactly keen to undertake a patrol of the flat, convinced she would have a heart attack if she so much as bumped into a cat. And yet it struck her that, considering the circumstances, she was peculiarly calm. Normally she was a bag of nerves over nothing more alarming than a gale forecast, even though they didn't have a trampoline in the garden or loose tiles on the roof. She sat on the loo, feeling rather pleased with herself for keeping her cool. But the feeling didn't last long. From the sitting room came the familiar sound of the laptop starting up. Her heart lurched, until she remembered that the computer had a habit of restarting once its automatic updates had finished. That must be it. After all, what kind of burglar would sit down to surf the web in the middle of a break-in?

That monstrous doll was watching her from the bathtub. Dísa averted her eyes and concentrated on peeing, but her gaze was drawn back irresistibly to the doll. She stared, mesmerised, at the plastic eye that seemed to be following her movements as she reached for the loo paper. It was an optical illusion, of course, like one of those portraits whose eyes seem to be watching you. There was nothing to be afraid of.

Another noise drove the doll from Dísa's mind. It wasn't the clatter of tins. Or a cat. Or a collision. Or a vase smashing to smithereens. And it certainly wasn't an earthquake. It was a familiar, everyday sound.

It was the loose block of parquet creaking in the hallway just outside the bathroom.

Dísa stood up, her pyjama bottoms round her ankles, and took a step towards the door that she had closed from habit. Before she could reach the lock, the handle was turned from the other side. The door opened slowly inwards and, as she saw the person standing there, Dísa could have sworn that the doll in the bathtub grinned.

The present
May

Chapter 2

The zip tore into the quiet of the night as Abby opened the tent flap. Earlier that day, the silence had seemed pleasant, with only the birdsong to remind her that she and her boyfriend weren't completely alone in this unfamiliar land. But now it felt oppressive. The birds had stopped singing and were no doubt asleep somewhere among the tussocks or in the knee-high birch scrub next to the tent. Ever since she and Lenny had left the city, it was as if nature had been given a crew-cut: nothing grew higher than a foot or so off the ground. It had taken a bit of getting used to, but before long she had come to appreciate the landscape. You could see for miles in every direction and she soon found that she didn't miss trees one bit. She had always been a little afraid of woods after all the fairytales she had grown up with about children losing their way among the endless, identical trees, never to be seen again in some cases. Mind you, the tourist website she had read before the trip had made it abundantly clear that you could also get lost in a country with no forests. And, as in the tales from her childhood, you might never be seen again.

The wind changed, carrying the smell of ashes over to Abby. They had built a small, round hearth of stones next to the tent. There may have been no trees here but you certainly couldn't complain of a shortage of rocks. For kindling they had used some dry sticks that Lenny had gathered among the scrub. These had burnt up so fast that the sausages had been charred on the outside and cold in the middle, but they had eaten them anyway. In fact, they had both been secretly relieved that the fire had died down so quickly. The moment the twigs caught, it had dawned on them that if the flames escaped from the rough stone circle they could set fire to the pasture, taking their tent and the two of them with it. This wasn't the first time they had belatedly become aware of their own foolishness. The trip itself was the best evidence of that. If they had only stopped to think beforehand, Abby wouldn't have been about to crawl into a cold, dank tent on a chilly spring night in a country that made up for its lack of trees with an overabundance of rocks and gusts of wind. Abby forced her mind back to the unbearable heat of Spain; to their fiery red shoulders, peeling from the merciless sun, and the sweat that had poured off them after any exertion greater than reaching for a water bottle. To be fair, Lenny had toler-ated the heat better than she had as his skin wasn't as pale and he'd found it easier to ignore the discomfort. He had even managed to venture out from under the sunshade. Their budget hotel had so few intact sun loungers or umbrellas that they'd had to wake up at the crack of dawn if they wanted to secure both. While Abby languished in the shade beside the swimming pool, trying not to pass out, Lenny had chatted a bit to the other guests or brought her food and drinks. She hadn't been able to move an inch until evening. Even then it had been unbearably hot, but at least she'd been spared the cruel sun.

When Lenny, returning from a stroll, had perched on her sun lounger and suggested giving up on Spain as a bad job and going to Iceland instead, she had almost burst into tears with relief. The very name had sounded like a cooling lotion. She had only just noticed that her toes had been poking out from under the towel that she had draped over her legs, and now they resembled angry little cocktail sausages.

Once evening came and the sun had gone down, the idea lost some of its appeal. All sorts of practical considerations reared their heads but like cheap fireworks, they appeared with a crack but fizzled out almost immediately as she chose to ignore them. If she and Lenny had stopped to give it a moment's proper thought, the idea would have been nipped in the bud. Initially she had been a bit worried about where they were going to stay and how they were supposed to get around, as hotels and travel in Iceland were bound to be way over their budget. Even Spain had been a luxury they couldn't really afford. They could pay their rent at the beginning of every month, but the further they got from pay-day, the more pinched their circumstances became. Their credit cards were already way over the limit and their debit cards nothing more than a gateway to their overdrafts. The supply of euros they had brought along as travel money was fast being depleted. All of this made a trip to Iceland an absurd proposition. But they had gone for it anyway; Lenny had talked her into it.

He'd said he could sort them a couple of free airline tickets from a man he had got chatting to at the swimming-pool bar. The man couldn't use the tickets himself and had told Lenny they were his if he wanted. It would cost them a small fee to change the names on the tickets, if they really felt that was necessary, but that was all. The man added that he'd rented two bicycles as well and couldn't get a refund on those, so he'd throw them in too if they liked.

It was a pity he hadn't booked non-refundable accommodation as well. Instead, he had given Lenny a tent and two sleeping bags he had bought for the trip. It was only later, when they got the camping gear out and saw what cheap tat it was, that they realised the gesture hadn't been as generous as it sounded.

Who needs hotels? Camping's way cooler and you're allowed to pitch your tent anywhere in Iceland. We can just head off wherever we like on the bikes. Iceland's so awesome that I'm sure we won't have to go far to see something amazing. We'll just bring food with us. After all, we'd have to buy it anyway if we stayed in Spain.

This is what they had told themselves, but many of their assumptions had turned out to be doubtful, if not wholly misinformed. For example, before making up their minds, they had read online that according to ancient laws, you were free to camp almost anywhere in Iceland. This had turned out to be only partly true. In practice, as references to these old laws were laughed off by angry landowners, they realised that the internet had interpreted them rather loosely. That first evening it had taken them hours to find a spot to pitch their tent. They had eventually opted for some mossy moorland on the outskirts of the city, only to be chased off at the crack of dawn the following morning. Hopefully things would improve now that they had crossed the mountains east of the capital and descended to the lowlands again. No one had objected to their new campsite yet.

Lenny had been insistent that they should get out beyond the city limits and wouldn't hear of taking things easy and spending the first night in Reykjavík as they had originally discussed. The plan had been to stay at the campsite in Laugardalur, to give them a chance to try out the famous open-air geothermal swimming pool. But Lenny had changed his mind and was adamant that they should get straight out of the city. This surprised her, since he'd never given the impression of being a nature lover before. Not until the built-up area was left behind did he relax and start to enjoy himself. She didn't comment on this about-face, just felt grateful that he was himself again. She had been afraid the trip would be ruined by his having second thoughts. To be fair, he had tried to hide his worries from her, but she knew him too well.

Abby crawled into the tent and zipped the flap shut behind her. They had eventually turned off the road and hunkered down among the absurdly large tussocks of a rough, dun-coloured pasture, beside some low birch scrub. Behind them rose a mountain that hadn't initially appeared that high or that steep, but had turned out to be a much tougher climb than they'd anticipated.

It was unlikely that anyone would chase them off this patch, in spite of the sign on the fence they had clambered over, which had warned that it was private property and camping was forbidden. They had decided to risk it anyway, as there seemed to be so few locals around. Apart from in the small town they had cycled past, most of the other people they had seen were tourists like them. It was almost as though the roads were reserved for the use of tour buses and rental cars. It appeared that none of the locals and hardly any of the other tourists were crazy enough to try and get around by bike, apart from one couple who had overtaken them without so much as a glance.

It was even colder inside the tent, if such a thing were possible. Although the weather was dry down here in the lowlands, it had rained while they were crossing the mountains and there was a strong smell emanating from the wet water-proofs that they had hung up on the poles inside. Abby was sure the clothes were just as wet now as when they had taken them off. The smell didn't improve when she removed her shoes, but she didn't care. Her aching body had been crying out for a rest all day and now at last she could lie down. Putting in her little Bluetooth earbuds, she selected her favourite song on her phone. She ought to be saving the battery but one more track wouldn't hurt.

With the poignant melody playing in her ears, Abby reached for the lantern at the foot of her sleeping bag and switched it on. It was shoddily made and she had to bang it several times before it would cast a weak glow over the chaos inside the tent. She frowned as she contemplated the mess. It looked somehow different from when she and Lenny had set out earlier that evening. But perhaps it was just the effect of the peculiar semi-darkness of the Arctic night.

Abby exhaled, her breath forming white clouds that disappeared almost immediately, unlike the thick, fragrant smoke of her Vape, which was buried somewhere under the mound of clothes and empty food packaging. She had a sour taste in her mouth but was too tired to root around for her toothbrush and water bottle. She'd make it her first task when she woke up in the morning.

Abby braced herself, then quickly pulled off her coat and began to undress. She had discovered the previous evening that the sleeping bag was more effective if you were almost naked. Her thighs and calves felt as if they were on fire once she had taken off her trousers. She couldn't bring herself to remove her socks as well, since her toes were still sore from the sunburn, so she would just have to sleep in them. The hard day's ride, topped off with a spot of impromptu mountaineering that evening, had just about finished her off. She was no cyclist – neither was Lenny, for that matter. They didn't even have a gym membership between them at home. *It'll only take us a day to break ourselves in,* he had said with unfounded optimism. How wrong he had been. She felt worse now than she had this morning.

She was aware, suddenly, of a desperate urge to pee. With a groan, Abby reached for the shoes at her feet. If Lenny could walk up the mountain in nothing but a thin pair of shorts, she should be able to survive a quick dash outside in her knickers. She aimed the lantern at the groundsheet in search of the toilet roll. Just then, the track she was listening to finished and she heard something that sounded like a cry. Taking out her earbuds, she listened. 'Lenny?' Could he have fallen over and broken his leg and be calling for help? She'd had the music turned up so high, he could have been shouting for a couple of minutes for all she knew.

She heard rustling outside as if someone was moving quickly through the dry scrub behind the tent. Abby relaxed. It must be Lenny. He had lagged behind on the walk back, having drunk most of the cheap red wine they had carried up the mountain with them. The climb had been his idea, conceived when he was halfway down a flask of the vile local schnapps that they'd picked up in Duty Free. It had tasted like cough mixture to Abby. Thick, dark, heavy, like one of those bitter medicines in which menthol is used to disguise the taste. A single sip had been enough for her, and nothing Lenny could say about schnapps keeping you warm had changed her mind. He'd had the flask to himself; not that he had seemed any warmer than her on the hike. If anything, the opposite appeared to be true. Certainly, red wine didn't possess any warming properties – after they had finished the bottle on top of the mountain, she had felt as if her whole body was encased in a sheath of ice.

She should have talked Lenny out of the climb. But, if she was honest, Abby had been tempted by the thought of the spectacular photos they'd get from the top: their feet in battered trainers, plastic cups half full of red wine and the scenery stretching out below. Unfortunately, she'd forgotten about the dusk, which had gradually crept up on them. By the time they were finally perched at the top of the steep slope, the light was too poor and the photos she did take, like most of the others on this trip, weren't good enough for social media. So far all her efforts had been spoilt by rain or grey skies or strangers blundering into her carefully chosen frame. If things went on like this, she wouldn't have anything worth posting. She'd be the first visitor to Iceland who hadn't filled her social media pages with enviable images.

To make matters worse, they only had one portable charger between them and once that ran out of juice, their phone batteries would die and there would be no more photos. There were no electric sockets out here to plug their phones into. So far, they had saved their batteries by keeping their phones switched to flight mode and turning them off when they weren't using them as cameras. But, even so, every time she switched on her phone, the battery had lost a little more power. Just as well tomorrow was supposed to provide some good opportunities for cool pictures. One of the things that had kept her going was the thought of getting to tell the world about the trip once it was over, by which time it would be too late for her family to be pissed off at their recklessness and extravagance. She had started getting cold feet as soon as the sweltering heat of Spain was behind them and she and Lenny were sitting in the chilly, air-conditioned plane. Mistake. Big mistake. She knew Lenny felt the same. As they took off, he had seemed nervous, as if he too were having regrets. But neither had said anything; they had just exchanged weak smiles, then stared in silence at the seatbacks in front of them.

In fact, Lenny had started having second thoughts before they'd even boarded the plane. The night before they set off she had woken to see him fiddling with the camping gear. She had raised her head and told him everything would be fine; they'd manage. Apparently embarrassed at being caught red-handed having doubts about their ability to survive a camping trip in Iceland, Lenny had told her he was going out for a vape and would take out their rubbish while he was there. She had fallen asleep again by the time he came back.

The rustling stopped and she wondered if Lenny had paused to take a leak. She strained her ears but couldn't hear any sound of trickling. Besides, it was unlikely given how often he'd already had to stop on the way down the mountain. That's why he had lagged so far behind. She had been too cold to hang around waiting for him.

Perhaps he was just catching his breath. The rustling had approached the tent fast, as if Lenny had been running. He must be in a hurry to get inside and lie down. She hoped to God he wasn't in the mood for sex. That definitely wasn't on the agenda, not after the chafing her inner thighs had suffered from the bike saddle.

The sounds had stopped altogether. 'Lenny!' Abby called at the top of her lungs, in the hope that her shout would rouse him if he was falling into a booze-induced sleep.

Spending the night outside in 4°C couldn't be a good idea. After all, no one would dream of taking a nap inside a fridge, especially not in shorts.

Lenny didn't answer. The silence was so complete that for a split second Abby wondered if she'd gone deaf. But then the rustling started up again, moving rapidly closer, as if Lenny were running towards the tent. He hadn't passed out then. But why wasn't he answering?

She called out again.

No reply.

As before, the sounds stopped the moment she shouted, as if Lenny paused every time she called his name. What was wrong with him? She waited until the swishing and crackling started up again, then yelled: 'Lenny!' No answer, just a sudden silence. When she heard the noise again it was right behind the tent. Abby slipped one foot into her shoe, wincing with pain as her blisters rubbed against the toe.

The lantern chose that moment to conk out, leaving Abby crouching there in the gloom, shivering in her knickers, T-shirt and one shoe. Her hearing was more sensitive now she couldn't see anything and she could make out every footstep Lenny took in the dry grass beside the tent until he was standing outside the door.

'Lenny!'

No answer.

'Lenny?' Abby didn't like this at all.

The harsh tearing of the zip was as unsettlingly loud as before, if not louder. It sounded like someone ripping through leather. Abby peered at the faint outline of Lenny outside the tent opening. He paused for a moment, then bent to come inside.

It was only then that Abby realised.

It wasn't Lenny at all.

It was a complete stranger.

The following morning, the farmer happened to be passing when he spotted a tent out in the pasture. Pulling over, he jumped out of the car, climbed over the fence and stormed across the rough, tussocky ground until he was standing in front of what turned out to be a cheap, rickety tent that would no doubt be blown out to sea the moment the wind picked up properly. He got ready to give the occupants a bollocking. From the bikes lying beside it, he assumed there must be two of them. But he hesitated when he noticed that the tent flap was open. There was no sound from inside and no one answered when he called out. He bent down to look in.

The tent was empty. There was camping gear and clutter everywhere, but no people. Seeing what a tip it was, he wasn't surprised the campers had ignored his sign. You couldn't see the groundsheet for their belongings, and everything, including the walls of the tent, was splattered with dark stains. It looked as if a tin of something inedible had exploded in there. How was it possible to make such a disgusting mess?

The farmer stood up and looked around. Anger began to course through his veins when he spotted the blackened remains of a fire not far from the tent. But he couldn't see any sign of the occupants. Not in the field, or in the birch scrub, on the mountainside or on the road. He dithered, irritated, wondering if they had maybe caught a bus to one of the popular tourist attractions in the region, like the Gullfoss Falls or the hot springs at Geysir.

Well, wherever they'd gone, there was no way he was going

to hang around waiting for them, so he turned and went back to his car. The breeze was growing stronger and he could hear the open tent door flapping behind him.

Bloody foreigners.

That evening he passed the same way again but by then the tent and the bicycles had gone. All that remained to show that anyone had ever been there was the patch where the fire had been, ringed with blackened stones.

August

Chapter 3

Friday

There were a number of things Huldar could have happily done without in this life, top of the list being corpses and boat rides, which made the present double whammy seem particularly unfair. He had been struggling manfully to hide his distress and was managing OK until the boat stopped its forward momentum and began rocking gently from side to side, up and down. Then, to his great dismay, his nausea began to rise and fall in sympathy.

The voyage out hadn't been nearly as bad: as long as the boat was ploughing through the waves he'd been able to cope, but now that it had stopped, everything was in motion inside him; an unhappy reminder of his one-off spell as a deckhand in his youth. That trip had begun well too but ended badly, with the result that he hadn't been invited back. Not that he would ever in a million years have accepted the offer. There had to be more to life than hanging over a rail, clinging desperately to the hope that he wouldn't lose his guts as well as his breakfast during the next bout of vomiting. When he disembarked he had promised himself that he would never again set foot on a boat.

But fate had other ideas. Since being a fisherman was out, he had trained as a carpenter, before subsequently joining the police, both of which had seemed safe bets if you wanted to avoid the sea. How ironic. You never could tell where life was going to take you.

'There you are.'

Huldar glanced round. He had taken up position by the rail, concentrating hard on the thin dark strip of solid ground visible between sea and sky. During his brief, abortive career as a deckhand, his crewmates had told him that focusing on a fixed point would help combat seasickness. But it hadn't worked then and time had done nothing to increase its efficacy. He was feeling just as bad now as he had been before he left the group by the other rail on the pretext that he wanted a smoke. Nothing could be further from his mind, but it had sounded better than saying: 'Excuse me while I go and throw up.'

'Feeling a bit under the weather?' Erla stopped beside Huldar, her head tilted to one side, examining his face. He didn't need a mirror to tell him that he was as white as a corpse. Now that he saw her close up, he thought she was looking a bit peaky too, but that didn't necessarily mean anything. No one in Iceland could boast a healthy tan after the wettest summer in a hundred years.

'No. I'm fine.' Huldar knew she wouldn't believe him but he didn't care. He'd been brought up never to betray any sign of weakness and it was too late to change now. That was why he hadn't hesitated for a moment when Erla asked him to accompany her on this trip – in spite of his old vow; in spite of the fact that he knew what the voyage would do to him. He wasn't only trying to save face: things between him and Erla had improved recently and he wanted to keep it like that. If he'd said no, she was bound to have taken it the wrong way, and he was fed up with constantly having to patch up their relationship. If only she were a man, he could have turned down the job without her reading anything into it beyond the simple fact that he didn't want to go. At least *he* was straightforward like that, he reasoned, whereas his five sisters never took anything at face value and were capable of interpreting the most innocent of comments in the worst possible way.

'What about you?' Huldar retorted. He'd seen her looking better.

'Nothing wrong with me.' Drawing slightly away, Erla blinked and swallowed. Her eyelids stayed closed a beat too long for her answer to be believable. So they were both in the same boat, so to speak. 'You're missing all the fun,' she continued, through clenched jaws. 'The submarine's found the spot. We saw something that looked like bones on the screen. Maybe from a finger or wrist. Small, anyway. It's possible they were carried off by a crustacean or something and that the rest of the skeleton's further away, but at least we're on the right track.'

A heavy cable had been paid out over the opposite rail down into the choppy sea. It was connected to a small, remote-controlled submarine that was busy scouring the seabed for human remains and sending back information via the cable. Huldar gathered that police searches of the seabed were usually conducted in deeper waters, which was a more laborious operation involving sonar and submarines that could only take stills which couldn't be viewed until the vessel had resurfaced. This was the first time the new sub had been deployed and, despite the inherent grimness of the situation, few of them could hide their excitement as footage of the seabed was instantly relayed to deck.

Apparently Huldar was the only person on board who wasn't riveted by the visuals on screen. Before nausea had threatened to unman him, he had stood with the others, underwhelmed by the footage of murky water and the uneven seabed, with the occasional small marine creature darting or scuttling out of view and the odd tuft of billowing seaweed; a drab, colourless world.

Even if Erla was suffering, it had apparently done nothing to dampen her interest. She was a real trouper. Normally Huldar would have claimed he was too, but there were limits. He had seen photos of the leg that had turned up in a fishing net at these coordinates and that had been quite enough for him. He felt absolutely no need to see the other one, should the submarine blunder across it on the seabed.

When Erla had shown him the photos he had been in better shape, capable of holding it together enough to scrutinise them carefully. A faded, lace-up Nike trainer, with two leg bones projecting from it, and a glimpse of something grisly in the shoe. He hadn't lingered on the picture taken after the shoe had been removed, since he had already seen enough to grasp the situation. A bare foot, size forty-one, belonging either to a woman with big feet or a man with small ones – or possibly to an adolescent.

Erla balanced nimbly as the boat took a sudden, vigorous plunge. For a moment she looked as if she were going to win her battle with the motion but then she gave up and grabbed the rail with both hands, sticking her head over it, closing her eyes and heaving a deep, gasping breath, as if she'd been underwater too long. There was no longer any doubt: she was seasick too. But Erla toughed it out. She turned her head back to Huldar and carried on as if nothing had happened. 'Anyway, hopefully there'll be other body parts nearby.'

'Yes, hopefully.' Huldar tried to force his lips into a smile. Of course he was hoping the rest of the skeleton would be found but his mind was busy working out the best way to avoid having to see it, particularly if they managed to bring it up. For this purpose, they had a second, specially equipped, unmanned submarine, since the sea here was still too deep for a diver, even though they were over a ridge on the continental shelf. The last depth reading Huldar had heard before he abandoned the others was eighty-three metres.

'It would be great if we found some that were intact enough to help us make a quick identification. I'd welcome a skull with a complete set of teeth.'

Huldar chipped in with what he would rather they found: 'Or a coat or other clothing with some form of waterproof ID or a credit card in the pocket.'

'Yes. Or that.' Erla didn't seem optimistic about the chances. The colour drained from her face again and she exhaled with a grimace. 'The real bugger is not having a clue how fast a body decomposes on the Icelandic seabed.'

'Yes. That is a bugger.' *Or not.* On their way to the harbour Huldar had forced himself to skim through the conclusions of the few existing studies on the subject. Before getting in the car, Erla had given him a printout of an article detailing the results of a foreign experiment on the decomposition of pigs' carcases that had been placed on the seabed in order to observe the process. According to the researchers, pigs resembled humans in that they were large, hairless and had the same bacterial flora in their digestive tracts. The decomposition rate of the carcases was therefore thought to be similar to that of the body of an adult human. In the event, two of the pigs had been reduced to skeletons within a month, while the third had taken considerably longer. Just reading about it had made Huldar so queasy that he had failed to take in exactly what it was that had caused the discrepancy. All he had grasped was that it related to the differing amounts of oxygen present in the water where the carcases were located. He hadn't a clue about the oxygen content of the sea off Iceland, or indeed of any other variables that, according to the study, could make a difference.

'The bones on screen looked completely clean, like the ones sticking out of the shoe. So we probably won't find any soft tissue, assuming we find anything else apart from those finger or wrist bones. Perhaps the rest of the skeleton is buried in the sand.' Erla's short hair was being whipped around by the wind and she tried in vain to tuck it behind her ears. 'It's bloody lucky the shoe had preserved some flesh. That should simplify the DNA analysis.'

'Yes.' Huldar turned his gaze towards land again in the hope that it would finally prove to be a fixed point. The thought of the rotting flesh in the shoe wasn't helping matters.

Erla's stomach seemed to be unaffected by the subject, judging by the way she persisted in discussing it. 'Let's hope the deceased's clothes were thick enough to delay the sea creatures' activity, like the shoe did. Though we're still left with the problem that the head has probably been picked clean. Unless part of the scalp has survived. I gather that hair works a bit like clothes in that way.'

Huldar took a deep breath. He had to change the subject if he wasn't going to lose his breakfast. 'Who do you think it is?' he asked desperately. 'A suicide? A tourist who was washed out to sea from some popular destination like the beach at Reynisfjara?'

Erla shrugged. 'Haven't a clue. Until we know how long the body's been in the sea, there's no point speculating. It'll go before the Identification Commission anyway. If anything suspicious turns up, they'll call us in to investigate. But that's unlikely.'

The commission had been set up to identify the victims of major accidents and natural disasters, as well as any random human remains that turned up, as in this case. Huldar had recently been offered a position on the board as deputy representative of the Police Commissioner, but had turned it down without a moment's pause. He had absolutely no desire to expose himself to any more corpses than the ones he already encountered in the line of duty.

Erla released her grip on the rail, enough to give Huldar a nudge. 'Anyway, come on. I didn't put myself through this to miss all the fun.'

Huldar mumbled that he'd come in a minute, and turned back to the rail the instant Erla had gone. He stared fixedly at the distant shore, trying to picture himself there, with both feet planted on terra firma. Then he closed his eyes and inhaled deeply, as Erla had done. Slowly but surely it worked and he felt well enough to rejoin the others.

No sooner had he reached them than the little group poring over the screen emitted a yelp of excitement. Apparently they had spotted the other leg. More clean bones emerging from a shoe that was mostly buried in sand.

The mood of the group quickly became subdued again when they remembered why they were there. This reaction wasn't uncommon in their job: successes or victories were no occasion for celebration when you were dealing with the dead.

Erla was the first to notice that Huldar was hanging back. Looking round, she gave him a genuine smile, the colour returned to her cheeks. It suited her and he responded with a pale smile of his own. 'You'll miss the whole thing if you don't come over. We've obviously hit exactly the right spot.' Clearly, the body parts hadn't been scattered far and wide by an army of crustaceans as she had feared. 'Don't you want to see?'

'I'm good.' Huldar's worry that Erla would insist proved groundless. Something else had appeared on screen to capture the group's attention.

'Those look like arm bones to me.' The representative of the Coast Guard tapped the screen. 'Don't you think?'

The man in charge of the submarine fiddled with the remote control as the group pressed in for a closer look.

Erla stretched, tried and failed to fold her arms over the bulky lifebelt, then let them drop to her sides. 'Yes. They can't be anything else. Aren't those fingers lying beside the bigger arm bones?'

'Possibly, though there are lots of other small bones that connect the arm to the hand and fingers, so it's hard to tell. There aren't enough there for a whole hand.' The diving expert appeared to be well up on human anatomy. Noticing everyone looking at him, he added in explanation: 'I worked as a paramedic for several years.'

They all turned back to the screen and the search continued. But despite circling the spot for some time, they didn't see much more. A few more finger bones and a single bone from an upper arm, poking out of the sand. No coat or other item of clothing, let alone any form of ID or credit card.

After that, there was nothing but sand and more sand, the

odd stone and, finally, the murky void. Eventually, Erla agreed to the captain's suggestion that they should abandon the quest for the moment and bring up what they had found so far. A deterioration in the weather had been forecast for that evening and the captain advised turning back as soon as possible.

Huldar knew Erla well enough to be sure that she would have preferred to carry on searching – to hell with seasickness and rough weather – until they all keeled over with exhaustion. Thank God, the decision wasn't entirely hers. Huldar had managed to soldier on so far, but if the sea got any rougher, he'd be lost.

The first submarine was hauled up on deck and the second one, which was equipped to collect the human remains, was lowered in its place. As the bones began to come up, one after the other, dread of seeing rotting flesh made it harder and harder for Huldar to control his stomach. The pitching of the bloody boat was to blame; the wind had picked up and the swell with it.

When the last batch, consisting of the other leg plus shoe, arrived on deck, Huldar was too late to look away. But what he saw surprised him so much that he temporarily forgot his curdling insides. He even bent closer to check he wasn't mistaken, then called from where he was crouching: 'Erla, have a look at this.'

She came up beside him. 'What?'

Huldar pointed at the shoe. 'It's not a Nike. It's an Adidas.'

Erla instantly squatted down beside him and inspected it. 'Shit, that's weird. Could the person have been in such a state that they jumped in the sea with odd shoes on? I suppose what you're wearing isn't going to be the first thing on your mind when you're about to end it all.'

Huldar disagreed. He had attended a number of suicide scenes over the years and some of the deceased had actually dressed up for the occasion. He didn't once remember having seen anyone in odd shoes. 'I'm pretty sure this shoe isn't a size forty-one either. It looks smaller to me.'

Erla, who hated to be proved wrong, persisted in contradicting him. 'If they were in a total state they could easily have put on different-sized shoes.'

'Maybe.' Huldar stood up, frowning and forcing himself to recall the image of the other foot. Then he got out his phone and searched for a picture of a skeleton. He handed it to Erla. 'See, the thick leg bones face inwards and the thin ones face out. If this was someone wearing odd shoes, the bones should be mirror images of one another. But they're not. These are both right feet, Erla.'

There was no way to put that down to someone being in a total state.

Erla raked her fingers through her salt-crusted hair and sighed. Then she turned to the representative of the Coast Guard and told him that she wanted to extend the search. Unfortunately for Huldar, the request didn't meet with any opposition when the man heard her reasons. If there were two bodies on the seabed, it was almost impossible that they were dealing with a suicide. Of course, this didn't rule out an accident, but there was a very real chance that the bodies had ended up there through the actions of a third party. If that was the case, their priority was to find as many bones or other remains as possible. What they'd found so far wouldn't be nearly enough to establish the cause of death.

The Coast Guard representative announced that the return

to shore would be postponed for as long as could be considered safe. Meanwhile, the search submarine would be relaunched to continue scouring the seabed.

Anyone would have thought the sea was delighted at the chance to toy with them for a little while longer. The boat immediately started rocking and pitching more than ever and Huldar took himself smartly back to the opposite rail.

Chapter 4

Freyja Styrmisdóttir stretched her shirt under the hand dryer in the ladies' and waited for the dark patch to dry. She had been trying to wash off the stain that she'd spotted in the mirror at the most inconvenient moment. She was about to be late for a meeting and had nipped into the ladies' in the lobby of the building to touch up her appearance, fluff up her hair, check her mascara and practise smiling at the mirror. But there had been no time for any of that.

She had been in the firing line that morning as she tried to force porridge down her little niece, Saga, who was staying with her while her mother was off sunning herself in Bali with a new boyfriend, and her father, Freyja's brother Baldur, was guiding a group of tourists on a ten-day trip around Iceland. He had only recently got out of the Vernd halfway house and Freyja didn't like to think what sort of guide he might turn out to be. He wasn't particularly well informed about Iceland's geography or history, as far as she was aware, let alone an enthusiast for outdoor pursuits like riding or hiking. But he looked good in a traditional *lopapeysa* jumper and would no doubt make a convincing impression on the tourists. At least this job was on the right side of the law too – as far as she knew –

though where Baldur was concerned, you could never take anything for granted.

When he was assigned the tour, Freyja had happily agreed to look after her little niece, even though her summer holiday hadn't yet begun. Things were quiet at the Children's House, the centre for the investigation of crimes involving children, where she worked as a psychologist, and the only other people around were unlikely to comment if she spent fewer hours at the office for a week or two. After all, they hadn't raised any objections when she was seconded to work on the special project that today's meeting was about, although it would mean temporarily neglecting her duties at the Children's House. Sometimes, she reflected, there were advantages to not being indispensable.

Saga had recently started at nursery school, which meant that Freyja would just have to get up that little bit earlier and leave work earlier in the afternoon. Nothing too complicated about that. She was well aware, however, that her role as auntie wouldn't consist solely of trips to the ice-cream parlour or to feed the ducks on Tjörnin, the little lake in the centre of Reykjavík. She knew exactly what she was letting herself in for. Her niece wasn't like other children, but that didn't make her any harder to deal with, just different.

That morning Freyja had made porridge for Saga. Since this had appealed to the child about as much as a bowl of worms would have done, Freyja had resorted to putting jam on it. Saga had clumsily scraped off and eaten the jam, then started energetically hurling porridge around the room. One splat had obviously landed on Freyja without her noticing, but then she'd had her hands full trying to limit the damage at the time.

The hot air switched off automatically and Freyja set it going again. The wet patch was fading but still visible. She sighed. She simply didn't have time to wait for it to dry properly. The choice was between arriving late or arriving punctually with a big wet patch on her front. Oh well. She could always keep her coat zipped up to the neck throughout the meeting, as if it were being held outdoors at the North Pole. If only she'd worn a thinner jacket, but the unusually cold, wet summer had made that impossible.

The dryer cut out again. Freyja tucked her shirt into her trousers, reminding herself that not everything had to be perfect. Not always. This was part of her ongoing campaign to sort out her life, which involved a thirty-day sex ban and three ground rules: one, enjoy what every day has to offer; two, don't set your goals too high; and three, take a break from the search for a partner. The last of these had proved the hardest to stick to and she kept having to remind herself that she wasn't alone, even if she wasn't in a relationship. She had her brother Baldur, and little Saga too. And the dog, Molly, whom she looked after for her brother when required.

Not to mention the snake that went with her flat.

She shuddered at the thought of this 'pet', which belonged to the flat's owner, who was currently doing time for crimes unspecified. Since moving in she'd had trouble sleeping, knowing that the python was in the flat, even though it was safely locked away. Every night when she closed her eyes she pictured the snake coiling its way across the floor towards the bedroom. The worst nights were the ones when Saga was staying. When she first moved in, Freyja had splashed out on a sweet little child's bed for her niece, but Saga still hadn't spent the whole night in it because Freyja invariably ended up fetching the sleeping child and putting her in her own bed. Only with the little girl safely in her arms could she relax, telling herself that if, by some unlucky miracle, the python escaped, she would be able to save her niece.

This was by no means a given, however. There was every chance the python would get the better of her.

On her way up in the lift, Freyja examined her shirt in the mirror. It was still wet. Clearly, unless some pop singer armed with a wind machine suddenly materialised in the lift with her, the stain would be glaringly obvious at the meeting.

But her first sight of the man she'd come to meet instantly put Freyja at her ease. He had a huge ink stain under his shirt pocket. Since the offending pen was still there, he presumably wasn't aware of the accident. Freyja carefully averted her gaze.

He was a thin man, fiftyish, with tired eyes and a notable absence of smile lines. His handshake, when he greeted her, was firm and purposeful, his palm smooth and uncallused, as befitted a true office worker. Freyja returned his greeting with her own equally soft hand, wearing a confident smile. He introduced himself as Yngvi, which was unnecessary since they already knew each other slightly through work. He was employed by the Child Protection Agency, she by the Children's House, which came under its aegis. Their paths had crossed a few times, at crowded meetings, workshops, Christmas drinks and annual parties.

Freyja wasn't disconcerted when Yngvi didn't return her smile. The little she had seen of him had suggested that he wasn't exactly a ray of sunlight. Even at the annual children's services knees-up she'd seen him sitting on his own, apparently wringing his hands over the state of the world. Since Freyja had been there to enjoy herself, she had quickly gone into reverse and sought out more entertaining company.

'Thanks for coming along at such short notice. We're really up against it at the moment as so many people are on their summer holidays. I don't know what I'd have done if you hadn't been willing. The case can't wait until the autumn.' Yngvi's eyes strayed from Freyja's face to the corridor containing the offices. It was clear that he wanted to get the meeting over with as soon as possible, so he could attend to other matters. It was no secret how much pressure the Child Protection Agency was under. 'If you'd like to follow me, we can get started. There's no reason to hang about.'

Freyja followed him into a meeting room which boasted little more than a table, some chairs and a projector screen drooping crookedly from the ceiling. She doubted it would be required on this particular occasion.

It had emerged that an employee of Reykjavík children's services, one Bergur Alvarsson, was being investigated by the police, suspected of inflicting sexual abuse on children – children in his care; children he was supposed to be nurturing and protecting. To make matters worse, the police had neglected to report the allegations against him, with the result that the man had continued working for a further three months. The matter only reached the ears of the Child Protection Agency when one of his alleged victims gave an anonymous interview in the press. Unsurprisingly, this had caused an outcry. It was a PR disaster for the police, the city council and the Child Protection Agency. Never mind that the man had been employed by the City of Reykjavík and was therefore unconnected to the agency. In the eyes of the public, however unfairly, the agency was held jointly responsible whenever anything went wrong.

Freyja wasn't offered any coffee. Instead, they got straight down to business. She and Yngvi took seats facing each other across the table. Freyja removed her coat and hung it over the back of her chair, repeating to herself the mantra: *not everything has to be perfect*. Yngvi's eyes were immediately drawn to the stain but he quickly lowered them when he realised he was staring. Freyja merely smiled and allowed herself a moment of schadenfreude when she imagined him going to the gents later and spotting the ink blot on his own shirt. She wished she could be a fly on the wall at that moment.

'Is it just the two of us?'

Yngvi nodded. Freyja had been hoping there would be others present but, then again, if it was just the two of them, she could focus on their conversation instead of feeling self-conscious about her wet shirt.

'My assistant's pulling together the files for you. They cover everything relating to the children in our care, from when they were first sent to the home in question, and include material handed over by the city council. You'll get them on a memory stick – we're trying to go paperless and we're discouraged from printing things out unless it's unavoidable.'

'No problem. I've got a printer at the Children's House.' Seeing his face tighten with disapproval, Freyja added hastily: 'I'll go through most of it on screen but I might have to print the odd page. We're being encouraged to cut costs too.' Her workplace came under the agency and was therefore subject to the same measures, which almost invariably involved cost-cutting.

Yngvi reminded her that she would have to follow standard procedure and, for reasons of confidentiality, destroy any documents she printed out. He also warned her not to make copies of the files. As far as she was concerned, this was basic stuff, but instead of pointing this out, she just nodded. 'You'll also be granted access to the shared files on our system about the young people concerned. It'll be either tomorrow or the day after. The IT department is under-staffed because of the holidays, so I'm afraid it hasn't been sorted out yet.'

The new data privacy laws required more stringent control of documents relating to the agency's wards. Previously, staff in her position had enjoyed almost unfettered access to the material, but now it was secured behind digital lock and key. Freyja nodded and Yngvi continued.

'Right, as I told you on the phone, the police have asked us to provide a child psychologist to sit in on their interviews with any witnesses who are under eighteen. Since Bergur has been running the home for thirteen years, many of his former charges are now older than that, so you won't need to attend every single interview. But I understand that they're planning to start with the kids who stayed there recently, all of whom are juveniles. If anything emerges from these interviews to back up the abuse claims, they'll carry on down the list of names.'

'I see.'

He went on: 'The arrangement requires that the psychologist in question should not have had any previous contact with the juveniles, either before, during or after their time at the home, since – understandably in the circumstances – neither the young people themselves nor their guardians have much faith in the professionals who have been handling their cases up to now. You fulfil that condition. And you aren't on holiday. Am I right in assuming that you're not about to take your annual leave in the next couple of weeks?'

'That's right, I'm not.' Freyja still hadn't decided when she would take her holiday, but it certainly wouldn't be any time soon. As she had no plans to go abroad, she had decided to wait until the weather improved here at home, but there was no sign of that happening yet. The forecast showed solid rain for the foreseeable future. If it went on like this, she would be left with a double allowance of leave this time next year.

Yngvi resumed: 'The job also involves checking to see if there's been any cock-up by us or by Reykjavík children's services. Obviously, they blundered by appointing Bergur in the first place, but it's hard to see how that could have been avoided. He had a clean record and there was nothing to suggest that he was struggling with paedophile urges. But we need to find out if the children in his care raised the alarm and were ignored, or if the social workers failed to take appropriate action. If so, the hole in the system needs to be plugged to avoid similar incidents in future. On no account must this be allowed to happen again; once is bad enough.'

He paused but didn't seem to be waiting for a response from Freyja so she remained silent. After sighing heavily, he went on.

'As you know, Bergur ran a temporary placement home for juveniles in the care of Reykjavík children's services. His charges were mainly adolescents, a number of whom had issues with drugs. They were placed with him for varying periods, some for longer than can strictly be regarded as a temporary placement, which doesn't usually exceed three months. Some only stayed with him once, others more often, when their home circumstances continued to deteriorate. As I said, he ran the home for thirteen years, right up until he was removed from the post last week. Naturally, they got rid of him the moment the news broke.'

You don't say, Freyja thought, but all she said aloud was: 'What about the staff who worked for him? He can't have run the place alone.'

'No, there were other staff there as well. There were always two people on duty morning and evening, but only one during school hours and at night. The city council has spoken to the staff currently working there and they claim not to have been aware of anything untoward. In fact, they speak well of Bergur. The police have started calling them in for interview, as well as any staff who've retired or moved on.'

'Did Bergur take the night shifts himself?'

It was clear from Yngvi's expression that he knew what she was implying. 'Yes, he did. About as regularly as the others.'

Freyja nodded. 'And in all those thirteen years there's never been a blot on his record, as far as we know?'

'Apparently not. I spoke to his manager at Reykjavík city council and she told me his record was almost perfect. Of course, like anyone working in the profession, he's been the subject of the odd complaint over the years, but never in connection with inappropriate behaviour or sexual abuse. Just complaints from children or parents who were unhappy about their situation in general. That's nothing new.'

'What about his private life? Is he a family man?'

'No. He's single. He was married but got divorced more than a decade ago. The marriage was childless.'

Freyja opened her mouth to ask another question but Yngvi interrupted. 'Let me save you the effort. There's nothing in the man's background or behaviour to give the slightest suspicion of wrongdoing. His boss described him as a model employee who never had a day's illness. The only leave of absence he's taken in the last thirteen years was when he went into rehab about ten years ago to get his drinking under control. He informed his employers and requested some time off, making no secret of the reason for it, and took it out of his summer holiday allowance, like many other people. But, according to her, he wasn't a daytime drinker or anything like that. She reckoned he was one of those rare individuals who recognise in time that they've got a problem and take action before it's too late. So you can imagine how surprised and shocked his colleagues are over these accusations.'

'Is he still in custody?' Freyja didn't remember hearing that he'd been released, but her attention had been taken up with other aspects of the story.

'Yes, he is. For now. But that's irrelevant for our purposes because you're not expected to attend interviews with him. Your role is to be available to the police when required, and also to comb through the files on the juveniles who spent time in his care, not just from the periods when they lived with him but also to check if anything significant cropped up after they were moved to alternative accommodation or sent back to their families. You never know when they might have disclosed what happened. If they ever did.'

At this point Freyja felt compelled to interrupt: 'What about the possibility that the children did speak up, but their allegations were never recorded or acted on?' There were precedents. It certainly wouldn't be the first time in Iceland that adults had let down children in similar situations. Often this was down to ignorance or poor judgement, but there had been cases in which the perpetrators had been protected due to their connections or position. 'Perhaps the adults thought they were making it up.'

'It's possible. Though anyone working in this area ought to know better than to ignore that kind of accusation. Still, who knows?' Yngvi hesitated, then said: 'They're considering whether to allow you access to recordings of the children's sessions with therapists employed by the City of Reykjavík from the period in question, as well as with our own people. Most of the kids attended one or more sessions during their time in care. As you're a psychologist employed by us to work on these types of cases, the request should hopefully be approved, but it's possible the powers that be will decide that the therapists who originally took the interviews should go through them. I hope not, because the interviews were taken over a long period and many of those involved have since moved on or left the profession. The thing is, I suspect these interviews are going to provide our best evidence. It's not unlikely that the children will have hinted at what was going on, and only someone motivated by criminal intent would have deleted that from a recording.'

'I see. How many children are we talking about?'

'The first batch consists of teenagers who were resident at the home over the last four years. Thirty-three of them are still under eighteen. The second batch are mostly over eighteen, so your presence won't be required much if the police decide to interview that group as well.'

Thirty-three adolescents. Freyja felt a pang. She was lucky she hadn't been numbed by repeated exposure to these kinds of cases. Not yet, anyway. 'So my role is basically to listen to the interviews I'm asked to attend and, in addition, to check whether any of these thirty-three children have previously tried to raise the alarm?'

'Exactly.' Yngvi laid his hands flat on the table as if he was about to stand up. But he remained sitting.

'I hope you won't come across any evidence of mistakes on our part. I dug up the name of the boy responsible for the original accusation – the one who came forward anonymously in the press – and ran through his file.' Yngvi removed his hands from the table and cleared his throat. 'He claims in the interview that he reported the abuse at the time, but I can't find anything to support that. I did go through it in a bit of a hurry, though, so it's always possible you'll come across something I missed.'

'What's his name? It would make sense for me to know that when I'm going through the records.'

'Tristan. Tristan Berglindarson.'

Freyja nodded. 'Do you know if the police regard him as a credible witness?'

'I have no idea. They've hardly shared any information with us.' Yngvi was becoming restless, although the meeting hadn't lasted long. 'I want to make it absolutely clear that your work is to be kept completely separate from the police investigation. They'll do their job and you're simply to sit in on the interviews and make sure that the young people are treated appropriately. You can intervene if you feel their rights are being infringed or they're being put under undue pressure. Apart from that, you're not to get involved. Don't ask any questions: they'll take care of that.'

'I've attended these sorts of interviews before, in the same role. I know what's required.'

'Good.' For the first time since Freyja had emerged from the lift, Yngvi seemed pleased. 'But don't forget about your other role, regarding the files. Your work is part of an internal investigation that we're conducting independently of the police inquiry. We absolutely can't be caught napping by any further statements in the press. We need to be forewarned about any potential problems, for the purposes of damage limitation.'

'Understood.'

'I should also stress that I expect you to be completely impartial when you're reviewing the files. You may come across the names of people you know from your work in child protection but you're to overlook any acquaintance. Though, having said that, none of the young people concerned have gone through the Children's House, so you needn't worry about encountering the names of any close colleagues. Or your own, for that matter.'

Freyja didn't bother to reply to this. There was nothing to add.

Yngvi's assistant appeared, out of breath, with the USB stick. It felt warm when she closed her hand on it, like a reminder of the inflammatory material it might contain.

Once the assistant had gone, it became clear that the meeting was over. Yngvi rose to his feet and she followed suit, though she did manage to slip in one more question that had occurred to her. 'Where are these kids supposed to go for help when this whole thing is out in the open? They're hardly likely to trust us.'

Yngvi looked her in the eye and answered without a moment's hesitation: 'No. That's pretty clear. But we'll deal with that when we come to it. Right now we need to establish the scale of the problem and wait for the police to complete their investigation. Only after that will we be in a position to consider our next steps.'

Freyja had to be satisfied with this answer. If she said any more, he was bound to remind her that it wasn't her job to oversee the case, just to concentrate on her contribution.

He walked her to the lift and waited with her for the doors to open. As she stepped inside they said goodbye, then, just as the doors were closing, Yngvi stuck out his foot to stop them.

'It would be good if you could give me a daily update.'

Freyja agreed. But Yngvi didn't withdraw his foot. Awkwardly, he opened his mouth to add something, then changed his mind. Then he opened it again and finally came out with what he wanted to say:

'It's only right you should know that there are plans to create a permanent position of liaison officer between children's services and the police, as a way of preventing further mistakes like the failure to report the allegation. The recruitment process will be starting shortly and I imagine you'd be well placed to send in an application. It's better paid than your current position and involves more responsibility too. A different kind of responsibility.'

'What about my job at the Children's House?'

'What about it? You'd have to resign, of course. The liaison officer position would be full time, and, as I said, better paid than your current job.' Seeing that Freyja was in two minds, Yngvi added: 'I know you're ambitious. You wouldn't have applied to be director of the Children's House back in the day if you weren't. But, to be honest, you won't get another crack at that job given . . . well, you know . . .'

Freyja managed to keep her expression impassive. How come it always hurt when people spoke 'honestly'? She was damned if she was going to be drawn into discussing the fiasco that had ended her career as director of the Children's House. 'Yes, well, there's no need to go into that,' she said curtly.

Apparently Yngvi wasn't entirely devoid of sensitivity. He clearly realised his gaffe. 'No, of course not. I just wanted to encourage you to apply. It would be a good move, career-wise.'

Freyja didn't know what to say. The man could hardly expect her to give him an answer there and then, standing in the lift with her finger on the button. 'Do I get some time to think about it?'

'Yes, of course. I just wanted to give you the heads-up – that if you're interested, there's more at stake than the present role, important as that is. If you do a good job, the position's yours. I can promise you that.'

Freyja thanked him. Yngvi's foot remained where it was.

'There's something I've heard but wasn't going to share with you, because I'm not sure it's true. But if it is, it may explain why the abuse went on for so long without coming to light.'

'What's that?' Intrigued, Freyja stepped into the gap between the doors to make sure they didn't close.

'I'm told that Tristan claims he was drugged – that he was asleep when the abuse took place. If that's true, it's possible that not all the young people involved are aware of what happened to them. Or of who was responsible.' He grimaced. 'Good luck.'

Freyja stepped back into the lift and the doors closed. She was clutching the warm USB stick so tightly that the edges cut into her palm.

Chapter 5

Tuesday

Huldar blew out a long breath and contemplated getting on top of his outstanding admin. He knew the Police Commissioner's quality-control officer would be over the moon. He might even feel a certain sense of satisfaction himself afterwards. He reached for his mouse to rouse his screen from its deep hibernation, only to jerk back his hand at the last minute. No way was he going to waste his time on that stuff. Not now, not tomorrow. Not ever.

He got to his feet. What on earth was he doing? He had actually, seriously, been considering getting on with some paperwork. Clearly, he needed an occupation. He peered over the monitor between him and Gudlaugur and saw that his colleague was sound asleep in his chair. No wonder he'd been so quiet for the last half-hour or so. Huldar briefly toyed with the idea of giving him a fright but thought better of it.

His relationship with Gudlaugur was back to normal after months of awkward silences and stupid misunderstandings. Nothing in particular had happened to bring about this reconciliation; Gudlaugur had simply realised in the end that Huldar couldn't give a damn about his sexuality. The message had finally sunk in when the reaction of their colleagues to the news that Gudlaugur was gay had been one of general indifference. They had – *almost* without exception – shrugged their shoulders. And Huldar had personally seen to it that any dinosaurs who did have a problem with it kept their mouths shut. He was only too happy that Gudlaugur seemed blithely unaware of the blows he'd struck to that end.

Against his better judgement, Huldar decided to see if Erla had any jobs up her sleeve for him. He knew she was bored out of her mind too. He'd been watching her through the glass wall of her office as she repeatedly reached for her phone, then drew back her hand. Presumably she was summoning up the courage to call the Identification Commission, and the reason for her hesitation was that she had rung them several times already.

Maybe he could distract her and himself at the same time. Of course, when Erla was in this mood she was apt to take it out on him, but, since he hadn't done anything wrong recently, she would have to find a pretext. Or dredge up some past misdemeanour. There was no shortage to choose from.

'How's it going?' Huldar went into her office, shutting the door behind him. That way there was less chance that she would drive him straight out again.

'Going? It's not bloody *going* anywhere. That commission's a bunch of fucking bureaucrats who have no idea of the need for a proper investigation. I expect they're falling over themselves hunting for some procedural rule that will let them off the hook.'

Huldar nodded, feigning agreement, while privately reflecting that the commission was made up of respected professionals who were dedicated to the task of establishing the identity of the deceased. It wasn't their job to investigate the cause of death. And it wasn't their fault that the Swedish lab required time to analyse the DNA. 'A week or two's nothing. And we should have the results of the age estimation before then.'

Erla was contemptuous. 'The age estimation? Don't get your hopes up. Apparently we don't have any of the "skeletal elements" that provide the best indication of age. Which means we'll get such a broad range that it'll be meaningless. It seems the most they're likely to be able to tell us is whether they were adults and whether they were past their prime. It's bound to be give or take ten years, if not even vaguer. Fat lot of use that'll be.'

'Won't we at least get an idea of their height?'

'Yes, apparently they can calculate that fairly accurately from the leg bones. But we won't be able to determine their sex from what we've got. So, in other words, we won't have anything useful until those bloody Swedes get their arses into gear and send us the results of the DNA analysis.'

'Isn't there anything we can get on with in the meantime?'

Erla snorted. 'Like what? Ring round the sportswear suppliers and ask if they've got a list of names of everyone who's ever bought Adidas or Nike shoes? We might as well resort to the telephone directory.'

'What about the missing-persons' list? Have you looked at that?' One of the jobs of the Identification Commission was to maintain a list of all the people who had disappeared in Iceland, the Register of Missing Persons, which could be referred to whenever a body turned up. Since it was stored on the police database, CID had access to it and could run the list together with other programs containing information about biological specimens, dental records and anything else that could shed light on an individual's origins. But they would have nothing to run through the system until they heard back from the commission. After one or even two long weeks.

Erla nodded. 'Nothing doing. Not as it stands.'

'Oh?'

'There are no instances of two simultaneous disappearances. Not for years, anyway. And no recent examples of people last seen wearing Nike or Adidas shoes.' Erla reached for a stapled bundle of pages. 'See for yourself.'

Huldar ran his eyes down the top page. There was no point looking any further back in time as the remains couldn't have been in the sea for years. It didn't require a PhD in pigs' carcases to work that out. It was self-evident that it wouldn't take the sea creatures that long to pick off the last scraps of flesh, even if they were protected by a shoe. And not even bones would last forever on the seabed. Huldar had discovered this much while killing time. The bones would be consumed by a variety of different creatures, just like any other organic matter that ended up in the sea. The process would take years but not decades. To narrow down the time frame, he had ascertained that the summer sea temperature off south Iceland was around 10°C. At that temperature, and given a favourable oxygen content, it would take around three months for the marine life to clean the bones to the extent of those they had found. And as the sea in wide bays like Faxaflói, which were open to the ocean, tended to be rich in oxygen, his was as good a guess as any other. So, logically, the bones couldn't have been in the sea for less than three months. Which gave a time frame of more than three months at one end and less than five years or so at the other.

They had carried on scouring the seabed with the submarine until the captain had put his foot down and insisted that the search be aborted. By then the weather had deteriorated to the point where everyone on board was clinging on for dear life just to stay upright. And Huldar, who had long since succumbed to his seasickness, had been too preoccupied with hanging on to his insides to take any further interest in the proceedings. Nevertheless, he had caught the moment when Erla stepped aside to throw up. She had been quick to return to the fray, though, carrying on as if nothing had happened. Paler, admittedly, but just as determined. He tried to comfort himself with the thought that seasickness didn't affect everyone in the same way.

But the extended search hadn't produced the desired results. All they'd got for their pains were three more arm bones, one thigh bone, a shoulder bone and several pieces of a coccyx. Neither skull had come to light, nor had any clothing, teeth or anything else that would make life easier for the Identification Commission. Some pelvic bones would have been helpful, as this would have speeded up the estimation of age and gender. None of the remains had provided any indication of the cause of death either, with the exception of a mark on one of the arm bones, the ulna, that could conceivably have been caused by an injury sustained while the person was alive. An expert would be brought in to examine the groove once the bones had been cleaned, but it wasn't impossible that it had resulted post-mortem, from being bumped around on the seabed.

Huldar glanced up from the list. 'Nothing leaps out at me.'

'No. Not a single bloody thing.' Erla took back the list. 'The shortest interval between disappearances is between the two top names. One vanished three months ago, the other ten. Sometimes there's a gap of a year or two between disappearances, but basically we're talking about fewer than fifty people in almost half a century. Not that the oldest instances are relevant, anyway, as no one in Iceland was wearing Nike shoes fifty years ago. Or even forty years ago, for that matter. In fact, none of the people on the list are thought to have been wearing Adidas shoes at the time they went missing and only two were wearing Nike. The most recent was five years ago, so I doubt the bones belong to him.' Erla glanced at her phone, momentarily distracted, then went on, 'I'm starting to think they could have fallen overboard from a ship or come from a wreck.'

'Hm, strange choice of footwear for fishermen. Could the men have been recreational sailors?'

'Men? Some of those bones could have belonged to a woman.'

Huldar had to concede that she was right. The Adidas shoe had looked smaller than the size forty-one Nike that had turned up originally. 'I didn't spot any women on that list.'

'There's one. But she went missing so long ago that it can't be her.' Erla made a face. 'Something's not right. Say it was an accident at sea: why isn't there any information about it? I spoke to a guy at the Commission of Enquiry into Accidents at Sea and according to him no sailor has died or been lost in Icelandic waters this year. Or last year either.'

'Foreigners, then?'

'Maybe. But if they'd come from international waters, they'd have been in a vessel with a transmitter, and the Directorate of Shipping would have picked them up on their radar if they were that close to shore. The guy I spoke to wasn't aware of any foreign vessels being lost off Iceland in recent memory. Not for many years, in fact. And he reckoned it was almost impossible that the bodies could have drifted there from a wreck that had gone down outside the two-hundred-mile limit. The same would apply to anyone who had fallen overboard in the Atlantic west of Iceland.'

Huldar pondered this for a while. 'What about a rowing boat or a kayak? Could they have been out in one of them? Small craft like that wouldn't be equipped with a transmitter, so they'd be unlikely to show up on radar.'

'In that case, it must have been a local one. You couldn't paddle all the way to Iceland in one of those. No, if they were tourists who'd rented a boat or a kayak and hadn't come back, the company responsible would have reported the incident. Anything else would be unthinkable.'

It would. But Huldar persisted. 'They could have brought a kayak or rubber dinghy to the country with them.'

Erla screwed up her face in exasperation. 'Oh, right. Would they have checked the kayak in or stuck it under the seat in front of them?'

'They could have come by ferry; taken the Norröna to Seydisfjördur.'

Erla's sneer faded. 'True.' She seemed annoyed not to have thought of that possibility herself. 'But it's still unlikely that two tourists would go missing here and not turn up on the register. It's not restricted to Icelanders.'

They were both silent. The truth was, there were no systematic checks in place to establish whether visitors who didn't turn up for their flights or ferry had in fact returned home by other means. There were a number of airlines operating flights to and from Iceland these days, which made it impossible to keep track of whether no-show passengers had left with other companies. Moreover, some airlines didn't operate passport checks on flights within the Schengen area, which made it theoretically possible to travel under a false name. Fortunately, few travellers, if any, had a reason to do so. But there had been examples of people coming to Iceland in order to take their own lives in the wilderness – travelling under their own name. The incidents had only come to light later, when their family or friends reported them missing.

'Is the plan to carry on searching the seabed?' Huldar asked, breaking the silence.

'Yes. They're waiting for repairs to the small sub. The bloody thing developed a fault. But the moment it's ready and there's a let-up in the weather, they'll resume the search. I'm told it's unlikely to be today, though.' Erla exhaled irritably. 'There have to be more remains out there. There was nothing to suggest the bodies had been dismembered. The bones were undamaged apart from the sea-creature activity and that one groove in the ulna. But since it's across the middle of the bone, apparently it can't have been the result of any butchery. So the bodies were probably intact when they ended up in the sea, which means the rest of the skeletons must be there somewhere. And hopefully their clothes as well.'

'Couldn't they have been eaten by sea creatures?'

Erla shrugged. 'Unlikely, if the bodies have only been in the sea for a matter of months. Clothes take much longer to degrade than soft tissue. Especially manmade fibres.' Evidently Erla had also been using the downtime to do a bit of online research. 'I just can't understand why we haven't found anything. If the bones are fairly recent, I can only conclude that the people weren't wearing many clothes. Maybe they were naked.'

'Naked, in shoes?'

'No, I suppose not.' The sudden note of irritation in Erla's voice was a warning sign that her patience was wearing thin. Perhaps she had finally steeled herself to ring the commission again. 'Anyway, what did you want?'

'I was hoping you'd have something for me to do. I'm willing to go to Hveragerdi and hunt for the cat killer, if nothing else.' It was no lie. It would be a pleasure to hand that sadist over to the justice system. Or to take him – if it was a him – round the back of a house and deal with the matter using a shorter, sharper method than the courts would allow.

Erla surveyed the open-plan office where the rest of the team were hard at work. 'How about using your time like your colleagues and getting on top of the outstanding paper-work from your past cases? I got an email from the quality controller the other day asking me to give you a nudge. None of us are good at this bloody chore but he singled you out for criticism. Which gives me a fair idea of how behind you are.'

Huldar gritted his teeth but managed to keep his cool. 'Don't you have anything more important for me to do?'

Erla snorted. 'More important? In my opinion everything's more important than fucking box-ticking.' She folded her arms across her chest. 'But I don't have a thing.' Seeing the disappointment on Huldar's face, she relented. Erla might be prickly, but she was capable of being human. Occasionally. Today it seemed his luck was in. 'I happen to know they're up against it down in Sexual Offences. They've got a child-abuse case that's plastered all over the headlines, which means everything they do is subject to close scrutiny. It doesn't help that they fucked up by failing to alert the city council when the original complaint was made. Anyway, they're short-handed because everyone's on holiday. If you're at the end of your tether, I'm sure they'd welcome you with open arms.'

Huldar didn't wait to be told twice. As the pressure on the various departments was impossible to predict, dictated as it was entirely by the caprice of the offenders, it was common for people to be seconded to other teams. Struck by a thought, he paused in the doorway. 'What about Gudlaugur? Can I take him with me?'

Erla pursed her lips, regarding him inscrutably.

'He's bored shitless too, and it would do him good to be occupied.' Huldar neglected to mention that Gudlaugur was at that moment having a nap.

When she didn't immediately answer, he added hurriedly: 'I'll tell them it's strictly provisional. If anything changes here, we'll be back like a shot.'

She agreed then, albeit reluctantly. Which was fine. He chose to interpret it as meaning that their work in CID was appreciated, until he remembered that she hadn't hesitated about letting *him* go. Perhaps it was only Gudlaugur's contribution that she regarded as indispensable.

'Hey!' Erla called after him before he could disappear. 'If you go to Sexual Offences, you won't be able to come out on the boat with us when we get the call.'

'Oh.' Huldar tried to look downcast. 'Yes. That's true.' He groped frantically for a way of justifying his absence, but Erla saved him the effort.

'Your loss. I'll find someone else.'

Huldar forced his features to register disappointment, then turned, mentally raising a triumphant fist to the sky.

Gudlaugur was awake and doing his best to give the impression of having been compos mentis ever since getting out of bed that morning. Huldar refrained from teasing him about it, merely slapped him lightly on the shoulder and told him they were being lent to Sexual Offences to help out with an inquiry there.

Gudlaugur's face brightened and he almost knocked down his chair in his hurry to get to his feet. Clearly, Huldar hadn't been the only one doing his nut with boredom.

Chapter 6

Freyja leant back in her chair and rubbed her eyes. She had been sitting in one position for far too long without stretching or getting up to refill her coffee cup. None of her colleagues had looked in and her phone had remained silent, emitting not so much as a ping to announce a text. It was as if the outside world, recognising the gravity of the case, wanted to ensure she had peace and quiet to work. As a result, she had made a good start.

She had gone through half the reports and other documents relating to the thirty-three pre-teens and adolescents who formed the focus of the first stage of the investigation. Of course, she hadn't yet been granted access to the files on the Child Protection Agency server, but those would mainly be useful for filling in the gaps, providing information about how the children had come to the attention of the agency and tracking their progress through the system. No doubt the amount of data on each child would vary enormously, depending on how long they had been involved with children's services. Some had been luckier than others, their cases easier to solve due to their particular circumstances. Others had been right through the system until they grew out of it. At the age of eighteen they were considered adults and most were then transferred to the care of social services.

Having divided up the children according to gender, Freyja had decided to focus on the boys first. As far as she could tell, the victim who had spoken to the press had just turned twelve when the perpetrator first abused him. This was consistent with the information Freyja had found in the files, which recorded that Tristan Berglindarson had been placed in temporary care with Bergur three weeks before his twelfth birthday. To her, this suggested that, rather than being a classic paedophile, Bergur was what was known as a hebephile, someone sexually attracted to pubescent children. Despite being controversial among psychologists, the diagnosis had gained a degree of recognition. From what Freyja had read, such individuals were usually only attracted to one sex, unlike paedophiles. As the victim who had come forward was a boy, Freyja suspected that Bergur's other victims would also turn out to be boys. On this basis, she put the girls to one side for the moment, intending to come to them later.

Nothing she had read so far provided any corroborating evidence of the man's crimes. There were various hints but nothing conclusive. Some of the boys had regressed after their time in his care; they had been caught using drugs and displayed signs of both physical and social deterioration. On the other hand, all these boys had been placed with Bergur following treatment for addictions, so it wasn't as if they'd had far to fall. Few people managed to sort out their lives after a single spell in rehab. An alternative explanation was that their regression could have been a result of abuse, but as yet she had found nothing that pointed unambiguously to this. Nevertheless, she conscientiously noted down any increased signs of distress. She thought she could detect a difference between the wellbeing of the prepubescent boys and the pubescent age group. The little boys seemed to have been in a relatively good state of mind, considering that they had been removed from their homes and sent to live with strangers. Sadly, however, this age group had been in the minority, as the home had mainly catered for teenagers. If her analysis was correct, this was unlikely to have been a coincidence. Child abusers are cunning at engineering situations which provide them with easy access to victims in the desired age group.

Freyja glanced back over her notes. The bulk of the material she was currently able to access consisted of information that was quantifiable, and questions that could be answered with a simple yes or no, and her comments were influenced by this. Much of what she had to go on were height and weight measurements, the results of drugs tests and answers to questions like: *How are you feeling on a scale of one to six?* None of the boys had scored a 'six'. She had seen two 'fours', but most peaked at 'three'. Two of the boys had apparently asked if they could answer 'zero'. When they'd first arrived at the home, they had put their wellbeing at 'two'. They were both in what she judged to be the at-risk age group. The same boys had complained of nightmares, of finding it hard to wake up in the mornings and of feeling sluggish when they did get up. Freyja thought it possible the man had abused these two after slipping them sleeping pills, which would have had similar side effects. However, the spot tests for drugs hadn't checked for the active elements in sleeping pills, which meant her theory was impossible to prove.

None of the boys had been given physical examinations for signs of sexual abuse during their time at the home. The occasional individual had been examined on first entering care, due to suspicions of earlier abuse, but they were the exception. Apparently it hadn't crossed anyone's mind that the boys might be at risk once they were in the hands of the system, since they were supposed to be safe there.

She would have liked to read transcripts of interviews with the boys taken by therapists or social workers, but frustratingly there were few on the USB stick. It was mainly reports by their support workers, a number of which could immediately be discounted, since the support-worker role had been performed by the alleged abuser during the children's stay at his home. Read with the benefit of hindsight, this was chilling stuff. All the reports spoke of happiness and good progress, except when Bergur noted that a boy was untruthful and had a tendency to invent stories as a way of seeking attention. Presumably these comments were designed to cover his back in case any of them complained. If Freyja's theory was correct, Bergur's comments would constitute a deliberate attempt to cover up his crimes.

In the case of these boys, she would have to rely on other evidence. The children had seldom been taken to see experts but had occasionally received visits as the result of an incident; uncontrolled behaviour, aggression or a failed drug test being the usual reasons. As a result, the experts' comments, recorded on file after the interview, mostly related to specific events. Although an attempt had been made to find out what had caused the outburst on each occasion, Freyja hadn't come across any insinuations by the boys that the man who ran their home was abusing them. It was easy to be wise after the event and criticise the experts for not pushing harder for answers but, to be fair to them, their approach had been standard procedure. All the children had a history of problems and the occasional lapse was only to be expected.

Freyja had been hoping one of the boys might have noticed something suspicious – been woken in the night by the abuser's activities, perhaps – but none of them had reported anything of the kind. There hadn't been many children accommodated in the home at any one time – at most three but usually only two. She didn't have a floor plan or any other information about the premises but assumed that the children would have been given their own rooms. Perhaps it had been enough for Bergur to close their doors, yet in spite of this it seemed odd that in all these years none of the kids had ever lain awake, heard strange noises and got up to investigate. When she stopped to think about it, though, it occurred to her that Bergur might have slipped them all sleeping pills when he was on night shift.

Freyja put the papers down on her desk and sighed. She'd have to head off soon. Her working day wasn't officially over, but she wanted to be punctual to collect Saga. Her niece wasn't wild about her nursery school, but then she didn't really like anything that could be called normal. What Saga liked best was being alone with one of the three adults in her life: her mother, her father or Freyja. Whenever her niece was staying with her, therefore, Freyja tried to limit the amount of time the little girl spent at her nursery school.

Before hurrying out of the office, Freyja rang Yngvi, as promised, to update him on the day's progress. The phone call was as dry and impersonal as a conversation between two computers. Freyja made no attempt to play down her fears that a number of the boys might have been abused. It didn't look good, despite the lack of solid evidence – not that this depressing conclusion came as a surprise to either of them. Once the mink's got into the henhouse, it doesn't stop at a single chicken. They ended the call as coolly as they had begun it. Neither made any reference to the new position of police liaison officer.

Freyja shut down her computer, put the USB stick in her pocket and headed out.

At the nursery school, Freyja was met by the familiar shrieking and wailing of tired children, bored of the battered toys and of each other. They looked up hopefully when she appeared in the doorway, their faces falling when they saw she hadn't come to collect them. Two started crying. Saga had raised her head too but didn't crack a smile on discovering that she was the lucky one. Instead, she simply abandoned what she had been doing alone in her corner, got to her feet and walked over to Freyja. Not in any hurry, though, as it wouldn't do to look eager. On reaching her aunt, she held out her small, moist hand and allowed Freyja to lead her out. They went into the cloakroom, where Freyja helped the little girl into her wellington boots and anorak. Saga's red puddle suit was hanging on her peg, but unlike the other children's water-proofs, it was spotless. There was no sign that she had been running around outside like the other kids. Knowing her, she had probably stood there with a bucket and spade in her hand, watching the others play. The psychologist in Freyja itched to go back inside and ask the teachers about Saga's social development but she curbed the impulse. She was only the child's aunt, not her mother.

The Doll

They drove out to Seltjarnarnes, the westernmost suburb on the peninsula on which Reykjavík was built, and Freyja parked her old banger in the almost empty spaces in front of the smart apartment block. The flat came with its own parking spot in the underground garage but this was occupied by the owner's vehicle while he was stuck behind bars. His car, like those of the other residents, was too expensive to be left outside at the mercy of the elements. Still, at least this meant Freyja never had any trouble finding a space. It was yet another advantage of the arrangement, which she owed to her brother and his colourful friend. If you ignored the snake, there was little to fault about the flat, apart from the fact that she didn't feel at home there. Most of the contents belonged to the owner, which made it feel almost like living in an Airbnb. No doubt the feeling would wear off over time, as she gradually made her mark on the place: her cosmetics in the bathroom, the Post-it notes on the fridge and the cafetière on the kitchen worktop were a good start.

The afternoon passed in a whirl of activity, which didn't leave Freyja with a spare moment to sit down. She went for a walk around the peninsula, with Molly on her lead and Saga in her buggy, meeting no one apart from other dog walkers, as no one in their right mind would go out in weather like this unless they had no choice. Heavy raindrops fell from a leaden sky, only to be snatched up by a cold northeasterly and flung horizontally into Freyja's eyes as she tramped doggedly along the coast path. After they got home, Freyja fed them both, then gave Saga her bath, while Molly cringed behind the sofa, afraid that she would be next. Once Saga was in her pyjamas, they sat on the sofa in the sitting room and Freyja read her niece some of the children's books she had collected. Storytime lasted longer than it should have done because Saga was determined to hear the same book over and over again. By the end, Freyja didn't even need to look at the page as she knew the story off by heart.

Once Saga had finally dropped off, Freyja tucked her up in her little bed. She pulled the duvet up to her chubby chin, after removing the favourite cuddly animal from the little girl's slack grip and putting it at the foot of the bed. It was supposed to be a dinosaur but looked more like a fox with a Toblerone on its back. A grubby, sticky fox, as Saga liked nothing better than to throw it as far as she could – a metre or so – for Molly to fetch.

Freyja cast an eye over the main news sites but found little of interest. The police investigation into the skeletal remains that had been found in Faxaflói Bay dominated the domestic headlines, while nothing of any substance had been added to the articles Freyja had already read on the abuse case. She turned her attention to social media but that turned out to be just as dull. Complaints about the wet weather were interspersed with the occasional sun-drenched photos of friends holidaying abroad. Freyja couldn't concentrate on any of it and there was nothing remotely tempting on television either. Since the last thing she was in the mood to think about now was the new job and whether she really wanted it, instead she fell to brooding on what she had read about the care home.

She lay back on the sofa, letting her mind wander. She recalled a recent study of adolescents' sleeping habits, which had concluded that girls had more problems sleeping than boys. Perhaps there was something significant lurking in the files on the girls who had stayed at the care home. Although

– assuming Freyja's theory was right – they would almost certainly have escaped the attentions of the sexual predator, they could have witnessed some odd behaviour in the night. Freyja got up from the sofa, fetched the USB stick and plugged it into her laptop.

It was only when she stood up to fetch a glass of water that she realised two hours had passed and she hadn't looked up once.

There had been far fewer girls than boys at the home; only seven in total. Most had stayed there for shorter periods as well, and their records were patchier than those of the boys. In the two hours, Freyja had managed to review all the available material on five of the girls and only had a couple left. The information was similar to that in the boys' files, except that none of the girls had mentioned having trouble waking up or feeling sluggish in the mornings. In contrast to the boys, their level of wellbeing seemed to improve the longer they stayed at the home, which would fit with Freyja's theory about the man's interest being restricted to boys. Since she had been extremely careful not to let her theory influence her interpretation of the records, she felt fairly confident that in the girls' case there was no evidence to suggest they had been abused in any way. She would go over the material again at work tomorrow to be on the safe side, but didn't expect that to alter her conclusions.

Freyja drank a glass of water, trying not to let the girls' sad stories get to her. The files had contained only incidental descriptions of how their stay at the home had ended. Mostly she'd had to read between the lines. If she had understood right, three of them had come from dysfunctional homes while the fourth had gone off the rails as a teenager. All had

had a tough time in one way or another, and how they'd turned out was influenced by a number of complex factors. Sometimes it seemed that chance alone had decided whether children managed to flourish in spite of being presented with a crap hand in life. Other kids seemed hell-bent on self-destruction, defying all efforts to help them. Yet the authorities had to try, and to go on trying, until the kids were eighteen and became somebody else's problem.

Freyja wondered if she should get out her yoga mat and do a few exercises before bed. Perhaps she would finally achieve the elusive peace of mind which was supposed to result from putting yourself through all those physical contortions. It wouldn't hurt to try, since she had no desire to go to bed while still preoccupied with the fate of those poor kids. The snake was bad enough as a disincentive to sleep.

It wasn't long before Freyja would have to feed the slippery creature again; a weekly event that still made her skin crawl. Between feeding times, she avoided going into its room, only going in once a day to change its water. The python seemed perfectly content with this arrangement and gave no sign of having missed her when she popped in. The flat head would slowly rise, the black eyes watching her through the glass wall of the big tank as she hastily changed its water bowl, then made a sharp exit. The animal showed a fraction more gratitude when she brought it the weekly mouse or hamster. Although the staff at the pet shop must have guessed what was in store for the poor little creatures, as she clearly wasn't the only person in Iceland feeding an illegal snake, they turned a blind eye. They couldn't afford to refuse any custom.

Now that she had allowed thoughts of the snake to distract her, any hope of concentrating on yoga was lost. Instead,

Freyja sat down with her laptop again and started looking through the files of the two remaining girls. The first had been at the home for less than a week and there was nothing of interest to be learnt from her case. The second, however, had been there more often and for longer periods, adding up to more than a year in total. That was quite a long time, given that she had first been placed with Bergur two years previously. In the three years before that she had been in and out of care. There were far more files on her than on the other girls – or boys, for that matter, though some of them had spent a longer time at the home.

Freyja started reading and didn't stop until she had finished every last word. Then she closed the laptop, feeling perplexed, not knowing how on earth to interpret what she had read. This girl was unlike any of the other kids at the home, not only in terms of the issues she was wrestling with but also of the answers she had given when questioned. What she did have in common with the others was the lack of specifics on file about her history and the reason she had ended up at the home. From the little information provided on the USB stick, it was clear that the girl's background was as untypical as she was. Freyja couldn't wait to get hold of some proper records and learn Rósa's story.

Chapter 7

Huldar was no longer bored at work. Quite the opposite, in fact. Not only did he have enough to do but he had a sense of purpose as well. He and Gudlaugur had been given a warm welcome by Hafthór, head of the child abuse inquiry, who had quickly found them jobs to do, with the proviso that they were there simply to assist and could forget about initiating their own lines of inquiry. This seemed fair enough to them since they weren't permanent staff in the Sexual Offences Unit and had next to no experience in that area. As soon as they had been briefed on the investigation, they went their separate ways.

They weren't required to be present during questioning of the suspect. Not for the moment, anyway. Huldar didn't mind this at first since he knew how challenging he would find it to have to sit and listen to the man's warped version of events. The perpetrator's perspective was always filtered through smoked glass. Huldar was used to this from the cases he dealt with in CID but knew he would find it much harder to listen to twisted descriptions of crimes against children, in which the blame was transferred onto them. Self-control wasn't exactly his forte and he couldn't afford any more anger-related incidents on his record.

But when Hafthór told them that the man refused to confess and was insisting on his innocence, Huldar changed his mind. He was quite competent at telling when an interviewee was lying and would have liked a chance to judge for himself. Although he wasn't infallible, he reckoned his instincts were pretty good.

The most serious consequence of the man's steadfast denials was that, unless they uncovered rock-solid evidence against him, such as witness statements corroborating the account of Tristan Berglindarson and any other victims who might come forward, it would end up being one person's word against another's. In that case it would make no difference how many victims there were, as strength in numbers had no validity in Icelandic law. The onus would be on every single victim to prove that a crime had been committed against them. Since Tristan had waited years to bring charges, there was no question now of a medical examination or record of injuries. This was the Achilles' heel of sexual offences: that it so often came down to one person's word against another's.

Tristan himself had already been interviewed once in front of a judge but the investigators still had to question a long list of Bergur Alvarsson's other former charges. They would be speaking initially to thirty-three young people who had been resident at his home in the last four years. Not all of them could be contacted, however. One had moved abroad with his family, two had been awarded disability allowance at eighteen and moved to Spain, and two were dead, one from an overdose, the other from suicide. That left twenty-eight names.

Gudlaugur was assigned to helping trace the kids they hadn't yet managed to contact; Huldar to attending the interviews. When Hafthór mentioned that the judge had insisted on the presence of a child psychologist, Huldar's spirits had lifted, though he tried not to let it show. But when he oh-so-casually asked the psychologist's name, the smile that spread over his face when he heard that it was Freyja gave him away. Gudlaugur, catching it, rolled his eyes.

Hafthór looked disconcerted. 'Do you know her?'

'She's assisted us with several cases.'

'All right, is she?'

'Oh, yes.'

The digression caused Hafthór to lose the thread and he couldn't remember anything else to tell them. After hovering in front of his desk for a while, Gudlaugur and Huldar left the room and went to their new workstations. Unlike those in CID, these consisted of booths with high partitions. Huldar assumed this was due to the sensitive nature of the cases dealt with here. The fewer people who saw what was on screen, the better.

The officers whose desks he and Gudlaugur had been allotted were on holiday. Judging by the three photos pinned to the partition, the man Huldar was standing in for was a weight-lifter. They showed him grinning triumphantly as he posed beside a succession of barbells loaded with impressive weights, designed for dead lifts, squat lifts and bench presses. Presumably each picture had been taken after he had beaten a personal record. It reminded Huldar of those idiots who had photos taken of them posing with their guns beside dead animals on safari – but far less harmful, of course. There were no photos in Gudlaugur's booth, or indeed anything else personal. The officer had departed on holiday as if he had no intention of ever returning.

Huldar switched on the computer and logged in under his own username. He found the inquiry folder and was relieved to be admitted without a hitch. The IT department obviously hadn't wasted any time in organising his authorisation. He checked to see what was stored in the folder but didn't click on many files while he was getting to grips with the overall picture. The oldest files dated from nearly three months ago, which was consistent with the fact that the original complaint had been filed at the end of May. Not much seemed to have happened between then and the recent appearance of the anonymous interview with Tristan in the media. After that it hadn't taken the police long to discover his identity and only then had the inquiry got properly underway. Since then files had been pouring in, even though this had coincided with the beginning of the summer holidays.

Huldar paused when he spotted a familiar name on one of the files. It belonged to a student taking a degree in policing, who had previously done a stint of work experience in Erla's department. She had last saved a file ten minutes ago. Huldar rose to his feet and peered around. Unable to spot her, he tried calling her name: 'Lína?'

Over in the far corner, a familiar red head popped up over one of the partitions. Lína smiled, waved, and came over.

They greeted each other with genuine warmth as they had got on well when working together in CID. Lína was a stickler for detail, prone to citing her textbooks, and not shy about pointing out other people's mistakes. This had done nothing to endear her to the rest of the team, not least because most were wary of the new generation of police officers who would come armed with university degrees. But Huldar wasn't resentful about progress or change, taking the view that neither he nor his colleagues would be able to halt the tide, so he had taken her under his wing.

Huldar explained what he was doing in Sexual Offences and asked why Lína was there herself. It wouldn't have surprised him to hear she'd graduated early.

'I'm here for the summer.' Lína blushed slightly and avoided Huldar's eye. 'I'm trying to build up a portfolio of experience in a number of different departments. That's why I didn't apply to come back to your team.'

Huldar grinned. 'Sensible decision. Just what I'd have expected of you.' He glanced around. 'Listen, perhaps you could teach me the ropes, since you've been here longer than me?'

The tiny Lína drew herself up to her full height, her head just reaching his shoulder. 'Yes, I should be able to do that,' she said, with the air of an old pro.

Huldar nodded, trying to look grave. 'Are you working on the case I'm helping out with?'

'Yes.' Lína shuddered and pulled a face. Huldar assumed this was due to the serious nature of the crime but he was wrong. Lína's disgust was motivated by something else entirely. 'Yes. And I can't begin to describe what a pig's ear they've made of it. How could they possibly have forgotten to inform Reykjavík city council about the complaint? And overlooked the case altogether? They didn't even interview the alleged perpetrator back in the spring.'

Naturally, Lína would be outraged by this kind of incompetence. He could have told himself that. She wouldn't be fobbed off with the explanation Huldar and Gudlaugur had been given, which was that a mistake had been made during the handover between investigators. The person who received the complaint had gone on sick leave shortly afterwards and his replacement had overlooked it. A typical unintentional oversight. Nor was Lína likely to have been impressed by the mistake made by the switchboard when the victim had tried to report the case directly to the City of Reykjavík. In her eyes, this level of incompetence would be unforgiveable – which it was, of course, but Huldar had no intention of getting drawn into the blame game. It was too late now to undo the damage. 'So, what job have they given you?'

Lína's scandalised expression cleared. 'I'm responsible for going over part of the material that was removed from the care home. I'm recording it and making a preliminary assessment of whether it constitutes evidence.' Pride shone from her porcelain-white face. 'There's an unbelievable amount of stuff. Apart from the contents of the flat, the storeroom was crammed with boxes containing all kinds of lost property. I was asked to sort through it. Some of it dates back to before the suspect's time, but it all needs to be catalogued anyway. It's not as if odd socks, notebooks or hairbrushes are labelled by year.'

Huldar tried to sound enthusiastic. 'Interesting.'

Lína wasn't only a good student, she was a shrewd judge of character and a mind reader to boot. 'You think it's pointless?'

'No. Of course not,' Huldar lied smoothly. He couldn't imagine anything more tedious than having to sift through junk from a storeroom. His own basement storage unit was half full of clobber he had transferred from his old place when he bought his flat. That had been seven years ago and he hadn't once gone down there since locking the door on the stuff. He would never use any of it again but nothing could be further from his mind than having a clear-out. He'd sooner go on a shopping expedition to the Smáralind mall with one of his sisters. And that would only happen over his dead body. 'Have you got far?'

'I'm about halfway through.'

'Found anything interesting? Apart from odd socks and hairbrushes?'

Lína glared at him. 'Ha ha. I have, actually. There are various items that could be significant. Some of the kids left all their belongings behind. I found a diary, for example, and two mobile phones that are recent enough models to date from the period we're examining. The IT department is working on unlocking them in case they belonged to anyone who turns out to have been a victim. They may contain messages or photos that could be relevant.'

'Oh, great.' Huldar smiled, hoping Lína would forgive his earlier scepticism. 'Whose diary is it?'

'One of the girls who was a resident there. I've yet to go through it but it's very densely written, so who knows? Maybe she saw or suspected something. If so, she might have mentioned it.'

'Let's hope so.' Huldar saw Hafthór waving to him from his office door. He gave Lína a pat on the shoulder and told her he was looking forward to working with her again.

Freyja was looking good. Even better than he remembered. She smelt good too; no sickly-sweet reek of perfume but a hint of expensive soap made from natural ingredients, like the sort he imagined you'd find in the bathrooms at health spas. They hadn't met for months but he got the feeling that in this case absence might have worked in his favour. The smile she bestowed on him was warmer than usual and she clasped his hand more firmly, which made it hard for him to concentrate on the interview Hafthór was conducting.

It didn't help that the interview room wasn't what he was used to. They'd attempted to make it a bit cosier, as part of the same arrangement that had stipulated the presence of a child psychologist. A padded armchair had been dragged in and placed in one corner; there was an ailing pot plant on the table and a familiar framed map of Iceland on the wall, with red crosses marking all the fatal traffic accidents of the previous ten years. It wasn't the happiest choice of wall decoration and Huldar hoped none of the kids would ask what the crosses meant. Something told him that the judge who had made this arrangement with the police hadn't come by to check up on how his orders were being carried out.

It was some time before Huldar could tear his mind away from these distractions and concentrate on what the interviewee was saying.

The boy's name was Bragi Lárusson and he was fourteen years old. He had turned up unaccompanied, saying his mother was ill and his dad was 'who knows where', adding off-handedly that he hadn't seen him for years. Bragi was thin, with shaggy hair and bad skin, like so many teenagers. His tangled, overgrown fringe might have been an attempt to hide his acne but, if so, it had failed. His trainers were filthy and soaking wet, as if he were three years old and had jumped in all the puddles on his way there. The trail of footprints could still be seen glistening on the floor. But apart from this, he was respectably dressed, in clean clothes and a coat suitable for the rain. Obviously someone cared about him; presumably his sick mother.

Bragi was nervous at first and had trouble looking any of them in the eye when answering their questions. Nevertheless, his replies, delivered in a low voice, were clear and to the point. He was perfectly aware of the reason for the interview and that he himself wasn't suspected of any wrongdoing.

To begin with, the questions were general. He was asked why he had been placed at the home, what conditions had been like, and who else had been resident there at the same time.

Bragi had spent just over two months in Bergur's care when he was eleven because his mother had been admitted to a psychiatric ward. Neither his paternal nor his maternal relatives had felt able to take him in, which was unusual, to say the least, but Hafthór, Huldar and Freyja carefully refrained from commenting on the fact.

Bragi said there had been two teenagers at the home at the same time as him, a girl and a boy, but he couldn't remember either of their names. They had been mean and ignored him. He did recall that the boy had monopolised the game console, although he was useless, and the girl had been on the phone the whole time, when she wasn't in a sulk and slamming doors. He had mostly stayed in his room. When asked what he'd done to pass the time, he told them he'd done nothing. Just sat there. After a moment he added that he had probably been thinking. They didn't ask what he'd been thinking about.

Once the general questions had been covered, Hafthór moved on to the trickier ones, the questions that required careful phrasing, designed to discover any possible abuse. Freyja had discussed with Hafthór how best to approach the subject. If he didn't go about it right, there was a risk the boy would retreat into his shell or try to deny what had happened, to avoid having to admit to something he found embarrassing or humiliating to talk about with strangers. Freyja had offered them access to the interviewing facilities at the Children's House, but Hafthór had turned this down. Although she didn't come right out and say so, it was obvious that she was unimpressed by their feeble attempts to make the interview room at the police station more welcoming. Hafthór had defended his decision on the grounds that they were under pressure to get results and there was no time to re-schedule the interviews, and Freyja hadn't pursued the subject, though Huldar could tell she thought he was making a mistake.

As Hafthór put his questions, Huldar reflected that he was doing a good job. On the rare occasions that he chose the wrong word or phrased something badly, Freyja came to the rescue. Together they guided the mortified boy through the points they needed to get straight. Some things required a number of questions, others had to be rephrased until he grasped what they were getting at. By the time it was over he was crimson in the face and his eyes kept sliding towards the door as if desperate to make his escape.

Huldar hadn't opened his mouth once. He was entirely focused on listening, as befitted his role as an observer, which enabled him to keep a close eye on the boy's reactions to questions that no one should need to ask a child. He was fairly confident that Bragi was telling the truth when he claimed that he had never been molested. He had never woken up to find the manager in his room or his bed, or any of the other staff either, for that matter. The man had never touched him in an inappropriate way or in any other way that Bragi didn't like. In fact, the manager had taken very little notice of him when he was on duty. He'd fed Bragi, made him do his homework at the kitchen table and told him when to take a shower. Woken him up in the mornings, given him breakfast and sent him to school.

Further, Bragi told them he had never been given any medicine in the evenings, only the yellow pill he had to take every morning on school days. He recognised that pill and was familiar with the taste, so he was sure it had never been swapped for a different one.

Next, Hafthór moved on to asking similar questions about the two teenagers who had been there with him. Had Bragi ever been aware of Bergur going into their rooms at night? Had he ever seen them taking medicine from him or noticed the manager putting anything in their food or drink?

The answers to all these questions were the same: no, no and no. Bragi hadn't been aware of anything untoward. Bergur had taken little interest in him and had mainly been concerned with the girl who apparently had a drug problem and required all his attention. Bragi followed this up with the assurance that he himself had never taken drugs and never intended to. He held his head a little higher after this declaration.

When it became clear that the interview was drawing to an end, Freyja slipped in a question of her own. Hafthór didn't object, as it was a perfectly natural closing question that he would probably have asked himself. Her voice was softer and friendlier, more likely to elicit an answer from the boy. 'Is there anything else you found strange at the time, or now, looking back?'

'Ummm . . .' Bragi licked his lips, thinking. When he spoke it was to Huldar and Hafthór. 'It was all so strange. Totally different from being with my mum. It wasn't like a home at all. They tried to pretend it was, but they were full of crap. None of us felt at home or wanted to be there. We were only there because we had no choice.'

Huldar and Hafthór both looked at Freyja, as if expecting her to trot out the standard response used by children's services to counter this kind of accusation. She didn't have a standard response, but answered anyway: 'Care arrangements have nothing to do with the police, Bragi. We're trying to find out if anything happened that struck you as weird or wrong at the time. Maybe nothing did, but if you do remember, it would be really helpful if you could tell us.'

'I don't remember anything.'

'All right. But something might come back to you after the interview. If it does, please get in touch.' Freyja glanced at Huldar and Hafthór. Realising what she meant, they got out their cards. The boy took them and stared, puzzled, at the small, rectangular pieces of card. Presumably he'd never been given one before. Fourteen-year-old boys had no truck with such things: it would have been more appropriate for them to swap Snapchat accounts.

Bragi looked up, still with the cards in his hand, seeming unsure whether he was supposed to return them or take them away with him. 'Like I said, I don't remember anything. Can I go now?'

'Yes. But keep the cards in case anything occurs to you later. They've got our phone numbers on them.' Huldar reached across the table to point at them.

There was no sign that the boy had any intention of following this advice as he pocketed the cards and rose to his feet.

Hafthór escorted him out, leaving Huldar and Freyja

behind. She surveyed the room, shaking her head, her lips compressed disapprovingly.

'It is a bit depressing, I'll give you that.' Huldar picked up the jug on the table and watered the doomed plant. Two more leaves fell off, which left only three.

Freyja shook her head again. 'What's that map? What are the markings?'

'Fatal traffic accidents in the last ten years.'

Freyja's jaw dropped. 'That's cheerful. Is that really all they could come up with?'

'Apparently.'

Freyja was still gaping at the poster. But when she spoke again it was to express her astonishment at the statistics. 'There must be more than a hundred crosses.'

'Yes. There are quite a lot. I can't say I know the story behind all of them but there are plenty I do remember.'

'Such as?'

He told her about the ones that immediately sprang to mind: the recent collision between a lorry and a rental car in which two tourists died; the car that rolled over in the south of Iceland, throwing a little girl, who wasn't wearing a seatbelt, to her death; the young couple whose car had turned over at the foot of Mount Akrafjall, killing them both; the drunk driver who had killed two pedestrians; and, one of the oldest on the map, the tragic incident ten years ago in the north-east, in which a six-year-old girl, left waiting by her father's broken-down car at the side of the road, had fiddled with the gearstick and died when the car ran her over.

'That's enough.' Freyja grimaced. 'For Christ's sake, don't answer like that if any of the kids ask about the crosses. Just make up some lie. But that map has to go. There's no way we want to plant images of broken and crushed bodies in these kids' minds, especially not of a little girl. Take the map down.'

There was no time sort it out now. More interviews had been booked and he handed her the list of names. Freyja skimmed it, then asked about a girl whose name wasn't there. Huldar told her that the Rósa in question was one of the kids they hadn't yet managed to contact. Before Freyja could explain her look of disappointment, Hafthór appeared with another boy. The next interview was due to begin.

Chapter 8

Tuesday

Gudlaugur neatly laid down his knife and fork as a sign that he had finished and his plate could be removed. Since the police canteen was self-service, this was a singularly pointless gesture, but Freyja caught herself doing the same thing. Huldar, who'd helped himself to twice as much as the others, was still shovelling down his food.

Freyja and Huldar had been given an hour's lunch break after the first three interviews. The next two teenagers, a boy and a girl, had told the same story as Bragi: neither had experienced anything untoward, or witnessed any improper behaviour. Both had turned up unaccompanied, though each gave a different explanation for this: 'Mum's working.' 'Mum's busy at home.' What the mothers considered more important than providing their child with moral support at the police station was not explained. As had been the case with Bragi, their fathers played no part in their lives. Having read the three kids' files, Freyja knew why. One was an addict, another had left the country and the third was basically a bastard. Bad behaviour doesn't always require complicated analysis to understand.

Freyja watched Gudlaugur take a sip of water, waiting for him to put down his glass so she could start grilling him.

She'd held back long enough not to appear rude – but it had been an effort.

At first she had been wary about accepting Huldar's invitation to eat lunch with him, but when Gudlaugur breezed over and joined them, she had changed her mind. She was longing to find out if he'd managed to get hold of Rósa yet. It was a sign of how eager she was for information that she was prepared to sit through a whole lunch hour with Huldar, putting up with his idiotic attempts to impress her. Mind you, she had to admit that he was looking bloody good and so far he hadn't said or done anything too embarrassing. In fact, he had behaved like a normal person. Wonders would never cease. At this point, common sense kicked in, reminding her that her self-imposed abstinence might be affecting her judgement.

The instant Gudlaugur put down his glass, Freyja seized her chance. 'I hear you're trying to trace the kids who haven't been contacted yet.'

Gudlaugur nodded dully, his eyes on his glass. 'Yes. I've only just started and can't really see how I'm supposed to go about it. I'm mainly checking social media at the moment, not that it's provided many leads. I found two posts from yesterday evening, by a girl and one of the boys. But they didn't tell me much beyond the fact that they're both still alive.'

'Well, that's something, at least,' Freyja said encouragingly. 'You'll find them in the end, I'm sure of it.'

'Yes, I suppose so,' Gudlaugur said, sounding unconvinced. 'I'm still waiting to meet the guy I'm supposed to be assisting – he's a specialist in missing children. But he's mainly active in the evenings and at night. Apparently he was up until four this morning, so he isn't expected in until later. I just hope I'll get to work on processing the information he's gathered, rather than having to join him on night shift.'

No sooner had Gudlaugur finished than Freyja jumped in again. She had limited interest in hearing about his shifts. 'The girl who posted. It wasn't by any chance Rósa? Rósa Thrastardóttir?'

Gudlaugur shook his head. 'No. I couldn't find anything on her. She's got profiles on most of the social media sites but she isn't very active on any of them. Her last posts are from a week ago, but she hasn't been missing that long.'

'How long has she been missing?' Huldar chipped in.

Freyja suspected him of feeling left out. He hadn't been as eager for Gudlaugur to join them as she had.

'Four days. She ran away from the foster home where she's only been staying for a month or so. I spoke to the woman she was living with and she told me that the girl has a habit of doing this. Apparently children's services have tried repeatedly to find more permanent solutions for her but she's never happy and always runs away. She keeps ending up in temporary placements while they're looking for a new foster family. I don't know if that's true or if the woman was just trying to make excuses for the girl's disappearance. Maybe she thought I was blaming her.'

'No, she's right. Rósa's a regular absconder.'

'Why are you interested in her? Do you have reason to think she might be a victim?' Huldar shoved a piece of bread in his mouth. He had used it to wipe his plate clean.

'No. Or at least I'd be surprised if she was. I think our suspect's interested in boys. Pubescent ones.' Freyja noticed that Gudlaugur had lowered his eyes to his plate as if embarrassed, and added hastily: 'Neither paedophilia nor a sexual preference for pubescents has anything to do with homosexuality. Or with heterosexuality, for that matter. These are specific urges.' If anything, Gudlaugur looked even more pained at this, so Freyja gave up and replied to Huldar's first question. 'The reason I'm interested in Rósa is that she came across as very unusual when I read her file. And her stay at the home coincided with Tristan's, which makes her a potential witness.' Freyja wasn't telling him anything new as the police already had information about when the various kids had been in residence.

Huldar swallowed the bread. 'In what way unusual?'

The duty of confidentiality prevented Freyja from revealing any details of the girl's case. 'Just atypical,' she said. 'Strange history, strange behaviour.'

Huldar and Gudlaugur continued to stare at her in the hope of further details, until it apparently dawned on Huldar what was stopping her. 'You realise we can access the information by other means?' he pointed out.

'Maybe you can, but that doesn't alter the fact that I can't discuss the Child Protection Agency's files on individual cases.'

'Coffee?' Gudlaugur got to his feet. Freyja and Huldar both accepted the offer. Neither spoke as they watched him pumping dark liquid into three mugs. Freyja thought Huldar was searching in vain for an opening but she was too preoccupied with pursuing her own train of thought to help him. She was wondering how much of what she had read was likely to emerge during interview, once the girl had been found. Hafthór's questions weren't designed to elicit the young people's back-stories or emotional state, and yet those were exactly the aspects Freyja had found most intriguing about Rósa.

Her interest had initially been roused by references in the reports to the girl's problematic relationship with reality. It was repeatedly mentioned that she had difficulty distinguishing real life from fantasy. But, oddly, the documents reporting this were accompanied by other reports on the girl that indicated she was perfectly normal. She was doing well at school and OK socially, was always clean and tidy, and had a healthy appetite.

There was no indication that the various professionals who had examined the girl or handled her case within the system believed she was suffering from a serious mental illness. At least, Freyja hadn't found any indication that Rósa had been sent for psychiatric evaluation or treatment. Apparently the only action taken had been to document the girl's problem with reality. And since when had documentation ever improved anyone's mental health?

But maybe Freyja was reading too much into the incoherent nonsense the girl had come out with.

The second piece of information that had alerted her interest was the girl's habit of running away. This was nothing new for adolescents in trouble. The same young faces were always turning up in the missing-persons' notices. Unlike Rósa, most of them were addicts. Her disappearances were not apparently motivated by the desire to get hold of drugs, but she could never be persuaded to explain why she kept absconding. Every time she was placed with a foster family, in the hope that the solution would prove permanent, she would take off. Her reappearances would be followed by a spell in temporary care, often with Bergur, while children's services were searching for another placement for her.

The USB stick had contained scans of letters relating to the girl's frequent disappearances, which had only increased Freyja's curiosity. Almost every time Rósa went missing, the Reykjavík branch of children's services received a letter, consisting of a single, printed sheet:

To the Child Protection Agency, Reykjavík.
Rósa Thrastardóttir, who ran away yesterday, is safe and sound. There is no need to be concerned about her welfare during her absence. She will come back when she's ready.

There was no signature and the wording was always the same. A report on the girl's disappearances mentioned that she refused to reveal where she went during her absences or who had written the letters. The person who compiled the report thought it possible that Rósa sent the letters herself but noted that the adult wording made this unlikely. Moreover, the girl's relatives all flatly denied sheltering her or writing the letters. Their author, and Rósa's whereabouts during her absences, remained a mystery.

Early that morning Freyja had finally been granted access to the juveniles' full records in the Child Protection Agency database. She'd managed to take a quick look at Rósa's file and get a better picture of her history before she'd had to come into the police station. The authors of the documents on the USB stick had made it tantalisingly clear that they were aware of her history, meaning that none of them had bothered to repeat it. This left Freyja feeling as though she'd switched on the radio in the middle of a programme and never discovered who was being interviewed.

What she read had left her thoughtful but no less baffled. Rósa had endured more than her fair share of traumas. She'd lost her father at six and her mother at eleven. The first of these traumas could have had a lasting psychological impact, but not of the type exhibited by Rósa. According to the reports, she displayed no signs of anxiety or separation angst. The second trauma was therefore more likely to have been the trigger for the peculiar symptoms recorded in her file, though the earlier loss had no doubt been a contributing factor; a devastating blow, followed by a second, even more shattering one. In Freyja's opinion, the loss of her father could have formed cracks in Rósa's mental health, which her mother's death a few years later had widened into chasms. The fact that her closest relatives had proved unfit to take her in afterwards must have turned these chasms into serious faultlines.

An eleven-year-old girl who had lost both father and mother would automatically fall under the remit of children's services. They would, as a matter of course, try to solve the problem of guardianship by approaching her closest relatives. But this wasn't always possible, as in Rósa's case. She'd had little contact with her father's family and, anyway, her paternal grandparents lived in Norway, which automatically ruled them out. The Child Protection Agency didn't send Icelandic children abroad in cases like this. The girl's paternal aunt, meanwhile, had learning difficulties and lived in a group home, which made her ineligible to care for the girl.

Rósa's mother had one brother who was unmarried and worked as a night security guard. Although he'd expressed willingness to change his working hours and provide Rósa with a home, he had failed to satisfy the authorities' stringent criteria. That had left Rósa's maternal grandparents, who had taken her in temporarily, but the arrangement had been cancelled when her grandmother lapsed and started drinking heavily as a result of the strain and grief following her daughter's death. All the couple's promises to clean up their act and go into rehab were futile. A mere six months after her mother's death, Rósa had ended up in care, as a juvenile with little or no family support. What had followed was a succession of foster homes from which Rósa had run away and refused to return to. Perhaps unsurprisingly, the foster carers had expressed few regrets over this fact.

For Rósa, it seemed, was adamant that her parents had been murdered; first her father, then, five years later, her mother. After reading her file, Freyja had been left with the impression that for the first three years after Rósa had been taken away from her grandparents, she had talked only of her mother being murdered. The addition of her father had begun about a year ago.

Childhood obsessions were difficult to treat. It was futile trying to reason with a child and the more peculiar the obsession, the more difficult it was for the child to see sense. Rósa's obsession clearly belonged in the most serious category. She didn't claim her mother had been murdered by a 'bad man'. Or a burglar. Or a rapist. Or a criminal.

No. The girl insisted that a demonic doll had caused her mother's death. How, she didn't explain. Nor did she say whether the doll had been implicated in her father's death as well. But one thing was crystal clear in Rósa's mind: she herself would be next.

The notes on the girl's obsession mentioned several times that both her parents had died in accidents. Their deaths had been investigated at the time and her mother's was considered to have had another, more obvious explanation than a murderous doll. Her father's death appeared to have been similarly straightforward. Yet nothing would convince Rósa to change her mind. Until recently, anyway. The latest report suggested that she might have abandoned the idea since she was no longer willing to discuss it – unless it had finally hit home that there was no point sharing her bizarre story with adults. Before this, she had brought up the doll in every single interview.

Gudlaugur came over to their table carrying three mugs. Turning from him to Huldar, Freyja said: 'There is one detail I can share with you, since it relates to the police rather than to the girl's personal circumstances.'

Huldar took a mug of coffee. 'Go on.'

'Rósa's mother died several years ago. The girl claims she was murdered but the police came to a different conclusion after investigating her death. Is it possible you could have made a mistake?' Freyja decided to leave Rósa's father out of it for now. Huldar and Gudlaugur were bound to be dismissive if she raised the issue of both parents' deaths. Her question sounded foolish enough as it was.

'It happens.' Huldar took a sip of coffee, which, from the way he winced, must have been scalding. 'But – a very big but – presumably the girl's theory would have been considered at the time, so I'm guessing it must be nonsense. Families sometimes get an idea in their heads and it can be hard to talk them out of it. Paranoia kicks in and they refuse to face facts. Instead, they start coming out with claims of a cover-up, and there's practically nothing we can do to change their minds. Did the girl elaborate on her murder theory? Or did she just grab hold of it as a way of avoiding dealing with her grief? That sort of reaction's not uncommon.'

Freyja hid behind her coffee mug while trying to come up with an answer to this. She could hardly tell him that Rósa claimed a doll had killed her mother. 'She had some vague theory but nothing concrete to build on.'

Huldar raised his eyebrows. 'Then what are you suggesting? That we ought to bring up the old case when we interview her? I can't see how it would encourage her to open up if we remind her that the police wouldn't listen to her crackpot ideas about her mother's death.'

'No.' The coffee was still far too hot and Freyja put down her mug. 'I just wanted to warn you in case she brings it up.' If any remnants of the doll theory remained in Rósa's mind, it wasn't impossible that she would mention it during the interview. She was unlikely to pass up the opportunity to put it to the police again.

Huldar blew on his coffee, then made another attempt to drink it. 'Let's hope she can tell us something useful, regardless. I understand, from Tristan's interview, that they became good friends. He claims he told her his secret, which makes it all the more urgent that we track her down, Gudlaugur.'

'She'll turn up. Apparently they always do,' said Gudlaugur. But he didn't look optimistic.

After lunch, they managed to fit in two more interviews before Freyja had to leave to pick up Saga. The plan had been to talk to three teenagers, but one of the boys, who was known to have a drink problem, hadn't turned up at the agreed time. Since he couldn't be contacted via his phone or Facebook, they'd had no choice but to sit and wait for the third.

During the break they left the little interview room and Huldar offered Freyja yet another coffee. She said no thanks, then asked if he'd given up smoking since he hadn't immediately nipped out for a cigarette. When he hesitated, she could see in his face that he was wondering whether to lie. But in the end he admitted that he was still smoking and asked, rather shamefaced, if she wanted to come outside with him. To Freyja's own surprise, she accepted, blaming the stuffy atmosphere in the interview room. Smoke-polluted air outdoors would be preferable to being starved of oxygen inside.

They lingered in the yard behind the police station long after he had stubbed out his cigarette, neither of them particularly eager to go back in. They chatted mostly about general topics, barely touching on the case. He asked after Saga and Baldur, and she answered at length about her niece, but avoided saying a word about Baldur. She had an ingrained dislike of discussing her brother with the police, however harmless the question.

Huldar seemed to sense this and stuck to the topic of Saga. She had assumed he was working his way round to inviting her out but, somewhat to her surprise, he didn't raise the subject. Aware of a vague feeling of disappointment, she put it down to her oath of celibacy. If she kept on like this, she would end up flirting with the fit guy in the advert at the supermarket that reminded men to go for a prostate check-up.

When Freyja left the police station after the final interview of the day, Huldar walked her to her car. Nothing useful had emerged from either of that afternoon's sessions. Freyja couldn't tell whether the kids were concealing something or telling the truth, and concluded that it would have been better to conduct the interviews in the more relaxed atmosphere of the Children's House. Then the subjects would have been less agitated and it would have been easier to work out from their body language whether they were being honest. She put this to Huldar before getting in the car and he promised to ask Hafthór if he'd reconsider, but added that he thought it was about as likely as the government and the opposition parties agreeing over the budget. In that case, she said, could he at least make sure the interview room was given a makeover. He agreed, but didn't seem particularly optimistic that anything would happen.

Freyja was out for a walk with Molly, pushing Saga in her buggy, when Huldar rang. She was on a slight slope at the time and had her hands full grappling with the lead and the buggy while simultaneously pressing the phone to her ear. Instead of getting straight to the point, he asked her if she could get out of the wind as he could hardly hear a word she was saying. She pointed out, rather acidly, that she was out at the end of Seltjarnarnes where there was no shelter of any kind to be found, then asked what he wanted, bracing herself to hear an invitation to go out to dinner, to a bar or even just to bed.

'I had a look at Rósa's mother's case after you left. I called up the old files.'

'And?' Freyja watched a crumpled shopping bag blowing along the path. Clearly, it had reached the end of its life.

'I'd like to go over it with you tomorrow as it throws up quite a few questions. The girl's statement, in particular. In some inexplicable way it appears to be linked to the case we're currently investigating.'

'Tristan's case? How's that possible? Did her mother know Bergur?'

Huldar coughed, then said: 'I'm not talking about that. I'm talking about the discovery of the bones in Faxaflói Bay. The story that's all over the news.'

Chapter 9

Rósa couldn't sleep. It wasn't the first time sleep had eluded her. Usually when it happened, she tried not to get worked up since she had long ago learnt that nothing in life came easily – not to her. It was unfair, of course, but that was just the way it was.

It had taken her a long time to come to terms with this fact. Most of her memories from the first few years after she had lost her mother were associated with anger. Anger at the people who had let her down; at her good-for-nothing grand-parents, the useless police, uncaring carers, uninspiring teachers and almost everyone who worked in children's services. None of the adults she'd had dealings with had ever come through for her: they had all failed her in the end. None of them actually loved her either. Most were paid to pretend they cared but they didn't. Not really. At least not in the way an actual parent would. Not like her mum had. Or her dad. Probably.

It wasn't hard to tell the difference. The people who pretended to love her touched her differently, looked at her differently, smiled at her differently and spoke to her differently. But worst of all they listened differently. Since she had been orphaned, no one had ever really listened to her. They heard the words she said but they couldn't be bothered to string them together and think about what they meant. It was less hassle for them to say '*yes*', '*uh-huh*' or '*let's talk about it later*', but of course 'later' never came.

So it was hardly surprising she had so much anger inside.

Anger got her nowhere, though, and in time she had come to realise that brooding incessantly on life's unfairness did nothing to make it any fairer in practice. She was still angry, but these days she had got better at keeping it under wraps. Most of the time. The sad part was that her change in attitude hadn't helped much. Although it made her dealings with the adults in her life less stressful, there had been no dramatic shift. Everything continued the same, just with fewer scenes.

Still, it was easier this way. The constant battles had taken their toll and she was tired, so she did her best to control her temper and keep the peace.

There were times, though, when her fury at the injustices she'd had to endure could no longer be kept in check. She knew the warning signs and usually took off for a while before she ended up exploding. She saw this as taking a mini-break from her situation. And it worked. She had borrowed a few self-help books from a library once but not one had suggested that running away from your problems was any sort of solution. On the contrary, every single book had advocated confronting your problems head on. Rósa seriously doubted that the authors had ever faced any real misfortune – not in the same league as hers, anyway.

If she could, she would run away and never look back. Leave her old life behind like a snake shedding its skin. But she couldn't. Not until she turned eighteen. Until then she was a ward of the state, and the state kept an inventory. It infuriated the minions of the system that they didn't know where she disappeared to when she ran away. But that was their problem. She thwarted her interrogators every time she returned by copying the adults who had never listened to her, simply repeating 'let's talk about it later' again and again until they gave up. And as her 'later' never materialised any more than theirs ever had, no one knew where she holed up. Which was a good thing. She even kept a burner phone to use when in hiding. She wasn't stupid.

The view of the ceiling overhead was getting boring. Rósa sat up in bed and reached for her phone on the table. She checked for messages but she hadn't received any since she'd put the phone down and tried to get to sleep. There was nothing strange about that. The only person she was in contact with was almost certainly sound asleep. She wondered whether to check this by sending a brief 'hi' but decided against it: she didn't want to come across as needy.

A shaft of moonlight entered the room through a gap in the curtains. She knew the moon was full tonight, but the sky had been dark when she'd gone to bed. The cloud cover had been so thick that you couldn't even guess where the moon was in the sky. But this thin beam of light suggested that the clouds were scattering.

Normally, Rósa would get out of bed, go over to the window and look up at the night sky. She loved gazing at the stars, trying to locate the planets and spotting the occasional satellite speeding along its orbit. It made her feel as if nothing here on earth really mattered. It put into perspective her worries about the future and her seemingly hopeless quest for the truth. In the great scheme of things, she and her problems were as insignificant to the universe as a speck of dust was to her. She found the idea soothing and often managed to fall asleep in the wake of it. But this calmer state of mind never lasted long. When she woke up in the morning, her worries and the persistent feeling that she had been let down would always be there, waiting to descend on her again like a heavy weight.

Rósa replaced her phone on the bedside table and lay back on the pillow. She tried to banish the thought that had prevented her from looking out of the window. It wasn't the knowledge that the relief it provided would be only fleeting. No. It was the irrational fear that if she drew the curtains, she would come face to face with the horrible doll, peering in at her. She knew it was stupid, knew it wasn't going to happen. But knowing this didn't help. A paralysing sense of dread prevented her from throwing off her duvet, swinging her legs out of bed, getting up and walking over to the window.

Fear was a much more effective barrier than any solid, physical obstacle.

She tried not to think about the doll. About that horrible, single staring eye, the matted hair and the rows of plug holes forming straight lines over half her scalp. Not to mention the barnacles and worms clinging to her naked, plastic body. Her mind could still conjure up a perfect picture of the doll, a picture she believed was exact almost down to each individual barnacle. This was so unfair when you considered that she found it almost impossible to recall what her mother had looked like. She had to rely on a photo now when she wanted to summon up her image in her mind's eye, while her father's face had gone for good.

Rósa felt a stinging in the corners of her eyes. If only the doll had been thrown back into the sea. If only.

The Doll

If only. Dangerous words for anyone trying to heal their wounds; the linguistic equivalent of ripping scabs off cuts before they had healed.

But she couldn't stop her mind from travelling down this path. What had happened was all her fault. She should never have insisted on taking the doll home. If only she hadn't done that, she might have been lying in her old room now, with her mum asleep next door. It wouldn't have saved her dad, but at least she'd still have her mum. She wouldn't be alone in the world.

Rósa drew a deep breath and held it in her lungs for a while before slowly exhaling. She reminded herself that taking the blame wouldn't change anything. Even if she blamed herself for insisting on keeping the doll for every minute of every day for the rest of her life, it would have no power to change the outcome. You can't go back and change the past. Not everything can be fixed. According to her science textbook, if you burn down a tree, there is no process in the world that can restore it from the ashes. She had never burnt down a tree, but she did know that once a person dies, it can't be undone. There is no undo button for life or death.

The clouds closed ranks and the shaft of moonlight disappeared. The room fell back into darkness and shortly afterwards raindrops began pattering on the window. The sound was comforting and Rósa could feel the pain relaxing its grip on her mind. With an effort, she managed to shift her focus from the negative to the positive.

Positive number one: she had a friend, a good friend. Two good friends, if an adult counted.

Positive number two: she had this room, which was always there waiting for her when she ran away. It was more *hers* than any of the rooms she had occupied since she'd entered the system. It was bigger than the ones she was usually given and it was a real room. Not a state-owned, state-furnished, pretend-this-is-a-real-room kind of room. And it was hers.

Positive number three: she was getting closer to finding out the truth about her mother. She could feel it. When that happened, she would finally be able to scream at everyone who had ever doubted her: I TOLD YOU SO. She couldn't wait for that moment, not least because she believed that when she had her answers, she would be able to put the memory of the doll to rest. It wouldn't haunt her any more.

Positive number four: there was no positive number four. Three was all she had.

But three was good. It was better than one or two or none.

Rósa could feel her mind relaxing and beginning to slip down the slope that led to sleep. Soon everything would be better. Tomorrow she would finally get her answers.

Her mind found the sentiment worth repeating: soon everything would be better.

Chapter 10

Erla sat in the passenger seat of the unmarked police car, staring out of the window at the small, rather dilapidated, wooden house, clad in corrugated iron, which was home to Rósa's maternal grandparents. Hverfisgata, the street on which it stood, had from time immemorial been over-shadowed by its bustling neighbour, Laugavegur, but with the increase in tourism, the area had finally undergone a renaissance, and the shabby house which would once have been perfectly in keeping with its surroundings now stuck out like a sore thumb. The tiny garden, condemned to exist in permanent shadow, looked even more forlorn than the house. A few sad pansies drooped in the flower bed among the weeds. Even the weeds and the ragged yellow grass were obviously struggling to grow in the sunless patch.

Lights were on in all the windows indicating that somebody was home.

'This is bullshit, Huldar.' Erla turned away from the house to scowl at him. 'I don't know what the hell I was thinking to agree to this visit.'

This was disingenuous. The fact was, her immediate reaction had been the same as Huldar's when she read the file on Rósa's mother's death. Was it a coincidence or, crazy as it seemed, could there be some link to the bones that had turned up in Faxaflói Bay?

According to the witness account, the demonic doll, which no one believed in, had been picked up in a net in the same area. At almost exactly the same coordinates. Of course, this on its own could be dismissed as coincidence, and there had been little else in the original files to arouse suspicion. Nevertheless . . .

In Huldar's opinion, the investigation into the woman's death had been adequate, if a little perfunctory. It was too easy to be critical years after the event, when you'd had no involvement in the original case. Sometimes it was just obvious that a death had been accidental and there was no need to conduct a more thorough inquiry. In this case, the sequence of events had seemed straightforward: Rósa's mother had gone to the loo in the middle of the night, tripped over her pyjama bottoms as she stood up, and fallen over, cracking her head on the edge of the bath. Knocked unconscious, she had silently bled to death on the tiled floor. There had been no sign of a break-in; no reason to think that anyone else had been present in the flat that night except the eleven-year-old Rósa. The girl had slept through to morning and discovered her mother's body when she went to brush her teeth.

Naturally, the experience had been traumatic and Rósa had been in shock when she was originally questioned by the police. All she could say was that her mother had been lying on the floor in the bathroom. The girl had been unable to tell them what time she had woken up, whether she had been disturbed in the night, or whether her mother was prone to dizzy spells or fainting. Nor could she explain the empty drinks cans that were scattered all over the floor in the dining area. The investigators hadn't managed to get any sense out of her.

The police had not been idle, however. They had taken photos of the scene, mostly of the bathroom, and the body had been sent for post-mortem, the results of which had been inconclusive. There was no indication of a stroke or any other medical reason for Rósa's mother Dísa to have fallen. Her blood had tested negative for alcohol and drugs, proving that she had been sober at the time. Fingerprint analysis of the drinks cans revealed that Dísa had handled all of them. Several other fingerprints had turned up on them as well, including Rósa's, but Dísa's prints were the only ones found on every single can. The police never found any satisfactory explanation for why they had been scattered all over the floor but they were not, on their own, thought to constitute evidence of criminal action. No one believed for a moment that the woman could have been murdered by a burglar who was after the cans for the deposits.

The flat was on the ground floor of a three-storey building. None of the neighbours had noticed anything out of the ordinary that night. As far as Dísa's friends and family were aware, she hadn't been experiencing difficulties with anyone or been involved with a violent boyfriend. The police had kept hitting a dead end, finding no evidence of a crime, a motive or a witness. All the indications were that her death had been a tragic accident.

Nevertheless, it was extremely rare for a young couple to die well before their time in unrelated accidents. First the husband, then the wife, five years later. A quick online search revealed that Rósa's father had died in very different circumstances. His obituary mentioned that he had died in the heart of the Icelandic countryside that had meant so much to him. Certainly, the bearded man in the accompanying photo gave the impression of being a lover of the great outdoors. There were no further details about the accident but Huldar had other, more important, things to do than to dig up the cause of death. It seemed out of the question that the couple's fates could have been linked.

The files became more interesting, the further he read. As time went on, little Rósa had started turning up repeatedly at the police station, demanding to talk to someone. On the first occasion, she had been seen by a friendly officer from the regular police, who took care of minor cases involving children. He had quickly realised that the girl's problem was very different from the usual round of lost bicycles, fights or snowballs thrown at cars.

After this, Rósa had been passed on to a detective who knew a little about her mother's case. That was when the business of the doll and the fishing boat had first come up. Rósa claimed not to have remembered this detail when she originally spoke to the police as she had been so upset at the time. Now, however, she wanted to know if there had been a doll in the bath when the police arrived and if the police had taken it away. She herself couldn't remember whether it had been there. Rósa had given a detailed description of the doll in question, which had obviously had nothing in common with the sort of thing Huldar's sisters used to play with.

The girl had taken it very badly when she was told that the doll hadn't been in the flat. She had left, only to show up again the following day, and that was when the fun had really started.

This time she had confided in the detective that her mother had almost certainly been killed by the doll. It was possessed by the devil, or perhaps by the ghost of the girl who had owned it; the girl who must be at the bottom of the sea. Rósa complained that no one would listen to her and that's why the police had to help. As he read, Huldar pitied the detective who had been forced to write a report of their interview. He felt even sorrier for him when Rósa started coming in regularly to harp on about the doll. To the man's credit, he had decided to look into the matter. Perhaps he did it to placate the little girl, perhaps because he was bored and had nothing else to do, or because he had been genuinely curious. Or a combination of all three.

The detective had tracked down Fridrik Reynisson, the owner of the fishing boat, who had been a colleague of the mother. Fridrik had confirmed that the doll was no figment of Rósa's imagination. It had been caught in the net, as the girl had said, and she and her mother had taken it home with them. He didn't have a picture of it but directed them to Dísa's Facebook page, although he wasn't sure if it still existed. He thought he remembered her posting a photo of the doll following the boat trip. It turned out that Dísa's page did still exist. Presumably it hadn't occurred to anyone to delete it. But there was no photo of the doll. The last thing Dísa had posted was a picture of Rósa in a grey hat, anorak and boots on her way to go fishing. If she had put up a post about the doll, she must have changed her mind and deleted it. Unless Fridrik had simply been mistaken.

He had been able to provide the exact location where they had caught the doll since it was his favourite fishing spot, which he had navigated to by GPS that day in the vain hope of improving their luck. At the detective's request, he had provided the coordinates.

The detective's investigation into the doll story had ended there. Nothing had come to light that couldn't be explained. Even the doll's disappearance wasn't really that mysterious. According to the boat owner, Rósa's mother had found the doll so gruesome that she had wanted to chuck it straight back in the sea. It seemed reasonable to assume, therefore, that she had thrown the horrible object in the bin when she got home, once her daughter had gone to sleep. By the time the policeman looked into the matter, nearly a year had passed since Dísa's death, so it was too late to search the dustbins or conduct a further examination of the scene. The flat had been sold and most of the money had gone into paying off debts. Once things had been settled with the official receiver and the loan companies, and the funeral and reception had been paid for, only 318,000 krónur had remained – a measly provision for an orphaned child.

The fact that the detective had included a personal comment like this in his report showed two things: that he'd taken a kindly interest in the poor kid, and that he hadn't expected anyone else to read the report.

This was all very interesting but there was nothing here to rouse Huldar's suspicions apart from the coordinates. The spot had turned out to be almost exactly where the bones had been discovered; within fifty metres, which was negligible when you took into account the immensity of the ocean.

'What the hell are we supposed to say when they want to know why we're showing up now, five years after their daughter's death?' Erla turned back to the house, as if hoping that all the lights would have been switched off, giving them an excuse to head back to the station.

'We'll say we're looking for Rósa – in connection with another case in which she's a potential witness. Well, it's true, isn't it?'

Erla blew out a breath. 'How did I let you talk me into this?'

'Oh, come on. I gave you the perfect excuse to start investigating the bones without having to piss off the Identification Commission.' Huldar opened the door and got out of the car. 'You can thank me later. Come on.'

She sighed but obeyed. They walked up to the house together and Huldar rang the bell before Erla could get cold feet. He kept his eyes to the front to avoid seeing the faces she was making at him while they were waiting. Even so, the wait had grown uncomfortably protracted before the door finally opened and an older man stuck out his head. He looked irritable and didn't appear mollified when Huldar introduced them both. That was nothing new, though. People seldom started cheering when the police knocked on their door.

'Is something wrong?' The man showed no signs of letting them in.

'We're here about your granddaughter, Rósa.' When the man didn't respond, Huldar added quickly: 'We're trying to find her. She's a potential witness in a case we're investigating.'

'She's not here.'

'Is there any chance we could come in and have a quick word with you?'

'I told you she's not here. It would be better for everyone if she was, but thanks to you lot she's not.'

'Us lot?' Erla snapped, in a tone unlikely to win the man over. Her recent course on interacting with the public didn't seem to have made the slightest impression on her usual brusque manner.

'You lot. The system. You're all part of the same bloody thing.'

Huldar intervened before Erla could get a word in. He hadn't dragged her round here to have the door slammed in their faces. 'I'm afraid we don't quite follow you, but I can assure you that we've had nothing to do with Rósa before. We're looking for her and were hoping that you or your wife might be able to shed some light on her whereabouts.' This wasn't strictly true but they'd agreed their initial questions would be along these lines. Only after that would they bring up the subject of her mother's death.

'Neither I nor my wife know anything that could help you. I hope she turns up, sooner rather than later. But she hasn't been here for two or three months, or been in touch with us at all. You lot made sure our ties with her were broken years ago.'

There was no point repeating that he and Erla could not be held responsible for the state of Rósa's relationship with her grandparents. 'We'd like to talk to you, all the same. To your wife as well. It shouldn't take long. I assure you it's important.'

From inside the house they heard a woman's voice rasp: 'Who is it?'

Rósa's grandfather called back. 'No one. Just some people who are leaving.'

The woman, presumably Rósa's grandmother, retorted: 'Don't talk rubbish.' They heard the sound of footsteps, then the door was wrenched fully open and an older woman appeared beside the man. She studied Huldar's and Erla's faces with a distinct lack of enthusiasm. 'You Bible-bashers?' The words were accompanied by a sweetish-sour smell of white wine.

'No. We're from the police.' Huldar held out his hand and introduced himself. He was surprised at how firm her grip was.

'What are you doing here? Has something happened?' An expression of fear briefly animated the slack facial muscles. Alcohol was never a good look. She swayed and had to lean against the doorpost to stop herself falling. Huldar wondered if her unsteadiness might have some other cause, as she didn't seem that drunk.

'They're searching for Rósa.' The man didn't look at his wife as he answered. 'She's run off. Again.'

Rósa's grandmother swallowed, twisting the collar of her jumper with one hand, holding on to the doorpost with the other. 'She's not here.'

'I've already told them that. That's why they're leaving.'

Huldar and Erla didn't budge. 'Could we have a quick word with you? It's extremely important that we find her.'

While the man was shaking his head, his wife moved aside and waved a hand. 'Come in.' Huldar and Erla didn't wait to be told twice and the husband was forced to give way. He didn't look pleased.

They followed Rósa's grandmother past the sitting room where the TV was on and they could see a half-empty wine glass on the coffee table. An open book lay beside it but the reader didn't seem to have got very far.

They were ushered into a small kitchen that was showing

its age, though it was clean and tidy. There were no saucepans on the hob or plates on the table, but then it was still a bit early for supper. A copy of the serenity prayer was stuck to the fridge with a little magnet shaped like a cocktail glass, though whether this was deliberately or unintentionally ironic was anyone's guess.

They sat down at the kitchen table. It was bare apart from a decorative vase on a small, round doily. There were no flowers in the vase.

'Where did Rósa run away from this time?' The grandmother took a seat facing them. Her husband had disappeared.

'She'd just started a foster placement here in Reykjavík. She hasn't been in touch with her foster mother and no one else has been able to get hold of her for several days.' Huldar tried unsuccessfully to fold his legs under the table. 'Your husband says he hasn't heard from her but is it possible that she's been in touch with you?'

Instead of answering, the woman turned the question back on them, making an effort to enunciate clearly: 'Rósa often takes off. I've lost count of the number of times, and when she does, the most they ever do is ring us. Usually it's some bloke from children's services. Sometimes no one bothers to get in touch at all and we only hear about it afterwards – when she's turned up again and tells us about it herself. Either that or we see a picture of her on the internet when they're appealing for information about her. So I'm asking myself why they've sent two cops round this time. Is Rósa in serious trouble?' The woman may have had a bit to drink but she was nobody's fool.

'No. She's not in any trouble as far as we're aware. The reason we're trying to get hold of her is connected to a case we're investigating. She's on a list of possible witnesses. She isn't suspected of any wrongdoing herself.' Huldar then repeated his original question about whether the woman knew where her grandchild was.

'No, Rósa never gets in touch when she disappears. And she never tells me where she's been when she turns up again. I don't ask either. I think it's better not to know. If she looked for shelter here she'd be welcome, but she never does. We have a bit of a strange relationship. She's never forgiven us for not fighting harder to keep her after her mother died and she was taken away from us.' The grandmother clasped her hands on the table. When she spoke again, it was with a note of regret and she seemed to have forgotten about trying to appear sober. Her voice slurred a little as she went on: 'Perhaps we should have done. But neither of us was in any fit state to fight the system. Everyone gives up in the end. You feel you have as much chance as a butterfly trying to break through a windowpane.'

Erla didn't have the patience to sit quietly through a rant on the injustices of the system. 'Has Rósa ever discussed her mother's death with you?' she interrupted. 'We understand that she believes it was murder.'

The woman snorted. 'Discussed? She wouldn't talk about anything else for years. It did my head in having to listen to it. The truth is that Dísa died in an accident but Rósa couldn't accept the fact. You can't really blame the poor kid. First her father, then her mother. She was only a child at the time, too young to have learnt how unfair life is. People are put through all kinds of misery and there's no rhyme or reason for it. It just happens.'

'We understand that a doll came into it?'

'Oh, give me strength! Not that bloody thing again.' The woman groaned. 'I can't bear to hear it mentioned. Rósa used to be obsessed with it. She couldn't sleep for fear that the doll would come and get her. Well, sometimes it was the doll, other times the girl who owned it. She used to go back and forth between the two.'

'Did you see a photograph of the doll on Dísa's Facebook page?' Huldar hoped the woman might remember, even though it was so long ago.

'Facebook? No, I wasn't on Facebook in those days. I am now. Have been for two years. When Dísa died, people my age didn't used to be on there so much. Now we've more or less taken over. Driven the young people away. I have two hundred and something Facebook friends. More than all the real friends I've made in my entire life.'

When neither Erla nor Huldar commented on this, Rósa's grandmother got back to the point: 'What's this case Rósa's supposed to be a witness in? I hope it's nothing serious. She's been through enough already.'

Before they could answer, she leant back in the kitchen chair, her eyes narrowing suddenly. 'Is it the paedophile who abused that boy? The case that's been all over the papers?' Reading the answer in their faces, she nodded slowly. 'I thought as much.'

'Did she ever mention anything about abuse to you?' Huldar found himself inadvertently leaning forward.

'Come to think of it, she did, yes. Not directly to me, but I heard her and her friend whispering about something that sounded like that. About sex abuse by someone who worked for children's services. When I tried to ask them about it, they went quiet and left soon afterwards. At the time I thought it was probably just some rumour going around among the kids in the system. It sounded so unbelievable. What an idiot I am.'

'When was this?'

'Now you're asking . . . In the spring, I think. In May. Possibly.' Rósa's grandmother had been managing to stay on the ball so far but now she seemed to lose focus and started fiddling with the little round cloth on the table as if to get it exactly in the middle. Although her efforts made no perceptible difference, she seemed satisfied.

'Who was her friend? Someone from school?'

'No. It was a boy she'd got to know at one of those care homes. As unlucky in life's lottery as her. Maybe that's why they became such good friends. They still are, I think. His name's Tristan.'

'Tristan?'

'Yes. He came round here with her a few times when they first got to know each other. Not that she came by that often.' The woman's eyes narrowed again. 'Is he the boy in the news?'

When neither Erla nor Huldar answered, she interpreted their silence correctly and seemed pleased at having guessed right. 'Of course, of course.'

Huldar bit back the urge to ask what impression she'd got of the boy. Tristan was the victim, not the perpetrator. What he was like was irrelevant. It didn't alter the crime.

'When did you last see them together?'

'About three months ago. At the end of May.' Rósa's grandmother thought. 'Yes, around about then. I was hurt when they took off. It was the first visit I can remember that she didn't start harping on about her mother being murdered.

Or her father – that was a new bit of nonsense that started about a year ago.'

Huldar raised his eyebrows. 'Was the doll supposed to have been responsible for that too?'

'No. The doll didn't exist when he died – if you can believe any of her story. Apparently it was caught in a fishing net the day before Dísa's accident. Thröstur died five years earlier. But Rósa didn't say how she thought he'd been murdered – I didn't give her the chance. I just couldn't bear to listen to it. Over the years I've kept hoping and hoping that she'd stop talking about her mother's death like that. I always thought she'd never get over her loss until she did. But when she started bringing her father into it as well, I couldn't take any more. When she came round last spring, though, she didn't mention it once.'

'Do you know what could have brought about the change?'

'No. Maybe it was just a coincidence. Maybe she'll talk about it non-stop the next time she appears. I thought she was getting better before, until she relapsed.'

'When was that?'

'About two years ago. She came round with Tristan. I think that was the first time I met him. Anyway, she wanted the condolence book from her mother's funeral reception. So I got it out and gave it to her, thinking maybe it was the first step towards coming to terms with her loss. There was such a pretty picture of Dísa on the front, and I'd put the order of service in there too and even stuck in a dried rose from the wreath on her coffin. I cut out the death notice, the funeral notice and the obituaries from *Morgunbladid* and stuck them in too. At the back I put in some photos of her as a little girl and as a young woman. It was a lovely book and I thought it would do Rósa good to look at it. But the next time I saw her, several months later, she was back to obsessing about murder again. I haven't seen the book since.'

Huldar, noticing that Erla was growing restless, hastily changed the subject. 'Might Tristan know where she is?'

'Maybe. Maybe not.' The woman's shoulders sagged. 'I simply don't know. But they were on the same wavelength. Young but carrying a heavy burden. Not your typical angst-ridden teenagers but genuinely weighed down by misfortune. I don't know how else to describe it.' She brightened up a little. 'You know what? In a way, I'm glad you're here about something serious. My first thought was that she must have gone to the police like she used to. About some nonsense like the murderous doll. She wouldn't stop pestering you lot at one time and I wouldn't have been surprised if her latest crazy idea hadn't sent her back to you.'

'What idea's that?' Erla didn't sound as if she was expecting any great revelation. She appeared to be suppressing a yawn.

'Oh, some nonsense about dead people in the sea. I ask you . . . What next?'

Erla's gaze sharpened. 'What exactly did she say?'

The woman shrugged. 'I didn't really get it. It was during the same visit that I overheard them whispering about abuse. She went off on some flight of fancy, claiming she knew about a couple of dead people in the sea. Something like that. I stopped listening – I've had about all I can take of that kind of thing. There's no way I can fake interest in those delusional stories of hers. I just can't. So I shut her up by offering them some pancakes, then went into the kitchen to make them. While I was cooking, it occurred to me that at least she wasn't going on about her parents being murdered. I should have been relieved, not angry. It was when I took the pancakes through to the sitting room that I heard them whispering about abuse, but they shut up the moment I came in. After that we just talked about normal stuff: school, the weather, football and their chances of getting summer jobs. Then they thanked me for the pancakes and left.'

It was Erla's turn to lean forwards over the table. 'And you're saying this was back in May? Not last week?'

When drunk people are offended, they demonstrate the fact with exaggerated gestures. Rósa's grandmother leant back in her chair and folded her arms across her chest, her face hard. 'Do you seriously think I'd mix up what happened last week with what happened months ago? I told you – she came round at the end of May. She hasn't been here since then. I'm sure of that. And I didn't dream or imagine the whole thing either.'

Huldar and Erla exchanged glances. News of the bones had only broken two days ago. No one could have had a clue about their existence at the end of May or beginning of June. No one, that is, except the person responsible for putting the bodies there – if that's what had happened.

And, apparently, Rósa.

Chapter 11

The horses raised their heads and stared at Hjálmar from under their long forelocks. Bulging brown eyes watched his approach until, eventually losing interest, they returned to their grazing. The grass was growing well after all the recent rain and the horses were looking plump and glossy. Plumper than usual. If things went on like this, they'd be in fine fettle by the time they were brought into the stables.

The field, which was situated between the villages of Stokkseyri and Eyrarbakki on the south coast, was well fenced and almost free from tussocks. There was a magnificent view of the ocean to the south and in good visibility you could make out the volcanic island of Surtsey. He was fairly sure that animals were indifferent to views but he still liked to think of them having all this beauty before them. Even though they hardly ever looked up from the grass. And even if the horses didn't care, he could at least enjoy the view himself whenever he visited them.

Not that it was much to write home about today. A curtain of fog hung just offshore, obscuring the view of the sea. The fine mist Hjálmar could feel on his cheeks as he walked over the rough pasture suggested that the fog was coming in over the land as well. Droplets glittered on the grass. He regretted not having put on the riding boots he kept in the boot of his car. His trainers were already soaking.

Hjálmar went up to the chestnut mare he had come here to check on. As he stroked and patted her neck, the mare ceased her grazing and turned her head to him with a vigorous snort. Her nostrils dilated, then reverted to their usual teardrop shape. He rubbed her soft muzzle and the mare seemed content. Then down went her muscular neck again and she carried on tearing at the grass. In the silence her munching was as audible as if he had laid his ear against her powerful jaws.

Moving slowly, Hjálmar slid his hand down her near hind leg. 'Easy, girl.' The mare had bent it and was resting her hoof on the ground, which wasn't a good sign, but when he examined the stitches, the wound appeared to be healing well; there was no sign of infection or fresh bleeding. Taking a small can of antiseptic spray and a cloth from his pocket, he palpated the area around the stitches as the vet had recommended. The mare's coat was damp and most of the antiseptic seemed to bounce off and run uselessly down her leg into the grass. Wetting the cloth, Hjálmar pressed it to the stitches in the hope that this would work better.

A flash of light on metal at the far end of the pasture caught Hjálmar's eye. It was near one of the fence posts but he couldn't see whether it was inside or outside the field. Once he reckoned he had got enough antiseptic on the mare's cut, he stuffed the cloth and spray can back in his pocket and walked over to the fence. The mare had been injured here in the field but they hadn't been able to find the offending object. The vet thought she might have rubbed up against a fence post and caught herself on a protruding nail. Hjálmar had asked if it could have been deliberate; if some sadist was going around harming horses. You heard stories from time to time. But the vet had been sceptical. Nevertheless, Hjálmar hadn't been able to find any protruding nails, despite walking right round the fence, so the cause of the injury had remained a mystery. Perhaps he had found it now, though in that case it occurred to him that he ought to have spotted it the other day, when he was searching the pasture.

In fact, the shiny object proved to be outside the fence. It appeared to be the pointed end of a metal pole which was sticking up from a ditch about two metres from his property. Feeling curious, Hjálmar climbed over the fence to investigate. His feet were so wet by now that there was no point going back to the car for his boots.

It turned out to be a tent pole, coated with green plastic apart from the sharp end that was poking up. On closer examination, he discovered that the tent itself was lying bundled up at the bottom of the ditch. He thought there was a sleeping bag there too, and other camping gear, including a single trainer and a muddy backpack. A little further off he spotted two bicycles. The stuff was all filthy and looked as if it had been lying there for quite a while. Hjálmar scratched his head and felt a sudden spurt of anger. Bloody tourists. They were clearly no better behaved than Icelanders at an outdoor festival; the type who dumped their tents and rubbish once the fun was over. The idiots had probably pitched their tent on the bank of the ditch or even in his field. Perhaps they had been defeated by the relentless rain, as there would have been no way to dry a tent this summer, and trying to pack up a wet tent was a horrible job. Before Hjálmar could start feeling sorry for the tent's owners, his eye fell on the bicycles again. No amount of rain could explain what they were doing in the ditch. There didn't appear to be anything wrong with them; the tyres were pumped up and the wheel rims were intact. There was nothing to suggest they were a write-off.

The whole thing was extremely odd.

It looked as if the tourists had cycled there, pitched their tent, then decided for some inexplicable reason to dump all their gear and continue on foot. Perhaps they had hitched a lift back to town and gone to a hotel after discovering that not every city dweller is suited to camping in the subarctic with only a thin sheet of canvas between them and the elements. But that didn't excuse the mess they had left behind.

Shaking his head, Hjálmar pulled out his phone to take a photo. There must be a group on Facebook dedicated to exposing the disgusting lack of respect some tourists showed for the Icelandic environment, and this was a perfect example. But however he positioned himself and whatever angle he tried, it was impossible to fit both tent and bikes in one picture. They were too far apart. He supposed he could climb into the ditch and take a picture from down there, but there was water in the bottom and Hjálmar didn't fancy getting wet up to the knee. Perhaps all the stuff had originally been in the same place but the tent and pole had been washed further along the ditch by floodwater. The pole could have been pushed upright when it caught in the canvas below. That would explain why he hadn't spotted it when he'd done the rounds last week.

Hjálmar took several pictures of the tent and some more of the bikes, then checked to see how they had come out on screen. He tried but failed to come up with a snappy caption. Never mind, he would think of something on the way home.

He walked back over the rough grass, pausing to pat and stroke the horses he passed on the way. They seemed humiliatingly indifferent to his caresses. But then love was rarely returned in equal measure.

He climbed up the slope to the road, got in his car and drove away. The horses had already forgotten his visit.

After he had gone, the fog condensed and turned into rain, and the water level in the ditch began to rise until in the end it covered the abandoned camping gear and the two bikes. Only the tent pole was still visible, poking up above the bank.

Chapter 12

The police car was unmarked, though Huldar didn't suppose this would make much difference since most of the kids they were looking for were bound to recognise it. The driver, Rafn, a kindly, middle-aged officer who had been sent to assist Gudlaugur, was responsible for tracking down missing juveniles. His success with this group had made him something of a legend on the force. No one doubted that he had found his vocation in life. As they drove, he had answered their questions by sharing his experiences and describing the techniques that had worked best for him. It seemed obvious when he spelt it out: approach the kids as a friend, not a policeman. Build up trust. Never chase them. Be understanding. Listen. Don't make threats. Don't judge.

Rafn was behind the wheel, Huldar in the passenger seat and Gudlaugur silent in the back. It was an unwritten law that the person with the least experience took the back seat on the rare occasions when more than two officers travelled together. Gudlaugur was clearly aggrieved by the arrangement, but that would change as he grew in seniority. Huldar had felt the same back in the day.

The night was as dark as it ever got in late summer, a heavy blanket of cloud smothering the moon and stars. It was a long time since the inhabitants of Reykjavík had seen clear skies, whether by day or night. Their hopes of good weather had been crushed to the point where now all people asked was that the clouds held off from emptying themselves for as long as it took them to dash outside to slap a lamb chop on the rusty barbecue. Not that anyone had barbecuing on their mind at this late hour. Most people were tucked up in bed as it was past midnight. The few souls they did see out and about appeared to be in a hurry to get home, plodding purposefully along the pavements of the city centre in thick coats more suitable for the onset of winter than late summer. The occasional foreigner with a wheelie case in tow could be seen peering around for street names or house numbers, presumably in search of their Airbnb. It was unlikely that the owner would have applied for the necessary permits but this was of no concern to Huldar or his companions. All their attention was focused on searching for Rósa, the teenage girl who was almost certainly a witness in two of the hottest cases of the moment.

They stopped at a red light at the junction between Laugavegur high street and Snorrabraut. Both streets were empty, there wasn't another car in sight, but even so Rafn resisted the temptation to jump the lights. He sat there patiently, his eyes on the road ahead. This was just as well, since, out of nowhere, two tourists suddenly crossed right in front of the car, barely visible in their dark clothes, and headed down Snorrabraut towards the sea. Huldar watched them until the light turned green and Rafn set off along Laugavegur.

'Do the kids often hang out in this area?' Gudlaugur piped up from the back seat. He didn't sound happy, exactly, but his mood did seem to be improving at last.

Rafn cruised along at walking pace, peering around in search of faces familiar from the missing-persons' notices. 'It happens. There are still several bars tucked away on Laugavegur, although the touristy "puffin shops" are pushing them out. The kids sometimes manage to sneak in when it's busy.'

Huldar looked down the empty street. There was no way you could claim it was 'busy' tonight but he held his tongue and copied Rafn by scanning their surroundings in the hope of spotting any signs of life. 'Are you looking for other kids as well as Rósa?'

'Yes. Three. Including her.'

'Is that a lot or a little?' Huldar hoped it was a record.

'Fairly typical. The average is about twenty kids a month, but of course they don't all go missing at once and some of them disappear repeatedly. The record was six, following the August bank holiday weekend. The public don't get to hear about all of them, as some aren't advertised as missing. We work on a case-by-case basis. Advertising doesn't necessarily help. It certainly doesn't make life any easier for the kids to have their problems flashed up in front of the entire country.'

'Do most of them have a drug problem?' Huldar assumed this was the case but still thought it worth asking.

'The majority, yes. But others have behavioural or mental issues. It's not a homogeneous group, if that's what you think. They come from very different family backgrounds and circumstances. It's not just the children of people who have problems themselves, which is a common misconception, although of course they're less likely to come out unscathed, since they have no back-up at home.'

'Do they all turn up?'

'Yes. We always find them in the end.'

'That's good.' Huldar was glad to hear something positive.

'Not necessarily. They always turn up in the end. But not necessarily alive.'

Silence fell in the car and lasted until Gudlaugur rejoined the conversation. 'Are you talking about drugs? Overdoses?'

'Yes. Opioids. Since they've come on the market, these kids have been at far greater risk. You don't have to miscalculate the dose by much for it to be fatal. It's not like they carry much body weight. Most of them are desperately thin.' Rafn glanced at Huldar. 'Take a look in the glove compartment.'

It turned out to be full of small square containers with long white stoppers, resembling bottles of clear nail varnish; but examining one, Huldar saw that it was something else entirely: the bottle was labelled Narcan Nasal Spray 4 mg. Huldar had heard of the spray, which could be used to revive the victims of overdoses. The numbers involved were daunting. In the worst periods, they were looking at almost one death a week from opioids. Not all these people were drug addicts, let alone kids, but the situation was serious enough that a committee had been set up to decide whether police officers should be routinely equipped with the spray. Their recommendations were unlikely to be delivered any time soon, though. 'Is it an antidote to opioids?'

'Yes.' Apparently catching sight of a movement, Rafn slowed the car almost to a stop and peered down an alleyway. A tabby cat strolled out and stopped dead, staring around in alarm as if expecting a police ambush. It paid no attention to the car, however, and after a moment continued calmly along the pavement in the direction of Hlemmur Square. Rafn shook his head and began to move forward again.

'Have you ever had to use it yourself?'

'Yes. Not often, luckily. But it's good to have it to hand if I do come across someone who needs it. There's no time to drive to A&E if a teenager's OD'd. By then, it's usually too late.'

Huldar put the little bottle back and closed the glove compartment. The atmosphere in the car was so subdued that it seemed better to keep quiet for a while and concentrate on what was happening outside. But he couldn't hold his tongue for long. As they passed the junction where Laugavegur became Bankastræti, he felt compelled to break the silence. 'I understand you've searched for her before. Rósa, I mean.'

'Yes. Several times. Though I can't claim I found her, except on a couple of occasions. She's an expert at lying low and usually only turns up when she's good and ready.'

'When's that? When the dope's finished so she might as well crawl back?'

'No. She's different from most of the other kids. She has various issues, but they don't include drugs and alcohol. Not yet, anyway.'

Huldar heard Gudlaugur muttering from the back that he already knew this. He'd been helping Rafn for several hours before Erla had imposed Huldar on them, directly after the visit to Rósa's grandparents. To Erla, nothing was more important at that moment than locating the girl and bringing her in for questioning.

Huldar, who had been hoping they would find Rósa without too much hassle, didn't feel he could complain about back-to-back shifts and lack of sleep. He was supposed to go in tomorrow morning for the interviews with more juveniles from the care home but it wouldn't be the first time he had done his job with dark shadows under his eyes, tanked up on coffee. From Rafn's comments, he deduced that Rósa was unlikely to be found on this trip, however. Nor on the next one, tomorrow evening. 'If she's not on drugs and doesn't drink, is there any point in looking for her at night? Isn't she more likely to be out and about during the day, like normal people?'

'Well, good luck searching by day. All she'd have to do is pull up her hood and you wouldn't be able to spot her in the crowd. Both times I've found her it was late in the evening or at night. Runaways all tend to use their freedom in the same way, whether or not they're addicts. They stay up as late as they like and go where they want. Adult restrictions no longer apply.'

They drove past a couple who were leaning together as they walked towards a taxi parked on Lækjargata. The couple sped up as it began to spit with rain, just making it to the car before the heavens opened. Rafn put the windscreen wipers on full, craned forwards to peer up at the sky and cursed. 'That's that, then. Even kids who are free to do as they please won't want to be outside in this.'

With the wipers labouring to cope with the downpour, Rafn drove out to Grandi. For once, he told them where they were going without having to be asked – to a colony of container housing for the homeless, located on the edge of a plot of land that was still used for various kinds of industry. They both knew the place Rafn was referring to. 'Housing' was a rather grand term for a cluster of re-purposed containers. Huldar had driven past them the previous winter and it had struck him then that the location was typical of the general policy towards those on the bottom rung of society. The few housing solutions on offer were all aimed at keeping the homeless out of sight. The plot in the industrial area of Grandi, to the west of Reykjavík harbour, was as close as you could get in a welfare state to sweeping the homeless into the sea.

Gudlaugur got in first with the question that had immediately occurred to both of them: 'Surely she won't go there if she's not a user?' The inhabitants of the container colony were mostly individuals with serious drink or drug problems; the long-term homeless who had reached the end of the road.

'No, probably not. But I once found her visiting one of the occupants. You know, the people who live in the containers are all right, despite their self-destructive tendencies. If the kids I'm looking for find their way there, they're usually given a warm welcome. The container folk try to help them as best they can. It's just a pity that their idea of help is different from mine. For them, getting the kids to go home isn't a priority. After all, they hardly know what the word means after years on the streets. I was very surprised the first time I ran into Rósa there, though, because, like I said, she's not into drugs.'

Rafn drove past the foundations that were swiftly rising on the sea front next to the Harpa Concert Hall. For the moment, there was nothing to hint at the promised super-luxury hotel they were to become; they were just grey concrete forms, along with the inevitable rubbish that accompanies construction projects. In this weather, they couldn't even see the glow of the concert hall. The light show had been switched off, presumably because the management had decided there was no point trying to compete with the gloom.

Huldar turned his gaze from the depressing view to the eagle-eyed officer at the wheel. 'Do you think Rósa could have been staying there all those times she vanished and couldn't be found?'

'No. I very much doubt it. If these kids stay anywhere, it's usually with people in their late teens or early twenties, who've been in the same situation themselves. People who've failed to grow up and can't drag themselves out of the mess they're in. You could say they're older versions of the missing kids – what they'll turn into if things are handled wrong. But Rósa hasn't been spotted anywhere like that, so there's no point looking for her there. And it seems she's only a visitor to Grandi. If we're in luck, we might find her there now.'

'This late?' Gudlaugur sounded disapproving.

Rafn looked round and smiled for the first time since Huldar had met him. 'Late? Like I said before, we're not talking about some nine-to-five existence. These kids' day begins at noon, at the earliest.'

Huldar waited for Rafn to turn back to face the road. Thanks to Gudlaugur's interruption, he'd been forced to postpone his own question. 'Where did she go to ground then? The other times she's disappeared. Does no one have any idea?'

'No. No one has a clue. But it was somewhere indoors, you can be sure of that. When she reappeared she was clean and neatly dressed, with freshly brushed teeth and combed hair. Not like a kid who's been sleeping rough in a tent or an underpass for days. Then there are those letters that suggest she's with somebody responsible. Sort of.'

'Letters?'

'Every time she runs away, Reykjavík children's services get a letter saying she's safe. Or something along those lines. Apparently they received one yesterday, but no one knows who sends them. Maybe she does it herself. She's an unusual kid, to say the least.'

Huldar tried to come up with a few suggestions, though he realised he wouldn't be saying anything new. All the places that occurred to him must already have been checked by the police. 'Could it be her grandparents? Another relative? Or a school friend, maybe?'

'No, none of those. No one they've spoken to will admit to sheltering her or writing the letters. And Rósa herself is as silent as the grave. I've tried to get it out of her to make life easier next time she does a runner, but it's hopeless. She just clams up and looks away. I try not to treat these poor kids like criminals. If I started behaving like I was interrogating them, I'd soon lose their trust. When it was clear she didn't want to tell me, I stopped asking.'

Once out on Grandi, Rafn parked in some spaces by the empty plot where the four container units had been lined up. They were unobtrusive, with pale-grey exteriors, though an attempt had been made to cheer them up by painting the doors in different colours. But when even the Harpa Concert Hall's light show couldn't overpower the dreary weather, these little dwellings didn't have a chance. To make the scene even more dismal, the surroundings were littered with all kinds of junk and scrap metal that the inhabitants had amassed. In the gloom, the area resembled the set of an apocalyptic film in which every piece of scrap had acquired the status of a treasure.

Curtains were drawn over the mean little windows high up on the walls beside the doors. The side walls were blank but Huldar knew there were large windows at the back, and assumed the curtains were also drawn over those, as the occupants weren't keen to share their private lives with the outside world. They appeared to be awake, however, as lights showed through the tatty curtains in all the units, though the rain swallowed up the faint glow so that it barely illuminated the wet gravel outside. Since there was no street lighting in the vicinity, the three police officers walked carefully over the uneven ground, trying not to trip over the endless rubbish.

Huldar surveyed the bleak surroundings of what had once been the beating heart of Reykjavík's fishing industry. He had come here as a boy with his father, on one of the family's few outings to the capital. His mother and sisters had wanted to visit the famous Kringlan shopping centre, but father and son had fled out to Grandi. Ever since Huldar could remember, his father had sought out any overwhelmingly male spaces, no doubt as an antidote to the gender imbalance at home. In those days, Grandi had been that sort of place: the fishing fleet in the harbour, a tangled mess of nets, and tubs of fish wherever you looked. His father had filled his lungs as they got out of the car by Kaffivagninn, the old café on the docks, and surveyed his surroundings with a broad smile.

Over doughnuts and hot chocolate, he had told Huldar bits and bobs about the history of the area. Huldar remembered little except the parts that had captivated him as a child, such as the fact that the end of the isthmus had once been an island, and that after the Second World War the citizens of Reykjavík had been treated to a display of exotic animals there, including monkeys, sea lions and polar bears, to celebrate the Fisherman's Festival. That had been before the days of the Icelandic Food and Veterinary Authority, with all its health and safety regulations. According to his father, there had been plans to turn the island into an outdoor recreation area for the city's inhabitants, but these had had to be abandoned in the face of the swiftly expanding fishing industry and oil depot. Work was begun on landfill around the Grandi or 'isthmus' that connected the island to the shore, and after this the oil tanks and other industrial buildings had quickly sprung up. Apart from the tanks, there were now few reminders of that time. Nor was there any way of telling where the old island of Örfirisey had ended and the landfill began. In the next street, the fishing industry had mostly been displaced by restaurants, art and design studios, and shops selling ice-cream, cakes and cheese. If the trend continued, the original plan of using the island as a recreational area would eventually come about organically.

Gudlaugur pulled up the hood of his jacket to protect himself from the rain. Rafn followed suit but Huldar didn't bother. There was no point. The water always got in where it wanted to in the end. He put his hand in his pocket and fished out a cigarette. A fat raindrop landed right on top of his lighter just as he was raising it to the tip and after that he couldn't coax a flame from it, however hard he tried. Disgruntled, he shoved the lighter back in his pocket and chucked away the now soggy cigarette.

'Should we knock on all the doors?'

'We only need to visit one. Rósa always goes to see the same guy. Binni Briefcase.'

'Briefcase?' Huldar raised his eyebrows enquiringly.

'They call him that because he used to be a white-collar type, once upon a time. Until he went off the rails. As far as I know, Rósa hasn't had any contact with the other people who live here, so we needn't disturb them.'

Huldar and Gudlaugur were relieved to hear this. The rain

showed no signs of letting up and the thought of tramping from container to container, hanging around outside the doors while they interviewed the inhabitants wasn't remotely tempting. But it was unlikely anyone would want to invite them in when they were all dripping wet. Each container was less than fifteen square metres inside, and none of the three officers were what you would call small men. If they were invited in, they'd have to cart some of the furniture outside to make room.

Rafn walked past two of the containers and stopped in front of the purple door of the third. They could hear the sound of a loud altercation but it seemed to be coming from next door. Although Huldar couldn't make out the words, he had the feeling the quarrel was the kind people have just for the sake of it. The kind that is common when both parties are too drunk to remember what they're arguing about and keep changing their standpoint as a result.

When no one answered Rafn's knock, he pressed his ear to the door. Huldar and Gudlaugur waited in silence. Then Rafn straightened up, grimaced and shook his head. Either there was nobody home or the occupant was out for the count. Rafn knocked again, just to be on the safe side, but no one came to the door.

'What now?' Huldar half hoped that Rafn would suggest going back to the station for a coffee. But it seemed his luck was out.

'I'm going to ask the guy next door if he knows where Binni is. It sounds like he's awake.'

The altercation seemed to have stopped and music suddenly started blasting from the neighbouring unit, the radio or music system almost drowned out by the tone-deaf cater-wauling of the people inside. Huldar didn't recognise the song as it wasn't his kind of thing. Too bland. No guitar riffs and hardly any discernible drumbeat.

Rafn had to hammer long and hard before the occupant finally heard and answered the door. He looked as if he was pushing sixty but in reality was probably much younger. He was bare-chested and so thin they could count his ribs. His dirty jeans hung off his skinny hips and he didn't appear to be wearing any underwear, or any socks on his filthy feet which were covered in puncture holes. His face was haggard, his knuckles were bloody and his dead-white arms and the backs of his hands were covered in needle scars like his feet. Some of them were raised and purple, others red and still others crusted over with scabs that were as white as his skin. His wrists were dyed black from all the metal bracelets he wore. 'Whoa!' he exclaimed. 'Who are you?'

Rafn introduced himself and explained that he was looking for Binni – Binni Briefcase. The man's watery eyes wandered from Rafn to Huldar and then to Gudlaugur, then repeated the manoeuvre. 'Hang on. How many of you are there? Two or four?'

'Three.'

'Wow, man. I could have sworn there were four of you. Or five, maybe.' Inside, his friend started his tuneless singing again. Huldar resisted the urge to put his hands over his ears.

'Do you know if Binni's home or if he's out somewhere?'

'Binni?'

The sunken-cheeked face looked more dazed than ever and the man rocked on his feet. 'He's not here.' He turned to Huldar. 'Got a fag, mate?' He wasn't so out of it that he couldn't unerringly spot the only smoker among the three – or four – of them.

Huldar fetched a cigarette from his pocket, then, thinking better of it, handed over four. From the way the man's face lit up as he took them, he was presumably under the impression that there were more. Thanking Huldar profusely he shoved one in his mouth and lit up. As a result of some odd chemical reaction, sucking in the smoke seemed to sober him up a little. He grew steadier on his feet and his eyes managed to focus on one point for longer than a couple of seconds. Huldar seized this opportunity to repeat Rafn's question about Binni.

'Binni? Binni's at home. Binni's always at home. He's broken his leg. Can't go anywhere.' The man took another drag, then played a riff on an air guitar, perfectly out of time.

'What about a girl? Have you seen a teenage girl hanging around here recently? Her name's Rósa. Dark hair. Small – about one metre sixty.'

'A girl.' The man puckered his brow. 'Yeah. There was a girl here earlier. I asked her to run over to the shop and buy me a Coke but she couldn't be arsed.'

They thanked him and, after the man had thanked Huldar again for the cigarettes, he returned to his private party.

Before trying Binni's container again, Rafn ran back to the car and fetched the nasal spray. He wanted to be prepared in case Binni had overdosed and was lying unconscious inside. After banging on his door so loudly it must have woken the entire container colony, they peered in through his windows but their view was blocked by the tatty curtains. Then Rafn thought of trying the door handle and discovered that it was open.

They didn't enter immediately. Rafn called Binni's name through the gap but there was no answer. He called again and was met by the same silence. Only then did Rafn step inside, while Huldar and Gudlaugur waited in the rain. When Rafn came out again, his face was white and he was still holding the Narcan spray, unopened. After Huldar had stuck his head inside, he understood that no antidote, drug or doctor could help Binni now.

They rang to report the discovery of a body, then waited in the car for back-up. The whole shooting match: Forensics, a pathologist, a photographer and a team from CID.

Judging by the scene inside, there wasn't even a theoretical possibility that Binni had died from natural causes. Or, for that matter, from an overdose.

Chapter 13

Wednesday night

There had been no let-up in the rain. The scene-of-crime team at work on Grandi had long ago abandoned the attempt to keep dry by putting up their hoods, donning waterproof ponchos or holding things over their heads. They had simply resigned themselves to being soaked to the skin, since once that stage had been reached, it was easier to concentrate on what needed to be done. Which was plenty. Secure the scene, carry out a preliminary examination of the deceased, photograph and fingerprint the interior of the container, collect biological samples, fibres and anything else that could conceivably qualify as evidence, and, trickiest of all, interview potential witnesses from the other containers. As yet nothing useful had been extracted from the neighbours, who were all either stoned or suffering from withdrawal symptoms; nothing in between.

Huldar watched as the dead man was carried out on a stretcher and taken to the ambulance that was waiting to transfer him to the National Hospital mortuary. The sheet covering him had slipped as the paramedics tried to ease the stretcher out through the narrow doorway, and hadn't immediately been twitched back into place. The leg, which according to Binni's neighbour had been broken, appeared to have been set at home and bound in whatever had come to hand. A long shoehorn had been tied tight against the bone using a colourful if grubby pillowcase and a dishcloth, all wrapped around with masking tape. They would never know how well this makeshift arrangement had worked.

Huldar averted his gaze, having seen enough when he stuck his head round the door earlier, when Rafn had found the body. After snatching a glimpse, he had hastily withdrawn. Apart from the horribly mutilated corpse, what had struck him most was how homely the place had been, if you over-looked the coffee table with its overflowing ashtray, collection of pills, tourniquet, syringe, lighter and aluminium foil, black-ened with soot. That could have come straight out of a film set for a scene involving an addict, but it was in stark contrast to the rest of the room. The furniture, obtained no doubt from the Red Cross, was shabby, ugly and dated – stuff that had been thrown out of the country's homes to make room for more modern pieces – but intact, nevertheless. A massive bookcase, taking up an unnecessary amount of the cramped interior, contained dog-eared books, ornaments and framed photos of people who Huldar took to be the man's closest family. People who would presumably now mourn his death. They were probably better prepared for the news than most, though. Rough sleepers seldom lived to a great age.

But it was rare, if not unheard of, for one of them to have his throat cut from ear to ear. It had taken Huldar several seconds to work out what he was looking at, after initially mistaking the wound for a wide grin.

Seeing Erla bearing down on him, Huldar hastily stubbed out the cigarette he had finally managed to light. Blowing smoke in her face would not be a wise move right now. Even people with a more placid temperament than Erla might be forgiven for going off the deep end after being woken in the middle of the night and dragged out in the rain to attend the scene of a murder.

'Can't we even send you on a simple mission like looking for a child without you creating havoc?' She took no notice of the raindrops trickling from her soaking hair down over her face and into her neckline.

'Nothing to do with me, Erla. I didn't top the guy.'

She didn't look remotely mollified by this statement of the obvious. 'You know what I mean. Like the whole situation isn't fucking confusing and complicated enough already. The last thing we need is another corpse. Who's supposed to work on this? All my most experienced officers are on leave.'

It was absurd for her to imply that Huldar wasn't one of them, but he was too tired, cold and wet to quarrel. 'Did they find the murder weapon?' He already guessed they hadn't, but the question stopped him from losing his temper with her and saying something he'd only regret.

'No. Not yet. They're still searching through the mountain of bloody rubbish around here. But the knife's not inside that container. I'm waiting for search warrants for the neighbouring units but I'm not optimistic about finding it there. We're too close to the sea where it could easily be disposed of for good, and anyway it's not certain the warrants will be granted as we don't have a lot of evidence to justify them. If we're lucky we'll get one. But there's no way we'll get permission to search all of them.'

Huldar agreed. The courts would be accused of displaying prejudice against this social group if they granted a blanket warrant. After all, when the average citizen was murdered in an apartment block, the police wouldn't automatically be given leave to search all the flats on their staircase. 'What do the neighbours say? Did they notice anything?'

'No. Not that they're admitting, anyway. There was a guy half asleep or dopey from withdrawal symptoms in one of the units. The blokes in the other two were awake but claim they've stayed indoors. People don't bother going outside to smoke here. We're not necessarily talking tobacco, either, which isn't helping us get statements out of them. We'll have to take them in for questioning, which is a bugger.'

'Questioning? Are you going to drag the whole lot down to the station?'

'No, not all of them. Just two. The occupants who were awake. They both had visitors but one had arrived relatively recently and the other was lying in a doped-up stupor on his mate's sofa. So I'm just going to take the two occupants.'

'On what grounds? Are either of them under suspicion?'

Erla shrugged. 'On the grounds that they're unlikely to remember a bloody thing in the morning. Not even our visit. I wouldn't put it past them to knock on the victim's door, asking for a light, once they wake up.' Sensing Huldar's disapproval, she carried on justifying herself. 'Come on. It's not unlikely that one of the people who live here or their visitors were involved. In fact, the odds are that it was one of them. They could have fallen out over drugs or debts. Real or imagined.'

It was possible. Binni could have had drugs that he didn't want to share. That wouldn't go down well with an addict tortured by cravings. 'Did they find any drugs in his place?'

'Fentanyl, OxyContin, Pethidine and Tramadol. All very likely smuggled to the country. There was also a two-litre

Coke bottle containing the dregs of illegal spirits. And Elephant beer in the fridge.'

'So whoever killed Binni wasn't after his stash.'

'No. Not unless they panicked and forgot to take the spoils with them.' Erla wiped a raindrop off her forehead before it could trickle into her eye.

Huldar had seen enough of the fallout from serious drug abuse in his job to realise that no addict who was desperate would have let a little thing like a dead body stop him or her from getting hold of the pills. If an addict had killed Binni for his stash, he or she would have stepped over the dead man, grabbed the gear, then got the hell out of there. Any pangs of remorse would only have surfaced later and no doubt have been medicated with more drugs, leading to another high, and so on and so on, down a slippery slope so steep it was almost vertical. 'Does that seem plausible to you?' he asked Erla.

'No. Not really.' Erla didn't contradict him as she usually did. 'I'm going back to the car to look up the names of the men we've already talked to. I'm almost sure one of them has a record of violence. I've seen him before. He could well have attacked Binni. His knuckles were bleeding.'

Huldar assumed she was referring to the man whose door he, Rafn and Gudlaugur had knocked on. 'How did he explain that?'

'He looked at his knuckles like he was seeing his hands for the first time since he emerged from his mother's womb. He couldn't explain the grazes. Needless to say, he's one of the two people we'll be taking down to the station. And not just for interview. We need to take samples from him. With any luck there'll be something under his nails.'

'Was there a fight, then?' Huldar hadn't seen any signs of one when he'd looked into the victim's container. It had seemed to him as if the attack had taken Binni by surprise as he sat on the rose-patterned sofa. Usually things got knocked over when people came to blows, however uneven the fight, especially in cramped conditions like that.

'Unlikely, though that's still not clear. Hopefully we'll get a better idea of the situation in the morning. It's impossible to think straight in this fucking downpour. It's as if it gets into your head and waters down your thoughts.'

Huldar had to agree. In his case, of course, it didn't help that he'd had no sleep and would only be able to grab a couple of hours at most before he had to go in to work again. If he complained, they wouldn't hesitate to give him the morning off, but he wanted to be there. The plan was to interview more youngsters from the care home and Freyja would be present. He wasn't going to miss out on an opportunity like that. The advantage of working for two departments simultaneously was that Erla and Hafthór didn't compare notes, just concentrated on the assignments he was doing for each of them separately. No one was keeping track of his overall hours.

'What about blood-stains? I took a look inside when we found the body and it was like his artery had been connected to a garden sprinkler. Was there any blood on either of the other occupants?'

'No. But they could have changed clothes or just escaped being splashed by coming at Binni from behind, cutting his throat, then taking a step backwards. The blood gushed forwards; none of it went behind him. There are two sets of footprints through the blood on the floor, which are being photographed and measured as we speak. If we get those search warrants, we may be lucky enough to find a pair of shoes with blood on the soles.'

Huldar remembered that the neighbour he met had been barefoot – perhaps because his socks and shoes had been covered in blood. 'Were the tracks made by a man's shoes?'

'One set. The other belonged to a woman or a man with very small feet. Or maybe a kid. The bigger prints lead from the pool of blood to the kitchen unit, then out of the door, while the smaller ones lead from the pool straight to the door. There are no tracks in the pool of blood itself, so it looks as if both individuals trod in it before it congealed. Which means either they were both there when Binni was murdered or they arrived shortly afterwards. Separately.'

Small shoes. Huldar remembered the original reason for their visit. 'Has anyone mentioned Rósa? We spoke to the man in the unit next door to Binni's and he said he'd seen her around earlier in the evening. She was friendly with the victim. That's why we were here.' Gudlaugur and Rafn had left but Huldar had hung around; he didn't really know why. It wasn't as if he was needed. The three of them had already made a full report, but he'd wanted to talk to Erla, who hadn't yet arrived by the time the other two went home. In the event, though, she hadn't been interested in talking to him until now. So he had hung around in the rain like an idiot while she was examining the scene and knocking on doors. 'The smaller prints could be hers,' he added.

Erla frowned. 'What the fuck? Was she here this evening? Is this some kind of frigging joke? Don't tell me she's a witness in three cases now?'

This aspect hadn't occurred to Huldar. He had interpreted

the drunken neighbour's remark as meaning that Rósa had been there quite a bit earlier in the evening, though he'd had no particular reason to think that. Perhaps the rain had watered down his faculties, as Erla complained it had done to her. Come to think of it, he didn't even know how long Binni had been lying there. He could have already been dead when Rósa arrived. Huldar hoped not, for the girl's sake. He prayed that the small prints had belonged to some other woman or small-footed man. The girl had experienced more than enough traumas in her life without having to stumble across another dead body. 'When do they reckon the man died, Erla?'

'Around eleven in the evening. According to a rough estimate based on his body temperature. I asked the pathologist if a badly damaged liver could affect the reading but he didn't answer, which usually means he thinks it's a stupid question.' Erla shrugged. 'So, he probably died around 11 p.m., about an hour before you lot showed up. You didn't see anything suspicious, did you?'

Huldar shook his head.

They stood and watched as a member of Forensics carried a box of personal effects out of Binni's container. Huldar wondered if the family photos were among them. His tiredness was obviously getting to him. 'I'm thinking of heading home.'

Erla glared at him as if wanting a bit of sleep constituted a breach of his contract. 'We're not done here.'

'Precisely. You're not done. But I am. As far as I can see, you've got all the people you need.' He didn't remind her of his statutory rest period, not wanting to come across as whiny.

'I'm recalling you from Sexual Offences. Our need's greater

than theirs. We're going to have to comb this entire area by daylight and, given the state of it, we could do with more hands.' She gestured at a derelict wooden house that stood nearby. It had once been a handsome building but now all the windows were broken and holes had been made in the walls in several places. What remained of the cladding was covered in graffiti, but even the graffiti artists obviously hadn't thought it worth making an effort. 'That dump, for example. We need to search every nook and cranny in there. Be back here by midday. I'll let Hafthór know about the change in arrangement.'

Huldar didn't protest, knowing it would be futile, but he resolved to go along to the morning interviews with the witnesses in the abuse case as planned. No need to mention the fact to Erla. He would return to his own department at lunchtime. With any luck he'd get away with it because Erla would come in late tomorrow, having been occupied here half the night. This would give him three or four hours in which to invite Freyja out, minus the time they spent doing the actual interviewing. So, around ten or fifteen minutes, then. He'd managed to secure a date in that short a window before. 'I'll be here. What about Gudlaugur?'

Erla didn't even pause to think. 'No, he can stay on loan. I want that girl found ASAP. Gudlaugur will be able to keep up the pressure on them to track her down.'

'Any news of the sub?' Huldar sent up a silent prayer that it was still out of order. Although he was prepared to work when he was exhausted, there was no way in hell he was going out on the boat again.

'Not yet. Though I'm hoping we'll be able to go out tomorrow or the day after. You won't be coming with us, though. I've got something else in mind for you.'

Huldar broke into a grin. 'What can I say? You're the boss.'

At that moment, a racket of screaming and shouting broke out in the container where the half-naked music lover lived. Huldar and Erla swung their heads round to see two policemen trying to drag the man out onto the narrow wooden step. They each had him by an arm but he kept writhing from side to side and it was all they could do not to lose their grip. The man had one of Huldar's cigarettes hanging from the corner of his mouth and managed to suck in and blow out smoke throughout his struggles. In the end, he was over-powered, and shuffled over to the car with the officers, still barefoot. He made several more attempts to escape on the way, though how he thought he'd succeed when the area was crawling with police was anyone's guess.

Before Huldar made his own, rather easier, exit, he thought it best to prepare Erla for the worst. 'I understand Rósa's good at hiding. She's vanished for days at a time on previous occasions. So it may be a while before you get to talk to her.'

Erla was scornful. 'Like it's that hard to trace a missing teen in Reykjavík. She'll turn up if they pull their fingers out. But just so it's clear, I doubt the girl had anything to do with what happened here this evening. The odds are against it. She can't be linked to three separate inquiries that crop up almost simultaneously. It's statistically impossible.'

'Unless the cases are connected.' Huldar couldn't see how, but then all three investigations were still in their early stages.

'Don't talk bullshit. You're obviously knackered. Go home and I'll see you at midday.'

Huldar caught up with the police officer who was on his way to the station with the contents of Binni's home, and hitched a lift with him. The entire way back, the man tutted over the disgusting mess around the containers. Anyone would have thought he was planning to build a summer house in the area. Huldar sat in silence, picturing the clean sheets awaiting him at home.

But once he had picked up his car from the station and driven home, chewed some sugarless gum in lieu of brushing his teeth, pulled off his clothes and collapsed into bed, he found he couldn't sleep. His tired mind wouldn't stop wrestling with the problem of how the three cases could be connected. The discovery of the bones, sexual abuse at the care home and now the murder of a homeless man. In the end, his brain abandoned the struggle and he fell asleep, still none the wiser.

Chapter 14

Thursday

Freyja sipped the watery police-station coffee that Huldar had brought her. It was tepid too. He'd obviously been a bit over-generous with the milk, but it was the thought that counted, so she tried not to make a face. He looked absolutely shattered; unshaven, his hair unkempt as if he'd towelled it dry without bothering to comb it. The two adolescents they had talked to so far that morning had clearly appreciated his seedy appearance and directed their answers largely to him. It was almost as if Freyja and Hafthór weren't there, although Hafthór was suppos-edly in charge of the questioning. But he didn't take offence, merely looked pleased that the teenagers were answering at all.

The map of traffic accidents had been taken down and replaced with an ancient, framed photo of Reagan and Gorbachev shaking hands outside Höfdi House during the historic Reykjavík summit of 1986. Freyja assumed it had been discovered gathering dust somewhere and they'd thought it would do. Apart from that, the room was unchanged – well, except for the pot plant, which had lost another leaf. If it went on like this, there would be nothing left but a bare stalk by the end of the week.

Today's interviews had also failed to produce anything of interest. One of the teenagers had plainly taken something which made him extremely jittery. His eyes were constantly flitting around the room and he seemed afraid that the ostensible reason for the interview was only a pretext and that really they were trying to nail him for drug use. Or for dealing. The other boy was much calmer.

But neither could tell them anything about the crime under investigation and Freyja was beginning to have her doubts. From her job she knew that active child abusers are rarely satisfied with a single victim. When the object of their desire evades their attentions or grows too old to be of interest to them, they are usually quick to identify the next victim. But so far the kids' statements hadn't provided a shred of evidence for this. Admittedly, there were still plenty of names on the list and it might just be a coincidence that the ones who had escaped Bergur's attentions had been the first to be interviewed, but even so it was troubling.

Freyja's suggestion that the interviews should be moved to the Children's House, in the hope that this would make the young people more willing to talk, had met with the same opposition as before: the matter was too urgent. Although she realised there was no point arguing, she had to bite her lip to stop herself. Meanwhile, Reagan and Gorbachev smiled down at her from the wall.

'I have to say, I'm a bit surprised we haven't heard anything at all to back up Tristan's allegations,' Freyja said, inadvertently forestalling Huldar, who had opened his mouth to speak. But he was a big boy; he'd have his chance later.

Huldar looked a little put out at the interruption but, recovering quickly, replied: 'Do you think they're lying? Covering up for the guy?'

'No. Their statements are believable, for the most part. Of

course, some of them reveal a distorted point of view, but in general they come across as honest. No, actually I was considering another possibility – that it's Tristan who's not telling the truth. False accusations do happen. Very, very rarely, but there have been examples, and it might be worth keeping an open mind.'

'Hmm.' Huldar sounded sceptical. 'I gather he's very convincing. I haven't heard anyone else suggest he might be making it up.'

'I'm just raising the possibility. Maybe what he says is perfectly true and we'll find a witness to back him up . . .' Freyja hesitated. 'But if the abuse did take place, it would be better if we could find someone to confirm it. You know as well as I do what happens when sexual offences cases go to court and it's one person's word against another's.'

Huldar nodded. Then he cleared his throat. 'By the way, what time is it?'

Freyja checked her phone. 'Ten past eleven. Whoops! We'd better get a move on.' From Huldar's pained expression, you'd have thought she'd just reminded him about a dental appointment. He'd be useless at poker. 'Good night, was it?' she asked with a grin.

'No,' he said flatly. 'I was working. On the incident that was in the news this morning.'

'Oh.' It had taken all of Freyja's powers to make it to the station in time for the first interview, what with having to dress Saga, give her breakfast, let Molly out, get herself ready, then drop her niece off at nursery school. There had been no time to check the news. 'Anything serious?'

'As serious as it gets.' Huldar suppressed a yawn. 'Murder. A nasty one.'

'Oh. Has the murderer been caught?' Freyja asked. Experience had taught her that in Iceland, murders committed during the night were generally solved before the morning news.

'No.' Huldar straightened up and knocked back the rest of his coffee. 'But we'll catch the person responsible, don't you worry. It's only a matter of time.'

Freyja nodded. She didn't doubt this for a moment. Then she forced herself to finish her own cup so she wouldn't have to take it into the interview room with her. 'By the way, any sign of Rósa yet?'

'You're still bound by confidentiality, aren't you?' Huldar asked. When Freyja nodded, he continued: 'Funny you should ask. She's the most popular girl at the party right now. She's a possible witness to last night's murder, incredible as it might seem.'

Freyja gaped at him. 'What?'

'Yes. A crazy coincidence, if you like. Though it's a bit too crazy for my taste.' Huldar suddenly looked more cheerful. 'I'm only here until midday. I've been recalled to CID because of the murder inquiry, so I should hopefully know more about the girl's whereabouts later today. How about I buy you dinner this evening and fill you in on what we've found out? She may have turned up by then. Since they're sure to want you there when we interview her, it's best to keep you in the loop.'

The offer was very tempting. Freyja was dying to hear more about Rósa, and an evening in Huldar's company didn't sound so bad. Guessing what was behind her change of heart, she reminded herself of her three ground rules. But, as it happened, there was no need for them in this case as she couldn't go anywhere this evening. 'I can't, unfortunately. I'm looking after Saga.'

Huldar's face fell and he looked as weary as he had before. There was no time to say any more as the next interview was about to begin.

Freyja parked by the bike rental shop where there were plenty of free spaces, as one might expect. She got out and started walking in the direction of the container colony, which was now all over the news as a result of the murder Huldar had mentioned. She'd managed to catch up on the story in her break and her curiosity was roused. Since Saga's nursery school was in the west of town, it provided the perfect opportunity to make a minor detour on her way to pick up her niece, and scope out the place everyone was talking about.

The last interview of the day had been postponed, as the same kid who had failed to turn up the previous day had let them down again. Finding herself unexpectedly with time on her hands, Freyja had gone up to Huldar's floor to plug him for news but was told he was interviewing witnesses with Erla. There had been no point hanging around as you never knew how long interviews would go on.

There wasn't enough time to drop by the Children's House, and besides there was nothing waiting for her there. Nor was there any point in dashing home, and she couldn't face doing a supermarket shop or taking the car to the garage. A quick drive out to Grandi was no worse an option than any other.

If it hadn't been for the police operation, she'd have missed the container colony altogether. Several officers were walking around with poles in their hands, poking at the ground. There was such a vast accumulation of junk lying around that it looked like a starter pack for a recycling centre. Although it would have been simplest for Freyja to park beside the police vehicles, she was afraid of attracting attention and being told to get lost. Better to park a little way off and stroll past casually like a lost tourist in search of the Valdís ice-cream parlour.

She started walking, relieved that the rain had finally stopped. Ahead she could see the long flat-topped hulk of Mount Esja, free of cloud for once, and a cluster of white oil tanks in the foreground. There were far more of them than she'd realised, since most were hidden from view when seen from the more familiar angle out on Seltjarnarnes. She also noted the signs that industry was still thriving there, despite the encroaching restaurants and shops in the next street.

Freyja turned her attention to the colony. At first sight, it would be easy to mistake them for four regular transport containers. These were a common sight on Grandi, after all. But the brightly painted doors gave them away, along with the dustbins, bicycles, chairs, mattresses and other objects associated with human habitation, though of course the average family didn't chuck this kind of stuff out of their front door and leave it lying around on the ground outside.

The police took no notice of Freyja. They were busy plucking objects out of the shopping trolleys that were lined up, side by side, like cars at a showroom. They examined them all, before dropping them carelessly on the ground at their feet. Freyja winced and looked away. This stuff had once been of value to somebody, perhaps to the dead man. Then again, she supposed that even if the things did belong to him, his relatives were unlikely to have any use for them.

What puzzled her was why a sixteen-year-old girl would have been attracted to a place like this. Rósa wasn't on drugs and there was nothing in her file to suggest that she drank either. She gave the impression of being totally clean, which was extraordinary when you considered her mental state. Alcohol and drugs were powerful comforters. Perhaps she had been given a bed here. According to Rósa's file, she often disappeared for days at a time. But she was sensible and must have realised that a place like this wasn't safe. In summer, she would surely have preferred to sleep in the open air. Freyja couldn't remember if her disappearances had coincided with summer or if she had absconded in winter too. If so, that would complicate matters. An Icelandic blizzard would make a cold bed. In that case, it would be preferable to crash on a sofa here, on the margins of society. At least the occupants would be unlikely to report her. Perhaps that was the explanation. Perhaps Rósa's desire for freedom had made it worth putting up with conditions like this.

But none of these scenarios explained the letters that arrived in the post. They were unlikely to have come from anyone in the container community, and if Rósa was sleeping rough, it was hard to imagine where she would get access to a printer. Maybe they had them in hotel reception areas, but Freyja guessed that an Icelandic teenager would stand out like a sore thumb in a place like that and would be chased out the moment she tried to use the amenities.

A painfully thin woman in an oversized quilted jacket now appeared between two of the tall stacks of timber which were dotted around the area, although they didn't seem to serve any purpose since there was no sign of any building work in progress. The woman was holding a rather sorry-looking bunch of flowers and had just stooped to lay it on the ground when she caught sight of Freyja. She hurriedly straightened up, looking self-conscious. It was hard to work out her age. She had short, thin hair and although her unusually gaunt face wasn't heavily wrinkled, the lines she did have were deeply entrenched, especially round her mouth, eyes and across her forehead. From a distance her cheeks had appeared a healthy red but Freyja saw now that they were covered in rosacea. The hands poking from the threadbare sleeves of her jacket looked blue, with bulging veins and swollen knuckles, like those of an old-age pensioner. Yet she couldn't have been that old. It was plain that life hadn't treated this woman kindly.

'Are you a policewoman?' Her voice was so hoarse she sounded like a chain-smoker who inhaled sand for kicks.

'Me?' Freyja smiled. 'No.'

'Work there, do you?' The woman pointed at a building bearing the name of a publishing house.

'No. I don't work there either.'

'What are you doing here, then?'

Freyja was slightly taken aback by her directness. 'I'm looking for a missing teenager. I understand she sometimes hangs out here.'

'Your daughter?' There was a flicker of sympathy in the woman's eyes.

'No. We're not related.'

'I hope she turns up soon,' the woman said. 'It's no joke being on the streets.'

Freyja decided to be equally direct in return, guessing the woman wouldn't take it amiss. 'What about you? Are the flowers for the man who died?'

'Yes.' The woman didn't seem remotely put out by her nosiness. It wasn't every day Freyja met someone that straight-forward. 'I used to know Binni well at one time.' The woman turned her gaze towards the containers. 'I cleaned up my act several years ago. He didn't.'

'I'm sorry.' Freyja didn't know what else to say. 'Did you often visit him here?'

'No, hardly ever. It's difficult enough staying sober among a group of bloody born-again types. It's almost impossible if you hang around with people who are still on the booze.'

'I can believe it.' Freyja didn't feel qualified to comment. Not from personal experience, anyway. She herself drank, usually in moderation, occasionally too much, but when this happened she always had the sense to take herself home. It wasn't really the alcohol she craved so much as the light-heartedness that went with it. Waking up in the morning wanting a drink was as alien a concept to her as waking up and wanting to go to the gym. As for drugs, she never touched them. 'You haven't run into the girl I'm looking for, have you? Her name's Rósa. She's sixteen, small for her age, with dark hair. Like I said, she used to show up here.'

The woman wrinkled her brow, thinking. 'I came over with some food for Binni once and there were a couple of kids at his place. A girl and a boy. Can't remember her name. It might have been Rósa for all I know. She had dark hair.'

'Was this recently?'

'No. Must have been about a year ago. Longer. It was shortly after Binni moved into the container. I remember that because he didn't have enough chairs for everyone and the boy had to stand.'

'Can you remember anything about the boy?'

'Not really. He was blond, I think – the pretty-boy type. He had a name that didn't seem to belong in a place like that. It sounded like something out of a poem. A prince's name. You know, like Alexander. But not.'

'Tristan?' The tragic knight who loved Isolde – because of a love potion, if Freyja remembered right. Medieval drugs sounded rather more romantic than the modern variety.

'Yes, that could have been it.'

'Did they mention what they were doing there?'

The woman thought again. 'No. Or if they did, I've forgotten. Maybe they'd brought Binni drugs. Not that they looked like dealers. Mind you, that would have made them ideal as carriers. So who knows? Gangs do use kids to deal and make deliveries.' She contemplated her bouquet with a dejected look.

'Aren't you going to leave it here?'

'No. I've changed my mind. The police will only take it, in case it's connected to the murder. They've got my fingerprints on file and I don't want to be mixed up in this. I've had enough of cops to last me a lifetime. I thought they'd have finished by now. It didn't occur to me that they'd waste more than a couple of hours on someone like Binni.'

'All murders should get the same treatment.'

The woman gave Freyja a pitying look. 'Yeah, right.'

Their conversation had run out of steam. Freyja noticed that one of the police officers was taking an interest in them. He was holding a clunky old grey desk phone that he had fished out of one of the trolleys. The receiver fell off and dangled on its wire just above the ground as the officer studied Freyja and the woman with the bunch of flowers.

'Do you need a lift?' Freyja gestured towards the bicycle

rental place where she had parked. She didn't feel like explaining to the police what she was doing there as it wasn't supposed to be her job to go out looking for Rósa. Her role was limited to sitting in on the interviews and being there for the young people.

The woman glanced at the policeman, who seemed on the point of heading in their direction. 'Yes, please.'

They walked quickly over to the car and got in. Freyja pulled away just as the policeman appeared between the stacks of timber. She hoped she was too far off for him to be able to read her registration plate. When she stole a peek in the rear-view mirror, she saw that he wasn't making a note of anything. He was just standing there, watching them drive away, still with the old phone in his hands.

The fridge was as bare as it had been that morning. It felt even barer, somehow. 'What do you say, Saga? Would you like Cheerios for tea?'

Saga seemed content with this. At least, her perma-scowl didn't get any deeper. Molly, on the other hand, sent Freyja a look of disgust. The dog had a vested interest in the subject since a large part of what Saga ate landed on the floor, where Molly would be waiting to hoover it up.

Freyja took out the milk and shook the carton. She was relieved to discover that there was enough in there for one bowl of cereal. She would have to find something else for herself. A tin of baked beans, perhaps. Her stomach grumbled in protest.

The doorbell rang. The owner of the flat had chosen a loud peal of bells that would be more appropriate for a cathedral than a modern apartment block. The first time a visitor had come round after Freyja moved in, she had half expected to find the Pope on the doorstep, but it had turned out to be her friends, a group who had precisely nothing in common with His Holiness.

This visitor was also from the lower end of the scale of human virtues. On the entryphone's video screen she saw none other than Huldar, holding up a bag from a burger chain and a colourful children's meal box. That was good enough for Freyja. She buzzed him in.

Chapter 15

Thursday

The kitchen table was littered with packaging from the fast food that Freyja had wolfed down with embarrassing greed. Huldar, not to be outdone, had demolished two burgers and more than his fair share of fries, before embarking on the remaining burger that Freyja had declined on the grounds that one was enough. The only person eating like a diplomat at an official function was Saga, who took neat little mouthfuls and dipped her chips in the ketchup with her pinkie crooked. She only showed her true nature towards the end of the meal when she'd had enough and started chucking the leftovers into Molly's gaping jaws, all refinement abandoned, as if the diplomat had overindulged in the complimentary booze.

Now that the food was finished, Freyja started having regrets. Huldar was a policeman; her landlord a criminal. The expensive furnishings had no doubt been paid for with ill-gotten gains, and although Huldar was unlikely to cause trouble, the situation still made her uneasy. Still, at least he hadn't come out with anything embarrassing yet. When he arrived, he had congratulated her on having found a flat and asked who it belonged to. Freyja had muttered something about a friend of Baldur's but omitted to explain why the flat had been available. Huldar had asked no further questions and she had relaxed, apart from inadvertently glancing at the door of the snake's room every few minutes. The thought alone was enough to make her eyes slide in that direction.

'What's in that room?' Huldar jerked his chin at the closed door. Her frequent glances had not gone unnoticed.

Freyja could feel her cheeks growing hot. 'Oh, just some stuff belonging to the owner. I never go in there. It's locked.'

Saga pointed a fat finger at the door and emitted a long hissing noise. Freyja immediately regretted having played 'What does the snake say?' when they were looking through a picturebook about animals. She could feel her face glowing even hotter and, flustered, she began collecting up the wrappers on the table.

'Aren't you curious?' Huldar's eyes remained fixed on the door.

'No. I'm not interested in someone else's belongings.'

Huldar grinned. 'If you say so.' When he still couldn't tear his gaze away, Freyja grew nervous that he would get up and press his ear to the door. Or even pull a skeleton key from his pocket and start picking the lock. To distract his attention, she asked the question that had occurred to her when he'd appeared at the front door, only to be driven out of her head by the sight of the food. 'How did you know where I live?' She wasn't registered at this address. Even the rental contract hadn't been committed to paper: Baldur's friend had sealed the deal by giving her a high five, which he had considered quite sufficient to complete the formalities.

'I'm a cop.' Huldar winked at Saga.

The little girl tried to copy him but couldn't do it. She kept blinking both eyes simultaneously.

'I can find anyone,' he added.

'What about Rósa?' Freyja retorted before standing up to take the packaging to the bin.

'Anyone except her.' Huldar didn't sound remotely offended. 'But we'll find her in the end. Gudlaugur's on the team and promised to ring if they track her down tonight, regardless of the time. It's getting pretty urgent.'

'So there's no news?'

'Nope. Next to nothing. We're still gathering evidence and taking witness statements in connection with the murder on Grandi. We should hopefully have a clearer picture by tomorrow morning.'

'You don't have any suspects?'

'Yes, we do, as a matter of fact. One of the neighbours had blood on the soles of his shoes and was arrested after being questioned at the station. The blood was sent off for analysis and turned out to belong to the victim. But I don't buy the neighbour as the killer. There's too much that doesn't fit. Mind you, having said that, I'm fairly sure the victim was killed by someone he knew. Someone drunk or totally off their head. Why else would anyone want to murder the guy? Maybe it *was* the neighbour, at the end of the day. Anyway, my bet is that it was just one of those messy killings that happen almost by accident. Nothing more complicated than that.'

'So that's all there is to it?'

'Yeah. Probably.' Huldar rose to his feet. Saga immediately reached both arms up to him and he lifted her out of her high chair. No one needs an interpreter to understand a child's body language. He sat down again with her on his lap and, apparently contented, she started fiddling with the buttons on his shirt. Luckily she was extremely clumsy and failed to undo them. A little ketchup got smeared on his shirt in the process but Huldar didn't seem to mind. As a police officer, he must be used to getting all kinds of muck on him. 'We may never know exactly what happened. But you can bet we'll find his killer.'

Freyja told him about the woman she had encountered on Grandi. She had given her a lift down to Lækjartorg Square, where the woman had said she would catch a bus home. Freyja hadn't asked where she lived. If the woman had wanted to share that information, she would have done so. They hadn't exchanged names either. Their paths were unlikely ever to cross again and there was no need to get sentimental and pretend they would. But her ignorance of the woman's name didn't alter the fact that Freyja sincerely hoped she would manage to stay on the wagon.

'According to this woman, she bumped into Tristan and Rósa – well, probably Rósa – when she visited Binni about a year ago. She didn't know why they were there but she got the idea they might be dealing or making a delivery. I don't know if she was right. According to the paperwork I've seen, Rósa's never tested positive for drugs. I suppose that's irrelevant, though. She could have got involved for the money. Or just gone along because of Tristan. Do you know if he's got a history of using drugs? He looks squeaky clean from his file.'

Huldar pinched Saga's nose and she screwed up her eyes with enjoyment. 'No. He's not an addict. Not as far as I know. I haven't heard any rumours about him dealing either. But then I don't know much about him. They're planning to talk to him this week, so maybe it would be an idea for me to sit in on his interview, on the grounds that he had a link to the murder victim. It wouldn't hurt for me to ask.'

'I'll be there.' Freyja fetched a clean cloth, wet it and began to wipe Saga's fingers. The little girl resisted so vigorously that Huldar had to tighten his hold to prevent her from tumbling off his lap. It was inevitable really that during the struggle Freyja and Huldar should touch and that it should trigger flashbacks to the night they had once spent together. Turning a little pink, Freyja backed off before all Saga's fingers were done. Only by sternly reminding herself that Huldar's expertise in bed was the result of a great deal of practice with any woman who was willing could she get a grip on herself.

'You missed two.' Huldar took the cloth from Freyja and finished the job. Saga sat there docilely letting him wipe her fingers clean. The little traitor.

Freyja hid her pink cheeks by turning to the kitchen sink and pretending to rinse it, though this was unnecessary as it was as sparkling clean as when she'd moved in. The owner couldn't have used it much; presumably he had lived on take-aways that he ate straight out of the carton. That would explain why the dishwasher looked as pristine as if it had just been installed and the kitchen cupboards had been prac-tically empty when Freyja took over the flat. Apart from one coffee cup and two forks, the contents had mainly consisted of wine glasses. Now the cupboards were full of IKEA kitchen-ware that Freyja had picked out in fifteen minutes flat during a whirlwind visit to the country's only labyrinth. The stuff didn't exactly match the décor in the flat but it did the job.

Once she reckoned her face had recovered its normal colour, Freyja turned back to the kitchen table. 'However hard I try, there's one thing I can't get my head round.'

'Just one? You're lucky – I can hardly get my head round a single aspect of this case. Or cases, rather.'

Ignoring his interruption, Freyja persisted: 'If Rósa didn't visit this Binni to get hold of drugs, what on earth was she doing there? It sounds as if she went there more than once too. That behaviour just doesn't fit with anything else I've read about her. I suppose you've visited the scene?' When Huldar nodded, she went on: 'I wouldn't have thought it was exactly a desirable hangout for kids who aren't on the scrounge for drink or drugs.'

'No. I agree.' Huldar pinched Saga's nose again, then blew in her face. The little girl gave every indication of being on cloud nine. 'Nevertheless, she was obviously drawn to the guy, so it stands to reason he must have had something to offer, even if we can't figure out what it is.'

Freyja didn't immediately reply. She was trying yet again to imagine what the attraction could have been. But it was as futile as searching for poetry in the wording of a website's privacy notice. 'Is it possible that she was related to him?' Although undesirable personality traits could destroy friendships or attraction, family ties were different. Blood was thicker than water and all that. Never mind what your relatives did, you couldn't change the fact you were related to them. 'If so, that might have been what took her to see him. People can forgive a lot when it comes to family members.'

'Well, I haven't heard of any relationship, so if they were, I'm guessing it would be very distant.' Huldar furrowed his brow. 'At least, I assume I'd have got wind of it. I suppose it's possible we didn't check, beyond looking up his next of kin to inform them of his death. I just don't know.'

'What's the man's history? Is there anything there that could explain the link? Interests, quirks, anything else that could have brought them together?'

'His history? It's no secret and it'll come out in the obituaries. Of course, that'll be the edited version and you'll have to read between the lines, but his life story should be there for all to see.'

'You know I'm bound by professional confidentiality, Huldar,' Freyja said, her voice rising in exasperation. 'I shouldn't have to repeat that every time I ask you something. It applies to all the information that emerges while I'm assisting the police, not just the stuff relating to the kids.'

Huldar looked hurt. His eyelids drooped a little and so did the corners of his mouth. 'Even though this is social, not a work meeting?'

Freyja sighed under her breath. She had two choices, either to hurt him even more by saying that, as far as she was concerned, this was strictly a work meeting. Or to soften the blow. She chose the latter course. 'Yes, Huldar. Even though this is a social *visit*.' She stressed the last word to underline that this visit couldn't by any stretch of the imagination be described as a date. For both their sakes. She had every intention of sticking to her vow of celibacy. She had only just over a week left of the thirty days she had set herself and there was no way she was breaking her vow for Huldar.

He cheered up again and gave her a brief summary of Binni's life. The man had been forty-six years old at the time of his death. He had been born in the town of Húsavík in the far north-east of Iceland and grown up there, before moving to Reykjavík with his family in his teens. He had gone to sixth-form college there, then to university to take Business Studies with Accountancy. After graduating, he had started working for a large shipping company, got married and had two children in short succession with his wife. So far so good, and no sign that he was about to fall off a precipice. Yet this is what had happened. His drinking, which had started off as purely social, had gradually got out of control, until he ran on alcohol the way a car runs on petrol. He had twice gone to rehab but the effects had only lasted for the time it took him to drive to the state off-licence on his way home from the clinic. In the end, his drinking had cost him his job, and after that he had spiralled into serious alcoholism, until one day, about ten years ago, he had walked out of his house and taken to living rough. His wife and children hadn't been able to compete with his addiction. Once on the streets, he was able to drink without a guilty conscience or having to put up with recriminations or exhortations to turn his life around: a fettered form of freedom, if you like. Understandably, he'd had only intermittent contact with his family during the remaining years of his life. And the situation hadn't improved when he began using drugs as well. At first glance, there was nothing in this brief biography that could possibly link him to Rósa. Nothing other than the desire for escape. But she was unlikely to have sought him out for his advice on that since she seemed more than capable of absconding on her own.

Huldar had begun to fidget. Following his gaze past the open-plan kitchen to the balcony door at the far end of the living room, it dawned on Freyja what was wrong. 'You can smoke on the balcony, if you like. I think there's a chair out there.' She hadn't gone outside herself yet. The weather hadn't exactly been tempting since she'd moved in. There seemed to be a perpetual gale blowing, so it wasn't as if the smoke would bother her neighbours. 'I can lend you a pot as an ashtray.'

From the gratitude on Huldar's face, you'd have thought she'd just given him a generous Christmas present. Freyja relieved him of Saga and put the little girl down on the floor. She made a beeline for the glass door to the balcony, with Molly hot on her heels, and pressed her face against it. They both stood there watching intently as Huldar leant over the rail, savouring his cigarette. Saga began to mimic him, raising her fingers to her lips and puffing. If the child ever took up smoking, it would be Huldar's fault. The same applied to the dog.

Before Huldar could finish his cigarette, he glanced down, then reached into his pocket where his phone was obviously ringing. He took it out and alternately listened and made brief comments. The door, which was triple glazed to keep out the traffic noise, prevented Freyja from hearing a word of the conversation. It was like watching TV with the volume on mute. She watched him anyway, trying to guess what it was about. He appeared relaxed but serious, as if discussing an important matter with someone he knew well. Perhaps he had a girlfriend who was asking why he hadn't turned up for the supper she had lovingly cooked for him. It would be totally in character. Yet he gave no sign of being in bullshit mode as he talked, so that probably wasn't it. Perhaps it was one of his mates, discussing their team's performance in the latest match. But Freyja had the feeling it was to do with work.

When he came back inside, accompanied by a strong smell of smoke, Saga and Molly, undeterred, greeted him like the prodigal son. He patted them both on the head and took care not to trip over them on his way across the living room as they repeatedly got under his feet.

Freyja was dying to ask him about the phone call, but their relationship gave her no right to demand information like that. Besides, she told herself, she was only interested in case it related to Rósa.

'I have to go, I'm afraid.' Huldar smiled a bit sheepishly. 'Duty calls.' He didn't elaborate.

'Is it connected to Rósa?' Freyja blurted out. 'Has she been found?'

'No, she hasn't been found.' This only answered her second question but Huldar gave her no opportunity to repeat the first. He took his jacket from the back of the chair and hovered awkwardly for a moment, as people tend to at the moment of parting. Everyone wants to say the right thing, which suddenly seems so elusive. Freyja was equally embarrassed, though she did at least have the presence of mind to thank him for the food. Saga, however, wasn't remotely shy. She said goodbye to Huldar by bashing him on the calf with a big yellow Duplo brick. Huldar was apparently used to this sort of treatment as he didn't even wince, and the blow had the effect of dispelling the momentary awkwardness. He went to the door, said goodbye and was gone.

Freyja was left standing there, still none the wiser about Rósa or her fate.

Chapter 16

The man in the cell was in such a state that the police officer on guard duty thought he should be taken to hospital. He'd had enough experience of dealing with addicts in custody to recognise withdrawal symptoms better than most. In his opinion, the prisoner's life might be in danger if he wasn't seen by a doctor soon, and as deaths in custody were naturally frowned on, his recommendation was taken seriously.

Why Erla chose Huldar to take the man to hospital was anyone's guess. As usual, he hadn't raised any objections, but he did wonder if by some sixth sense she had known he was with Freyja and had deliberately chosen to ruin his evening. If so, she'd done a brilliant job.

Huldar closed the hatch in the cell door. 'How long's he been like that?'

'It started around midday while he was being questioned and he's gone dramatically downhill over the last couple of hours.' The police officer lifted a hand to the bolt. 'The trouble is, I don't know what drugs he's dependent on. If it's opioids, his life's probably not in danger, but if it's alcohol or something else, he could be at risk of a seizure or a heart attack. The same applies if it's a cocktail of substances. The doctors at the National Hospital will know what to do, so it's best they handle it. Anyway, from what I hear, it seems unlikely he's the killer.'

Huldar nodded. Before leaving work, he had skimmed the prisoner Týr's statement. When Týr had heard that the blood on his shoes was Binni's, he'd managed to retrieve a scrap of memory from the haze: he had gone over to Binni's place to borrow a Coke. From the transcript, it seemed he had been deeply affronted when asked if he was referring to the drink or the powder. According to him, he had just needed a mixer.

When Binni didn't respond to his request, Týr had simply gone ahead and helped himself to a can of Coke from his fridge. Týr seemed to have been completely oblivious to the fact that Binni was slumped dead on the sofa. But then it had quickly become apparent that Týr's eyesight was totally shot and since, by his own account, he had lost his glasses years ago and never got round to replacing them, it was quite plausible that he simply hadn't noticed the gaping wound in Binni's throat.

The footprints provided further evidence that his statement was broadly correct: someone had walked straight across the blood-spattered floor to the fridge, without going over to the sofa. Týr's visitor had backed up his statement, recalling that his host had vanished briefly to fetch some Coke. The men's credibility as witnesses was equally shaky but, taken together, their stories did appear to add up to the truth The two Coke cans discovered in Týr's unit, bearing his and Binni's finger-prints, further supported this version of events. Three identical cans had been found in the victim's fridge. There was no sign of the blood-stained murder weapon in Týr's container either, or indeed of any other knife that could have inflicted the wound and subsequently been washed clean. By the time he had finished reading, Huldar was fairly satisfied in his own mind that the man in the cell had had nothing to do with the killing. Not least because of the drugs that had been lying around for all to see in the dead man's container. Nothing of the kind had been found at Týr's place, which suggested he hadn't stolen any pills. It would be a strange kind of addict who'd had the presence of mind to take away two Coke cans but had left the stash behind, however off his head he had been at the time.

On the other hand, Týr had failed to dig up from the recesses of his mind exactly when he had seen Rósa. The only time frame they could get out of him was that she had been around before Týr went to fetch the Coke. He didn't think much time had passed between these two events but became confused when they tried to get him to be more precise. He thought he had waited quarter of an hour. But maybe it was half an hour. Or even an hour. So the information was of little use for establishing whether or not Rósa had been at the scene when the murder was committed. Finding the girl was now the police's top priority – not that this had done anything to speed up the process. She was still missing.

Huldar braced himself for the stench that was bound to hit them the moment the cell door was opened. The prisoner was lying on the couch, with the sick bucket, of which he appeared to have made copious use, on the floor beside him. Despite being prepared for the worst, Huldar had to cover his nose and mouth with his elbow as the heavy steel door swung outwards. 'Christ!'

'I'm dying.' The man lay curled up in the foetal position, his eyes shut, though he obviously wasn't asleep. He raised his head a little. 'You've got to help me.' He turned hopeful, red eyes on Huldar. 'You! I know you, don't I? You've got to help me. Please, give me something – anything.'

'Do you two know each other?' The guard glanced at Huldar in surprise.

'Not exactly. We met when the body was discovered.' Huldar turned to the prisoner. 'I'm here to take you to hospital. They'll help you feel more comfortable.'

'Hospital?' The man's voice was threadbare. Even hoarser than it had been on the evening of his arrest, which Huldar would hardly have believed possible. 'I don't need a hospital to make me feel better. Haven't you got any dope? Stuff you've confiscated?'

'Nope. Not a thing.' Huldar felt an extreme reluctance to set foot in the cell and hoped to God the man would be able to get up and make it outside under his own steam. 'Come on. It'll do you good to get a bit of fresh air. I'll drive with the window open. Come on, mate. I've got an energy drink. A nice cold one.' Huldar waved the can inside the cell door. It worked.

Týr struggled to his feet, tottered, clutched his head and sank down again. Then he made another, desperate effort and this time he was successful. Huldar felt sorry for the poor bastard. He had never experienced full-on withdrawal symptoms himself, despite having graduated from the university of hang-overs. According to those in the know, withdrawal symptoms were like the kind of turbo-charged hangover you'd get by knocking back a bottomless well of beer that had been brewed among the radioactive waste from a nuclear reactor. 'You'll feel better once you've got this down your neck.' He opened the can for the man, since he looked too frail to pull the tab.

'Huh.' Although clearly unimpressed by Huldar's medical

advice, Týr took the can and gulped down its contents. Then he stiffened and for an agonising moment it looked as if he was about to regurgitate the lot. Mercifully, however, it stayed down.

'Have you got a coat for him? An anorak or something?' Huldar asked the officer. Týr was wearing the same filthy jeans as when he had been arrested, but had been lent a T-shirt that was far too big for his skeletal frame. The prison storeroom always had a supply of shabby old garments from lost property. The T-shirt was decorated with a spoon from which thick yellow liquid was dripping. Beneath it was the logo of Lýsi, the cod-liver-oil producer. Huldar doubted the company would be particularly grateful for the association with Týr. 'It's cold outside and he already looks like he's freezing.' Huldar gestured at the goose pimples covering Týr's poor, punctured arms.

'That's due to the withdrawal symptoms. It's got nothing to do with the temperature in here.' Although the guard seemed to know what he was talking about, he obligingly went to fetch a coat.

'Please, mate. You must be able to fix me something. Just one Oxy. Please.' Týr wrapped his arms around himself in an attempt to stop the violent fits of shivering that were assailing his frail body. The moment he had finished speaking, his teeth – the few he had left – started chattering.

'I haven't got anything. Honestly. They'll give you something in hospital.'

'Shit. The stuff they give you there is shit.' Týr was still shaking. 'What about a beer? Have you got a beer? Or a shot of something?'

He was persistent all right. 'You know I haven't got anything like that,' Huldar said. 'I'm a cop, remember? And I'm on duty.'

The other officer returned with an old anorak that more or less fitted the prisoner and would be quite warm enough for a chilly summer night. Huldar helped Týr put his arms into the sleeves and zipped it up, since the man was trembling too badly to do it himself. Then Huldar took hold of his bony shoulder and steered him down the corridor and out into the fresh air. He helped Týr into the back of the car but didn't bother with the belt as the man immediately collapsed sideways onto the seat.

It wasn't far to the hospital but Huldar drove slowly to be on the safe side. He tried to keep Týr talking in the hope of distracting him from his nausea. 'Did you know Binni well?'

'Well?' The pain in the husky voice was an eloquent testimony to the man's sufferings. 'Quite well. You know.'

'Did you ever talk?'

'Sometimes.'

'What about?' The moment he had spoken, Huldar realised how foolishly optimistic he was being. Týr was barely capable of giving more than one-word answers in his state.

'Football.'

Of course they had talked about football. What had he been expecting? The Middle East peace process? 'Tell me something. Do you think there's any way you could have killed Binni without remembering?'

'No—' Týr broke off and retched, without bringing anything up, then added: 'I remember everything. More or less. I remembered you.'

Fair point. It would be an odd order of priorities for his memory if it had covered up an act as drastic as murder but clung on to the recollection of a man knocking on the door shortly afterwards and hanging around for a few minutes.

'Did Binni have any enemies? Was he in debt to someone for drugs or booze?'

'Drugs. Booze.' Longing dripped off the words. Týr sounded like a man in hell talking about heaven.

'Was Binni in debt? To someone who could have killed him over it?'

'No. Binni had drugs.'

Huldar understood what Týr meant. If Binni had been in debt to his dealer, he would have run out of pills. Of course, there was every chance he would have organised another dealer or dealers to keep him going while he owed money to the first guy, but that didn't alter the fact that no dealer in his right mind would let his customers accumulate debts so big that they could never pay them off. And a dealer wouldn't be in a hurry to kill off a debtor, since, if he did, he would never get his money back. The executors were unlikely to take drugs debts into consideration when settling the victim's estate.

'What about other friends, apart from you and your neighbours? Or acquaintances? Did he have any visitors that you remember?'

Týr retched again and Huldar cursed himself for not having had the presence of mind to bring along any more cans of the energy drink. He offered the only thing he could think of. 'Want a cigarette?' He could drive back to the station with the window open to get rid of the smell. But the offer proved to have been unwise, since it triggered another bout of heaving and this time Týr went ahead and vomited. Of course he did. Not even Huldar could smoke when he was in the throes of a killer hangover. The mere sight of a cigarette packet was enough to make his stomach turn over.

Fuck. Huldar fumbled for the buttons that controlled the windows and opened them all, front and back. He had to fight the urge to stick his head out of the window and drive the rest of the way to the hospital like that.

When Týr had finished his spasmodic heaving, he groaned and lay back on the seat. After a few more groans, he answered Huldar's question: 'Binni was popular. He often had mates round.'

'The dark-haired girl, Rósa – the one you asked to buy mixers for you – did she often visit him?'

'I wasn't counting, man. Stop grilling me.' Týr sniffed, then gagged again.

'OK, I'm done.' Huldar put his head out of the window and snatched a gulp of fresh air. 'Nearly there.' Hearing the man's breathing growing laboured, he put his foot down on the accelerator. 'How are you doing? All right?'

Týr emitted a rattling sound. 'I'm dying.'

'You'll survive. I promise.' Huldar could say this with some confidence as he was pulling into the hospital car park as he spoke.

'Will you do something for me, mate?' The hoarse voice sounded as if the man was losing consciousness.

'I don't have any drugs, remember?' Huldar searched for a parking space near the night entrance that wasn't reserved for the disabled or ambulances.

'I know. I need a little favour.'

'What?'

'I've got a cat. A black bugger. Could you feed him for me?'

There was no one about by the containers on Grandi, which wasn't surprising given that the number of residents had halved over the previous twenty-four hours. Of those who lived in the four containers, one was dead and another was in hospital. Huldar had left him there, shivering and shaking in the hands of the professionals, after he had dealt with the formalities, which included forbidding any visits and reminding them of the rules pertaining to the care of prisoners under arrest.

'Puss, puss!' Huldar called into the gloom, as loudly as he dared without risking waking the occupants of the other two containers. He was holding an open tin of tuna that he had bought on his way back from the hospital in one of those depressing shops that are open all hours and used only by the desperate. Although the tin was dusty and past its sell-by date, Huldar doubted the cat would turn its nose up at it. The choice had been between that or a plastic-wrapped sandwich with yellow mayonnaise oozing out between the crusts. 'Puss, puss. Come here, kitty.'

Huldar peered into the surrounding gloom but couldn't see any movement. Perhaps the cat had mewed its way in with one of the neighbours, or gone down to the beach to catch its own supper. Cats could look after themselves. If the human race vanished off the face of the earth, the cats would cope. Dogs, on the other hand, wouldn't have a chance. Huldar put down the tin of tuna on a rusty cooker that stood abandoned by one of the containers, and lit a cigarette.

He'd smoked it halfway down when he heard the sound of an approaching car. Turning, he watched as an old wreck pulled over and stopped under a streetlight. It had a large spoiler fixed to the back and a go-faster stripe along the side facing Huldar, though the engine couldn't have had more than four cylinders, judging by the noise it was making, and would probably have come off worse in a race against a mobility scooter. The car was weighed down, with two people in the front and three in the back. When the rear door opened to let out a passenger, booming music briefly destroyed the peace, before being muted to a dull bass beat as the door slammed shut again. Huldar guessed they were sightseers, come to get an eyeful of the murder scene and maybe take a selfie to post on social media.

A skinny young woman had clambered out onto the gravel. Her shoes with their ridiculously thick platform soles weren't exactly suited to the rough ground and she teetered as she picked her way over. She was wearing a bulky, purple waist-length jacket made of fake sheepskin, and black leggings. In that get-up her arms, windmilling wildly to help her keep her balance, appeared thicker than her thighs. 'Hey! You!' Clocking Huldar, she came hobbling towards him.

'Hi!' Now that she was standing in front of him, he saw that she was only a teenager. The darkness couldn't hide how clumsily her thick make-up had been applied, the purple lipstick matching her jacket. 'Do you live here?'

'Me?' Huldar was too taken aback to be offended. 'No.' Feeling compelled to explain what he was doing there, he added: 'I'm looking for a cat.'

'Oh.' The girl's face fell. Perhaps she'd been hoping to get some juicy details about the murder from one of the occupants. Nothing people did surprised Huldar any more. But after a moment she brightened and gave him a knowing wink. 'Oh, right. I get it. Cat.' She beamed. 'Do you know if there's any going?'

'Any?'

'Yeah. You know.'

He didn't. 'I'm not quite sure I follow you.'

'Oh.' The girl hesitated, looking past Huldar at the containers. 'I was told . . .' She broke off, belatedly regretting that she had ever struck up a conversation with him.

Huldar finally twigged. 'You mean dope? Right, yeah, that's what I'm here for too. The cat was just an excuse.'

The girl smiled again, visibly relieved. 'Yeah. God, I thought so, but, like, then I thought maybe you were one of those . . . you know, like, one of those uptight types.'

'Me? No way.' Huldar returned her smile. 'Hey, do you know who it is that's selling? I wasn't told exactly where to go.' He nodded towards the containers, giving silent thanks that he was in his civilian clothes.

'The guy in that hut. The one with the purple door.' She pointed at Binni's unit. 'Hey! Whoa! It's, like, the same colour as my jacket!'

Huldar grinned. 'And your lipstick, don't forget.'

'Yeah, right. It matches, you know.'

Huldar nodded gravely. 'What's the guy selling?'

'Anything, man. Anything you want.' The girl made a pathetic attempt to sound worldly. 'Though, actually, I don't know exactly. I've never been here before. We only just heard about him, so we thought we'd check him out. There's a party tomorrow. You know.'

This ordinary teenage girl was a perfect example of the latest depressing trend in the drugs scene. Previously, it had only been problem kids who went looking for hard stuff of the kind that had been found at Binni's place. Now, though, perfectly normal, respectable teenagers were being drawn to this shit.

'Can I give you a piece of good advice?'

'Huh?'

'Do you want to live like that?' Huldar jerked a thumb at the containers.

'No way. Are you crazy?'

'Then stay away from drugs. Don't go looking for another dealer. Skip it.'

'What? Another one? What's wrong with this guy?'

'Nothing. Oh, apart from the fact he's been murdered. Don't you follow the news?'

A blast of the horn indicated that the occupants of the car were growing impatient. The girl gaped at Huldar, unsure what to do.

'I'd get yourself back over there. Tell them the police have got their registration number, so you'd better all steer clear of drugs in future. We'll be keeping an eye on you. Believe me. Cops don't lie.'

'Cops?'

'Yeah. I'm a cop. Oh, sorry, did I forget to mention that?'

The girl spun on her heel and tottered off in her ludicrous shoes. When she reached the car and got in, it screeched away as fast as an old wreck could move. The girl didn't even have time to slam the door but it swung shut under its own momentum as the car lurched forwards.

Huldar watched it go but didn't bother memorising the number plate. They were just stupid kids. The Drug Squad didn't have the manpower to keep them under surveillance and there was no point arresting them. It would only marginalise them and risk turning them into criminals. He would just have to hope that he'd given the girl a bad enough scare to keep her away from that bloody crap. But he wasn't holding out any hope.

Finishing his cigarette, he called, 'Puss, puss, tsk, tsk, tsk,' a few more times, then gave up and left the open tin of tuna on Týr's step. Although he'd failed to find the cat, it hadn't been a completely wasted journey. He now had evidence that Binni had been dealing. That changed things a bit.

When he reached the car, he glanced back once and saw a small black shape crouching over the tin outside Týr's container.

Chapter 17

Any possessions of Binni's that were thought to merit closer attention had been placed in two cardboard boxes, which were now sitting on the floor beside Huldar's desk. He hadn't yet taken a look inside but he had picked them up and found them depressingly light. Some of the man's belongings had been left behind in the container but, going by photos of the scene, Huldar reckoned two more boxes would have been sufficient to empty the place of all loose items.

The unsettling thought occurred to Huldar that the same would be true of his own flat. He hardly owned any personal items; if you couldn't plug it in, he wasn't interested. Apart from the contents of his basement storage unit and wardrobe, his possessions would probably fill a shoebox – or one for boots, anyway. So he wondered why Binni's half-empty boxes should have affected him so much. If he himself could choose to live a life stripped of all but the bare essentials, why shouldn't the dead man have done the same? There was nothing to suggest that Binni had been forced into the role of ascetic since moving into the container. He could have chosen that life, as Huldar had chosen his. But the photos and Huldar's brief glimpse of Binni's living quarters had told a different story. Unlike him, Binni had put up a handful of ornaments – scrappy and recently acquired, maybe, but then he was unlikely to have carted around shelves of books and knick-knacks during his years living rough.

It wasn't the first time Huldar had been touched by melancholy at the sight of a deceased victim's worldly possessions. Anyone who came into contact with death would be familiar with the feeling. Few of the things that were precious to people while they were alive had any intrinsic value for others. Viewed in the cold light of day, without the sentiments associated with them, the objects were revealed as worthless. It was better to own nothing but electrical gadgets.

The photos taken outside Binni's container hadn't stirred up the same emotions. Huldar had seen the rubbish with his own eyes the night they discovered the body, and it wasn't improved by a second viewing. There was no telling who owned what as the scrap metal and other junk was strewn all over the place, most densely around the containers, then thinning out the further you got from the little colony. In time, the whole area would be covered in junk. You'd have thought the occupants were human magnets. What they wanted with all this crap was hard to guess. But no doubt their intentions were good and, if they hadn't collected it, the stuff would only have gone to the dump.

Huldar clicked through the most recent photos that had been loaded onto the server. It wasn't part of the job Erla had assigned to him; he was supposed to be sorting through and listing the items in the boxes. Thanks to the tip he had brought Erla about Binni's dealing, he had got out of being sent to Grandi to search through the junk on site. He had also got out of viewing the CCTV footage of the area. The man to whom that task had fallen was hollow-eyed from long hours staring at his screen.

The Drug Squad had been notified of Binni's alleged activities. According to Erla, they had been nonplussed, as it was the first they had heard of him. In fact, they claimed it was unthinkable that the man could have been active for long without crossing their radar. But then what else were they supposed to say?

There was something rather disheartening about the empty seat at the desk facing him. Although Gudlaugur could be withdrawn and moody, he was quite good company at times and Huldar enjoyed talking over cases with him. But Gudlaugur had been up half the night searching for Rósa and wasn't due in until after lunch. The search had drawn a complete blank and, although no one had actually said as much, the team was growing increasingly concerned. How could a teenager vanish off the face of the earth for days at a time? Usually, no sooner had the missing-persons' notice and photo been circulated online than the news came in that the kid had turned up. Sometimes the second notice to report the fact appeared hot on the heels of the first. But not in Rósa's case.

A request for information had been put out the day before. The news had stayed there a while, before slipping ever further down the screen, displaced by fresh items. Few people seemed to have paid any attention to the notice and it wasn't even on the list of the most read articles. Still, it wasn't as if the whole country needed to see the news; it would be enough for one person who knew the girl's whereabouts to come forward. In practice, missing kids were rarely found as a result of information from strangers. And Rósa had no obvious distinguishing features to make her stand out from any other teenage girl.

So far, nobody had called. Or nobody with genuine information. They'd had the usual cranks and time-wasters, but the officers manning the phones were trained to see through this kind of thing and quickly cut off any idiots.

Huldar got up to fetch a pair of gloves. If he didn't get his arse into gear soon, Erla might notice and tear a strip off him, which was never a good start to a day. Especially when she was already as prickly as hell due to the shortage of manpower, which hadn't improved despite her attempts to recall officers from their summer holidays. So far, only one had obeyed the call. The others were all out of town; either chasing chinks in the clouds in the north or east of Iceland, or sunning themselves on foreign beaches. Although Huldar had heard on the news that one in three Icelanders had fled the country because of the relentless rain, he was struck by the perhaps cynical suspicion that most of his colleagues had bought their tickets the day the discovery of the bones hit the news. They knew that if they were in town, they risked having days shaved off their holiday. Huldar would have acted no differently in their shoes; he'd have booked a plane ticket or jumped in the car and headed into the wilds.

Unable to find any gloves in his size, he had to make do with a pair that were too small. The fit was so tight, they felt like a second layer of skin.

The first box turned out to be half empty. The scene-of-crime team hadn't bothered to bag each item separately since none were likely to be of any relevance for the murder inquiry. The handful of objects that did enjoy that honour – the pill packaging, the ashtray and its contents, beer cans and anything else the killer might have touched – were already down at Forensics, being checked for fingerprints or biological traces. An old mobile phone that was thought to have belonged to the victim was also being examined. It was a battered model of the cheapest kind that even a pre-school kid would have turned up their nose at these days. Since the SIM card was prepaid and unregistered, the phone had presumably been used for drugs deals. If so, it would be a goldmine for the Drug Squad, though they were sceptical that it would be possible to find out who procured Binni's drugs by tracing messages or numbers. His suppliers were bound to use their own unregistered SIM cards and would have ditched them the moment news of the murder got out, regardless of whether they had any link to the case.

Forensics thought it unlikely that the murderer would have handled any of the objects that had been on the shelves or in the kitchen cupboard. The man hadn't had his throat cut with a picture frame, after all. Nevertheless, although it wasn't a priority, everything would be carefully examined once Huldar had listed it.

Huldar took one of the photos out of the box and put it on his desk, then opened the registration form that filled the screen, every box empty apart from the case number and the number that would be assigned to the object in question. He picked up the picture frame and started writing an uninspired description. *Blue plastic photo frame, 13 x 18 cm, containing a photo of Brynjólfur when he was younger, with two children, a girl and a boy. White concrete wall visible in background. Photo a little faded and battered.* Huldar assumed they were Binni's kids but the form wasn't designed for speculation. He shoved the frame in a bag and wrote the evidence number on it. Then he picked up the next picture and repeated the process. *Oak photo frame, cracked glass, battered, 13 x 18 cm, containing a photo of Brynjólfur before he became homeless, probably aged around forty, with two men of a similar age. All three wearing waders, each holding a salmon. Picture taken on an Icelandic riverbank, location unknown.* Huldar wondered who the men were and why Binni had kept the picture on display. It was in a much better condition than the one of his children, though the frame appeared to have fallen on the floor at some point. There was no sign that the picture had been carried around in Binni's pocket during his years sleeping rough.

The third and last framed photo was a studio portrait of a young man wearing a student's cap. Huldar filled out yet another form, bagged up the frame and labelled it with a number.

Three photos. Three more than could be found in Huldar's own flat. He couldn't be bothered to frame the few pictures he took himself, or the photos of his nephews that invariably accompanied Christmas cards from his sisters. Since he had five sisters, he simply didn't have room for the entire collection. Nor did he particularly want his flat to look as if he were the proud weekend dad of a pack of boys. A gallery like that might lead to unfortunate misunderstandings when he invited women home.

Erla came up to his desk and looked down into the box. 'You're not making much bloody progress, are you?'

'I know.' There was no point arguing. 'But at least I've made a start.'

Huldar hadn't expected a pat on the shoulder for this and didn't get one. 'You do realise that we don't have time for fannying about?' Erla snarled. 'We're so short-staffed, we can't afford to have you slacking.'

'No. Understood.' Huldar gave a perfunctory smile. Erla had obviously forgotten that she'd called him back to work the previous evening, causing him to miss out on his statutory rest period yet again. Not that he minded: he'd make up for all the lack of sleep when he was dead. What he did regret was the company he had been forced to forgo in exchange for a crap assignment. Spending the evening with Freyja and Saga was infinitely preferable to ferrying a puking drug addict to hospital. Fortunately, the vomit on the back seat of the unmarked police car wasn't his problem. He'd dropped the car off at the station, feeling profoundly grateful that he didn't have to clean it up himself, and unceremoniously informed the person in charge that it would need to be valeted. By then, it had been nearly two in the morning and he had been too tired to be anything other than blunt.

'I've just got the post-mortem report,' Erla said. 'Not many surprises there. Brynjólfur died as a result of his throat being cut, severing an artery, as any fool could see. They estimate he'd have lost consciousness within ten seconds and been brain dead after two to five minutes. Up to that point he'd have been gushing out blood. He wouldn't have been able to call out or scream in those few seconds because his windpipe was severed below the larynx.'

'So inflicting the wound would have required quite a bit of strength?'

'Not necessarily. Not if the knife was sharp and the person using it had the sense to pull his head backwards. Analysis of the wound indicates that it was made by a penknife or similarly short blade. The killer appears to have been right-handed.' Erla sighed. 'Týr's left-handed so he's unlikely to be the culprit. Which means we're back to square one. They didn't find any other blood or biological traces on the victim that could have come from his attacker – nothing under his nails or anything else to suggest a fight. The most likely scenario is that the killer approached him from behind and took him by surprise.'

'What about Týr's knuckles?'

'They found his blood on the wall of his container, which would fit with his having punched it repeatedly. The wall panel was dented. So that probably accounts for his skinned knuckles.'

'What about the tox report on the dead man? What emerged from that?'

'He had a considerable amount of alcohol in his blood-stream. The test also confirmed that he'd taken oxycodone. Traces of it were found on the aluminium foil and syringe, indicating that he injected it. But that's nothing we didn't already know, so really we're no better off. The window for the time of death hasn't been narrowed down much either. He died around 11 p.m. His stomach contained *skyr*, which is consistent with the empty pot found in the kitchen. He's thought to have eaten it about an hour before he died.'

'Anything else?'

'Various things, obviously. But nothing of any use to us. Inevitably, he had hepatitis C, and he had a leg injury too. No broken bones but a badly sprained ankle. His body was covered in scars, puncture marks and fading bruises. His lifestyle took its toll.'

Erla picked up one of the photos that Huldar had bagged up. 'Are those his kids?'

'I assume so.'

'We're expecting the son in later. I'll ask him.' Erla replaced the frame. 'You'd better join me for that interview. Everyone else is up to their ears. Be ready for 1 p.m. Don't make me go looking for you in the smokers' yard. It's vital that the interview begins on the dot and finishes ASAP. The submarine's in working order again and I'm due to go out on the boat at three.' Erla looked a little pale and swallowed as she said this, perhaps reliving the memory of the last trip.

Huldar just nodded. Once Erla had gone, he noted down the time of the interview on a yellow Post-it note and stuck it to his computer screen. Better safe than sorry. Then he reached into the box again and took out a painted figurine of a shepherd boy that would have looked more at home with an old lady in a retirement home than a drug addict in a container unit.

Binni's son, Thorgeir, went by his matronymic, Salvararson, rather than his patronymic, Brynjólfsson; a clear sign that his relationship with his dead father hadn't been particularly close. That was understandable enough. Binni had walked out on the family when his son was at a sensitive stage of adolescence. At that age, Huldar had hardly been able to face going to the shops with his dad for fear that he would say something cringeworthy. He couldn't imagine how it must have been for Thorgeir to be afraid of running into his father in the gutter every time he went into town with his mates. For a teenager, it would be hard to think of anything more mortifying.

Thorgeir had light brown hair and unusually dark rims round his eyes. He had frowned as he introduced himself and the expression hadn't left his face since. He rested his hands on the table between him and the two detectives, as if poised to get up and leave the moment he got a chance. He hadn't unzipped his jacket either, an unequivocal sign that he had no intention of sticking around any longer than was strictly necessary.

There was a certain resemblance between the young man and the old photographs of his father. But Thorgeir was nothing like the man Huldar had seen lying dead on the sofa. To be fair, though, with that obscenely gaping wound in his neck, Binni had hardly been looking himself.

'Is this a picture of your father with you and your sister?' Huldar passed the exhibit in its labelled plastic bag across the table.

Thorgeir loosened his grip on the table edge and picked up the photo, barely glanced at it, then pushed it back to Huldar. 'Yes, that's me and Sunneva. And Brynjólfur.' Poor Binni had clearly forfeited his right to be called 'Dad'.

'Do you know who these men are?' Huldar handed him the bag containing the photo of the salmon fishermen.

Again Thorgeir took the picture, gave it a cursory glance, then replied: 'Some blokes. Friends of Brynjólfur's from the old days, maybe. That's him in the picture. But of course you already knew that.' He slid it back across the table. 'Why are you asking me about some old photos? What have they got to do with anything?'

'Did you visit your father regularly?' Erla asked, ignoring his questions.

'No. I can't say I did. We weren't close. There was no doubt about where me and Sunneva came on his list of priorities. It's not like we mattered much to him. But I did look in on him once or twice when he was living in that container. I didn't stay long, though.'

'When was the last time you were there?'

'About two weeks ago. Or a bit less. It was on a Saturday.'

'What did you talk about?' Huldar removed both pictures from the table. He didn't bother to ask about the third photo as the student in the portrait was unmistakeably sitting in front of them.

'Nothing, really. He asked how Mum was doing. How Sunneva was doing. How I was doing.' He stopped. Huldar and Erla remained silent. Silence was the most effective lubricant for an interviewee's vocal cords. After a pause, Thorgeir went on: 'But it was obvious he wasn't interested. He was drunk. Or stoned.' Thorgeir smiled with a sudden savage contempt. 'Just for a change.'

'He didn't mention anything about being in trouble? Or involved in a dispute with someone?'

'No. It was all very superficial. As usual. He wouldn't have told me even if he had been in trouble.'

'Can I ask why you went to see him? Was there some specific reason?' Erla's expression was stony, about as animated as one of the heads on Easter Island. Her complexion looked suitably grey as well.

'Reason? Yes. I wanted to let him know that Grandma – his mother – is in hospital, dying. I thought he might want to say goodbye to her. I even offered to drive him there but he wouldn't go. Just asked me to send his regards.' Thorgeir uttered a brief, sarcastic laugh. It conveyed the young man's perpetual disappointment in his father better than any list of all the times Binni had let him down.

'So he didn't go and see her?' Huldar guessed Binni hadn't been able to face it. A more charitable interpretation would be that he had thought it kinder for his mother to depart the world without having the image of him in his scarecrow state as the last thing she saw. It would be better if she remembered him as he used to be, before his life had unravelled. People suffering from serious addictions had lucid intervals when they were all too aware of their situation and their future prospects; an awareness that only deepened their craving for drug- or booze-fuelled oblivion.

'No. As usual, he couldn't think about anyone but himself. He said his ankle was killing him. Big deal. Like that's comparable? To be dying of pain from an injured ankle or to be dying, full stop?' Thorgeir broke off and lowered his eyes to the table, ashamed of his outburst. He was plainly battling with conflicting emotions: loss and relief, grief and anger.

'Do you know where your father got his drugs from?' Huldar asked, though he didn't for a minute expect the son to possess this kind of information. Or indeed to care.

Thorgeir looked surprised. 'No. When I was there he said he'd quit the drugs. Said he'd been forced to; that from now on he'd stick to drinking.'

A hint of pity softened Erla's forbidding expression for a moment, before her face grew hard again. 'We found drugs in his container. Opioids. So I'm afraid he was still using. Possibly dealing too. Do you know anything about that?'

Thorgeir's startled look was convincing. He hadn't heard. Then he recovered, being no doubt unsurprised by anything where his father was concerned. 'No. I hadn't a clue about that. But then it wasn't like he'd discuss it with me.' Thorgeir straightened up. 'I know nothing about drugs. I don't even drink. Any more than I'd play Russian roulette. With my genes, alcohol would be the bigger gamble. A fifty-fifty chance of a fatal outcome.'

Erla changed the subject. 'Have you any idea who might have wanted to kill your father? Did he keep anything valuable in his container that would have been worth stealing?'

'I wouldn't know – either who killed him or if he owned anything valuable. I don't even know what sort of thing the crowd he hung out with would consider valuable. Does murder always have to have a motive? Couldn't it just have been something trivial? It's not like his life had any logic to it. If you're right that he was dealing, couldn't that have been the motive? That he stole from the people who gave him the dope? It's not like he could go abroad to buy it or grow it himself in his container. You must be looking into that possibility?'

Again, Erla brushed off his speculation. She and Huldar were there to ask questions, not answer them. 'Are you by any chance acquainted with a teenage girl called Rósa? She knew your father. She's sixteen years old. Small. With dark hair.' Erla handed Thorgeir a photo. It was the one they had been circulating in the media.

'Isn't that the girl who's missing?' Thorgeir looked from one of them to the other and they both nodded. 'Is she a suspect?'

'No, she isn't. We just want to talk to her.' Huldar could

have kicked himself. Everyone knew that when the police *wanted to talk to someone*, it wasn't just for a witness statement.

'Well, I know nothing about her. I don't recognise her. I've never come across her – in connection with Brynjólfur or anywhere else.' Thorgeir sighed. 'And I haven't a clue who'd have wanted to kill him. Not a clue.'

And the worst of it was that neither had they.

Chapter 18

Friday

Tristan Berglindarson declined the offer of orange juice or water. Instead, he asked for a black coffee. This was unusual for a boy who had just turned seventeen and when he got the cup he barely touched it. Freyja guessed that he had opted for coffee not because he liked it but because he wanted to make himself appear more grown-up. She remembered ordering coffees herself during her formative years, sitting in a café with similarly gauche friends, trying to look as mature and sophisticated as the other customers. But the way their faces puckered at every sip, as Tristan's was doing now, had given them away.

He was impossibly good-looking, yet he seemed unaware of his beauty, not even bothering to pose. His conventional clothes, free from all logos or other form of ostentation, gave the impression that he wasn't bothered about fashion either. He was much neater, too, than the adolescents who had preceded him in the chair. If Freyja hadn't known better, it would never have occurred to her that the boy came from a problem family. She would more likely have taken him for an up-and-coming footballer.

But if you looked closer, you could discern the marks of stress on his face that betrayed his difficult upbringing. The smile that touched his lips when he spotted the picture of Reagan and Gorbachev had quickly faded, and Freyja got the feeling that none of his smiles would last long. His face grew sombre again, as if his features naturally fell back into that expression.

He had turned up at the appointed hour and, so far, had answered all Hafthór's questions conscientiously. These had related to the care home and were designed to fill in any gaps in his previous interviews, as well as tidying up a few details that had emerged from questioning the other kids. Tristan came across as calm and convincing. He stuck to his guns about the abuse and didn't budge from his earlier testimony. He said he couldn't comment on anyone else's experiences as he'd found it hard enough coping with his own problems during the period in question and hadn't given any thought to whether others might have suffered the same mistreatment. Because the kids' stays at the home only tended to overlap by a few weeks, they rarely became close. It was therefore perfectly natural, in Freyja's opinion, that their welfare hadn't been uppermost in Tristan's mind, any more than people worry about the wellbeing of other patients in a doctor's waiting room.

Hafthór appeared to have run out of questions. He glanced at Huldar, raising his chin a little as a sign that he should take over. Before the boy arrived, they had agreed that they would talk about the care home first, before moving on to other matters. The time had now arrived to start quizzing Tristan about Rósa. The only person who wasn't aware of this turning point in the conversation was Tristan himself.

Huldar came straight to the point. 'You're a friend of Rósa Thrastardóttir, aren't you?'

The question threw Tristan. His eyes widened as he turned to Huldar, who had been sitting in silence up to now. 'Er . . . yes.'

'Did you know she was missing?'

'Er . . . yes.'

'Do you know where we can find her?'

'Er . . . no.' Tristan's answers had suddenly become a lot more monosyllabic than when Hafthór had been asking the questions.

'Are you sure about that?' Huldar kept his eyes fixed on the boy's face. 'It would be best for you, for us, and most of all for her if you helped us find her.'

Tristan didn't say anything, just took a sip of coffee. It didn't appear to make him feel any better.

Huldar pressed on. 'Of course, you'll remember saying you'd confided in her about the abuse at the time. That's correct, isn't it?'

Tristan nodded his blond head. 'Yes.'

'If we could get Rósa to confirm this, it would back up your statement. So let me ask you again: do you know where she is?'

'No, I don't.' Tristan took a breath before continuing. 'If I did, I'd tell you.'

'When did you last speak to her?'

'I don't remember. It was, like, a while ago.'

'You'll have to do better than that. When was it? A week ago? Two weeks? A month?'

'Maybe a week ago. Ten days. Something like that.'

'Did you talk on the phone?'

'Yes. I think so.' Tristan fiddled with the leather band he wore round his right wrist like a bracelet. The ends were threaded with tiny coloured beads that he now began to play with.

'Then could you check the exact date on your phone for me?' Huldar gestured towards the pocket of the boy's jacket.

Tristan went on twisting the beads without looking up. 'No, sorry. My phone's in for repairs. I'm using a borrowed one from the shop.'

Huldar gave no sign of believing this but left the question for now. 'All right. When did you first meet Rósa?'

'I was thirteen. She was twelve. So, four years ago.'

'Was that at the care home run by Bergur?'

'No. We were at a different home. They were looking for a foster family for her. I was in temporary care. I think we were there for, like, three or four months together. We became friends and stayed friends, though we weren't always in the same homes.'

'So you didn't overlap again until later, at Bergur's place?'

'That's right. Two years later. When she was fourteen and I was fifteen. That's when I told her. It was a secret I couldn't talk about to anyone. But she'd noticed I was unhappy. I asked her not to tell anyone, though. Don't you believe me?'

To Freyja, this account sounded rehearsed, as if he'd often trotted out the same sentences in the same order.

Huldar left the boy's question hanging. 'On another matter: how did Rósa know Binni?'

'Binni? Binni who?' Tristan's look of puzzlement struck Freyja as fake; his eyes were too wide open, his facial muscles too tense.

'Binni. Brynjólfur. Binni Briefcase. He lived in the container colony on Grandi.'

'I don't know him.'

'Oh? You've never been there, then? With Rósa?'

'Er . . . no. At least, not that I remember.' Assuming Binni's friend, the woman Freyja had bumped into on Grandi, had been telling the truth, Tristan must be lying. The agitated way he was fiddling with the saucer of his coffee cup and avoiding eye contact reinforced this impression.

'Sure?'

'Yes. Quite sure.'

'That's strange. A witness claims to have met you round at Binni's place a year ago. With Rósa. Would you like a moment to reconsider?'

Tristan flushed and silently accepted this offer. But he seemed intent on wasting it by staring at the little beads and twiddling them between his fingers. To prompt him, Freyja decided to intervene with a few friendly words. She was here to look out for the boy and the sudden turn the interview had taken seemed to have thrown him badly. One minute he was being questioned as the victim of abuse, the next he found himself being caught out in a lie as a witness in a completely different case. 'It's not an offence to have visited the man, Tristan. The questions are just part of the effort to trace Rósa. The police also need to find out how Rósa knew Binni and why she used to visit him – not just the time you went with her. It's part of a different investigation that's unconnected to yours. It's just an odd coincidence that Rósa's name happens to have cropped up in both.'

Her friendly tone worked. The flush left Tristan's cheeks and the muscles of his jaw relaxed a little. Soon he'd feel confident enough to raise his eyes. It was hard being caught out in a lie. Freyja thought it best to rephrase the question herself rather than let Huldar ask it again, as there was a risk he might sound too harsh. 'Don't you have any memory of going out to Grandi with Rósa? And dropping into Binni's container? A year's a long time, so no one would be surprised if it didn't immediately come back to you.'

Tristan raised his eyes gratefully to her. Letting go of his leather wristband, he cleared his throat. 'Yes. Now that you mention it, I do vaguely remember. I did go there with her.'

'What did she want?' Huldar took over the questioning again.

'I don't know. Rósa said she had to talk to the guy. I just tagged along. We took a bus from Hlemmur—'

Huldar cut him off. How they had got there was irrelevant. 'Didn't she tell you what she wanted to talk to the man about?'

Tristan shook his head. 'No. She didn't.'

'Weren't you curious? Didn't it strike you as odd that a young girl like her should want to go and see a rough character like Binni?'

'I didn't know he was an addict,' Tristan protested. 'Not until we got there. I'd never been there before.' He added quickly: 'Of course I'd been out to Grandi before, but not to the containers. You can't see them from the main road.'

'From Grandagardur, you mean?' Freyja offered the street name since Huldar and Hafthór were looking uncertain.

Tristan nodded. 'Yes. Something like that. The one with the ice-cream parlour.'

Huldar smiled. 'OK. Going back to the actual visit. You say Rósa didn't tell you what it was about, but once you got to Binni's place, you must have heard what passed between them? The container's too small for private conversations.'

'Yes, I know. But she never got to the point. Some woman turned up and Rósa didn't get a chance to have her talk with

Binni. When the woman left, Binni got his drugs out. And after that you couldn't get any sense out of him. So we went. Rósa seemed a bit down afterwards and I tried to cheer her up. I didn't ask about the visit because it had obviously gone wrong. It would have been like – like rubbing a wound in salt, you know.'

Freyja, Huldar and Hafthór all cleared their throats automatically, but none of them corrected the boy. This wasn't a lesson in idioms.

'I never went back there. I swear it. And Rósa never mentioned him again, so I avoided talking about the visit. It was all so embarrassing and stupid somehow.'

'So you weren't in the area the day before yesterday? On Wednesday evening?'

Tristan gave Huldar a wondering look. 'No. I just told you. I only went there that one time. And I definitely wasn't there on Wednesday evening.'

'Where were you, then?'

'Me?'

'Yes.' Huldar gave a slow nod. 'You. What were you doing on Wednesday evening?'

'Er . . .' The boy appeared to be racking his brain. Then he brightened. 'Oh, yes – I was at home.'

'Can anyone confirm that?'

His elation evaporated. 'Er . . .'

'Did a friend visit you? Or was your mum home, maybe?'

Tristan appealed to Freyja. 'Does it matter? I said I was at home.'

'Your answer matters, Tristan.' Freyja didn't explain why it was important since Huldar hadn't yet mentioned the murder on Grandi and the boy gave no sign of having heard the news. If he had, he would have instantly made the connection.

'Mum was home. She can tell you I was there.' Tristan almost spat in his eagerness to get the words out. Freyja didn't believe him. He hadn't been home that evening. She didn't for a moment believe he'd been out on Grandi, committing murder, but she'd bet anything he hadn't been at home.

'Moving on to another matter . . .' It was impossible to tell from Huldar's expression whether he believed the boy or not. 'We know you went round with Rósa to see her grandparents back in the spring. While she was there, she mentioned something about a couple who were in the sea. Can you give us any idea what she meant?'

Tristan shifted in his chair. 'I don't know what she was on about. But I do remember that visit. Her gran gave us pancakes.' He licked his dry lips, then continued. 'Look, Rósa gets these crazy ideas sometimes and I have literally no idea what she's talking about. I can't really explain.' Tristan reached for his coffee, but changed his mind as his fingers touched the cup.

'Would you like some water? Your coffee must be cold by now.' Freyja pushed over the water jug and handed him a glass. He accepted it gratefully, poured himself a glass and gulped down half in one go. Then, snatching a breath, he carried on talking in a high, tight voice. 'Does that mean she's an unreliable witness? Does it mean it won't help if she swears to the judge that I told her about the abuse at the time?' There was genuine fear in his eyes.

'Don't you worry about that,' Hafthór intervened. 'Your main concern at the moment should be whether Rósa turns up. Are you absolutely sure you don't know where she goes when she does a runner like this? It sounds like you're good mates. Have you never asked her about it?'

'We're friends. But we don't meet up every day or anything like that. Just occasionally. I never know when she's run away. We're mostly in touch on our phones. We message each other and that kind of thing. I don't always know where she is when she answers me.' He paused, then went on, looking a little embarrassed. 'We're not going out with each other, if that's what you think. We're just mates.'

The interview continued along the same lines until it became clear that the boy had run out of answers. Nothing new had emerged to lead them to Rósa, either because Tristan couldn't help them or because he was covering up for the girl.

Freyja and Huldar watched as Hafthór escorted the boy out. Freyja got the impression that Tristan had to force himself not to break into a run, so relieved was he that his ordeal was over. There was nothing odd about that. No one, whatever their age, enjoyed being interrogated by the police. Sticking a pot plant in one corner and a picture on the wall didn't make the slightest difference. She and Huldar followed them out of the room.

It struck Freyja that Huldar was unusually relaxed compared to how he normally behaved when she met him at work. She attributed this to Erla's absence. Apparently she was on a boat in Faxaflói Bay, searching for more bones. She certainly had the perfect weather for it: sunshine, not a cloud in the sky and a flat calm. It was as if the summer had finally realised it was late to the party and had determined to make up for it by pulling out all the stops for this one day. Rain and wind were forecast again for tomorrow.

'Do you know what happened to Rósa's father?' Freyja glanced at the clock and saw that she would need to get herself down to Sexual Offences in a few minutes to attend the next round of interviews.

'I have to admit I haven't looked him up. All I know is that he died in an accident.' Huldar glanced at Gudlaugur who was back at his desk. 'Do you know anything about him?'

Gudlaugur shook his head. 'Same here. I only know that it was an accident. A long time ago. I can't see what he has to do with our search for the girl. We've got enough on our plates without investigating long-dead family members.'

Freyja felt compelled to justify her interest. She was used to being taken seriously at work and was miffed at having her question dismissed as a waste of time. 'It just occurred to me that she might be drawn to places associated with him, to feel closer to him perhaps.' Lame as this sounded, it was the best she could do.

Huldar and Gudlaugur both looked at her dubiously.

'Places associated with him? What do you mean?' Huldar couldn't suppress a smile. 'The place where her parents met or something?'

'No.' Freyja felt herself backed into a corner. 'Not necessarily that kind of thing. I don't know *where* exactly, because I know nothing about the man. I read the obituaries but they were the usual stuff: people scraping around for inoffensive anecdotes about the deceased to illustrate his character. They never tell you the whole story, as Rósa's mother might have told it. Or the man's parents.'

'So you're suggesting . . . what? That we call his parents?'

'No, that's not what I'm suggesting,' Freyja retorted, her voice becoming shrill. 'Look, it was just a thought, OK? It's not like you're having much success at tracking her down with the methods you're using. Which are what, by the way? Hoping to run into her by chance?'

Neither man answered this and an awkward silence fell. The most embarrassed of the three was Huldar, who now sat down at his computer and started tapping hurriedly on his keyboard.

'I'll see what I can find. Seeing as he died in an accident, he's bound to be in the system.'

Freyja felt ashamed of her emotional outburst and wondered what had come over her. She would hardly be suited to the job of police liaison officer if she reacted so badly to the slightest disagreement. This wasn't a psychology clinic where contact with her colleagues was limited to the kitchen. This was a police station, where the staff knew their job better than she did. But before she could apologise, Huldar found what he was looking for.

'Here's a brief summary.' Huldar read for a moment before relaying the contents to them. 'OK. There's nothing suspicious about the accident, at any rate. The man drowned while salmon fishing in the Öxarfjördur area. He'd been drinking and waded out into a river he wasn't familiar with. He was planning to fish in a deep pool, which was easier to get at from the other side, so he tried to wade across the shallows below it, where the riverbed was rocky and the current was very strong. He lost his footing, his waders filled with water and he was carried downstream. There was nothing the witnesses to the accident could do. His body was found several hundred metres further down.'

Gudlaugur grimaced. 'That's grim. Was his wife there?'

'No. It's only a summary and doesn't name the witnesses

but there seems to have been two of them and they're both referred to as male. One was a friend. He saw what happened. Then there was a stranger who was fishing nearby. In other words, there were two witnesses, one of them independent. It wasn't murder, like the girl claims.'

'Presumably there was an inquest?' Freyja regretted her question as soon as it was out of her mouth, since it sounded as if she was querying Huldar's version of events. But all she wanted was to be absolutely sure there was no hint of anything untoward. If it happened the way Huldar had described, Rósa couldn't have got the wrong end of the stick about her father's death due to some unexplained detail in the series of events. Besides, she had only produced her theory when she was fifteen, no longer a credulous little girl as she had been at the time of her mother's death.

It looked as if Freyja's original assessment had been correct; that Rósa had serious psychological problems. This did nothing to allay her concern about the girl's disappearance and failure to turn up.

'Yes, of course. The Thórshöfn police dealt with the incident, according to what it says here.' Huldar paused. 'Strange they didn't send any officers from Húsavík. I'd have thought that would have been closer and the station there is bigger.' He looked up, adding apologetically: 'I come from the east myself, so I know the north-eastern region quite well.'

'Do you think there's something dodgy about it, then?' Freyja couldn't picture a map of the area. She had never actually travelled right round Iceland; never got any closer to this remote region than Akureyri, the capital of the north.

'No. It doesn't make that big a difference in terms of distance. But still.' Huldar fiddled with the mouse, frowning at the screen. After a while he turned back to Freyja. 'Ah. Here it is. Apparently the Húsavík force were busy dealing with a fatal road accident involving a child. That explains it. These country police stations aren't very big outfits. A serious incident like that would have required all their manpower – if you can use that term for a police team of two or three officers. Anyway, regardless of who was in charge of the investigation, there's no doubt that Rósa's father's death was an accident.'

Huldar reached for his mouse again, saying: 'Don't look. I'm going to open the photos from the scene of the accident. You definitely don't want to see those.'

Warnings and prohibitions only make things more intriguing, and Freyja moved round behind Huldar so she could watch over his shoulder. He raised his eyebrows but didn't chase her away. Perhaps he thought she was still offended and didn't want to risk riling her any further.

He scrolled quickly through the photos from the riverbank and its immediate surroundings. It was evident from the colour of the vegetation that they had been taken in autumn. The grassy banks overhung the water and many of the pictures would have been suitable for a tourist brochure were it not for the body in the foreground. Rósa's father was lying on his back several metres from the river, presumably after being dragged onto dry land by his friend and the witness. His arms and legs were splayed out, as if he were making a snow angel. He was clean shaven and looked younger than in the bearded photo that had accompanied his obituary. As a result, his gaping mouth was clearly visible. Freyja guessed someone had tried and failed to give him the kiss of life. His eyes were fixed wide open in a permanent stare.

Freyja averted her gaze as a close-up of his face flashed up on screen.

'Bloody hell.' Huldar peered closer. 'I've seen him before.' He pushed back his chair, reached for the cardboard box by his desk and pulled out a plastic bag containing a picture in a frame. He laid the bag on the desk and smoothed out the clear plastic. 'Look. Isn't that the same man?'

Freyja bent down to examine the picture as Gudlaugur came round to join them. The photo showed three men in angling gear, each holding a salmon. And, yes, she could have sworn that one of them was Rósa's father.

Chapter 19

Friday

The framed photograph lay on the coffee table, still in its plastic evidence bag. Seated in a circle around it were Gudlaugur, Huldar and Salvör, ex-wife of the late Binni, who had invited them to take a seat in her tidy sitting room. Huldar had called Erla with the news that Binni had known Rósa's father, but as she was still at sea, searching for more bones, she had delegated the interview to him. It had been his decision to take Gudlaugur along. He wasn't in the mood for the company of any of his other colleagues that afternoon, or indeed any afternoon, but particularly not on a Friday.

At first, Salvör had been rather short with him on the phone, protesting that her ex-husband's death had nothing to do with her: she and Brynjólfur had separated for good when he walked out on her and the kids ten years ago. When Huldar explained that they wanted to ask her some questions about her husband's life before he went off the rails, she had reluctantly agreed, on condition that she didn't have to come into the station. She would rather they came round to hers instead. Huldar had jumped at the excuse for him and Gudlaugur to escape the Friday-afternoon torpor in the office.

Salvör lived in a fairly new estate near Lake Ellidavatn

in Kópavogur, the town immediately to the south of Reykjavík. The neighbourhood had sprung up about a decade before and spread out in a pattern of streets so confusing that it was impossible to find one's way around. Huldar, who was driving, had to rely on the satnav once they'd left the main road. Gudlaugur, yawning away in the passenger seat, had little to say. It was no coincidence that night shifts were paid at a higher rate, given the way they sapped people's energy.

Salvör lived in a modest, low-rise white building. The woman herself turned out to be as modest and unassuming as her flat. She was unusually petite and slender, with wavy, shoulder-length ginger hair and a fringe so short, it looked as if she'd had an accident with a pair of scissors. Her face was covered in large, light-coloured freckles, made up of clusters of countless smaller ones, and she wore no make-up apart from black mascara, which had smudged on one eyelid. Her black lashes and the smudge were very conspicuous against her otherwise pale face.

After letting them in via the entryphone, she had met them at the door in the carpeted corridor. Her greeting wasn't exactly effusive: they shook hands and introduced themselves, though they already knew each other's names from the phone call. She had then invited them in, with the comment that today was the last day of her summer holiday and this wasn't at all how she had envisaged spending it. Neither Gudlaugur nor Huldar saw any reason to apologise for their visit since she still had the whole weekend ahead of her, though admittedly it didn't look as if the good weather would last.

'I've got coffee but no milk. I'm lactose intolerant.' Salvör was sitting stiffly upright in her chair. 'Would you like some anyway? I've got water too, of course. But no Coke or anything like that.' When they both declined her offer, she leant back, looking a little less tense.

'We won't detain you long; we just need to ask you a few questions about Brynjólfur. Nothing uncomfortable or embarrassing, though.' Huldar smiled. 'Shall we just get started?'

'Yes, please do.' Salvör glanced at the Fitbit on her wrist, clearly intent on making sure that they stuck to their promise of getting it over with quickly.

Gudlaugur gestured at the picture lying on the coffee table. 'We'd like to begin by asking you to take a look at this photo and tell us if you recognise any of the men in it. We believe it was taken while you were still married.'

The woman wrinkled her brow as she reached for the evidence bag. 'Can I take it out?'

'No. I'm afraid you'll have to look at it through the plastic.'

She smoothed out the bag and peered at the photo, then put it back down. 'That's Brynjólfur with two of his friends. One was called Thröstur. He's dead. He drowned on one of their endless fishing trips. Binni was there and the accident did nothing to help his problems with alcohol, as you can imagine. His drinking got completely out of hand afterwards.'

Huldar nodded. After talking to Freyja and reading the summary, he had tracked down the files on the accident. When he read the witness statements, he had discovered that Binni had been the anonymous friend referred to in the summary. Yet so far this information had got them no further with regard to Rósa. He pointed now to the other man in the photo in the evidence bag. 'What about him – do you recognise him?'

Salvör shook her head. 'I know the face but I can't remember what he was called. He used to go by a nickname. Sibbi – I think that was it. I assume it was short for Sigurbjörn or something like that.' Her eyes darted back to the bag. 'But it's such a long time ago, and I didn't have much to do with that group of friends. They mainly met up to organise their trips, which were always men-only affairs – us wives were never invited along. I only remember Thröstur's name because of the way he died. It was such a horrible shock and Binni took it terribly to heart. Perhaps he blamed himself. Because he was too drunk to save him, maybe. Who knows? He wouldn't discuss it with me. Any more than his other problems.'

The conversation was getting off track. They hadn't come here to talk about the state of Salvör's marriage to Binni. 'Were they childhood friends?' Huldar asked, getting back to the point. He felt that he was better placed to question her about an all-male group of fishing mates than Gudlaugur, who had absolutely no interest in that kind of thing and simply shook his head whenever Huldar invited him along. This was disappointing, as his own group could have done with some new members. Recently, numbers had been thinning out at such a rate Huldar would soon be the only one left. The others were slowly but surely being swallowed up by the world of coupledom and kids. 'School friends, maybe?'

'Partly. But some of them got involved with the group through fishing. They were all around the same age, though. There were more of them than in that picture. Probably about seven or eight in all.'

Huldar pulled out a notebook in anticipation of her answering his next question. 'Do you know any of their names?'

'There was one called Siggi, if I remember right, and a Raggi. Then the Sibbi in the picture. And Thröstur. I'm afraid I've forgotten the others. I hardly knew them, as I said. I got the feeling they deliberately kept wives and girlfriends out of it. That way they could be sure there would be someone at home when they went on their trips and no hassle about having to find a babysitter. I don't suppose they wanted us tagging along, anyway. They could drink themselves silly without getting any stick from us. I wasn't surprised when Thröstur had his accident. They used to take such stupid risks. I made sure Brynjólfur knew what I thought about it but he didn't listen to my warnings. Any more than the others did.'

There was an unmistakeable hint of schadenfreude in Salvör's face; the satisfaction of someone whose warnings had gone unheeded for years but who had finally been proved right. *I told you so.*

Huldar waited until the expression had faded before putting his next question. 'Do you know if Brynjólfur stayed in touch with his mates after he ended up on the street?'

'I have no idea. We went our separate ways. He walked out and that was that. It didn't occur to me to try and persuade him to come home again. Thröstur's death affected him so badly that it finally sent him over the edge, but it wasn't like he was a model husband one day and a homeless drunk the next. It had been a long time coming. I just can't understand why I didn't throw him out before.'

Misfortune had a way of insinuating itself almost

imperceptibly into people's lives, which was why a situation had often become unbearable before they finally did something about it. Salvör wasn't alone in looking back and not being able to understand why she had put up with so much crap for so long. 'So you didn't see Brynjólfur again after he walked out?' Huldar was careful to keep the disbelief out of his voice. But the fact was, they had split up ten years previously and it was almost impossible that their paths wouldn't have crossed in a town as small as Reykjavík.

'Of course I saw him after that. But only when I had no choice, or by accident. For example, I had to track him down to get him to sign the divorce papers. And I occasionally bumped into him in town. In fact, I deliberately stopped going into the centre, to avoid running into him.' Salvör paused. 'I don't understand what you're after. Am I a suspect in his murder?'

'No. You aren't,' Gudlaugur said firmly. Perhaps a little too firmly, given that they had no real suspects as yet. 'Although it was a long time ago, it would be helpful if you could think of anyone who might have had it in for Brynjólfur.'

'I know nothing about the people he associated with after he left me. And I can't believe you think someone would have been harbouring a grudge for a decade and only got round to attacking him now.'

Huldar and Gudlaugur waited with studied patience for her to answer the question.

'Well, if you're really asking me that, then I'll have to disappoint you because I don't remember any sworn enemies or anyone who had it in for him. Brynjólfur hadn't fallen out with anyone – except me, that is. But if I'd wanted to kill him for being a bloody awful husband and father, I'd have done it ten years ago – and spared my kids the humiliation of seeing their father in the gutter.'

Gudlaugur steered the conversation back on course. 'To return to the men in the picture, were you acquainted at all with Thröstur, the man who drowned? Apart from knowing his name and how he died, obviously.'

'No, not really. I seem to remember that he was an aircraft mechanic. But I assume you already know all that if you're interested in him. He can hardly have killed Brynjólfur, though, seeing as he's been dead for years.'

Huldar ignored her sarcasm. 'Did you know his wife? Her name was Dísa Högnadóttir.'

'No. I only met her twice, as far as I remember. The second time was at her husband's funeral. Us wives were allowed to come along on that occasion.' Salvör snorted. 'The next thing I heard, she was dead herself. I saw the obituaries and recognised her from the photo. It was all terribly sudden.'

'What about the daughter, Rósa? Have you had any dealings with her – either at the time or more recently?'

Salvör looked surprised. 'No. I've only seen her once and that was at the funeral – her father's funeral. She was only small. Five or six. It was desperately sad to see the poor little thing. I can't imagine how she must have felt when she lost her mother as well. But of course I didn't go to Dísa's funeral. Like I said, I really didn't know her.'

'So you haven't had any contact with Rósa?'

'Contact? Me? No. I don't know why on earth you'd think I would. I've had enough on my plate over the years with coping as a single parent and trying to look after my own kids. I don't go sticking my nose into the lives of other people's children.'

'She's missing,' Huldar interrupted. 'If you have any idea where she might be, we'd be very grateful for the information.' He studied Salvör's face, searching for tell-tale signs of concealment, but he couldn't see any.

'Missing? Is she the girl they sometimes put out notices about?'

When Huldar said yes, Salvör gave her head the tiniest shake, like people do when they hear something sad. 'Oh, God. I can't help you find her, I'm afraid. I really wish I could. That poor girl has had more than her fair share of grief. I do hope she turns up soon.'

Huldar asked his next question: 'Have you any idea why Rósa might have wanted to visit Brynjólfur?'

'Visit Brynjólfur? Did she visit Brynjólfur?' Salvör's astonishment appeared genuine.

Huldar nodded, without elaborating.

Salvör went on: 'I wasn't aware of that, and I've absolutely no idea why she would have gone to see him. In search of drugs, maybe?'

'She's not into drugs,' Gudlaugur cut in, as if feeling compelled to defend the girl's honour, though Salvör's question had been perfectly natural in the circumstances.

'Oh? Then maybe she wanted to talk to someone who used to know her father. That would be my guess, if she wasn't after drugs. Perhaps she wanted to hear first hand about his accident.'

Naturally, this had occurred to Huldar as well. He thought her visit was highly unlikely to have been motivated purely by a wish to meet an old friend of her father for a general chat. The police had contacted Rósa's paternal grandparents in Norway and her uncle as well, but apparently she had never been in touch with any of them to ask about her father. You'd have thought they would have been her first port of call, if all she'd wanted was to hear stories about him. If she'd wanted information, what would have been the point of going to see a man like Binni, who was off his head most of the time? Unless she was after something that no sober person would dream of telling a teenager – like how her father had come to drown. In that case, Binni would have been ideal.

'Changing the subject, what happened to Brynjólfur's belongings when he walked out? Did you throw them away or did he take them with him?' On the short walk from the hall to the sitting room, Huldar hadn't spotted any reminders of Salvör's ex-husband. There were several photos on the wall in the hall but he wasn't in any of them, not even in the ones where the children were small. Huldar guessed that Binni's possessions had probably ended up at the tip, or been flung out of the window after him, like in the movies.

Salvör hesitated. 'He didn't take anything with him, except the clothes he was standing up in. And a half-empty bottle of rum. When it became clear that he wasn't coming back, I packed his things into boxes, in case he wanted them later.' She added, a little embarrassed: 'Brynjólfur was very decent about the divorce. He didn't make any fuss about my getting the flat, the car and almost everything else. Of course, I took on all our debts too, but he could have claimed his share of the flat and forced me to sell. I couldn't have afforded to buy him out, although we're not talking about a particularly large sum of money. Anyway, I didn't feel I could pay him back by burning his belongings. I wanted to, but I just couldn't bring myself to do it. So I packed his things in boxes and put them in storage.'

'Are they still there?' As he said it, Huldar felt Gudlaugur's foot pressing against his. Presumably he didn't want them to be lumbered with a load of old junk – yet another job for their understaffed department, which was bound to fall to him and Huldar.

When Salvör answered, 'Yes, actually, they are,' Gudlaugur increased the pressure, hard enough to move Huldar's foot.

Avoiding his eye, Huldar asked if they could possibly go through the stuff. A fleeting expression of anger crossed Gudlaugur's face, but he managed to rearrange his features before Salvör noticed.

'Well, I don't know what use it would be to you. It's only clothes and books. A few other bits and pieces, but nothing that could possibly explain what's happened – either with Binni's murder or the girl's disappearance. Trust me, I packed the things up myself.'

'Even so, it would be good if we could have them,' Huldar said. He had no intention of backing down. 'We need to examine quite a few things in the course of our enquiries that might seem strange to the public.'

Gudlaugur cleared his throat, but before he could say it was fine, they didn't really need the boxes, Salvör replied: 'I'll have to fetch them. I hired a storage unit for them back in the day. I wanted to be able to send Brynjólfur there if he ever came back for his junk. I didn't want him setting foot in my new place.' Her gaze wandered round the room. 'I moved once the divorce had gone through. I wanted a change of scene and to be free of the old memories and ghosts. At the time, this area was perfect. It was too new to have any memories associated with it. A fresh start.' Salvör's eyes dropped to her Fitbit. 'I'm afraid I can't do it today, though. I'm going to use the rest of the afternoon for something more enjoyable. But I can fetch the stuff at the weekend, or after work on Monday, if the miserable forecast turns out to be wrong and the good weather lasts a bit longer. I don't suppose the delay will make any difference to you.'

She didn't offer them the key, which would have been simpler, and Huldar didn't ask for it, for fear that she would change her mind. He'd never be able to persuade Erla to apply for a search warrant for the storage unit; she was bound to side with Gudlaugur in the matter of the boxes. So he told Salvör that would be fine. Shortly afterwards, when it became clear that there was nothing else to be gained from their visit, the two men rose to their feet, said goodbye and returned to the car.

Gudlaugur wasn't as quiet on the way back as he had been on the drive there. 'What were you thinking of?' he complained. 'Who's supposed to go through all that crap? You?'

'Actually, I was wondering if we could borrow Lína. She's on work experience in Sexual Offences at the moment. They had her go through the lost-property items from the care home.'

'They won't let her go. They're as short-staffed as we are.'

'Come on, Gudlaugur, this is Lína we're talking about. Be honest. Wouldn't you have lent her out like a shot if another department had requested her? Even if only to get a break from the endless commentary?'

Gudlaugur didn't answer. He didn't need to. They both knew he'd have jumped at the chance.

'You never know what might emerge from those boxes.'

'Nothing but moths, I expect,' Gudlaugur said gloomily, then relapsed into silence until they got back to the station.

Salvör watched the policemen pull out of her drive and take the wrong turning – if they were hoping to exit the estate, that was. It was always happening. She waited at the window until she saw the car reappear, going in the right direction this time. Only then did she go back and sit down in her chair, thinking back to the day when her husband had walked out. She remembered how she had swept the things off Brynjólfur's dressing table, emptied out his desk drawers and tossed everything that belonged to him into cardboard boxes without even bothering to sort through it. What would have been the point? At that moment she had severed the connection with her husband, so cleanly that there wasn't a single tie left between them. For her, the clear-out of the house had been like disinfecting the hospital room of a dead patient who had been a complete stranger to her. As far as she was concerned, Binni had to all intents and purposes been dead already. It hadn't required a knife to finish him off.

There was no doubt in her mind: she would have to go through the contents of the boxes before turning them over to the police. No way was she going to hand them over without knowing what was inside them. What if there was something incriminating in there that would completely destroy Brynjólfur's reputation? Hadn't the children been through enough? Hadn't *she* been through enough?

Outside, the only gorgeous day in what had been a wash-out of a summer awaited her. Was she really going to waste it in a storage unit, rummaging through dusty boxes? No. That could wait until tomorrow or Sunday, when the forecast was miserable again.

Right now she was going swimming. Salvör got up, fetched her costume and headed outside into the sunshine.

But the thought of Brynjólfur and the way their life together had ended, all those years ago, cast a shadow over the beautiful day. A downpour would have been more in keeping with her mood.

Chapter 20

Friday

Freyja couldn't ignore her aching calves any longer. She heaved a deep breath and focused grimly on her block of flats that was so near yet still so terribly far away. The sun was blazing down and she had a free hour before she had to collect Saga from nursery school. Without even thinking about it, she had pulled on her tracksuit and running shoes and headed out. This summer she had found it worked best to switch off her brain before going for a run or to the gym. If she paused to think, it wouldn't happen. Even so, she had let things slide for the last three weeks and was paying for it now with her burning calves.

It wasn't as though she'd broken any records for speed or distance either. She'd run round the Seltjarnarnes Peninsula, following the footpath along the northern shore, with a panoramic view of the mountains – Esja, Skardsheidi and Akrafjall – across the gleaming waters of Faxaflói Bay. Having reached the westernmost point, stopping just short of the lighthouse at Grótta, she had turned south and run to the golf course, before following the gravel bank of Bakkagrandi along to Sudurströnd, then home. She'd lost count of the birds she had seen watching her from the air, land and sea as she jogged past, all of them looking equally baffled by the vagaries of human behaviour. Molly, in contrast, gave every sign of being highly satisfied as she loped along at Freyja's side without even panting. The dog could easily have done several more circuits of the peninsula, whereas it took every ounce of Freyja's will-power not to give up and drop to a walk for the last hundred metres.

She felt better when she met two women walking along in their running gear, both scarlet in the face and gulping down water from their bottles, obviously shattered. It was good to know she wasn't the only one. Everyone else she'd encountered had seemed so focused: cyclists acting as if they were taking part in the Tour de France; lean, fit runners pounding along, eyes fixed purposefully on the horizon.

With one last inhuman effort, Freyja made it to the car park in front of her building, before bending over with her hands on her knees, panting in great, tearing gasps. Molly watched in disgust and turned her head away when Freyja finally straightened up and limped the last few metres to the front door. Perhaps that was the advantage of having a snake as a pet: it only had the one expression and never judged you. Probably because it was too busy contemplating where best to bite you.

The hot shower performed its usual miracle and when Freyja stepped out, reinvigorated, the taste of iron, the burning lungs and sore calves were no more than a distant memory. By the time she'd dressed and had a coffee, the memory had disappeared. Instead, her head was buzzing with ideas about the case. She allowed her mind to pursue them at will, as in this rejuvenated state it was easier to think things through properly. When she was tired, her thoughts tended to drift aimlessly until they hit a rock.

This time, her mind was occupied with Tristan rather than Rósa. Another batch of interviews had been completed, but still nothing had emerged to corroborate the young man's story. Even the boys Freyja had expected to back up his allegations with similar experiences of their own had denied having any problems of the kind. They had shaken their heads, adamant not only that no one had laid a finger on them but also that they hadn't noticed any inappropriate behaviour towards the other kids. When Freyja had intervened with questions for those who'd reported having trouble waking up in the mornings, they had responded that they'd always found it hard to wake up and still did. One couldn't even remember having said it.

The terrible suspicion that Tristan might be lying was growing ever stronger. Yet he'd seemed so convincing when they'd questioned him. Perhaps Bergur had only abused the one boy. She had searched for academic studies on patterns of abuse by paedophiles to see how common it was for them to be content with a single victim, but had found frustratingly little on the subject. Most of the research was concerned with what happened to child abusers after they had been released from prison, which had no real bearing on the case she was investigating. The offenders in question knew what would happen if they didn't toe the line. It didn't help that most of the articles originated in America where sentences were much longer than those in Iceland and prison conditions considerably harsher. She doubted that Icelandic sexual predators would shake in their shoes at the thought of a spell in Litla-Hraun.

She needed to know how likely it was for a sexual offender, who had never been caught, to turn over a new leaf of his own accord. Needless to say, there were no articles devoted to this subject since, by the nature of the crime, only the perpetrator and the victim would be aware of what had happened. All she found were statistics about the number of paedophiles who had only one, historical crime behind them at the time they were charged, and these had more to do with criminology than psychology. Since she'd failed to unearth a single study or abstract on the subject, she would simply have to trust her own common sense, which told her that nothing could be ruled out. Tristan could be telling the truth, in which case Bergur was guilty, or the boy could be lying or misremembering, in which case Bergur was innocent. Perhaps things would be clarified when the police tracked Rósa down, but this couldn't be taken for granted.

At any rate, on the basis of what had emerged so far, there wasn't much likelihood of charges being brought, or of Bergur being found guilty if they were. For that, they needed more substantial evidence. But the chances of that were diminishing with every interview that failed to come up with the goods. Even a statement from Rósa that Tristan had confided in her several years ago was unlikely to weigh particularly heavily. For the case to be watertight, she would need to have witnessed the assaults.

Freyja looked at the clock. There was just time to ring Yngvi at the Child Protection Agency to give him the daily update. He listened to her report but had little to contribute when she shared her thoughts on the findings so far. Although she hadn't been expecting him to have a firm view on whether Tristan or Bergur was more likely to be telling the truth, she had hoped that his experience of similar incidents might provide a little insight. Then again, maybe he didn't have any experience. The situation was highly unusual, after all.

The phone call wasn't an entire waste of time, though, because Yngvi informed her that she'd been authorised to listen to recordings of the children's sessions with therapists. After warning her that there were fewer interviews than he had been expecting, Yngvi added that the recordings had been uploaded to the agency's server, and she could access them there. He had also uploaded all the existing interviews with Rósa, including those dating from before her residence at the care home, since Freyja had seemed so interested in her during their last phone call, and so concerned about what might have happened to her. With any luck, they might provide some clues that could help to track her down. Freyja then listened obediently as he mechanically recited the relevant privacy and confidentiality laws and reminded her of the ethical rules by which psychologists were bound. Although she knew it all off by heart, she let him finish before confirming that she would observe the rules in everything. As always.

Before ending the call, Yngvi asked if Freyja had made up her mind whether to apply for the police liaison position. She said she'd been giving it a great deal of thought but hadn't yet decided. The truth was that she'd hardly thought about it at all. It was a big decision, and when you had a lot on it was all too easy to put decisions about the future on the back burner. Hopefully she'd manage to sit down and make up her mind before the future became the present, or even the past, and the opportunity had slipped through her fingers.

Freyja threw on her coat and went to fetch Saga.

At the nursery school she was handed a note containing a message that nobody wanted to hear: THE NITS ARE BACK! The exclamation mark implied this was something to be celebrated but the small print underneath made it clear that it was anything but. Parents and guardians were kindly requested to start the necessary treatment immediately, and brief instructions followed. Freyja felt a momentary impulse to chuck the note away and run for the door; leave Saga behind, phone Baldur and tell him to ditch his tourists and come back for his daughter. She could feel her scalp crawling at the mere thought of headlice and the nursery school teacher who handed her the note had no difficulty in interpreting her horrified expression.

'It's nothing serious.' The woman folded her arms. 'It happens from time to time. Especially in autumn. If the golden plover is the traditional herald of spring, nits are the herald of autumn.'

Freyja couldn't smile at this. She couldn't say a word. The woman carried on talking, describing how nits spread and the importance of everyone taking the treatment seriously. With every word, the itching grew worse. It was a relief when the woman finally shut up, but the respite was brief, since she added that Freyja should remove everything from Saga's peg and take it home to wash. Freyja glanced round in vain for a pair of rubber gloves but all she could see was a plastic bag lying on one of the benches. Picking it up, she turned it inside out and put it over her hand for protection. As she was stuffing the clothes one-handed into Saga's bag, she took care to stand as far from the wall as she could, for fear that lice would drop on her from the other kids' hats and coats.

Unfortunately, she was still at it when the teacher returned with Saga. The woman looked unimpressed but took pity on Freyja enough to say: 'If it's any comfort, Saga isn't one of the children who've been scratching. But I see I can trust you to take the treatment seriously.'

Oh, she would do that all right.

Freyja managed to lead Saga to the car, manoeuvre her into her car seat at arm's length and drive off, all without their heads ever coming into contact. But her feeling of triumph didn't last long. She had hardly left the car park before she caught a movement in the rear-view mirror as her niece raised her little hand to her head and began to scratch. Freyja had to restrain herself from jumping the lights and ignoring stop signs all the way to the nearest chemist.

The flat reeked of nit shampoo. Poor Molly, who didn't appreciate the new smell one bit, had taken herself outside onto the balcony and refused to come in. Saga's hair had been washed and combed so often that it was standing up in a halo of static electricity, and Freyja's was little better, though it was too long and heavy to stick up like her niece's. All the towels Freyja owned had been put on a boil wash, and on the floor beside the washing machine were tightly tied plastic bags stuffed with clothes and bedding awaiting the same treatment. The dustbin in the basement contained another, equally well-sealed bag, full of nit combs and the results of the combing, which Freyja was trying to wipe from her memory. She'd be damned if a single louse or nit had survived the purge. Louse-mageddon. It wasn't over yet, though, as she had bought enough shampoo to repeat the job for several days in a row. No chances would be taken in this house.

It crossed her mind to ring Baldur and demand his gratitude for a job well done. But she knew he wouldn't let her complain for long before he interrupted her on a lighter note and before she knew it he would have lifted her out of her sulk. She wasn't in the mood for that. Sometimes you had to be allowed to wallow in grumpiness and a sense of martyrdom.

By the time Saga was in bed, Freyja had more or less recovered. She even dropped a good-night kiss on the little girl's forehead once she was asleep. It would be a while before she kissed her on the top of her head or let her sleep in her bed, though. At least the snake was sated for now after being fed earlier that evening – another operation she would rather not think about.

Once she and Molly were alone, Freyja decided to try listening to the interviews with the kids from the care home. She succeeded in connecting to the server but the connection was slow and she had to wait for the files to load. She would have preferred to wear headphones but if she did there was a risk she wouldn't hear if Saga woke up, so she had to make do with the loudspeaker on her laptop.

As a result, the first time she heard Rósa's voice it was distinctly tinny. The interview was four years old, taken the year after her mother died, when Rósa was twelve. This was two years before her stay in the home run by the alleged abuser and three months before she met Tristan.

Freyja closed her eyes to concentrate and to shut out the sight of Molly, who was staring at her fixedly, as if she hadn't had enough to eat.

To begin with, the therapist did all the talking, trying to coax the girl into responding. She was a middle-aged woman who specialised in providing counselling for children; Freyja knew her by reputation and had heard only good things about her. She listened as the woman asked in a calm, friendly voice whether Rósa would like to take her coat off. Her question was met with silence. The woman got the same reaction when she repeated the question, pointing out that it was quite warm in the room. Then she offered Rósa a glass of water, asked if she was comfortable and continued with general questions and remarks that were aimed at breaking down the wall of silence the girl had created around herself. Nothing worked: Rósa remained stubbornly mute.

The therapist then said she was going to give Rósa a list of questions – standard stuff, nothing for her to worry about – but still the girl didn't respond. Only when the woman asked if the problem was that she couldn't read, did Rósa finally open her mouth to reply indignantly that of course she could, pride overcoming her obstinacy.

'*So you know how to read and you can talk too. That's a relief.*' The woman still sounded as warm and comforting as *skyr* with sugar and cream, and perfectly sincere, with no hint of sarcasm or teasing in her voice.

'*You already knew I could talk: they'd have told you if I was dumb.*' Now that Rósa had come out with a whole sentence, Freyja could hear how deep and husky her voice was. Assuming she didn't have laryngitis, she could have a bright future as a blues singer. A tragic life story would do nothing to harm her prospects.

'*You're quite right: I already knew you could read too. I've been told you're doing very well at school, which would be difficult if you couldn't read.*' This was met with silence, so the therapist continued: '*Seeing as you're a clever girl, you probably know why we're sitting here. Is there something you'd like to tell me about that?*'

'*No. There's nothing to tell. I didn't want to live there, so*

I just left. No one should have to stay somewhere if they're not happy. Or maybe you think they should?'

Evidently, she had run away, probably for the first time since ending up in the hands of children's services. Freyja wondered how the therapist would tackle Rósa's attempt to turn the tables and assume the role of interrogator.

'There are other ways of dealing with it, Rósa. By talking about it, for example; by telling someone. You've got the perfect opportunity to do that now. Don't throw away the chance. Would you like to tell me why you weren't happy with the family?'

'They didn't want me there. It wasn't like home. Not for me, anyway. Maybe for them. But I know what a proper home's like. I had a proper home until my mother died.'

'Yes. That was a major upheaval for you. Everyone around you is very conscious of that, Rósa. You must remember to ask for help when you're feeling unhappy. Running away won't help. The problem will still be there when you come back. I expect it follows you when you run away as well. No one has ever managed to escape from grief. It's something you have to confront. But there are ways of making your loss and your other problems easier to cope with.'

Freyja thought the therapist was using rather mature language for a girl of that age. Perhaps it was because the girl's voice sounded so grown-up, or because Rósa came across in person as older than she really was. The traumas she had gone through would have had the effect of forcing her to mature early.

'I've tried talking. No one will listen. No one. You won't either. Though you say you will.'

'That's not true. Why don't you try me? Not all adults are the same. I promise you I'll listen.'

'My mother didn't die in an accident. My mother was killed.'

This time it was the therapist's turn to fall silent. Freyja could understand why; this was an unexpected development. But it didn't take the woman long to recover.

'I'm afraid I know very little about your mother's death, Rósa. Only that it was sudden, an accident. Accidents happen. Sometimes they're the result of pure chance and there's no reason for them. That's why they can be so hard to accept.'

The deep, husky child's voice gave a contemptuous snort. 'I knew it. You don't believe me. You would if I was a grown-up.'

'No, Rósa. You can't be sure of that. Whether you're a child or an adult, it's not enough simply to claim something and expect everyone to believe you. If you really believe your mother was killed, you'll have to do better. Explain to me why you think that. Maybe, just maybe, you'll change your mind when you put forward the evidence. Then again, maybe you won't. Go ahead, anyway. Try to convince me that you're right. It'll do you good to talk about it.'

There was silence as Rósa considered this. It had been a good move by the therapist. If the girl's obsession was getting in the way of her ability to mourn her mother, it would have to be tackled. Unresolved issues could have a serious impact on people's mental health.

'There was a doll in the bath when my mother died. It had disappeared the next day, when my mother was found.'

'There could be a perfectly natural explanation for that. It's unlikely that someone would have killed your mother just to steal a doll.'

'But what if the doll was evil, sent by the devil? Maybe it was the doll's fault.'

'I don't believe there's any such thing as an evil doll. I don't even believe in the devil.' The therapist paused, then went on in a level voice: 'What made you think that, Rósa? Was there any particular reason?'

'I don't remember.'

'Did you think that straight away? The day you heard your mother had died?'

'I didn't hear about it. I saw it. I found my mother. By the bath.'

'The bath the doll was in?'

'Yes. There was blood everywhere. The floor around my mother was red. I didn't look in the bath. Only at my mother. And the blood.'

'Was it your doll? Had you been giving her a bath?'

'No. She wasn't mine. She came out of the sea. My mother wanted to throw her back but I wanted to bring her home. If I hadn't done that, everything would have been all right. For my mother. And me.'

'You're not responsible for your mother's death, Rósa. You have to understand that. I think we should focus on that for now, because it's extremely important that you understand that.'

Self-reproach was a common reaction to stressful events. People blamed themselves wrongly, both for things they had done and for things they had no control over. Rósa belonged to the former category. This was the more common type of self-reproach and fortunately it was fairly straightforward to treat. With the right handling, it was possible to prevent it from spiralling into the kind of low self-esteem, depression and self-loathing that were characteristic of the most serious cases.

Rósa didn't respond. Instead, she asked a question that completely threw Freyja: *'Do you know a man called Bergur? He works with children. I want to live with him. Can you help me get a place with him?'*

Freyja paused the playback to check the date. The interview had taken place two years before Rósa went to stay at Bergur's home and three months before she'd met Tristan. Freyja had no idea what to make of it. Could it be a coincidence?

Where had Rósa heard about Bergur and why did she want to live with him? Could she have met another child in the system who had said nice things about him? Or was her interest motivated by something quite different?

Freyja started the playback again. But the interview did nothing to clarify the issue. If anything, it just muddied the picture even further.

Chapter 21

Friday

The barbecue was proving a bit of a flop, in spite of the good weather. The guests were so out of practice that they had forgotten how to handle a windless, sunny day. If they weren't cursing the flies that buzzed harmlessly around their heads, they were moaning about the heat or what a wash-out the summer had been. A few even managed to blame the whole thing on the government. No one appeared capable of enjoying the long-desired balmy weather. The situation could hardly have been more Icelandic.

Still, the party was bound to liven up later. People had only just arrived and they'd forget their complaints once they'd relaxed and got a few drinks inside them. This would happen sooner for some than for others, judging by the sickly, spicy smell of pot wafting under Frikki's nose. He carefully avoided looking round to see who was smoking the joint. The other guests didn't seem bothered and he didn't want to come across as a square. He felt out of place enough as it was.

Frikki bit into the burger that his younger brother, Fjalar, had given him. Frikki'd had to find a place at one of the tables lined up in the garden before his paper plate buckled under the weight of the burger, which was at least three times thicker than normal. This was typical of Fjalar, who never did anything by halves: whether it was Christmas presents for their parents that made Frikki's modest parcels look like stocking fillers; expensive bottles of fine wine brought along to informal family suppers, or the ton of fireworks he let off on New Year's Eve. Fjalar always had to outdo everyone else around him. The only aspect of his brother's life that wasn't characterised by unbridled extravagance was his attitude to the fishing boat they co-owned with their father and uncle. In that case penny-pinching was the order of the day: Fjalar insisted on carefully weighing up the cost of every screw, washer, nut or bolt that needed replacing; sometimes for so long that by the time he had finally come to a decision, the cost had gone up.

Frikki had often wondered why his brother behaved so differently when it came to the boat and concluded that it was because the people who sold spare parts for boats and ships didn't accept maxed-out credit cards. They had to be paid cash in hand, not with an airy promise of payment some time in the never-never. The only possible explanation for Fjalar's lifestyle was that it was financed with loans. On the rare occasions that he mentioned his little tourism business, it was to boast about how incredibly well it was doing. But whenever Frikki visited him, he couldn't help noticing that one or two of the three campervans Fjalar rented out were invariably parked in his broad drive. Sometimes they were all there. Frikki suspected that demand was similarly patchy for the holiday apartment in the Med that Fjalar rented out to Icelanders, or for his summer house here at home. Every time the brothers met, Fjalar offered Frikki the use of his summer house, which suggested that it was mostly vacant. He never offered the foreign apartment, though, so hopefully that had turned out to be more of a money-spinner.

'Here. Have a beer, man.' Fjalar appeared with a glass in each hand. Oversized, of course, and the beer chilled no doubt to freezing point: naturally, Fjalar had to keep his fridge colder than anyone else's.

Frikki took the misted glass his brother handed him and put it down on the table. Drops of condensation ran down the sides, forming a little puddle around the base. It would only grow, since Frikki had no intention of touching the drink. He was driving, though he didn't mention the fact again since he had already pointed it out and declined a drink twice since he'd arrived. Fjalar had quickly changed the subject, not wanting the others to notice that his brother wasn't in the party mood that he expected of his guests.

'How's it going? Good?' Fjalar plonked himself down on the wooden bench beside Frikki, slamming his beer on the table. There wasn't much left in the glass, which meant he wouldn't stay sitting for long.

'Sure, fine.' Frikki put on what he hoped was a carefree smile, in an attempt to blend in with the crowd, only to realise that in order to achieve this he would have been better off grumbling about the flies.

Fjalar was wearing a T-shirt that looked as if it had been bought in a charity shop but was almost certainly by some famous, bland designer. It had probably cost more than the only suit Frikki had in his wardrobe. Fjalar's arms, revealed by the short sleeves, were brown and muscular; he was one of the few people in the garden with a tan. As far as Frikki knew, Fjalar hadn't been abroad that summer, so it must have been acquired in a salon or from a tube. In fact, on closer inspection it was obvious: the hand holding the beer glass was a bit stripy. The thought made Frikki cringe.

Fjalar slapped him matily on the shoulder. 'Why aren't you mingling, man? The place is full of fun people and here you are, sitting alone in the corner.'

This was a little unfair, since the table was bang in the middle of the garden. It was the other guests who were lining up along the fence. The only person who had been at the table when Frikki sat down had got up and left, abandoning his half-eaten burger that would soon make a feast for the flies. 'I was only planning to drop in. I told you that. Besides, I don't know anyone.'

'Don't know anyone? Bullshit, man. You've met these guys loads of times.' Fjalar drained the rest of his beer and waved at a woman standing in a small knot of people, who appeared to be looking their way. She smiled and waved back before turning to her companions.

Technically, Fjalar was right. Frikki had often been invited to parties at his brother's place with this same crowd. But he had never got talking to any of them. He couldn't put a name to a single person here. 'I'm afraid I've got to go.'

'Oh, come on. Like you've got anywhere else to go. Home? There's no one waiting for you there, remember?' Fjalar jabbed an elbow in his side, causing Frikki to wince. 'Did you see the chick I was waving at? She's just broken up with her boyfriend. I bet she's up for it. Go and talk to her. She was giving you the eye, man.'

The woman had been looking at Fjalar, not at him. If asked how many people had been sitting at the table when she waved, she'd have said one. People tended to mistake Frikki for the invisible man.

'She's not my type, Fjalar.' It was true. The woman was far too dolled up for his taste. She was wearing a summery dress, which was fine on its own, but she'd paired it with ludicrously high heels that kept getting stuck in the grass. If she decided to dance round the garden, Fjalar wouldn't need to aerate his lawn this year. Her hair was dyed unnaturally blonde, the curls about as genuine as the breasts she'd obviously paid for. Even the long, pink talons on her fingers looked as if they were glued on. A type like that would never be happy with him. And he certainly wouldn't be happy with her. He fantasised about a woman in hiking boots; someone who'd be willing to go out on the boat with him. Not a Barbie doll who'd be happiest at the launch party for a new shop, in the hope of being papped with a plastic glass of white wine in her hand and making it into the 'Seen About Town' section of the online news sites.

Sadly, he didn't know where to go looking for his ideal woman, but he did know he wouldn't find her in his brother's garden. It had been years since he'd found a woman he thought might be the one. He remembered how he had taken her and her daughter out on the boat and believed the trip had been a success. He had really thought it might be the first step towards a more serious relationship. But fate had had other plans. He had never seen the woman again and her sudden death had put him off dating – for far too long if he was honest.

His brother brought him back to the present. 'Your type, my ass. Eyjalín's everyone's type, man.'

Frikki muttered something about not everybody having the same taste, only to regret the comment, though it had hardly been audible. Why the hell was he discussing some woman with his brother, like they could decide between them that she should be his? 'Great burger,' he said loud and clear, to be sure his brother caught it. Fjalar would be off any minute now that he'd finished his beer, and Frikki had to say something positive about the barbecue. They might have been chalk and cheese, but they were brothers. Fjalar meant well by inviting him to his endless round of parties. Frikki mustn't forget that.

'Shit, man. I need another beer.' Fjalar rose to his feet. 'Drink up. That's a pathetic effort.'

Frikki nodded in a pretence that he would step it up. He sat there until he had finished his burger, then tipped out the beer on the lawn when no one was looking – or so he thought. Glancing up, he caught the eye of the woman who had waved at Fjalar. She was staring at him in astonishment and didn't return his embarrassed smile, just raised her eyebrows, pouted and turned away. She'd certainly picked her moment to finally become aware of him.

Frikki got up and waited until Fjalar was standing with his back to him, absorbed in talking to his guests, then slipped away without anyone paying him the slightest attention.

He knew his brother would be hurt when he realised he'd left without saying goodbye, but the night was young and the beer was flowing. When Fjalar woke up in the morning with a headache the size of the Vatnajökull ice cap, the memory would have gone, purged from his mind with spirits.

Frikki parked on the drive in front of his small terraced house. He got out, aimed the key fob behind him and locked the car as he was walking up to the front door.

He unlocked the outer door and called as he closed it behind him: 'Hi! I'm back!'

Fjalar had been wrong when he'd said there was no one waiting for Frikki at home.

Or had he? There was no answering call from inside the house.

Frikki called out again as he slipped off his shoes. 'Rósa! I'm back! What do you say to a trip on the boat tomorrow morning?'

She didn't answer. Only then did he notice that her shoes weren't in the hall. She wasn't back yet, but then he could have told himself that as it was still relatively early. So he *was* alone at home after all.

Chapter 22

Gudlaugur had shadows under his eyes and stubble on his cheeks; his shoulders were sagging and he couldn't stop yawning. He was like a dusty edition of himself. The night shifts were clearly taking their toll. It was ridiculous that he should have been called in on a Saturday but they were all having to sacrifice their days off due to the shortage of manpower. They had been promised a rest on Sunday, though.

'Get some coffee down you.' Huldar had found this the best cure when he himself had been working late shifts as a uniformed officer. In fact, it was his cure-all for any number of ills. Everything appeared a little more manageable after a shot of caffeine. Perhaps that was why they provided coffee free on tap in A&E.

'No thanks, I've already had my daily allowance.'

'There's no such thing as a "daily allowance" of coffee, Gudlaugur. Any more than you can have a daily allowance of breath.'

Gudlaugur gave him a weary look. 'You can breathe too much, actually.'

Huldar decided not to argue with him, as he suspected Gudlaugur was right. This was confirmed by Lína's expression.

She was standing in the station yard with them. She and Gudlaugur had come out for a bit of fresh air; Huldar for the poisoned variety; the kind that no one doubted could kill you. He took a drag and the wind carried his smoke up the wall and in through an open window on the second floor. Huldar just hoped the person sitting next to it was a smoker. Not that it mattered if they weren't, since Erla wasn't around to complain to: she had rushed off to a meeting of the Identification Commission in the hope of hearing some news. The fact the commission had come together on a Saturday was almost certainly due to her persistent phone calls. When she came back, she'd be too busy processing the information to bother with the complaints of delicate flowers who you literally couldn't even breathe on.

Gudlaugur yawned. When he prised his eyes open again, they were no more than slits.

'How are you getting on with sorting through the lost property, Lína?' Huldar asked, to deflect her from commenting on how tired Gudlaugur was and delivering a lecture about the regulations on statutory rest periods.

'Me? Oh, I finished that ages ago. I did it so systematically that it took me no time at all. Good organisation is key.' Lína made no attempt to disguise her smugness. She looked at them both in turn from under her thick red mane, which she had for once allowed to fall loose to her shoulders. She was so much shorter than them that she had to tilt her head back to see their faces. 'Every minute spent planning a job saves you quarter of an hour in the execution.'

Gudlaugur rolled his eyes, too tired to snipe at her. But Huldar smiled. 'Did you find anything of use for the inquiry?'

Lína's smugness evaporated. 'No, actually. There was

nothing of interest on the phones.' Then, recovering her composure, she added: 'Shame it took IT so long to unlock them. It's infuriating having to waste so much time waiting in suspense, only to be disappointed. It's better to get the bad news straight away. I can't understand why they don't take on more summer support staff. More students like me, who can lend a hand, even though we haven't graduated yet.'

'No, it's extraordinary that it hasn't occurred to anyone.' Huldar suppressed an ironic grin by taking another drag on his cigarette. 'What about the diary?'

'It didn't contain anything of relevance to the abuse case. Tristan's mentioned twice by name, and Rósa once, but not in connection with abuse. I took the diary down to the Drug Squad because the girl wrote quite a bit about using. She was an addict herself, poor thing, and I came across details about how she got hold of her drugs and other stuff that might be useful to the police. She also mentioned that she'd been asked to do some dealing in return for getting her dope cheaper or even free. But it won't be easy to decipher the information because she doesn't name any names. She was prostituting herself as well and the descriptions of that are horrible. Unfortunately, she didn't mention any names there either. I just hope the Drug Squad can do something with the info.'

'Maybe they could ask her directly. Or don't they know who the diary belonged to?'

'Yes, they do. But she's dead. She killed herself.'

Huldar blew out a thick stream of smoke. He couldn't begin to describe what was going through his head, at least not in words he could use in front of Lína. After a moment, he pulled himself together and said: 'It's possible you'll be asked to sort through more stuff like that.'

'Oh?' Lína's eyes widened. No doubt she'd already started mentally planning the task. 'Where from?'

'From a storage unit. It belongs to the man who was murdered on Grandi. It's not impossible that his murder was linked to something that happened in his past. Unlikely, but not impossible.' Huldar watched Gudlaugur lean back against the wall and close his eyes. If he nodded off in that position, perhaps he'd slide gently down to the wet tarmac. If so, Huldar was tempted to watch until Gudlaugur had almost reached the bottom before prodding him. He wanted to see what would happen. With an effort, he turned his attention back to Lína: 'With any luck, the stuff should be delivered to the station early next week, so it would be great if we could borrow you from Sexual Offences.'

'Fine by me.' Lína was radiant, in stark contrast to the exhausted and indifferent Gudlaugur beside her, who looked ready to conk out any minute.

'Tell me, Lína. You're young, closer in age to Rósa than we are. Plus, you're a girl. Where would you hide if you decided to run away?'

'Why should a girl be any different from a boy?'

Huldar shrugged. 'Just humour me for a minute. Where would you go if you ran away?'

'Ran away? Why would I want to run away? I'm not a prisoner, I can go wherever I like.'

Huldar regretting asking. Lína was too literal minded to enter into the spirit of the thing. 'I realise that. But say you did want to run away, where would you hide?'

Lína frowned as she thought about it. 'I'd try to find somewhere indoors. Not outside, because there are too few places where you can stay warm and dry – and safe. It's more dangerous for women to sleep rough than it is for men, so safety considerations would play an important role in choosing a place. But where? An underpass, maybe, though I'd be reported immediately if someone saw me sleeping there, and of course it would be risky for a woman alone.' She paused again to consider. 'I don't know. Maybe I could pretend to be a backpacker and hang around at the airport. But it wouldn't work – a friend of mine works there and she'd recognise me. There's really nowhere you can go outside without the risk of being recognised. Iceland's such a small country. Unless you can stay with someone you trust not to give you away.' Lína frowned again. 'But then why run off in the first place? If you're going to end up a prisoner anyway, stuck in someone's house, unable to set foot outside?'

Huldar turned to Gudlaugur. 'Have we definitely checked all her associates to see if they've been sheltering her?'

Gudlaugur answered sleepily. 'Yeah, we've asked school friends, relatives, even her boss and co-workers at the bakery where she had a summer job. She's not staying with any of them. Or at any of the homeless shelters. She hasn't got a credit card and there haven't been any transactions on her debit card since she took off. Which means she can't be at a hotel, a hostel or an Airbnb. We've checked everywhere. All we can think of is that she must have holed up somewhere that's not immediately obvious.'

Lína gnawed at her upper lip, trying to think of a possible hiding place that everyone else had overlooked. It was a new experience for her to be stumped like this. Still, there was a first time for everything, and if she couldn't come up with an answer, then it was pointless for Huldar to go on racking his brains over it.

He had almost finished his cigarette by the time Erla drove into the yard. He nudged Gudlaugur, whose breathing had become suspiciously slow and deep. However much Huldar had wanted to see him slide down the wall, he'd rather Erla didn't witness it. Gudlaugur started, pulled himself upright and did his feeble best to look alert. Lína didn't have to pretend; as usual she looked as if her batteries were fully charged.

'What are you three doing out here? Plotting a mutiny? Or a strike?' Erla was looking uncharacteristically pleased, which must mean the meeting had exceeded her expectations. Perhaps the Swedes had delivered the results of the DNA analysis on the bones. 'Drop by my office, Huldar, once you've finished your little meeting.' She smiled and went inside without waiting for an answer.

'Am I imagining things or was Erla actually in a good mood?' Lína couldn't have been more amazed if Erla had turned up carrying a live great auk.

'It's not totally unheard of, you know.' Huldar took a final puff, then stubbed out his cigarette and threw the butt in the overflowing bin on the wall. Then he hurried inside after Erla, leaving Gudlaugur and Lína behind in awkward silence. It would do them good to have to talk to each other, if only on their way back upstairs.

Erla's coat was hanging on the peg and she was sitting behind her desk. She beckoned Huldar into her office, still looking uncharacteristically sunny. She had also been jubilant when she returned from her boat trip the day before. Thanks to the good weather, they had managed to sweep quite an extensive area beyond the one they had already searched, in the process recovering several more bits of skeleton, including a jaw bone, a skull, a number of vertebrae and a hip bone.

The jaw bone and skull didn't match but at least they now had the upper jaw from one person and the lower jaw from another. None of the bones displayed any signs of injuries that could explain the cause of death. Even more puzzling was the fact that no remnants of clothing had been found. The searchers had thought they'd spotted a zip in one of the photos taken by the submarine, but they hadn't managed to track it down with the gadget that was used to recover the remains from the seabed. The conclusion was that the bodies must have been either scantily clad or naked.

'What did you find out?' Huldar plonked himself down on the chair in front of the desk.

'The results of the DNA analysis are in. They managed to get them onto the priority list.' Erla's smile was triumphant. 'The remains belong to a man and a woman, neither of them Icelandic, or at least neither of them of Icelandic descent. The bulk of their DNA comes from the British Isles. Only two per cent originates from Scandinavia in the man's case and one per cent in the woman's. Then there's a sprinkling from southern Europe, but that's irrelevant. The main thing is that the results rule out the possibility that they're Icelanders, unless they're immigrants, of course. But we can find no incidents in which a British or Irish tourist has gone missing here. Let alone two of them.' Erla rubbed her neck. 'I also got some findings back about the bones. The couple appear to have been in the twenty-five to thirty-five age bracket and, judging by their leg bones, they reckon one was about one eighty-five, the other one sixty-seven metres tall. Presumably the taller one was the man.'

'What are you thinking, then? Could they have come from a ship or a boat?'

'They must have done. Nobody in the Register of Missing Persons fits their description. And the same applies to all those who have been lost overboard in Icelandic waters. How they got here is a complete mystery. The Identification Commission are inclined to believe that they must have fallen overboard but that their disappearance wasn't reported. From a cruise ship, possibly. Anyway, they've sent the information to Interpol and, as the people are very likely to be from the UK, to the British police department responsible for missing persons. We should get an answer soon, especially now that we've got their teeth. It's just as well since apparently about two thousand people go missing every year in Britain, so it's a bloody long list.'

Huldar raised his eyebrows. 'Wow.' Their foreign colleagues had a whole different world to contend with. 'If they're foreigners from a cruise ship, it's pretty clear that Rósa can't have been a witness to what happened or have any information about them. It must have been a coincidence that she talked about people in the sea.'

Erla shrugged. 'I reckon it must have been. She can hardly have been in contact with a foreign ship. At the end of the day, she's only a little girl. I'm coming round to the idea that she's just a bit unbalanced, which wouldn't be surprising when you consider what she's been through. But don't think I've lost interest in finding her. She's still a potential witness to murder. Speaking of which, what a fucking nightmare. Have you seen the news sites?' Erla's mood darkened suddenly in the kind of swing that she had perfected during her time as head of department.

Huldar nodded. He could understand why Erla was pissed off about the coverage. In the opinion of those working on the investigation, the articles were unfair. Stories about police incompetence were interspersed with reports on the appalling neglect suffered by the homeless and drug addicts in Iceland. But in practice there was little the police could do other than let these people spend a night in the cells when they were desperate. Anything else was outside their remit. This should have been clear to the public, but some readers no doubt regarded the police as the chief obstacle to these people being given humane treatment, while the institutions who were in fact responsible for their welfare were unlikely to leap to the police's defence.

'If we don't make any progress soon, the press are going to have a field day. I can just imagine the rash of articles about how we're not giving the inquiry our proper attention because we don't give a shit about people living on the margins of society and whether they live or die.' There was no trace left of Erla's earlier good mood. Instead, her habitual scowl was firmly back in place. 'And what'll happen then? I'll have the top brass on my back, giving me a bollocking for ruining the image of the force.'

Huldar felt a frisson of pure pleasure at not being in her shoes. 'Why not remind them that our image is still shite after a suspected rapist was allowed to carry on working in a care home while his case was supposedly being investigated? The hostile coverage we're getting now is a step up from that.'

'Huh,' was Erla's only reaction to this suggestion. 'What the hell's going on with that girl? How is it possible that they haven't managed to trace her? Could she have left the country? Have they checked the passenger lists?'

'Yes, they have, from what I hear. Her name wasn't on any of them. Of course, that doesn't rule out the possibility that she's left the country under a false name. But in that case somebody else must have bought the ticket for her. You can't pay in cash and there's no transaction on her debit card for the purchase of a plane ticket. So she has to be in the country.' He paused. 'I just hope to God she's alive.'

'Oh, no thanks. Don't even go there.' Erla gestured at him to get lost, as if afraid he was tempting fate. 'We've got enough on our bloody plate without the poor kid turning up dead. Go away and do something useful instead of making me depressed and worried.' Her phone rang and she turned away to answer it, forgetting about Huldar.

He hadn't been sitting at his desk long when the door of Erla's office opened and she came out. Huldar stretched out his leg as far as he could and trod on Gudlaugur's toes. His colleague was sleeping like a baby in his chair on the other side of the desk. Gudlaugur jerked awake, sat bolt upright, grabbed his mouse and pretended to be absorbed in his computer screen. Huldar wasn't sure if Erla had noticed that Gudlaugur had been out for the count. Only now did he realise that she was white as a sheet and looked extremely upset. 'Could we have a quick word?' she asked him.

He followed her back into her office. She perched on the edge of her desk, her arms folded across her chest, as if she were inadequately dressed for a blizzard, hugging herself to keep warm.

'I've just had some very bad news. The worst.'

'Oh?' Huldar guessed this wasn't something he wanted to hear. For a split second he thought of intervening to prevent her from opening her mouth for a few moments longer, but he was too late.

'We've had a report of a body.'

'Oh.' Usually, when this sort of thing happened, Erla's reaction would be to pull on her coat and get straight over to the scene, shutting down all human emotions. He couldn't ever remember seeing her react like this before; in fact, he got the impression she was close to breaking down. 'Have they found an ID?' he asked.

Erla shook her head slowly. 'No. But I have a horrible feeling that what you said earlier could be about to come true. It's a teenager. Very likely a girl. With dark hair, wearing black jeans, a red hoodie and a dark-blue anorak with a fake-leather collar. Does the coat sound familiar to you?'

Huldar drew a deep breath. 'I'll get my coat. I'm coming with you.'

Erla dropped her eyes to the floor. She stayed where she was on the desk, her legs dangling motionless. She didn't appear to be going anywhere.

'Is everything OK, Erla?' Huldar kept his voice slow, quiet and kind. 'You need to get a move on. They'll be waiting for you.' When she didn't answer or raise her eyes from the floor, he added: 'You've run murder investigations involving kids before. And coped like a trouper. This won't be any different.'

Erla looked up and met his eye. 'Huldar, I'm pregnant.'

It was his turn to be momentarily paralysed.

She rolled her eyes, suddenly herself again. 'Relax. It's not yours. I'm not an elephant whose pregnancies last for years.'

'That's not why I didn't say anything.' This was a lie: he'd been frantically trying to remember how long it was since they'd slept together. Panic had done nothing to improve his mental arithmetic; he had still been counting the months when she interrupted his thoughts. 'I suppose I should congratulate you?' he said.

'I don't know what you're supposed to do. I'm no expert.'

Huldar resolved not to ask who the father was. He preferred to stay out of that particular minefield. 'Er . . . now I get why you're so upset about the body. Carrying a child must do that to you. I can see why the death of a kid would hit you so hard. Hormones and so on.'

Erla raised her head to glare at him. 'God, you're an idiot. Pregnancy doesn't make you more sensitive. I'm just struggling with fucking horrible morning sickness. Though morning sickness is a misnomer, because this bugger doesn't just affect me in the morning, it lasts twenty-four fucking seven, which is why I'm not my usual chirpy self. That's all. Jesus. "Hormones and so on"? What's "so on" supposed to mean?'

Huldar backed two steps towards the door and fumbled behind him for the handle, relieved when he felt the cold metal in his grasp. 'I'm going to fetch my coat. I'll be ready when you are.' He got himself out of there.

Gudlaugur was wide awake now. Curiosity, no doubt. He tensed when he saw Huldar but managed to wait until he got to his desk before asking what was up, rather than yelling it across the open-plan office for all to hear, as he would no doubt have liked to.

'Almost certainly bad news. The body of a teenage girl has turned up. The description fits Rósa.'

The excitement faded from Gudlaugur's face. His shoulders drooped and he looked exhausted and crushed. 'Shit.' He rubbed his face, then splayed his fingers and looked through them at Huldar. 'Where was she found?'

Huldar realised he'd forgotten to ask. 'That's all I know. I'm going to the scene with Erla. I'll have more information later, if you haven't gone home by then.'

'I'll be here. If it's Rósa, there's no point continuing with the search, so no more night shifts. Should I let Rafn know? He was going to do another circuit of town this evening and he asked me to come along.'

'As long as you tell him nothing's confirmed yet.' Huldar pulled on his coat, though he knew he might have to wait a bit longer for Erla to be ready. He found it easier to deal with misfortune this way. In his coat he felt ready for action – or he looked ready, at least. Inside, he was gutted. He had been banking on their finding Rósa alive. The alternative hadn't seriously occurred to him, even though he'd raised the possibility. The fact that the bad news had come from Erla did nothing to help matters. It wasn't as if death and new life cancelled each other out. When it came down to it, one person didn't come into the world to take another's place.

The fact was, he was shattered by the news.

So shattered, that when Freyja rang, he couldn't disguise the flatness in his voice. But she didn't seem to notice anything, so her psychologist's insight clearly wasn't working. She got straight to the point.

'I came across an interesting fact about Rósa yesterday. It was in an old recording of a session she had with a therapist. I wanted to tell you, though I'm not allowed to say exactly what it is. Not yet. I have to apply for an exception to my duty of confidentiality, which is a Herculean task. But, if I were you, I'd take another look at Rósa's connection to Bergur. There may be some link dating from before she was placed at his care home and before Tristan mentioned him to her.' Freyja added quickly: 'I'm not violating confidentiality by telling you that.'

Huldar exhaled slowly. 'Thanks for that, Freyja. Look, things are a bit hectic here. I'll have to talk to you later.'

'Oh.' Freyja sounded like a concert-goer who was standing, ticket in hand, outside the venue when it was announced that the singer had a sore throat and the show had been cancelled. 'Oh.'

Huldar hesitated, then decided to tell her: 'If the duty of confidentiality is with regard to Rósa, the situation may have changed. That's to say, if it only applies to the living.'

There was a long silence.

Chapter 23

Saturday

The sky was mirrored in the smooth sheet of water and an almost uncanny stillness hung over the scene. The modest summer houses dotting the shores of the lake appeared to be shut up and empty. There was no crying of moorland birds or any other sign of life. Even the police officers kept their voices to a murmur on the rare occasions that any of them opened their mouths. In spite of the all-encompassing beauty of the mountains, the lake, the green meadows and pockets of trees, it was the most depressing scene they had attended in a long time.

The slight figure was floating face down in shallow water at the southern end of the lake, one arm stretched towards the jutting grassy bank, as if to prevent her from drifting out into the middle. Dark hair spread out from the back of her head, seeming to hover as it was lifted by the gentle ripples. Her head had been turned just enough to establish that it was indeed Rósa and not some other girl in similar clothes.

The man who found her had been heading south along the road past Lake Hafravatn, thirteen kilometres to the east of Reykjavík, when he'd spotted a dark-blue coat floating close to the bank, at a point where it was possible to drive down to the water's edge. He had immediately pulled over and jumped out to take a closer look. The moment he saw that it was a person, he had waded into the water without stopping to think, his first reaction being to rescue them. But when he reached her, he realised that it was too late. Neither the kiss of life nor CPR would work now. He had let go of her shoulder and her body had fallen back into the same position as before. He had been so stunned that it had taken him three attempts to dial the number of emergency services. Now the man was sitting in the back of the police car, his legs soaked, shivering from cold and shock. Soon, he would be allowed to go home, which was where he had been heading when he made the discovery. He had been called to his father's sickbed at an old people's home in Mosfellsbær, north of Reykjavík, and decided to take the longer – usually more scenic – route past the lake on his way home to Nordlingaholt, the newest estate on the eastern edge of the city.

Huldar was hanging back, watching the Forensics team and photographer at work. Erla had waded out into the lake with them. Her boots had long since filled with water but she didn't seem to care. Every now and then she looked up and their eyes met. He didn't smile or wave in acknowledgement and neither did she. They both had other things on their minds.

Huldar took a deep breath and gazed over at the summer houses on the northern shore. There were no lights on yet or any other sign of occupation. A handful of cars had driven past since their arrival but only one had stopped. Huldar had gone over and told the driver to move along.

He knew the lake fairly well, having fished for trout here several times with his mates and once with one of his nephews. He had tried to scare the boy with tales of the *nykur* or water monster that was supposed to live in the depths, but it seemed today's kids weren't afraid of monsters. The boy had been unimpressed by his description of a grey horse with hooves that faced backwards, and said there was no way he'd be fooled into climbing onto its back and being dragged down to a watery death. The boy had sat there on the bank and continued fishing without turning a hair. Stories about the creaking and groaning of the ice in winter when the *nykur* was trying to break its way through to the surface, or about the underground channel that supposedly connected the lake to Tjörnin in the centre of Reykjavík, had left the boy completely unmoved. In the end, Huldar had been forced to admit to himself that the *nykur* was a pretty lame kind of monster.

When it came down to it, reality was far grimmer than any imaginary terrors. His nephew was more likely to have shrunk back from the water if Huldar had described the scene that was before his eyes now.

'What do you reckon? Did he drive her here and drown her, or just dispose of her body in the lake?' One of the scene-of-crime team, who appeared to be surplus to requirements, had come over to stand beside him. His voice seemed unnecessarily loud to Huldar. At times like this it was more appropriate to keep it down.

Huldar surveyed the lay-by that was just large enough for two vehicles. 'Hard to tell,' he said curtly. 'We'll see.'

He was in no mood to chat and hoped the man would bugger off. If he'd felt like it, he could have told the guy that in his opinion the murderer had probably just dumped the body there. It was far too close to the road to have been the scene of the killing. However off the beaten track it was, there was always a risk that someone might drive past. Then there were the summer houses. Although no one appeared to be using them at present, the spot was too overlooked. And from his fishing trips, Huldar also remembered how well sound travelled across the lake. If Rósa had screamed, the noise would have sounded as close as if it was coming from the deck of one of the summer houses. Anyone staying there would have looked outside to see what was going on.

'Terrible case.' The man still hadn't got the message, in spite of Huldar's terse replies. 'I understand it's the girl they've been doing the big search for. You have to ask yourself what's happening to this country. She was only just sixteen.'

'Mm.' Huldar pulled out a cigarette in the hope that the man would be put off by second-hand smoke. No such luck.

'Ah, a hardcore smoker, I see. I vape myself.' The man extracted a Vape pen from his pocket and began producing clouds of steam. 'Do you think she's been dead long?'

'No. I doubt it.' Huldar had already thought about this. It seemed unlikely that the murderer would have waited long before disposing of her body. Rigor mortis normally peaked twelve hours after death, lasted for another twelve, then receded over the next twelve. Transporting a body in an average-sized family car during that phase was easier said than done. Of course, it was possible the perpetrator had been driving a van or pick-up, but even then it wouldn't have been simple. He would still have had to manoeuvre her into the back without being seen. Dead bodies were unwieldy objects.

From watching his colleagues' activities in the water, Huldar had got the impression that Rósa's body was at peak rigidity, though the pathologist would be a better judge of that, of course. But Huldar wasn't expecting a very precise time of death as the cold water was bound to affect the calculations and no one knew how long she had been lying there or how long her body might have been hidden somewhere else before-hand. As nothing was yet known of her movements prior to her death, it wouldn't be possible to rely on her stomach contents either. If you could pinpoint the time of a victim's last meal, you could assess how far the food had been digested and work out an estimated time of death from that. Dead bodies don't digest.

'Who would do a thing like that?' The man blew out a cloud so thick, it reminded Huldar of the vapour that billows out of a cooling tower. 'I mean, what's wrong with people?'

'Plenty. There's plenty wrong with some people.' Huldar wouldn't have had any more to contribute on this theme even if he'd been in the mood to chat. He just couldn't get his head round the cases they were currently dealing with. CID were getting nowhere with the investigation of Brynjólfur's death and Huldar couldn't have been the only one who'd been staking everything on hearing Rósa's account of her visit to his container that evening – assuming the visit had ever happened. It was hard to place any trust in the statement of a half-blind witness who had been so high that he saw four people when only three were standing in front of him. Well, they'd never get a chance to hear Rósa's testimony now.

And that wasn't all. This tragic twist in the girl's tale had left him so shaken up that he was in no state to process Erla's news. He had blown his chance to ask the million-dollar question and it was hard to see how he'd ever get another. Erla couldn't stand it when people stuck their noses into her business. She'd never let down her guard again.

How far along was she? Who was the father? Would she bring up the child alone? How long would she be off on maternity leave? Did anyone else know or was it a secret? Might she be planning not to keep the child? Would she ask for a transfer back to the regular police while it was young? And if she did, what then? Who would take over from her?

His mind tormented by an endless stream of questions, Huldar puffed away beside his companion who had mercifully shut up at last. They watched in silence as their colleagues waded around in the water. The photographer, who seemed to have finished, climbed out onto the bank and began to take shots of the immediate surroundings. He took particular care over a patch of dried mud next to the gravel-surfaced lay-by. It looked untouched and Huldar guessed that no one had walked or driven over it since the last time it had rained. Still, better to err on the safe side. There were no tyre tracks or signs that Rósa had been dragged along the ground, nor were there any footprints. The perpetrator must have had the sense to stick to the gravel.

'When do you think they'll pull her out?'

'Soon.' Huldar had no idea.

'Perhaps she was drowned in the lake?'

'No. She didn't drown.' Huldar took a last drag on his cigarette, then added: 'If she'd drowned, there wouldn't be any air in her lungs and she'd have sunk. To start with, anyway. Same as if her body had been put in the water face up: her lungs would have gradually emptied and she'd have sunk, only to float up later. But her body's clearly not at that stage. Which means she wasn't drowned and the person who dumped her here wasn't used to disposing of bodies in water. Assuming the plan was for her to sink.'

The vaper, encouraged by this long speech, took it as an invitation to resume his questioning. 'So, in other words, he could have dumped her in the lake in a different place and she could have drifted here?'

'Sure. Quite possibly.' Huldar regretted having encouraged the man and didn't intend to fall into that trap again. He needed peace and quiet to think. The vaper, getting the message at last, didn't ask any further questions.

Erla waved to the men who were standing by with the stretcher. It was time to remove the body and take it to the pathology lab. With any luck, some evidence would turn up in the post-mortem, more than had been found here at the scene, anyway. Huldar wondered whether Erla would be able to attend or if her morning sickness would prevent her. He shuddered when it occurred to him that she would probably ask him to go in her place. He hoped to God she'd be able to tough it out.

Erla waded to shore and made a beeline for the Forensics van, water sloshing from her boots at every step. The rear doors were open and she perched on the back to remove her boots and empty them, before putting them back on.

Huldar left the vaper and walked over to join her, determined not to show the embarrassment he still felt following their conversation earlier, though he knew it would be tricky. Erla was sure to regret having confided in him and was guaranteed to be all weird, like it was his fault. Though frankly, if she'd given him the choice, he'd have preferred to have been kept out of her private life. They were both hopelessly clumsy when it came to touchy-feely emotional stuff, and in this case two minuses did not make a plus.

'We need to comb the banks. And interview the summer-house owners. The choice is yours.' She was avoiding eye contact.

'I'll comb the banks.'

'We're talking three kilometres. At least.'

'Fine.' It would do him good to go for a walk and concentrate on what was immediately in front of him. Nothing complicated, nothing messily emotional or intangible.

'Then take that guy with you – the one you were smoking with. The rest have got their hands full.'

Erla didn't give him a chance to protest. Instead of the peaceful walk he had envisaged, Huldar was now doomed to trek all the way round the lake, being bombarded by pointless speculation and questions. Unless he got lucky and the guy was taken by the *nykur*.

Erla was watching the lake over his shoulder. Huldar turned to see the men struggling to lift Rósa onto the stretcher. The conditions were challenging and nobody seemed to have come suitably dressed for the job. The men carrying the stretcher appeared unhappy about the fact their boots weren't high enough to keep their feet dry, whereas the others had got used to the icy water and had no doubt lost all feeling in their toes some time ago.

They succeeded in the end, and the murmur of talk fell silent as Rósa's stiff body was carried to the ambulance.

It was impossible not to be reminded of the scene when Binni's body had been brought out of his container; too short a time had elapsed in between.

Huldar had found that scene bleak enough but this was worse, so much worse. Binni had at least lived to adulthood. And although you couldn't envy his lot, he could theoretically have taken charge of his own life. Rósa, on the other hand, had been the plaything of fate; nothing she said or did could have changed the situation she was in now. It was impossible to know how she would have turned out, but Huldar thought she would probably have made a go of it. Gone to university and become a scientist, wielding a test-tube in search of a cure for cancer. Or trained to be an actress and trodden the red carpet in a low-cut dress. Or followed in Lína's footsteps and ended up as Police Commissioner.

Or simply have been happy, without needing to be at the pinnacle of whatever profession she chose for herself.

'I want to find the person who did this and I want to find him now.' Erla was speaking through gritted teeth. 'We'll work day and night until we do. If necessary, I'll drag that lot back from holiday by their bloody ears.'

'You can count on me.' Huldar's words sounded hollow, even to him. What good was his contribution? Did he think he was going to trip over the murderer's ID lying about on the shore of the lake? Solve the crime during his ramble? Sadly, there was no likelihood of that.

Huldar tried to catch Erla's eye to convey the tacit message that she could also count on him with regard to her pregnancy. If there was anything he could do to make life easier for her, of course he would do it. Finally, she met his gaze. She knew him well enough to guess what he was going to say even as he opened his mouth.

'No. Not a word. I'm not discussing it with you.'

'Discussing what?' Playing the role of the innocent, Huldar hurriedly pulled something else out of his hat. 'I was just going to say that Freyja's found evidence in the Child Protection Agency records to suggest that Rósa knew Bergur, the care-home manager, before she was placed with him.'

'How?' Erla's curiosity was roused.

'I don't have any details. The information's subject to

confidentiality. But it might be relevant to . . .' He jerked his chin towards the ambulance.

Erla frowned. 'I don't see how. But who knows? Get hold of the information. I don't give a shit about confidentiality. The girl's dead.'

Huldar nodded without speaking.

Erla stood up. 'One more thing.'

'What?' Huldar was ready to do anything. The only way of getting over the grimness of this tragedy was to work. To keep on slogging away until they found some answers. Find an outlet for the rage that was seething inside him and already pushing the sadness aside. 'I'm ready to do anything.'

'Good. I need you to attend the post-mortem. It's happening on Monday and my sickness is worst in the mornings. I can't have people finding out that I puked up in the middle of it.'

Huldar forced his frozen facial muscles into a smile of acquiescence. He nodded. He had no choice.

Chapter 24

Sunday

Tristan peered at his phone. The screen was covered in a spider's web of cracks but he couldn't afford to replace it, let alone buy a new phone. As soon as he got a proper job, the first thing he'd do was go out and get one, even if it cost every last króna of his pay.

But in the circumstances, he couldn't get a full-time job – he found it hard enough taking the few shifts he was offered at the pizza place. He had other, more important duties, which operated on a quite different timetable.

He had to look after his mother.

Tristan avoided thinking about how unfair it was. There was no point. Only sometimes he couldn't help it: most of his contemporaries were so lucky that the comparison really hurt.

Their parents fussed over them, not vice versa.

There was nothing of interest visible between the cracks on his screen, just notifications of likes and comments on his recent posts. No message from Rósa, as he had been expecting. But that was nothing new. She went her own way and refused to be pushed around, as intractable, in a way, as his mother's addiction.

'Drink this.' Tristan handed his mother a smoothie. He

had blended *skyr* with some frozen berries that had been on special offer. 'It'll make you feel better.'

'Thanks.' His mother sat up, took the drink and sipped it. Then she put the glass down on the coffee table and lay back on the sofa, spreading the blanket over herself. The glass would remain there until evening when Tristan took it to the sink. 'What about . . . ?'

'I couldn't find any painkillers.' Tristan was lying. He knew exactly where he had hidden them. They weren't supposed to be addictive but it didn't pay to take any chances if his mother was to stay clean. It wouldn't be the first time something had happened to make her relax her vigilance and lose sight of her goal. 'Or any cigarettes either.'

His mother looked up and met his eye. Her face was red and her eyes were unnaturally bright, as if she had a fever. 'Would you mind going to the newsagent?'

'There aren't any newsagents around here any more, remember? Only the supermarket, and they don't sell fags.' This was a lie too but it was more likely to work than telling the truth. They couldn't afford to smoke – either of them.

'Are you going out this evening?' The question was supposed to sound innocent but Tristan knew exactly what she was doing. She wanted him out of the way so she could get her hands on something. She'd done it only the other day. Come home so off her head that she'd forgotten to hide what she'd been up to. He had flushed the rest of the pills down the toilet while she was sleeping it off.

'No. I'm staying in. We can watch Netflix together.'

'Oh. OK.' She did her best to hide her disappointment. 'Have we got any Valium? It would help me sleep. I need to rest.'

'No. We haven't got any.'

'Flunitrazepam?'

Tristan shook his head.

'Imovane?'

'No. We haven't got anything. Not even ibuprofen. I told you.'

'Oh.'

Tristan turned away. If he started to feel sorry for her, he would only end up relenting and fetching her a sleeping pill. Pretending he'd discovered it at the back of the cupboard. 'Drink the smoothie. It'll make you feel better and then you'll be able to get to sleep.'

His mother nodded but made no effort to reach for the glass. Instead, she pulled the blanket up to her chin. It wasn't cold in the flat, in fact it was too hot for him, but his mother was so painfully thin that she was perpetually freezing. If she went outside, she had to be well wrapped up or her fingers, and sometimes her face, would literally turn blue, even in summer.

'I'm just going online for a bit. Will you be OK?'

'Sure.' There was no conviction in her voice. 'Could you turn on the TV for me? Just whatever's on.'

He did as she asked. They only had the state broadcasting service and Netflix, but his mother's English was so poor that if she was alone, she found it hard to watch programmes or films without subtitles. The state channel was showing sport but that would have to do. With any luck she'd find it so boring that it would send her to sleep. He put the remote control on the coffee table beside the glass, knowing she wouldn't touch it any more than she would the smoothie.

Tristan went into his room and threw himself down on his

bed. It was time to wash the sheets but he had prioritised his mother's bedding when he'd put on a wash the day before. They had been stained with blood from a bad coughing fit.

He pulled over the battered laptop given to him by a friend who'd received a smart new one as a confirmation present. Tristan had found it excruciatingly embarrassing to have to accept the gift of the clapped-out machine, but his longing for a computer had outweighed even his embarrassment. Nevertheless, casually enquiring what his friend intended to do with the old one had been one of the most difficult questions he'd ever had to ask – and he'd had to say a lot of pathetic, humiliating things in his life.

He opened the laptop carefully as the hinges on the screen were on the point of giving way. Tristan didn't know what he'd do when the machine finally conked out. It couldn't be long now. It already had to be permanently plugged in as the battery had died. The next thing to break might not be so easy to get around. But seeing as he couldn't afford to replace the screen on his phone, he would hardly be able to scrape together the cash for a new laptop. He even had to use his neighbour's wi-fi because he and his mother couldn't afford an internet connection themselves. He'd struck a deal with the guy next door that he would take his turn at cleaning the stairwell in return for the password to his wi-fi. This was an excellent bargain for the neighbour, whose data allowance was almost unlimited. It worked out well for Tristan too, since no one bothered to clean the communal areas properly anyway.

It would have been far better to have their own internet connection and avoid this hassle but they lived on his mother's benefit payments, which didn't stretch that far. Not even when supplemented with the peanuts he earned at the pizza place. Rent, food, electricity, heating, clothes, phone, bus, doctors and related costs. School books for him and cigarettes for her when things were good. Which they rarely were. If he watched every króna they could survive February, but months with thirty-one days were harder. Somehow, though, they just about managed. Except when his mother fell off the wagon. Then everything went to pieces.

The small amount of money they had went nowhere near satisfying her need for drugs. These burnt through krónur faster than a woman with a shopping addiction let loose in a shoe emporium. He knew how she went about keeping herself in drugs when their bank account was empty but he preferred not to think about that. There were limits. He just prayed that those days were over.

Tristan waited while the laptop booted up. It took so long that his mind wandered. He hoped Rósa had got in touch and it was just that his useless phone hadn't received her message. She was the best friend he had, because she understood him. All the other people he knew lived a life wrapped in cotton wool, but not her. If anything, she had been dealt an even worse hand in life than him. At least he still had his mum, whereas Rósa was alone in the world. However flawed his mother was, she was better than nothing. Anyway, she was going to get her act together, one of these days. It couldn't be that far off. She had to stay clean for six months before she could undergo treatment for hepatitis C and she knew that it was now or never. She would do it for herself and for him. She had shown before that she was capable of it. If only her fellow addicts would leave her alone – not to mention the people who had a vested interest in keeping her hooked on drugs. Tristan hated them. More than he could possibly express. At times the hatred was so overpowering that he thought it would burn him up. Everything else faded into the background and, while it lasted, the fury was so violent that it felt as if it was hammering on the inside of his skull, demanding to break out.

Rósa had helped him cope with it. As she had with so many other things. Although she was younger than him, she was in many ways more mature and steady. She was very clever too and did well at school. It was she who had encouraged him to continue with his education and helped him when he couldn't make any sense of his homework. Thanks to her, he'd managed to struggle through a whole term's worth of credits.

The advice Rósa gave him for dealing with his fits of violent rage was to concentrate on breathing and revel in the certainty that the targets of his hatred would get their comeuppance in the end. That was life. He just had to sit back and wait. Of course, the alternative was to help the chain of events along a bit – or a lot. It was his choice. Either do nothing. Or do something.

Rósa herself had chosen to do something.

After going from pillar to post, trying in vain to get the authorities to re-open the inquiry into her mother's death, Rósa had taken matters into her own hands. She had given up on the useless authorities and the adult world when her search for justice had hit a brick wall. Her eyes glowed every time she spoke of her plan, yet she didn't seem able to focus on anything while she was talking. Her pupils darted back and forth, up and down, from side to side, as if she was watching a drunken fly. Perhaps that was why he found it so hard to discuss the business of her mother with her. Things didn't improve when her father got dragged into the story and the logic became even more warped. By pretending to listen, and changing the subject whenever possible, he managed to cling to the belief that she knew what she was talking about. That was good enough for him. Friends stood by each other, through thick and thin. Rósa had said that too.

The computer emitted its stupid chime to inform him that it was ready. Tristan went straight to his messages but Rósa hadn't been in touch. He stared at the screen, unable to shake off the unsettling feeling that something was wrong. She had been her usual self when they'd said goodbye on Friday evening, and promised to get in touch. The plan had been to meet up at the weekend, but it was Sunday now and he still hadn't heard from her. It was typical of her to drop out of contact from time to time, but not at all like her to break a promise.

To distract himself, Tristan checked his social media accounts. It was how he kept track of what was going on, both in his circle of few remaining friends and in Iceland and the outside world. He couldn't be bothered to read the news sites with their endless reports about politicians breaking promises, eruptions that didn't happen, negative stuff about tourists, wittering on about which paint colours were 'in' and the latest Trump scandal.

Noticing that he had been tagged in a discussion that had received a lot of comments from his friends, he opened the thread and read the first post. His heart missed a beat and he slammed the laptop shut. Then he opened it again, after recovering enough to be able to breathe normally. He could hear Rósa's deep, husky voice saying: *Just breathe. In, out. In, out. Nothing else matters.*

But she had been wrong. There was so much else that mattered apart from breathing. Like the fact that, according to the news, she was dead. That mattered to her and it mattered to him. Whereas breathing meant nothing to her now.

Tristan clicked on the link to the news report containing Rósa's name. He ignored the question from the person who had posted the entry: *Tristan, isn't that your weird friend who's dead? That Rósa?* Nor did he read the comments below, since they might contain anything from sympathy to jokes about her death. He couldn't face that.

The news confirmed in detail what he had read in the post. Rósa's body had been found and the police were treating her death as murder. There couldn't be many sixteen-year-old girls called Rósa Thrastardóttir, could there? He tried sending her a message, in spite of their tacit understanding that it was always Rósa who instigated any contact. But of course there were exceptions, and what better time for that than now?

He stared at his computer screen and phone in turn, hoping against hope for a reply. Nothing happened.

His breathing grew increasingly fitful and laboured. His ribcage rose and fell as if he were surfacing after spending too long underwater, yet he felt as if he were suffocating. He saw his room in its true light again and closed his eyes to avoid having to see his soulless, ugly, empty surroundings. The desk from the Good Shepherd charity shop that had been scrawled all over with marker pen by its former owner in a fit of madness, with the drawer you couldn't open. The yellowing light bulb dangling from the ceiling. The World Cup poster, a present from his mother, that he had stuck on the wall to please her, although he had no interest in football, let alone the national team. She had waited in such suspense to see his reaction that he'd had no choice but to fake gratitude.

He had to get out of here. Away from the laptop and the news that had knocked the ground out from under his fragile happiness. He flung the machine aside, not caring that it couldn't withstand any further damage. Then he stood up and waited a moment, until he was sure his knees wouldn't buckle, before walking to his bedroom door. One step at a time. Breathing in, breathing out.

That way he would make it to the sitting room and his mum.

She needed him. Every day. Always.

But now the tables had been turned: she had to be there for him. There was nobody else. He clung to the door handle, feeling a tear running down his cheek, followed by another. He could taste salt.

Tristan opened the door to the hallway and called into the sitting room: 'Mum?'

Chapter 25

Sunday

The young man rooted around in the metal wall cabinet, searching for Salvör's keys. He hadn't commented when she'd shown him her photo ID, saying that she couldn't remember the number of her storage unit. Nor did he seem remotely surprised that she was coming to check on her belongings for the first time since she had shut the door on them ten years ago and asked reception to keep the keys. He had looked her up without a word and given her the number of the unit. Presumably she wasn't unique in this. Apart from the two of them, the big warehouse on Grandi was empty and so was the car park in front of it, though there must have been more than a hundred storage units on the site. But then, by its very nature, the storage facility was used for things people no longer needed, and the level of activity around them was correspondingly low.

The man closed the cabinet and handed Salvör two keys on a metal ring. 'It's on the second floor. The lift's at the front, by the stairs. There are plenty of trolleys if you need to move anything heavy to your car. Just take what you need,' he recited, as if he'd said it countless times before. His dealings with the rare customers who came by were no doubt limited to these few standard phrases.

Salvör selected a good, heavy-duty trolley that looked as if it would have room for all the boxes in the unit. She'd packed them so long ago that she couldn't remember exactly how many there were, only that it had been quite a lot. She hoped she was wrong. One's memory has a tendency to exaggerate, making snowfalls heavier, summers warmer, slopes steeper and road distances longer in times gone by.

She hauled the trolley to the lift and pressed the button for the second floor. The place was a maze but with the help of the signs she eventually tracked down her unit. Heaving a deep breath, she inserted the key in the padlock on the bright-yellow door and undid the latch. But instead of pulling the door open, she stood quite still for a moment or two, bracing herself. She knew she was about to be hit by the smell of her old life with Binni, which wasn't a prospect she relished. However much she had grown to hate the man and the direction his life had taken, the fact was that she had loved him once. With all her heart. Or at least that's how she remembered it, though it wasn't only tangible things that the memory had a tendency to distort, amplify and shower with glitter.

When Salvör finally steeled herself to open the door, she was met by nothing but a stale, enclosed smell. The odour of dusty cardboard. She stared at the stack of boxes and sighed, conscious of the irony that Binni's later existence should have ended only a few hundred metres from the remnants of his old life.

She picked up the first box and loaded it onto the trolley. But the silence in the warehouse got her thinking that maybe it would be simpler to go through the contents there and then. Otherwise she would have to lug all the boxes out to her car, then unload them and cart them into her flat, then, once she'd gone through them, she'd have to carry them back out to her car and drive them down to the police station. Whereas if she got the job over with now, she would save herself a considerable amount of effort. She was unlikely to be disturbed or in anyone's way here. The worst that could happen was that the receptionist might wonder what had happened to her, but in that case he could just check that she was all right. He would have no reason to comment when he saw what had delayed her. She decided to get the task over with.

The first two boxes contained clothes: jackets, shirts and trousers that she remembered well. She had even bought some of them herself for her ex. He had never been keen on clothes shopping. Overwhelmed by a sudden rush of nostalgia, she had to remind herself sternly that she hadn't come here to finger his crumpled garments and indulge in reminiscences. Her purpose was to make sure there was nothing in the boxes that could cause her children grief. That was all.

Salvör removed the garments one by one, checked all the pockets, then folded them neatly before putting them back. At the time she had been so overcome with bitterness and rage that she had ripped the clothes out of Binni's cupboards and drawers and stuffed them into the boxes any old how. She'd just wanted to get rid of everything in the flat that reminded her of him. But she found nothing in the pockets apart from a half-empty packet of dried-out cigarettes, fifty-three krónur in change and a few old receipts. She hastily replaced them so the police wouldn't suspect her of having gone through the clothes. She would have liked to drive the boxes straight to the recycling bins at the dump and spare the police the thankless task of going through them. But she had mentioned clothes when she told them about Binni's belongings, so she would have to make sure they were there, to avoid arousing suspicion.

At the bottom of the last box of clothes she found a plastic bag, knotted at the top. Salvör vaguely remembered finding it at the back of Binni's wardrobe and chucking it into the box. At the time, she hadn't cared what was in the bag; anger had sucked all the oxygen from her blood vessels, smothering all other feelings, including curiosity.

Now, she untied the knot and peered into the bag. More clothes. She shook the bag and a pair of jeans, a checked shirt and a white T-shirt tumbled out onto the painted concrete floor. When she picked up the jeans, she saw that there was a large stain on the crotch and at the top of the thighs, and dropped them involuntarily on the floor. Ugh. Urine. That's why Binni had hidden them from her. Then she narrowed her eyes, frowning at them thoughtfully. Binni had never owned a pair of jeans like that. Let alone a checked shirt. She picked it up by pinching the fabric between finger and thumb, and held it at arm's length. If there was urine on the trousers, God knows what there might be on the shirt front.

Quite right. There was a dark patch on the shirt as well. She forced herself to hold it by the shoulders and spread it out. A large, round, brown stain was revealed, reaching from the waist to just below the breast. Salvör peered at it, puzzled. What was it? Not vomit, and certainly not urine. Possibly gravy or red wine. Or blood. Looking back at the jeans, she realised that of course the stain on them wasn't urine. It was as dark as the one on the front of the shirt. She put the shirt down and examined the T-shirt. There was a similar stain on that, in more or less the same place. If it was blood, it had seeped through the material, either from the inside out or the outside in.

Where had these clothes come from? Salvör put down the T-shirt and picked up the jeans again, making a face as she did so. She poked her fingers into both back pockets without finding anything. In one of the front pockets, however, there were some folded scraps of paper that she smoothed out. A credit-card receipt and a bill. At the bottom of the bill was the same kind of dark stain as on the clothes, while the top part was clean like the receipt and legible. It was a bill from a restaurant in Akureyri for the purchase of a hamburger, chips, and two beers, one large, one small. The name of the person who had placed the order was printed at the top. *Table five, Thröstur.* She checked the date.

Salvör threw it down in horror.

The date fitted with the fateful trip Binni had made with his friend to the north-east of Iceland. If she wasn't mistaken, Thröstur had died that very day. She had been holding a receipt for the man's last meal. The clothes at her feet were the ones he had died in, which was extremely odd given that he had drowned. Salvör stared thoughtfully at the blood-stains. It was possible that he had suffered a major wound to his stomach as he was floating down the rocky river. Perhaps that explained it. She shuddered.

How the hell had his clothes ended up in Binni's possession? Were people stripped at the scene of an accident? If she remembered right, he had been dead by the time help had arrived. What reason would they have had to undress a dead man?

There were no answers to be found in the heap of clothes.

She stuffed the garments back into the bag and knotted the top again. But she didn't put it back in the box. These clothes definitely weren't going to the police. The last thing she needed was for them to start asking questions about a ten-year-old accident.

Salvör rolled up her sleeves. Her efforts hadn't been completely pointless after all. She got down to examining the rest of the boxes.

These took rather longer to go through. They were full of papers and other bits and bobs from Binni's study. She had to pore over every page and inspect every item, just to be on the safe side. But she didn't find anything apart from a credit-card statement that she laid to one side, then tucked into her wallet. She and Binni used to have a joint account and the statement showed all her transactions as well. However innocent, they were none of the police's business. Besides, Binni's payments couldn't be of any significance to his murder investigation. Every other transaction was at the state off-licence and if they needed proof of his drinking, they would have to be satisfied with her word for it.

The stack of boxes was mounting up on the trolley. How on earth could she have thought they would all fit in the car? Admittedly, she was in an estate car and it was possible to put the seats down, but it was still unrealistic to think she could squeeze this lot into the back. Perhaps she should make two trips and take some of the clothes boxes to the dump on the way. The police needn't know, and she was doing them a favour really. They wouldn't ask any questions, as long as they got a couple of boxes of clothes, if they even remembered that she'd mentioned clothing. They would hardly need the whole lot.

Yes, that would be the best solution. They could hardly expect her to rent a van to transport the boxes to the police station. She had already done more than could be expected of a member of the public. She deliberately ignored the fact that the police had offered to fetch Binni's effects themselves. All this effort was to serve her own interests – hers and her children's.

She wasn't going to put the plastic bag in the recycling bin. There was something revolting about giving away clothes that the owner had died in. And it wouldn't be worth the expense of getting them cleaned. Yet, strangely, she couldn't bring herself to throw them away. If Thröstur's daughter was after information about how her father died, you never know, the clothes might be important to her. She was too young to be given them now, but perhaps Salvör could see that she got the bag later, when she was older. By then, the inquiry into Binni's death would hopefully have faded into just one more upsetting memory of her ex-husband. It wasn't a decision Salvör wanted to make now, though. She laid the bag aside to prevent it from getting mixed up with the stuff that was to go to the police or the dump. Her basement storage unit at home may have been rather full, but there was room for one more dirty little plastic bag.

The decision filled her with renewed energy. She was almost done. There were only a few boxes left on the floor of the storage unit and it looked as if she might even make it home in time for the news. But the boxes turned out to be full of papers, files, receipts and statements which would take ages to wade through. She probably wouldn't get to see the news after all.

By the time she got to the last box, her back was aching

from all the bending and her bag was stuffed full of papers she'd rather the police didn't get their hands on. Since most related to her and Binni's finances, there was nothing in them that could possibly be of interest to them anyway.

Her spine cracked as she stretched. The sound was unnerving but she felt better afterwards. Then she rubbed her sore shoulder and tried to summon up the energy to finish the task.

The last box was lying on its side at the back of the unit, as if it had been chucked inside, over the other boxes. Or had it perhaps been teetering on top of the stack and fallen down behind them? It was different from the others she had sorted through. They had all been identical as she had bought a job lot from IKEA and assembled them herself for the clear-out. But the remaining box was smaller and more battered-looking. It was from the state off-licence, labelled front and back with the name of a cheap red wine. Salvör frowned, puzzled, then remembered that Binni had rung her up years ago and asked if she could store a few things for him. Her initial reaction had been a flat refusal, but then she had taken pity on him and directed him to the storage unit. He had thanked her and she had let the company know that he was to be given access to the unit. It hadn't occurred to her that he would actually take her up on the offer, but apparently he had.

The box was taped shut, top and bottom. Salvör struggled slightly as she tore it open, then immediately put a hand over her nose. The contents stank like fish slime or a dirty beach. She assumed it must be old fishing tackle; hooks maybe, or a priest – a club for stunning salmon – with rotten bits of flesh still attached to it. Perhaps Binni had got hold of some fishing gear after he'd taken to sleeping rough and started catching his own food, then lost enthusiasm for it but hadn't wanted to throw the valuable tackle away. When Salvör looked inside, however, it turned out to be nothing of the sort. After lifting a layer of crumpled paper out of the top, she was confronted with something totally unexpected.

It was a doll, if you could even call it that any more – all she could see was matted hair on a partially bald head, and shoulders and legs covered in small barnacles and dead worms. It belonged under a jetty, not in a child's toy box.

Salvör used the paper as a glove to lift the doll out. It must be the source of the nasty smell and she had no wish to touch it with her bare hands.

Laying the doll on the floor, she stepped back a little, raising an arm to cover her nose and mouth, though the smell wasn't quite as strong as when she had first opened the box. Perhaps it had dispersed among the shining-clean aisles between the units. Hopefully it would be gone before the next person had any business on this floor.

She stared at the doll in bewilderment. Where had this horrible thing come from? And what on earth had Binni been doing with it? Why hadn't he just thrown it in the dustbin? All she could think of was that he must have been drunk, caught the doll on a hook or in a net and shoved it in a box, taping it shut to keep in the stench. Sometimes there was no rational explanation for people's behaviour, especially when alcohol was involved. One thing just led to another.

Once Salvör was sure the worst of the smell had dispersed, she bent down to take a closer look at the doll. There was a fine chain of what appeared to be tarnished silver hanging around its plastic neck and down over its chest where it vanished from view under a thick layer of barnacles.

Salvör shook her head and straightened up, feeling suddenly uncomfortably aware that she was the only person on the whole floor, in this maze of endless aisles. It was time to get moving. In any case, there was nothing to be gained from standing there, gawping at the doll. She could do that for hours, days, months even, without being any the wiser. Binni had taken the story of the doll with him to his grave.

Salvör stuffed the vile thing back in the box and shut the flaps, then put it on top of the other boxes on the trolley and set off in the direction of the lift.

Chapter 26

Sunday

The food tasted like cardboard. There was nothing actually wrong with it, but distress and a paralysing fear tended to affect the tastebuds. Frikki put his fork down after pushing the food around his plate to make it look as if he had eaten more than a single mouthful.

'Is everything OK?' His brother Fjalar met his eye across the table, his loaded fork poised halfway to his mouth.

'Yeah. Just a bit tired.' Frikki tried to force his stiff lips into a smile. Lowering his gaze, he reached for his glass and took a gulp of beer. He had asked for a sparkling water but as usual, Fjalar wouldn't hear of it.

'There's a bug going round,' their father chipped in, and the brothers waited for the inevitable: 'You two should get flu jabs.'

It was pointless reminding him that they hadn't started the latest round of flu vaccinations yet and were unlikely to do so until after New Year. Sometimes their father had to be allowed to talk bullshit if he wanted to. The brothers owed it to him, especially now that he was a lonely widower. Frikki just hoped he wouldn't start boring on about the hog roast parties he and their mother used to attend in Spain in the good old days. There were limits and Frikki had heard the stories more times than he could remember. But if Fjalar went on topping up their father's glass like that, there would be no escaping the tide of reminiscences. Their father tended to come over all nostalgic once the booze went to his head.

'No one's got flu, Dad. Frikki's just dying of frustration because he hasn't got a bird.' Fjalar winked at their father without making any attempt to hide it from Frikki.

'Aren't we all?' This was a bit near the knuckle from their father. Frikki felt briefly cheered, perhaps because the comment had annoyed Fjalar. His brother was in no position to take the piss out of Frikki's love life. Sure, Fjalar hooked up with a woman from time to time, but they rarely stuck around. 'Have you heard about something called Timber?' their father went on. 'I'm told that's where people look for partners these days. Maybe I ought to give it a go. You two definitely should.'

Frikki and Fjalar caught each other's eye and silently declared a truce. They had no intention of taking dating tips from their father and this overcame their irritation with each other.

Their father didn't notice anything. He shovelled a forkful of food into his mouth, swallowed and went on talking. Fortunately, though, he had changed the subject. 'Eat up, Frikki. Your brother's gone to the trouble of making a meal for us and if you're coming down with something, it's important to eat well.'

Since their mother had died, their father had taken over the role of doling out maternal advice that neither of them followed, any more than they had when their mother had done it.

Frikki put a tiny morsel of food on his fork and stuck it

in his mouth, to show willing. Anything to stop them nagging. 'I'm afraid I can't stay long.'

Fjalar put his fists on the table, knife and fork clenched upright in each. 'For Christ's sake! You could have told us before, while I still had the chance to move the meal to another day.'

Frikki knew perfectly well why his brother was so annoyed. He didn't want to be left alone with their drunk and maudlin father, having to endure his endless stories of long-ago hog roasts.

'What the hell's so urgent? Your work's not likely to call you on a Sunday.' Fjalar stabbed his fork into a chunk of meat and began violently sawing at it with his knife. 'It's not like you get weekend emergencies at the Marine Research Institute.'

'It has nothing to do with work.' Frikki cast around in vain for an excuse that would placate his brother. 'Something came up that I need to take care of. It's nothing I could have foreseen.'

'What? A blocked gutter?' Fjalar said with his mouth full, chewing as he spoke. He made no attempt to hide his displeasure, but then he never did. He had been an open book ever since he was a child. 'You've got to take the car in to be cleaned?'

'No.' Frikki left it at that. Once Fjalar was in a bad mood, there was no going back. It didn't matter what excuse he made, his brother wouldn't listen. If he'd said he was on his way to hospital to donate a kidney to save a child's life, Fjalar wouldn't have accepted it as a valid excuse.

But Frikki wasn't about to tell his father and brother the truth. They would be speechless if he confided in them that he was linked to the young girl whose body had just been found and whose name had now been released. If he started talking, there was a risk he wouldn't be able to stop. It wouldn't be fair to worry his father by telling him that he was afraid the police would soon be knocking on his door, asking why he had been sheltering the girl and hadn't got in touch when they appealed for information about her. Or, worse, that he was terrified he was about to be arrested, suspected of being involved in her murder. The worry was killing him. How was he supposed to explain his relationship with Rósa to the police when he didn't understand it himself? He supposed he had felt sorry for her and also in some way responsible for her psychological problems. If the doll had never landed in his net, Rósa might have found it easier to accept her mother's accident. But the idea for the fishing trip had been his.

No, the police would never buy this explanation. They would take it as read that he'd had some perverted interest in the kid. It was about the most horrible thing you could be suspected of. He would never be able to clear his name. The moment the rumour spread that he'd had a sexual relationship with the girl, his reputation would be destroyed, even if the investigation subsequently revealed that it wasn't true. The institute would find a pretext to sack him and he doubted he would ever be able to leave the house again.

No wonder his food tasted like cardboard.

Frikki excused himself and went to the toilet. He desperately needed to be alone for a minute to stop himself breaking down at the table. He stood in the little guest cloakroom, gripping the basin with both hands and staring down at the white china bowl. Focusing hard on breathing, he counted the round holes in the drain. Then he let go, raised his head and met his own gaze in the mirror. That was a mistake.

His pale, red-eyed face wasn't exactly an encouraging sight.

He splashed cold water on his cheeks, blew out a long breath, then did his best to force his features into a more natural, unconcerned expression. It worked to some extent. He was still pale and his eyes were still bloodshot, but anyone who didn't know him would think he was fine. It was just unfortunate that his present companions were the people who knew him best in the world.

Frikki emerged from the cloakroom. He didn't care if his father thought he had a stomach bug and started bombarding him with unsolicited advice.

No sooner had he stepped out into the hall than the phone started ringing in his pocket. He wasn't expecting any calls and when he saw a number he didn't recognise, his stomach lurched with fear. It was bound to be the police, calling him in for questioning or informing him of his imminent arrest.

While he was staring transfixed at his phone, wondering how horrendous his life was about to become, it rang a second, then a third time. From the dining room his brother bellowed at him to answer the bloody thing. Closing his eyes, Frikki did so.

An involuntary giggle of pure hysteria escaped him when it turned out to be the security company that looked after his house. The caller was momentarily taken aback, then he recovered and asked if Frikki was at home. The alarm had gone off and the man wanted to know if he had forgotten to enter the code. Hearing that this wasn't the case, he asked if Frikki would like the company to send round a security guard to check out the house.

It had happened before, more than once. Frikki had left a window open and the neighbour's fat Norwegian forest cat had squeezed in and set off the alarm. After the cat's first break-in, Frikki had agreed to a visit by a security guard and paid a fortune for the service. Ever since then he had said he would check on the situation himself.

The call had come at the perfect moment. Now he would have a genuine excuse to leave. Too bad he hadn't waited a few more minutes before announcing that he had to be off. Perhaps it was a sign that he shouldn't expect the worst. Perhaps the police wouldn't contact him after all. The thought cheered Frikki up a little.

Fjalar didn't look up when Frikki came back into the dining room with the excuse that now he really had to leave because his burglar alarm had gone off. But his father looked worried and opened his mouth, no doubt to share some advice about how to avoid visits from unscrupulous thieves. Frikki hastily forestalled him. 'It's probably just the neighbour's cat again but I'll have to go and see, all the same.' He went over to his brother, who was attacking his steak as if it was to blame for everything. Frikki laid a hand on his shoulder in an attempt to make peace. 'Thanks for the meal, Fjalar. Sorry about this. It won't happen again.'

Fjalar snorted. 'Yeah, right.'

Frikki didn't want to leave his brother like this. It would be trickier to make peace with him over the phone, but having their father on the sidelines, constantly interrupting, didn't make it any easier now. 'Could you walk to the door with me?' He gave Fjalar's shoulder a light slap and a squeeze. It was probably the closest physical contact they'd had since they'd hugged at their mother's funeral. The hug hadn't lasted long but they'd managed nevertheless to slap each other on the back a few times while it did.

Frikki's ploy seemed to work. Fjalar put down his knife and fork and got up. Frikki said a hurried goodbye to his father, then hastily left the dining room before the old man could get in another word.

'Sorry. Again.' Frikki hovered by the door to the hall where his coat was hanging on a peg.

'Yeah, yeah. Whatever.' Fjalar was still pissed off but didn't seem quite as angry as before. 'Another raincheck then?'

'It's my turn next.' As he stood face to face with Fjalar, Frikki felt a sudden wave of affection for his younger brother. In spite of their differences, they were connected by blood. 'Should we maybe set up a joint Tinder account? Brothers in search of sisters?'

Fjalar grinned, and with that the barriers were down. 'Yeah, right. Then you might be in with a chance at last; you could get off with the older sister of some chick who's crazy about me.'

'Or vice versa.' Frikki grinned back. The chances of this were slim. If he was arrested, they would be non-existent. But he could at least allow himself to enjoy the prospect while there was still hope. 'Next time you invite me to a party, I promise to chat up a girl.'

Fjalar gave him a brief smile. Everything was all right again between them. Yet Frikki still felt a bit melancholy. Behind every joke there was a grain of truth. They were standing beside a shelf on which Fjalar had placed framed photographs of himself; pictures he wanted his guests to see. From these it was apparent that Frikki wasn't the only one who ached for a long-term relationship. His brother had put up pictures of the only two women he had lived with in his life, though both relationships had been over a long time ago. His other girlfriends hadn't been accorded the same honour. But perhaps they would be relieved, because there was something a little disturbing about the way the pictures of the two women had been placed among Fjalar's most successful kills: Fjalar with a metre-long salmon, Fjalar with the carcases of eleven geese, Fjalar with a redfish weighing at least twelve to fifteen kilos, Fjalar with sixteen ptarmigan, Fjalar with a giant cod. Fjalar with Gudrún. Fjalar with Emilía.

Frikki was a little hurt that there was no picture of the brothers together. Or of their father and mother. Fjalar might as well have been an orphan. But then he was no different himself: he didn't put up pictures of his family at home or at work. Nor did any of the other men he worked with; only the occasional woman would have little framed photos of her children on her desk or as wallpaper on her computer. But the pictures were never of her husband.

Frikki felt an impulse to ask his brother if he had ever considered trying to get back together with Emilía or Gudrún, but this wasn't the right moment. If Fjalar was sad about losing them, Frikki didn't want to give the impression that he was rubbing his brother's nose in it.

They said goodbye and promised to be in touch but didn't make any firm plans.

Frikki drove home as fast as he could without breaking the speed limit. He didn't want to risk being stopped by the police; if he so much as heard a siren the stress would kill him. The cops would be sure to suspect him of being on drugs if he opened the window, all sweaty and shaking. It did nothing to help his anxiety that he had taken a swig of beer earlier, when he was flustered.

When he finally pulled up in his drive, he heard the wail of the burglar alarm that the security guard had said he would leave on. If the culprit was a thief rather than an overweight cat, he would be more likely to flee if the alarm continued its screeching.

Frikki hurried inside and switched off the deafening noise. But the oppressive silence that followed was no more comfortable. He tried calling the cat but couldn't hear its bell or any sound of mewing. When he glanced into the sitting room, he saw the reason why. Someone had smashed the glass in the garden door, reached in through the gap and opened it.

Seeing that the door was still ajar, Frikki froze. He stared open-mouthed at the broken glass scattered all over the parquet floor. This could hardly have been the work of the cat. It wasn't what he had been expecting at all and he now regretted having turned down the offer of a visit from a security guard. He wondered if he should go back out to the car, ring the security company and say he'd changed his mind: he wanted a man here straight away. Although he was more than a match for a large cat, he was unlikely to be able to overpower a crazed burglar.

On second thoughts, nothing seemed to have been touched. His laptop was still on the coffee table where Rósa had left it. The TV and music system were in their usual place. The rest of the stuff in the sitting room was hardly worth anyone's while to cart out of the house and try to flog. Perhaps the thief had had second thoughts; broken the glass, opened the door, then legged it when the alarm went off. That must have been it. The only thing that didn't fit with this scenario was the fact that there was a large sticker advertising the security company on the door, so the ear-piercing wail of the alarm shouldn't have come as a surprise.

Perhaps it had been an inexperienced thief. A kid.

Frikki listened but all he could hear was his own breathing. Nevertheless, he tiptoed towards the open-plan kitchen and picked up the marble kitchen-roll stand from the island which divided the kitchen from the living room. Taking off the kitchen roll, he gripped the cold marble cylinder. The stand had been a Christmas present from his employer. He doubted that the person who had wrapped it in festive paper would have envisaged it being used as a weapon, but its heft in his hand gave him a feeling of security. He peered round the island to check there was no one crouching on the floor behind it, then went into the hallway, moving as softly as he knew how.

He started with his own bedroom, having read in the papers that this was where thieves generally concentrated on searching for jewellery and cash. But everything was just as he had left it. The unmade bed, the open book on the bedside table, the clothes hanging over the back of the chair by the window. The wardrobes were closed and the television was still in its place on the wall facing the bed.

The same was true of the bathroom. Nothing had been touched in there.

But when he opened the door of the bedroom Rósa had been using, it was a different story. The place had been turned upside down.

Frikki clung to the doorpost, tightening his grip on the kitchen-roll stand. What did it mean? Who knew she'd been here? Rósa had always sworn that no one was aware she hid out with him, and he'd believed her since the police had never come looking for her. Perhaps her killer had forced her to reveal where she had been hiding. If so, the person in question must know about him too. Frikki sent up a fervent prayer that whoever it was had found what he was looking for. Judging by the mess, however, that seemed unlikely. Frikki's heart missed a beat when he realised that this could result in another visit. The killer probably thought Frikki was the most likely person to know the whereabouts of whatever it was he was after.

During supper at Fjalar's, Frikki had thought the worst that could happen was that he would be found to have been sheltering a runaway teen. A young girl. But now the situation was far more dire than that.

From the sitting room he heard a familiar miaow. That bloody animal must have seized the chance to slink in through the open door. A sudden pungent odour of cat pee wafted into the hallway.

Just when he'd thought things couldn't get any worse.

Chapter 27

Monday

The briefing, which had been going on for more than an hour, had finally ended. The police officers filed out, one after the other, in silence. The mood in the room was gloomy. Apart from Erla, who had called the meeting, hardly anyone had spoken. They all seemed angry, not with Erla but with the person who had murdered a teenage girl; the person they were now grimly determined to catch. Freyja wasn't surprised at their reaction. She herself was seething with violent hatred for the killer. He didn't deserve any pity, whoever he was. Nothing could justify what he had done.

Little of what had been discussed was relevant to Freyja. Mostly they had talked about the assignment of tasks and reviewed what the police already knew, which was worryingly little. It seemed they didn't have any theories, about the motive, the killer, or the exact time or cause of death. The post-mortem was in progress and Huldar was apparently in attendance. A few people emitted dry chuckles at this news; obviously some in-house joke that Freyja didn't get.

Apart from Erla and Freyja, there was only one other woman present, a young redhead called Lína, whom Freyja vaguely remembered meeting before. She had taken the seat beside the young woman. Huldar wasn't there, Gudlaugur was nowhere to be seen either and Freyja felt she could use a friendly face, not least because Erla had made no secret of the fact that she didn't want her there. Before the meeting began, she had actually told Freyja this to her face. It was lucky no one else had heard. Freyja wasn't particularly keen for everyone to know that she had been imposed on them by orders from on high, directly contrary to the wishes of the officer in charge of the investigation.

Freyja's presence had been required because a number of teenagers acquainted with Rósa were due to be interviewed, top of the list being Tristan. Freyja needed to be across the latest developments in the case if she was to be of assistance to the investigators, both during the interviews and afterwards, when they were being processed. In the current atmosphere, however, she doubted Erla would accept any help beyond what the police were obliged to request. Still, there was a chance Huldar might avail himself of her help after the interviews.

Her neighbour, the young Lína, who seemed supremely confident that she already knew everything that mattered in life, was unlikely to turn to anyone for help. She was one of the few people who had ventured to ask any questions during the meeting, but Freyja wasn't in a position to judge whether they were sensible or a waste of time. Erla had reacted with impatience, but Lína didn't seem to take it personally, or if she did, she hid it well.

Freyja and the redhead were not so different in that respect. Freyja had schooled her face not to show any emotion while Erla was going through harrowing images from the crime scene, with Rósa's body in the foreground. The photos were upsetting, horrible, unspeakably, unbearably sad, but Freyja had managed, with an effort, to freeze her facial muscles into an impassive mask. The glances Erla shot her every time she changed the photo on the big screen were an extra incentive to demonstrate self-control, since Freyja sensed that the other woman was hoping to see her wince or avert her eyes. Well, she was in for a disappointment.

Even so, it wasn't easy to play the cold, detached professional with those images blown up on the screen. Freyja would have found it less of a challenge if she'd been viewing them on her phone, but projected on this scale, the horror magnified so that no one could miss a single detail, it was almost worse than having been at the scene in person.

At one point Freyja nearly betrayed herself with an involuntary gasp. That was when Rósa's body had been turned over and her death mask first came into view. The pictures of Rósa's father that Freyja had seen on Huldar's computer screen had been nothing in comparison to this. Yet the girl's face wasn't distorted or marked in any way. It just looked oddly rigid and her open eyes might have been the painted eyes of a doll. At that moment Freyja was completely in sympathy with the thick miasma of anger emanating from the other people in the room. What had once been Rósa was Rósa no more. She had gone; her husky voice had been silenced for good. All that remained was a lifeless corpse. An empty carapace.

It wasn't until the images shifted to focus on the surroundings of the crime scene that Freyja began to recover. Nevertheless, she was still feeling badly jolted and wondered if this was what she had to look forward to if she became the Child Protection Agency's police liaison officer. She had been witness to some terrible things in her job at the Children's

House, but only indirectly, through interviews with the kids involved. That had been bad enough without the addition of giant images of their sufferings. Perhaps she wasn't suited to police work after all, though she would no doubt develop a thicker skin over time. The question was whether she wanted to.

Freyja stood up. She had waited for most of the others to leave the room as she was unsure what would happen after the meeting. The last thing she wanted was an altercation with Erla in front of everyone. Lína had hung back with her, probably for the same reason.

'Do you have any influence on who gets to attend the interviews with Rósa's friends and the other witnesses?' Lína was staring straight into Freyja's eyes from under her pale lashes. 'I'd really like to be there.'

Freyja gave her a rueful smile. The chances of Lína's wish being fulfilled were minimal if Freyja were to suggest it to Erla. 'I have less than zero influence on that, I'm afraid.'

Lína shrugged. 'No harm in trying.' She hurried off, since there was clearly nothing to be gained from Freyja. Hopefully not every member of the team would share that opinion.

Freyja followed in Lína's wake. Once she had left the meeting room, she saw that the team had returned to their desks, eager to get started on the jobs they'd been allotted. If cases could be solved by zeal alone, the murderer would be found by the end of that day, but sadly she knew it wasn't enough.

After standing around awkwardly for a while, Freyja could feel her temper rising. When no one else was prepared to stand up for you, you had no alternative but to stand up for yourself. She wasn't going to let Erla's foul mood prevent her from doing her bit to solve the case. She stormed over to her office, knocked, then walked in without waiting for a reply.

'Hi.' Freyja didn't bother with a fake smile. 'You forgot to tell me what I can do to help. The interview with Tristan isn't until after lunch, so I was wondering if you wanted me to run through a few things with the officers who will be present? Or perhaps I could read transcripts of the earlier interviews with him. You never know, I might spot something.'

Erla looked so sick when Freyja barged into her office that you'd have thought the next thing on her agenda would be to throw up in the bin under her desk. She stared back, pale and glassy-eyed, but didn't say a word.

Seeing that Erla wasn't going to answer, Freyja closed the door behind her, went over to the other woman's desk and sat down. The office struck her as coldly impersonal, with bare walls and shelves of identically coloured folders. The coffee mug on the desk was a plain white, with no decoration or lame slogan on it. Not that different from Freyja's own office, come to think of it. 'Look, I get that you don't like me,' Freyja began, 'but you're a grown-up and you're in charge of this investigation. Surely you can put aside your feelings for the duration?' Freyja immediately felt better after this bit of straight talking. She should have done it a long time ago. They were never going to fall into each other's arms and become best buddies, but they ought to be able to work together instead of behaving like school kids. Especially given the gravity of the situation.

Erla still didn't answer. She clamped her lips shut and put a hand over her mouth. Freyja couldn't tell if she was trying to stop herself from bawling her out, or if she had been rendered speechless by Freyja's bluntness. But the woman's unexpected reaction took the wind out of her sails. She'd been sure Erla would fly off the handle. 'Do you want me to talk to someone else?' Freyja asked, wrong-footed. 'Huldar, for example – when he gets back?'

This did not go down well. Erla narrowed her bleary eyes and looked as angry as anyone can with half their face hidden. When she spoke through her fingers, her voice sounded muffled. 'You talk to me. It's just not a good moment right now.' Closing her eyes, Erla drew a deep breath through her nose, then seemed to get a grip on herself. She opened her eyes, lowered her hand and swallowed audibly, then said, as if through clenched teeth: 'Come back later. Have a coffee. Go online. See if you can get permission to tell us what's in the files on Rósa. Surely you can look after yourself for an hour? We don't hold people's hands here, if that's what you're used to.'

This was more like the reaction Freyja had been expecting from Erla. She actually felt relieved. It was always a bit disconcerting when people you couldn't stand reacted normally or showed their better side. The world was simpler when people reverted to type. Freyja smiled and this time it was sincere. 'No problem. I'll sort myself out.' She prepared to stand up. 'I'll need somewhere to work, though. A computer, a desk and a chair. The sooner the better.'

Erla rolled her eyes as if she'd never heard such effrontery. Then she blenched and gestured furiously at Freyja to get out, muttering that she'd sort it. Her voice sounded strangled and odd. In fact everything about her behaviour had been downright strange ever since Freyja had entered her office.

Freyja still hadn't been allotted a desk by the time Huldar appeared. Instead of being able to sit down and get on with something useful, she had been reduced to wandering aimlessly round the department, stopping briefly to speak to Lína, who hadn't even tried to disguise her lack of interest. Her gaze had kept sliding back to her computer screen and when she smiled it was brief and fake. Freyja had given up and continued her wandering, eventually finding a chair by the wall to perch on. She had moved it nearer to a socket, plugged in her almost batteryless phone and embarked on an unsystematic and ultimately fruitless online search.

Huldar couldn't have arrived at a better moment.

Noticing that he looked almost as off-colour as Erla, Freyja wondered if there was some virus going round CID. But his face lit up when he saw Freyja rise to her feet and practically fling out her arms with pleasure at seeing him.

'How was it?' She glanced at the clear plastic sleeve he was carrying. It contained some papers but she couldn't see what they were as the page facing her was blank.

Huldar gave an involuntary shudder. 'It's over, anyway. The report won't be completed until tomorrow but most of the conclusions are already available.'

'Such as?'

'Rósa was dead before being dumped there. The cause of death was strangulation and she probably died just after midnight, in the early hours of Saturday morning.'

Freyja blew out a breath. 'None of that is particularly helpful for the investigation, is it?'

'Sure it is. Or it will be later. But it won't solve the case – not that anyone was expecting it to.'

'So she didn't have any hair or skin under her nails? Nothing to help you trace the killer or prove it was him when he's caught?' Freyja had seen her share of crime series on TV.

'No.' Huldar shook his head. 'Even if there had been anything, it would have been washed away by the water, though she probably hadn't been in the lake for more than six or seven hours, tops. Unfortunately, there were no fingerprints on her neck either.'

'What about evidence that could explain where she's been hiding for the last few days?' Freyja tried to remember all the questions that had been raised at the meeting earlier. It distracted her from thinking about Rósa and prevented Huldar from marching straight off to see Erla. Freyja was fed up with being sidelined and ignored.

He shook his head again. 'No. Nothing obvious. She had her phone in her coat pocket but had taken the SIM card out. It was in her other pocket. Which explains why her phone hasn't appeared on the system since she went missing.' Huldar perked up a little. 'But one thing did come to light.'

'What?'

Huldar turned the plastic sleeve round and handed it to Freyja. She examined the printout of a photo showing a painfully thin wrist. The whole arm appeared to be covered in bruising. She couldn't immediately work out what was so interesting about the picture. 'The bruises?'

'Nope.' He took the plastic sleeve back. 'Those aren't actually bruises, by the way. The skin turns that colour when the blood pools in the body after death. No, I meant the bracelet.'

Freyja looked at the brown loop tied around Rósa's wrist. Two coloured glass beads dangled from the ends, triggering a fleeting memory that she couldn't pin down. 'I know I've seen it before but I can't think where. Go on, where's it from?'

'It's the one Tristan was wearing when we had him in for questioning. I swear it's identical. If I'm right, it means they must have met recently. I'm hoping they didn't both have matching ones but I doubt it. It looks homemade, not like it was bought in a shop.'

Freyja ran a hand through her hair, which still felt strange from the nit shampoo. 'Are you going to ask him about it?'

'You bet I am. But first I want to see if he's still wearing his bracelet. Clearly, we need to bring his interview forward. There's no way I'm hanging around until this afternoon. The bloody little idiot probably knew all along where Rósa was hiding. If he'd opened his trap sooner we might have been able to avert this tragedy.' He added: 'Don't go anywhere. I need to talk to Erla but I'm sure she'll agree with me. I assume she'll have the boy brought straight in, so you'll need to be prepared.'

Freyja nodded, then blurted out: 'Could Erla be coming down with something, Huldar? She looked almost green earlier. Can the interview go ahead if she's not there?'

At this, Huldar looked oddly shifty. 'She's fine. Don't worry.' He strode off in the direction of Erla's office without elaborating.

Chapter 28

Monday

Tristan had been shown into the meeting room. This change of venue was because the usual interview rooms weren't big enough to accommodate all those who needed to be present. The police hadn't seen any reason to transfer the pot plant, picture and armchair as well, though Huldar couldn't ever remember having seen such a crowd turn up for the taking of a witness statement. He was there to assist Erla, who would lead the questioning; Freyja was there to represent the Child Protection Agency; Hafthór the Sexual Offences Unit; Gudlaugur as a witness; and a lawyer, an older man by the name of Bjarni Einarsson, was there on behalf of Bergur, the accused in the care-home case. Finally, there was a young man from IT who was responsible for the audio-visual recordings of the proceedings. He was a silent participant and did his best to melt into the background.

But that wasn't all, because outside in the corridor there were two more people: Tristan's mother, Berglind Sigvaldadóttir, and a lawyer called Magnús Eyvindarson, who had announced that he would be accompanying the boy. He had not been permitted to enter the room, however, since witnesses were not entitled to have a legal adviser present during questioning. As far as the police could discover,

Magnús was there on standby in case Tristan's status changed during the proceedings. This had done nothing to diminish speculation about the boy's possible involvement in the case, but the lawyer wasn't giving anything away.

Tristan's mother had presumably come along to provide moral support, but she wasn't allowed to go in with her son either since he was over fifteen. In fact, it was hard to see how her presence was supposed to help him since she appeared barely capable of looking after herself. Apart from mumbling a greeting as she avoided eye contact, she hadn't spoken at all. Anyone could see that she was in a bad way and that this wasn't simply due to anxiety about her son. The woman looked ill. She was skeletally thin, with glazed eyes, a blotchy red face and entrenched dark circles under her eyes that reached right down to her prominent cheekbones. Her hair hadn't been washed for days and her badly cut fringe straggled over her eyes. She was clutching one of her arms and kept rubbing it repeatedly through her shabby anorak. The nature of her ailment was blindingly obvious to anyone familiar with addicts. Next to the stout, formally dressed lawyer, Huldar thought she looked like the little match girl.

He had got his way and the interview had been brought forward, despite the logistical difficulties of assembling all the people who needed to be there. The first obstacle had arisen when Tristan announced that he wasn't coming. The police had tried to stop the media getting hold of the story, particularly the part about Rósa's death being treated as murder, but they must have failed since Tristan had obviously got wind of it. Until now he had turned up punctually to interviews.

Erla couldn't compel him to attend, as he wasn't a suspect.

When friendly persuasion failed to do the trick, she informed him that if he didn't turn up, he would be summoned before a court and made to give a statement there. And if he failed to turn up for that, he would be in contempt of court and could be arrested. Tristan, who was no fool, realised he was beaten. Refusing to speak to the police now would only be postponing the inevitable.

No sooner had they managed to talk Tristan round than they'd got a call from Bergur's lawyer, Bjarni Einarsson, who insisted on being present when the boy's statement was taken. Erla had given his request short shrift, pointing out that the interview had nothing to do with the boy's allegations of abuse, whereupon Bjarni claimed to have information to the contrary. Hafthór, the head of Sexual Offences, had mentioned to him that he would be attending. The only way the lawyer could interpret this was as an indication that his client's case was likely to come up. Bjarni added that he had it on good authority that the police believed the two cases might be linked, though he refused to reveal his source. Perhaps he had simply put two and two together. After all, Rósa had been a resident at his client's care home and was therefore a potential witness in his case.

Erla had told him curtly that she would be in touch, after which the lawyer's demand had gone on to create waves on almost every floor in the building. But Erla couldn't prove that the man's presence would be prejudicial to the investigation or cause problems for Tristan. Nor did she succeed in convincing her superiors that the interview would be restricted to matters relating to Rósa's death, since this clearly wasn't true. Rósa and Tristan had met at the care home: it would be almost impossible to question the boy about her without touching on the home and what had allegedly taken place there.

In the end, the top brass had concluded that refusing the lawyer's request wouldn't be worth the risk. It wasn't the first time Bjarni had asked to attend Tristan's interviews, though Erla hadn't been aware of this, since it had been handled by Sexual Offences. But now that he had stepped up his demands, the Commissioner's office had decided to give in. No watertight evidence sufficient to secure a conviction had turned up in the abuse case, and the police couldn't afford any irregularities if it went to trial. If a single mention was made of the care home during the interview, Bergur's lawyer would pounce on the fact and use it to his advantage. He would complain bitterly to the judge that he had asked to be present, as was his right, only to be refused, and judges invariably took a dim view of that sort of thing.

Erla had no sooner reluctantly informed the lawyer that his request had been granted than a new problem raised its head. There was a second lawyer on the phone. This one introduced himself as Magnús Eyvindarson and explained that he was Tristan's legal adviser. Erla was taken aback. Tristan was a witness in Rósa's case and there was no reason for him to hire a lawyer. Not yet, at any rate. Magnús reminded Erla that, as the victim in the care-home abuse case, Tristan had every right to employ an advocate at his own expense. Magnús would naturally also assist the young man in any dealings he might have with the police arising from other matters. Erla had to concede this point but stressed nonetheless that Magnús would not be permitted to attend the interview about Rósa. A witness was not entitled to have a lawyer or advocate present when their statement was taken and that was final. Magnús had then tried to get Erla to review Tristan's status, reminding her that if she had the slightest doubt about whether the boy was a witness or a suspect in Rósa's case, it would be more natural to interview him as a suspect. Erla put her foot down, insisting that, as matters stood, Tristan's status was not in doubt and Magnús would have to remain outside the room. The lawyer was plainly eager to get his feet under the table, presumably to stop his client if he showed signs of becoming too talkative.

But fate had kept the worst till last. Erla had also had to field a phone call from Rósa's grandfather, who had learnt of her death via the media. Unsurprisingly, the man had gone ballistic. She had sat there, scarlet in the face, enduring a storm of vitriolic abuse so loud that it carried to those sitting nearby, who also turned red. Whenever Erla could get a word in, she had tried to explain that there had been a misunderstanding: the police had assumed that children's services would inform the next of kin since Rósa had been their responsibility at the time of her death. CID had therefore reported the matter to the Child Protection Agency, but either the message hadn't been passed on because it was the weekend, or somebody there had slipped up. Rósa's grandfather had treated these excuses with contempt and finally hung up on Erla, after threatening to sue. Though exactly who he wanted to sue was unclear.

After all this, Erla still had to prepare for the interview itself and make sure that she and the Sexual Offences Unit were on the same page. This was done in a rush as it was almost time to start.

Some days were nothing but hassle.

Erla began the interview with the formalities. She noted

the time and informed Tristan that a statement was to be taken from him as part of the inquiry into the death of Rósa Thrastardóttir.

Huldar kept his eyes trained on the boy's face as Erla was speaking. Tristan swallowed hard and began to gnaw at his upper lip. He didn't ask any questions or show any signs of surprise, so Rósa's death obviously wasn't news to him.

Erla went on to stress that Tristan was being interviewed as a witness. He was obliged to provide a truthful account and leave out nothing of relevance to the case. If he failed to abide by these rules, he would be liable to conviction, as bearing false witness was a criminal offence.

The boy nodded, and, when asked to answer aloud for the recording, said, 'Yes.' Then he dropped his eyes to the table in front of him and asked: 'What does liable to conviction mean? Does it mean I'd go to prison?'

Erla replied: 'The penalty for making a wilfully false statement is a fine and a prison sentence of up to four months. As you're over fifteen, you're considered responsible for your actions.'

Huldar noticed Freyja leaning forwards and trying to make eye contact with Tristan. The boy went on staring down at the table, so she spoke to him directly: 'Tristan. You're too young to go to prison. You're not eighteen yet, though you're old enough to be held responsible for your own actions. So the most you could be facing is a fine and a suspended sentence, or else a custodial sentence at one of the Child Protection Agency homes.' Freyja turned to Erla. 'We must be careful not to cause the witness unnecessary distress. May I remind you that he is only just seventeen.'

Erla's face tightened but she bit back the angry tirade she

would clearly have liked to unleash on Freyja. Huldar gave a private sigh of relief. Before the interview, he had been so worried that Erla might have to rush out in the middle to throw up that he had forgotten to worry about how she would react to Freyja's presence. Perhaps he had got his priorities wrong. Freyja was here to protect Tristan's interests; Erla to extract the truth from him. A clash was inevitable.

'Is it clear that you must provide a correct and truthful statement?' Erla asked Tristan, who nodded again and was once more prompted to answer aloud for the recording.

'Yes. It's clear.'

'Good. Then we'll begin.' Erla arranged her notes on the table in front of her. 'When did you last see Rósa, Tristan?'

'When did I last see Rósa?'

'Yes. Rósa. Rósa Thrastardóttir. When did you last see her?'

'A while ago. Quite a long time ago. Like I already told you. I don't remember exactly when, but it was whatever I told you last time.' The boy clearly couldn't remember how he had answered before. If his response had seemed unconvincing then, it was doubly so now. Had he told the truth, he would have been able to remember.

'You'll need to be more precise than that.'

Tristan's expression was despairing. His eyes darted back and forth between the people sitting at the big conference table, lingering longest on Freyja. He was obviously hoping for support from her but he wouldn't get it. She knew her role and it did not consist of helping the witness to avoid answering perfectly reasonable questions.

'When did you last see Rósa?' Erla didn't try to hide her impatience. In fact, Huldar thought she was deliberately making sure the boy heard it.

Tristan lowered his gaze again and appeared to be thinking. When he looked up, he seemed to have recalled the lie he had told last time. He answered tentatively, like a caller to a radio quiz show, who's hoping to be stopped and given another chance if he gets it wrong. 'It must have been about ten days ago.'

'Ten days?'

'Yes. Ten days.'

Erla nodded slowly. 'Where did you meet? What was the occasion?'

'Umm . . . We met in town and wandered about for a bit. We bought a Coke and talked. As far as I can remember, we walked up Laugavegur and down Hverfisgata, past her grand-parents' house. But we didn't go in and say hello. We just wanted to be alone. To talk.' The boy's face was burning and his discomfort was plain to all.

'Would you mind showing me your hands, Tristan?'

'My hands? Why?' Tristan shifted in his chair and it looked to Huldar as if he was sitting on them, perhaps unconsciously. If a policeman asks you to do something, the natural response is to refuse.

'You'll find out. Can I see your hands, please?'

While Tristan was making up his mind, Huldar noticed that Bergur's lawyer was sitting up and taking an interest. Presumably he thought Erla was looking for scratches or other marks that might implicate Tristan in Rósa's murder. Naturally, it would be extremely convenient for his client if his accuser turned out to be a suspect in a murder case.

Finally, Tristan laid his hands on the table, palms down, fingers spread out. Erla leant over and used her pencil to lift the sleeves of his coat. Then she sat back in her chair. 'Where's the bracelet you were wearing, Tristan? When you came here three days ago you had a leather band knotted round your right wrist.'

'I don't remember.' Tristan had turned pale. 'I think you must be mixing me up with someone else.'

'No chance of that. Do you remember me telling you that our conversation would be recorded?'

'Vaguely.'

'Right. Well, we've got a video recording that shows the bracelet very clearly. So, where is it now?'

'I can't remember. I must have lost it. It was always coming off.' Tristan licked his lips.

Erla drew a sharp breath through her nose. 'Let me remind you to tell the truth, Tristan. When you were here three days ago it was on your wrist. Two days ago we found Rósa's body with the same bracelet round her wrist. Exactly the same leather band with small coloured glass beads on the ends. So, when did you last meet Rósa? Logically, it must have been after we spoke to you three days ago but before she died two days ago.'

Tristan looked aghast. 'You don't think I killed her?'

'No.' Erla answered loud and clear for the recording. It was vital to have this on record. If they were caught interviewing a juvenile suspect under the guise of his being a witness, it would have serious repercussions for Erla and for the case. 'May I remind you that you're here as a witness?'

This didn't appear to reassure Tristan. He glanced round the conference table again in search of support or a friendly face, but the expressions of those present were grave. He gulped. Huldar sent up a silent prayer that the boy would stop digging in his heels. He was their only hope of finding a quick solution to the mystery of where Rósa had been hiding.

'I didn't kill her,' Tristan exclaimed, his voice rising. 'She was my friend. I'd have to be crazy to have hurt her. And she wasn't just my friend, she was my witness too. Why would I want to get rid of her? It doesn't make any sense.'

'No one's implying you killed Rósa. We just want to know when you last saw her and where she was. We have good reason to believe that your paths crossed shortly before she died. We also need you to tell us everything you know about where she was staying while she was in hiding. That information will help us catch the person who killed her. If you were truly her friend, you'd tell us what you know.'

Tristan hesitated and there was silence in the room apart from a low beeping from the recording device. The IT man flushed dark red when Erla shot him a glare. She was on the point of repeating her question when Tristan suddenly started talking. His voice was flat and he spoke so quietly that Huldar wasn't sure it would be picked up by the microphone. 'OK. I saw Rósa. On Friday, after I'd talked to you. On Friday evening.'

Erla's shoulders relaxed a fraction. She was over the hardest part: the boy had cracked. 'How did you arrange the meeting and where did you go?'

'She contacted me. Via Messenger.'

Erla flicked a glance at Huldar. According to IT, Rósa's Facebook account hadn't been accessed since she'd vanished. Nor had her messaging app. 'According to our information, she hadn't logged in or used Messenger recently. Not since she went missing. Are you sure you've remembered that part right?'

'Yes. It was on Messenger. Rósa had a fake profile that she sometimes used. Not to post anything, just to send messages. She thought the Child Protection Agency were spying on her and wanted to keep it private.' Tristan turned to Freyja. 'Was she right? Were you spying on her?'

Freyja considered carefully for a moment before answering. 'Well, I'm not from the Child Protection Agency, so I can't answer for them, but I would be very surprised if they were.'

Erla appeared satisfied with this response, though of course she would never admit it, Huldar thought: she was incapable of seeing Freyja in her true light. 'Going back to my questions: where and what time did you meet?'

'We met at Smáralind and went to see a film. She suggested we meet at seven and get something to eat first, so we could talk. We had some burgers, then went to the cinema, and carried on talking a bit in the car park afterwards, before going home.'

'What?' Erla exclaimed, outraged. 'Are you seriously telling me Rósa could just swan around the shopping mall at Smáralind without anyone noticing? Her picture's all over the media.' Then, narrowing her eyes suspiciously, she asked: 'Did no one point at her or come over to talk to you?'

'Look, no one cares, OK? When kids are reported missing in the news, no one bothers to remember their faces. Everyone just assumes they're looking for a junkie. Rósa looked respectable. She just wore a beanie and that was enough. It wasn't the first time she'd walked around without being hassled after she was reported missing. If you don't behave like you're hiding, it doesn't occur to people that you are.'

Erla proceeded to interrogate him about which film they'd seen and exactly what they'd eaten, scribbling it all down.

The police would contact the cinema and restaurant in an attempt to verify the story, though it was unlikely anyone would remember them since the shopping centre was always heaving on a Friday evening and two teenage kids wouldn't have attracted much attention. If all else failed, the police could look for the food order Tristan said they had paid for in cash. That alone wouldn't prove his claim, though, since the restaurant had probably sold hundreds of meal deals consisting of burger, fries and Coke that evening. But it wasn't beyond the bounds of possibility that the CCTV footage would still be available.

'What did you talk about while you were eating, and afterwards in the car park? Did Rósa say where she was going after you parted ways?'

'She didn't tell me that, no. But she was in a really good mood and we talked about all sorts of things. She kept going on about her mum and all that. Like I said, I just used to switch off when she started obsessing about that stuff. It made me uncomfortable. I didn't want to get mixed up in it, if she decided to do something crazy.'

'How do you mean, "crazy"?'

'I don't know. Like I said, I didn't want to ask. Sometimes, it's just better not to know.' Judging from the boy's expression, this motto hadn't been chosen at random. He must have had to close his eyes to a lot of ugly stuff his mother had done over the years.

'Did you get the feeling she was planning to do something that evening?'

'No. I didn't get any kind of feeling. We caught the bus together. She got off, but I went all the way to Mjódd and changed there to go home.'

'Which bus did you both catch and where did she get out?'

'We caught the twenty-four after the film, so it must have been at around eleven. We were going to change at the Mjódd bus station. I live in Fellahverfi, so I took the number four. Rósa was going to take the number two to Seljahverfi. I know that, because she's done it before. But this time she didn't. She jumped out soon after the bus left Smáralind. At the third stop, on Dalvegur.'

Erla noted this down. 'Why did she get out there? You must have asked.'

'There was no time. She just suddenly took off. She said she'd be in touch but I never heard from her again.'

'Why did she suddenly take off? Did she see something out of the window?'

Tristan paused to think. 'No. I don't think so. I remember she was digging around in her pockets, searching for some chewing gum. Then suddenly she groaned, got up, rang the bell and jumped out as soon as the bus stopped. It all happened so fast. She only had time to say what I just told you: that she'd be in touch at the weekend.'

Erla was silent while she was working out the next question in her head. 'You know we can check the CCTV recordings from the bus, Tristan, and find out if you're telling the truth?'

'I *am* telling the truth.'

'All right. Did you see where she went after she got off the bus? Did she start walking towards Seljahverfi, where you say she was originally heading?'

'No. She went in the opposite direction. Towards Kópavogur. Towards Hjallahverfi, or whatever it's called.'

'Do you know if she was staying there or knew anyone who lived in the area?'

Tristan shook his head. 'No. I haven't a clue. She never mentioned it.'

'What about Seljahverfi – did she used to stay with someone there when she ran away?'

Tristan took a deep breath. 'Before I answer that, there's something I want to say.'

'Go ahead.' Erla put down her pen and folded her arms across her chest, ready to listen.

'I want to tell you something. I'm going to take back what I said about Bergur and the care home. As far as I'm concerned, you can stop investigating that now.'

Bergur's lawyer's eyes were on stalks. 'What?' he blurted. 'You want to withdraw your allegations?'

Erla rounded on him furiously. 'I'm doing the talking here. If you have any questions for the witness, you pass me a note, like we discussed.'

Erla's reprimand had no effect. The lawyer said: 'I demand to be allowed to ask the witness why he made a false allegation against my client. I also insist that the boy should forfeit his status as a witness or accuser in my client's case, now that he has openly admitted making false allegations against him.'

Tristan looked at Erla. 'I want to talk to my lawyer.' Boom. So that was why Magnús Eyvindarson was sitting outside. He'd obviously been forewarned about what was coming. Tristan had presumably asked his advice about the possible consequences of withdrawing his complaint. If so, Magnús had been quite right to accompany him to the police station. This was going to have major repercussions.

Erla had lost any semblance of control. Bergur's lawyer was on his feet, phone to his ear. Tristan had clammed up and appeared unlikely to say anything else. Hafthór from Sexual Offences was making for the door. And the young man from IT was looking stressed because the camera only covered the conference table but the people he was supposed to be filming had scattered around the room.

Huldar reached over the table and grabbed Tristan's arm. 'It looks like the interview's over, but you can't in good conscience leave here without telling us where Rósa used to hide when she was on the run. Come on, spit it out, dammit.'

Tristan snatched back his arm. 'She used to stay with some bloke who was a friend of her mum's. They used to work together. He lives in Seljahverfi. That's all I know.' Then he clammed up again and refused to say another word as everything fell apart around him.

Chapter 29

Monday

Huldar sat on the edge of Erla's desk, letting her vent. He didn't take in the finer points of her diatribe since he was only there as a punchbag, but then Erla had no interest in what he had to say – which was just as well, since he had no solutions to offer. He merely shook his head gravely in the right places and chucked in the odd *yeah* whenever it was called for. That was all that was expected of him.

'Oh, God. What the fuck does *she* want?' Erla scowled and Huldar turned to see who had attracted her ire through the glass wall.

He was relieved to see that it wasn't Freyja but Lína. She was hovering outside, visibly engaged in an inner struggle about when to knock on the door. She had probably been waiting politely for Erla to run out of steam, then realised that she would be waiting a long time in that case. She had a bunch of papers in her hand.

Huldar got up, beckoned to Lína to come in and was rewarded with a punch on the thigh from Erla. A wide smile spread over Lína's freckled white face as she stuck her head round the door. 'Is this a bad moment?'

Erla threw up her hands in exasperation but Huldar smiled back at the young trainee. 'What have you got there?'

Lína stepped inside and closed the door behind her. 'I've finished going through Brynjólfur's boxes.'

Salvör, Binni's wife, had turned up with the boxes the previous evening, after the few people who had come in on Sunday had already gone home. She had left them in reception and the pile had been waiting for Erla when she'd arrived that morning. Erla had been baffled, since Huldar had forgotten to tell her about them. Once he had explained, she'd been on the verge of losing it when her face had turned a nasty shade of green and she'd had to dash to the ladies'. By the time she came back she had a bit more colour in her cheeks and had got over the worst of her temper. Nevertheless, she had barked at Huldar and Gudlaugur to carry the boxes upstairs. Since Huldar had asked for them, she reckoned they were his problem. Gudlaugur was regarded as equally culpable since he had gone to see Salvör with Huldar. Neither man complained since it made a pleasant change to deal with something that required physical rather than mental effort. Once they had ferried the boxes upstairs, Huldar had asked to borrow Lína, who was still hanging around CID, to sort through them. As predicted, Sexual Offences had proved embarrassingly eager to let her go.

Huldar wasn't waiting with bated breath to see the list of contents any more than Erla was. It was just one more chore that needed to be crossed off the list.

Lína went on, with mind-numbing enthusiasm: 'I numbered all the boxes and created a table to show the contents of each. In my opinion, they contain nothing of interest for the inquiry.' She held out the papers. When Erla showed no sign of taking them, Huldar obliged. He put them on Erla's desk and praised Lína for her diligence. He hadn't expected her

to finish the job that quickly. Even Erla must surely acknowledge that the young woman was a human bulldozer, though
she was unlikely to start praising her any time soon.

'There's something else too.' Lína ploughed on, oblivious
to Erla's irritation.

'What? Do you have any fucking idea how busy we are
right now?' Erla snarled, her scowl deepening dangerously.

'Switchboard asked me to take a phone call from a guy
who runs a bike rental.' No one could touch Lína when it
came to shrugging off Erla's rudeness, Huldar reflected. She
was probably the toughest nut on the floor, if not in the whole
building.

'Some bike rental guy?' he asked. This sounded calculated
to tip Erla over the edge. He didn't know enough about pregnant women to tell whether sudden rage could bring on a bout
of sickness, but the evidence seemed to suggest that it could.

'Yes, he claims he called in the spring to report some stolen
bikes but never heard back from us. Then recently someone
drew his attention to some photos of bikes in a ditch that
were posted on Facebook. He's sure they're his.'

Erla stared at Lína in disbelief. 'Bikes?'

Huldar hastily intervened. 'Lína, I think that'll have to wait.
We're up to our necks here.'

But Erla appeared to disagree. 'Where is this ditch?'

'On the south coast. Between Eyrarbakki and Stokkseyri.'
Lína sounded uncertain, wrong-footed by Erla's sudden
interest. Huldar was similarly puzzled. He wondered if he
should hustle Lína out of the door.

'Well, as you've finished going over the boxes,' Erla said in
a deceptively mild voice, 'I suggest you deal with the bike
business. Borrow a car and get yourself over there.'

'Me?' Lína glanced enquiringly from Erla to Huldar. 'What am I supposed to do when I get there?'

'Sort it out. Bring the bikes back to town and give them to the rental guy. Take a report from him about who rented them and enter it in the system. Case closed. Everybody happy.'

Not least Erla, who would be rid of Lína for several hours.

'Couldn't we have used her for something more urgent?' Huldar asked, once Lína had closed the door behind her. 'She's unbelievably meticulous, Erla.'

'Oh, please.' Erla shuddered. 'I haven't got time to look after a trainee right now. In case you hadn't noticed, we're dealing with the bones of two Brits – who got here fuck knows how. We've got a murdered homeless guy who seems to have been dealing drugs on the side. We've got a murdered teenage girl. And now we've got a boy who decides to withdraw his allegations in the middle of an inquiry. A boy who's sitting on vital information that we can't now question him about.'

Tristan's decision to retract his statement had been a bombshell, not only for the abuse inquiry but also for the investigation into Rósa's death. Bergur's lawyer had gone on the warpath, demanding that it be put on record that he was considering suing Tristan for wrongful accusation. This looked bad for the boy and had the effect of sending him into lockdown. He had refused to comment on the reasons for his retraction. His legal adviser had quickly become involved and asked to be allowed to confer with his young client, and Erla had felt it best to suspend the proceedings while they had their chat. The interview had been derailed anyway; a short break would be a good thing.

What she hadn't expected was for Tristan and his lawyer

to walk out of the station and go incommunicado. The break that should have been brief had now lasted nearly two hours. Bergur's lawyer had lost patience and gone home. The same applied to Freyja, who still hadn't been allotted a workstation in CID.

'How's Gudlaugur getting on with tracking down that colleague of Rósa's mother?' Erla ran both hands roughly through her short hair, leaving it standing on end.

'When I left him he'd established that no one living in that area still works at her mother's old office. So it must be someone who's quit and moved on. But the guys at the Transport Authority are very eager to help and they're busy compiling a list of everyone who worked there in her day. Do you want me to check on their progress? See if the list's ready yet?'

'No. Gudlaugur should have the sense to come to me the instant it's available.'

Huldar agreed, though he didn't think there was any need to wait for the list. 'The man who took Rósa and her mother out on his boat the day before she died lives in Seljahverfi. I looked him up. His name was on file from when the business of the doll was being looked into. It's mentioned there that they were work colleagues. I'm betting he's our man.'

Erla nodded. 'Could be. I still want to see that list, though. He may not be the only candidate. But I agree he sounds likely.'

She carried on reviewing the situation. Every other word was a curse.

All of a sudden, Huldar was hit by a violent longing for a smoke. Glancing at the clock, he saw that they'd been talking for over an hour since Lína left. 'Anyway,' he said, 'we're not achieving anything here. I'd better get back to work.'

'Yeah, fine, go and have a fag, then.' Erla shook her head wearily. They knew each other too well.

As he stood in the yard, listening to the rumble of traffic, Huldar couldn't help envying the commuters on their way home from work. He tried to imagine what it would be like to do a job that didn't follow you home at the end of the day: receptionist, dentist, baker, driver, builder – something unrelated to human misery and death. Yet he couldn't see himself in any of those occupations. And he had grown accustomed to wrestling with intrusive thoughts about the victims – and sometimes the odd perpetrator too – that he came across in the line of duty. There was no way of switching the thoughts off, even if he wanted to. Not even when he was watching football.

He remembered the advice of a veteran officer he had worked with in the early days, who had told him that when the violence and the distressing stuff that went with the territory ceased to get to you, it was time to pack it in. You weren't supposed to become inured to it. So Huldar supposed he could comfort himself that he was still in the right job, but this didn't make the thoughts any easier to bear.

He resolved to stop going over and over the case in his mind and concentrate instead on the drone of traffic. He stubbed out his cigarette and immediately lit another. Why not?

It didn't taste that good, though. It was like having two ice-creams with chocolate sauce in a row. The second one never lived up to the first.

To distract himself, Huldar decided to run through Lína's tables. It would be better than listening to the traffic noise and dreading the year 2030 when Iceland would have switched over to one hundred per cent electric cars. What would it be like standing here, smoking and listening to the purr of traffic that sounded like a procession of Roomba vacuum cleaners?

The contents of the boxes turned out to be as uninteresting as Lína had said. There was nothing on her list that would help them find the motive for Binni's murder. After all, it was highly unlikely that it was connected to anything in his past. By far the most plausible explanation was that the man's murder had been linked to his drug dealing, though that line of inquiry hadn't thrown up any results as yet either. The Drug Squad said that Binni hadn't been on the payroll of any of the importers they were aware of. But of course they weren't aware of all the suppliers: how else to account for all the drugs on the streets? In spite of this, they remained extremely sceptical about the idea that Binni had been dealing, since he hadn't cropped up on their radar. Though they did qualify this by adding that he might only have started recently, as it took dealers time to make a name for themselves.

Huldar didn't know what to think. The killer couldn't have been an addict since there had been pills lying around in plain view when the police got there. Unless the container had been full of other drugs that the killer had taken away with him? Maybe he had been cunning enough to leave some behind to fool the investigators. But if all Binni's clients were anything like the ditzy girl Huldar had met, this seemed improbable. She hadn't exactly belonged to the premier league of users.

The CCTV footage culled from various cameras on Grandi hadn't produced any results. There was quite a bit of traffic on Grandagardur, but less on Fiskislód, the nearest street to the container colony. When the footage from the various different cameras was put together, it appeared that none of the cars passing along the road had stopped there. Logically, therefore, if the murderer had arrived by car, he must have parked somewhere else. The police were compiling a list of all the registration numbers they could read from vehicles parked in nearby spaces at around the time of the murder. But none of the pedestrians caught on camera had been identified as yet, and no camera had been found that showed the area around the containers.

Huldar ran his eyes down Lína's list. Clothes, clothes and more clothes. Shoes. Fishing gear. Old textbooks in English. A watch and an alarm clock. Books on angling and fly-tying. Stationery, including a pen with Brynjólfur's initials on it. A packet of dried-up cigarettes. Whisky tumblers. An old can of aftershave, a razor, a comb and nail-clippers. Miscellaneous documents that Lína had skimmed and categorised according to content – all of which belonged in the shredder, in Huldar's opinion. A big waste of time.

He took a last drag and turned over the final page, which consisted of a single line. It was a description of the contents of the last box, which, unlike the others, had contained only one object.

Huldar forgot to breathe when he read the description. '*A doll*', followed, in brackets, by: '*disgusting*'. He was still coughing as he bounded up the stairs to his floor, taking them two at a time, then paused for a moment outside his department to catch his breath before going in.

'Where did Lína put those boxes?'

Gudlaugur looked up, instantly on the alert when he heard the note of urgency in Huldar's voice. He gestured to the far end of the room. 'She stacked them in the empty workspace in the corner. The one they're planning to give to Freyja.'

Huldar strode off without a word of thanks. He heard Gudlaugur push back his chair and get up to follow. When he reached the pile of boxes, he set about searching for the right one, using the numbers Lína had methodically written in marker pen on each. He'd been prepared to have to dig down to the bottom of the pile but for once he was in luck. The box was in the top layer, as it was smaller than the rest.

'What's up?' Gudlaugur was standing behind Huldar, watching him shift the boxes, then stared at the small wine box that Huldar was holding as he scanned the room for an empty desk to put it on.

'Could you grab me some gloves?' Finding no space on the nearby desks, Huldar headed to the meeting room. He laid the box on the conference table and waited impatiently for Gudlaugur to reappear. When he did, Huldar broke his personal record in pulling the gloves on.

He cut the tape with a penknife. Lína must have assumed the box would never be opened again, which was no doubt true of the rest.

'Right.' Huldar opened the box, peered inside and grimaced. 'What the hell is this?'

Gudlaugur, bending down to see, mirrored his expression of disgust. He didn't look any less revolted when Huldar took the thing out. 'I think we'd better give Erla a shout.'

Huldar put the doll on the table where it sat in all its glory, glowering at Huldar from its single eye, while Gudlaugur went to fetch Erla. He could feel his spine crawling and had no difficulty at all in understanding why a little girl might have become fixated on the idea that the doll was possessed.

Besides only having one eye, its head was covered in tiny holes where half its hair had fallen out. In place of clothes it was encrusted with barnacles and worms. He had often seen mooring bollards but had never felt this kind of revulsion for the ecosystem clinging to them. When they were on a doll, though, with its resemblance to a human baby, the effect was deeply disturbing. He felt an irresistible urge to take out his knife and start scraping the horrible stuff off. But he checked the impulse. Instead, he picked the doll up and peered underneath it. He could just see the shape of a small, round plastic plug under the doll's buttocks. He couldn't tell if it had been made like that or if the plug had been a later addition, though from what he could see of the hole, it looked clean and smoothly curved enough to have been made in a factory. He shook the doll against his ear just in case, but couldn't hear any loose object rattling around inside.

'You've got to be kidding!' Erla marched in and came straight over to the table. 'That's never the fucking doll?'

'I think it must be.' Huldar straightened up. 'How's that for a coincidence? From the list of the guy's possessions, there was nothing to suggest he had a thing for kids' toys. The rest was all adult stuff.'

Erla bent down to get a better look, her face wrinkling with distaste as Huldar's and Gudlaugur's had done – as any normal person's would if they set eyes on the gruesome object. 'If it's the same doll that vanished the night Rósa's mother died, how the hell did it end up in Binni's possession?'

Huldar shrugged. 'Maybe as a result of a perfectly natural sequence of events. Binni knew Rósa's father. After he died, it's possible Binni stayed in touch with the mother and maybe visited her after the girl had gone to bed. Though I admit it's

trickier to explain how the doll ended up in his possession.'
He paused. 'Then there's the other possibility, of course: that
Binni didn't go round to pay a friendly visit but with something much darker in mind. That he knocked her against the
edge of the bath, grabbed the doll and got out of there.'

'But why would he have stolen the doll?' Gudlaugur was
staring incredulously at Huldar. 'Who'd want it?'

Their eyes were drawn irresistibly back to the doll but none
of them could think of an answer.

'Take that revolting thing down to Forensics. Get them to
photograph it every which way, take any fingerprints they
can with those barnacles on it and check if that chain's
valuable. Who knows, perhaps that's a priceless necklace
under all the crap. They might be able to find out the exact
make of doll as well and when it would have been sold – in
case it's connected to this whole business, far-fetched as it
may seem.'

There was nothing else to be done. They could stand
there, gaping at the doll and thinking until their brains
burnt out without coming up with any answers. What role,
if any, could the doll have played in the deaths of Binni,
Rósa and her mother? Sometimes strange objects found
their way into people's lives as a result of a series of coincidences. But in this case there was no one left alive to tell
the tale.

Or was there? Huldar turned to Gudlaugur. 'When did
Binni's wife say she'd put his stuff in storage? Wasn't it shortly
after he'd walked out on her? That was about five years before
the doll was fished up out of the sea. So how did it end up
in the storage unit?'

Gudlaugur scratched his head. 'Now you're asking.'

Huldar exhaled slowly. 'If his wife put the doll in storage later, she must have come by it in a legitimate manner or she would never have passed it on to us.'

'Maybe she'd forgotten about it.' Erla was still staring at the doll. 'We'll find out in the end. Clearly, we need to talk to the woman again. But that doesn't alter the fact that I want that horrible object taken down to Forensics ASAP.'

Huldar put the doll back inside the box. He felt strangely relieved once he had closed the flaps. But just as he was about to pick it up, his phone rang. It was a mobile number belonging to the police but not one that he'd saved as a contact.

It turned out to be Lína. 'Huldar, I've found the bikes.'

'Great, Lína.' Before he could tell her that it wasn't a good moment, she interrupted.

'There's more stuff here.'

'Oh?' Huldar said, his thoughts still on the doll.

'I think you need to send Forensics out here. There's something very strange about all this.'

'Are you down in the ditch, Lína? It's not unusual for rubbish to collect there.'

'This isn't rubbish. Or rather, it is now, but none of it looks to me like the kind of thing anyone would throw away.'

'Normal people don't abandon rental bikes, Lína. If you've found other unusual items, they're bound to have belonged to the same people. I wouldn't waste too much time on it.'

'But—'

'It's not our job to conduct the preliminary investigation of environmental crimes like fly tipping. Is the rubbish in the ditch likely to cause serious pollution or damage to the environment?'

'No.'

'Then it's not our problem, Lína, except for the stolen bikes. Bring them back with you and we'll report the rubbish to the Environment Agency. Just get yourself back to the office.'

'Can I send you some pictures?'

Huldar sighed under his breath. 'Yes, all right. Go on.'

They rang off and as Huldar went down to Forensics with the box, his phone kept bleeping to indicate that it was receiving a stream of picture files from Lína. Once he had handed over the doll and filled out the forms they shoved at him, ticking all the relevant boxes, Huldar opened the photos one after the other.

They showed an ugly mess and he could understand why an inexperienced, politically Left-Green trainee cop might think there was reason to investigate further. The ditch contained a weathered tent that appeared to have been lying there for some time in the constantly changing water level. One pole was poking up in the air, resting against the bank, while the canvas and the other poles lay in a heap at the bottom. As far as he could tell, there was nothing there to shock Lína unduly, since they'd all seen enough pictures in the media of the aftermath of outdoor festivals. In fact, this was mild compared to the usual chaos that looked as if a hurricane had sent the festival-goers fleeing for home, abandoning their rubbish where it lay.

The final photos were of a rucksack and of the tent, which Lína seemed to have rearranged to reveal what was inside it. Huldar had to admit that this looked pretty odd. The tent was full of everything people usually take with them when they go camping. By enlarging the image, he was able to make out sleeping bags, clothes, food, a shoe, coats and two quite nice-looking vape pens. All very peculiar. Even festival-goers would have the sense to take their most valuable possessions with them when they headed home.

As a smoker, he put a big question mark by the abandoned vape pens. Of course, he couldn't know how much other equipment these people had had with them, but it looked almost as if they'd decided to start a new life, given up vaping, chucked all their worldly goods in the ditch and walked away as naked as the day they were born.

Huldar zoomed in again when he spotted a familiar logo on the shoe that was lying amidst the rubbish: the three Adidas stripes. He studied the shoe. It looked exactly like the one on the end of the leg bone they had fished out of the sea. Closing the photo, he rang Lína as he climbed the stairs. 'Lína. Go back and stand guard by the ditch. We need to take a closer look at this.' Then he added: 'Well done. I shouldn't have doubted your instincts.'

After ringing off, he made straight for Erla's office. If she wasn't willing to send Forensics out there, he'd go himself. It could be a coincidence, but the events of recent days had taught him that coincidences weren't always what they seemed.

Chapter 30

Monday

Freyja said goodbye to Yngvi from the Child Protection Agency, and hung up. Her ear was red and sore from a conversation that had achieved little, despite lasting more than half an hour. She had told him about the latest developments in the Tristan case and they had discussed exhaustively what impact this could have, before ending their conversation in the same state of uncertainty as they had begun. Yngvi kept returning to the same question: *Do you think he might change his mind again and revert to his original testimony?* To which Freyja had replied: *I honestly don't know.* Another question he kept repeating was whether Bergur would now be released from custody. Freyja's answer to that was the same. There then followed speculation about whether the Child Protection Agency could be held responsible for depriving the care-home manager of his freedom, should he decide to sue. Would he have a right to demand reinstatement to his former position? Again, Freyja couldn't answer this. In fact, she had hardly been able to answer a single question, as the situation was still up in the air.

It was a sign of how shocked Yngvi was by this news that he forgot to press her on the question of whether she was planning to apply for the position of police liaison officer.

This was a relief as she still hadn't made up her mind. She just hadn't had time to give it any thought. Her job, Saga, the nits, Molly and the snake were already almost more than she could handle. But Baldur was due back in town the following day, and after that she would have more opportunity to think about her future. If her brother got held up in the highlands with his tourists, she would simply have to toss a coin.

Following Tristan's shock announcement, she had waited with the others for the boy to come back with his lawyer. After an hour, she had begun to have her doubts and twenty minutes later she had given up. Since they still hadn't bothered to sort out a workstation for her in CID, she had told Huldar she was going down to the Children's House until the situation was resolved. He'd promised to keep her informed but she hadn't heard from him yet.

Freyja leant back in her chair, her eyes on her screensaver, which featured stunning scenery in some exotic country that she would never visit. The image changed regularly and every time it did, she felt a pang that she didn't travel more. It wasn't as if she'd chosen her current existence. She reminded herself firmly of her three ground rules for sorting out her life: enjoy what every day has to offer, don't set your goals too high, and relax in your search for a man. There were only a few days left of her self-imposed period of abstinence, and seeing as she had done so well on that, the rest shouldn't be a problem. To her chagrin, she realised that her musings on this subject had led her thoughts inevitably to Huldar.

There was a knock and Elsa, who had taken over from Freyja back in the day as director of the Children's House, stuck her head round the door. 'How's it going?'

Freyja forced a smile. 'So-so. Slowly getting there.' In point of fact, this was a lie. Freyja was as clueless about Tristan's case now as she had been when she was assigned to it. And she was even more in the dark about Rósa's story and how it could have ended in tragedy.

'I hear there's been a spot of bother about Bergur.'

Freyja made an effort to hide her anger. How leaky could the system get? Had Yngvi got straight on the phone to Elsa after they'd talked? She had repeatedly stressed that their conversation was confidential; the case was at a delicate stage and more surprises were likely. 'Oh? Where did you hear that?' she said, trying to sound casual.

'Bergur's sister is my cousin's best friend. She rang me after his sister got in touch, over the moon because Bergur's lawyer had told her the case might be dropped. Is that true?'

Little Iceland syndrome. Freyja derived great satisfaction from nipping this juicy piece of gossip in the bud, even if it meant treating the truth in a rather cavalier fashion. 'I don't think anything like that's on the cards,' she said. 'At least, not as far as I'm aware.' Bergur's lawyer had demanded that his client should be released on the spot. Once Tristan had retracted his accusation, there was little to justify keeping Bergur in custody. But Hafthór from Sexual Offences had put his foot down, saying that such an action would be premature given that Tristan might well change his mind again. It wasn't unusual for people who brought accusations in sexual abuse cases to become disheartened during the process. More often than not, they subsequently found the courage to stick to their guns, as the lawyer was well aware.

'Oh, right. I thought it sounded a bit strange.' Elsa showed no sign of leaving. She fiddled with the big wooden beads round her neck. 'Do you know when you'll be free to come back to us?'

'No. But I expect it'll be soon.' Freyja wondered if her boss had got wind of the fact that she might be handing in her notice. Probably not. She imagined Yngvi had kept it to himself. 'These investigations have to end sooner or later.'

'Hmm.' Elsa looked doubtful. She knew as well as Freyja did that inquiries could drag on for months, until eventually the investigators gave up, closed the files and stuck them on a shelf somewhere.

'I'll let you know as soon as I have any idea.' Freyja could see that this didn't satisfy her boss. 'I should find out shortly.'

'Yes, let's hope so.' Elsa hovered in the doorway. 'The summer's nearly over and, as you know, we'll start to get busy soon. If you're still going to be tied up with this special assignment, I don't quite know how I'm going to manage the staffing here.'

Freyja couldn't enlighten her, and since she was no longer in charge herself, it wasn't her problem. 'I don't know what to say. But Yngvi asked me to do this, so if it drags on, you'd better to talk to him. Perhaps he has a spare psychologist who could stand in for me temporarily.' Or permanently, if she went ahead and applied for the new job.

'Yes. That's true.' Elsa heaved a world-weary sigh. Some people loved problems, especially when this gave them a chance to make everyone around them aware of the great burden they had to bear.

'By the way,' Freyja asked, forestalling any further complaints, 'do you know Bergur at all? Have you come across him in a professional context?'

'Me?' Elsa gripped her wooden beads more tightly. 'Not

much. But I have had some contact with him. I've had to request reports from him several times about the kids in his care. They were always thorough and gave me no reason to have any doubts about him – though I have to say, his spelling left a bit to be desired. When cases go to court, it doesn't look good to hand in documents littered with mistakes.'

Freyja wasn't remotely interested in Bergur's ability to spell. 'What does his sister say about the case? Have you heard?'

'She's stunned. In total shock. According to my cousin, she hasn't dared to look at the papers or online news since the interview appeared, for fear they'd publish a picture of Bergur. The moment that happens, he's done for, regardless of how the case turns out. He can change his name but not his face. And my cousin told me something else I found interesting: Bergur's sister has never been worried that he was interested in children or teenagers. Apparently, it was the mothers she was more concerned about. She'd got the impression he might be a bit too interested in them. Though, of course, that could have been a smokescreen to hide his real inclinations.'

'Sorry, but did his sister tell your cousin that Bergur might be going after the mothers of the kids in his care?'

'Yes. Though there may be nothing in it.'

'But what if it's true – wouldn't that be against the rules?'

Elsa twisted the beads on her necklace faster and faster, clearly regretting ever having brought up the subject. 'I don't think it occurred to anyone to put that in the carer's contract. But I imagine it would be frowned on.'

So it should be. The mothers of children who ended up in care tended to be extremely vulnerable themselves, due to mental problems or substance abuse. Many of them were easy prey for the unscrupulous. Freyja immediately thought of Tristan's frail mother, who had looked as if a puff of wind would blow her away. Was it possible that Bergur had tried it on with her? Maybe even used her, then dumped her? Could that be why the boy had invented his story? If Bergur's conduct wasn't against the rules, there would be little Tristan could do to get formal justice for their relationship. And even if such relationships had been prohibited, the only consequence for Bergur would have been a written warning.

'Do you know if Tristan's mother's name came up when Bergur's sister was talking about her concerns?'

Elsa let go of her beads and shook her head. 'No, I don't think she was aware of any specific instances. And her worries may have been groundless, if what the boy claims is true. Though there are some men who'll go after anything that moves when it comes to sex. It's rare but not unknown.'

Freyja merely nodded. Whatever the truth, she was fairly sure that Tristan hadn't lied just for the hell of it, to get an innocent man in trouble. If Tristan was telling the truth, Bergur was the worst kind of sexual abuser. If the boy was lying to get revenge for Bergur's treatment of his mother, then the man was a predator who went after vulnerable women. His job offered him the perfect opportunity for contact with any number of potential victims when they were at their most defenceless, when their children had been taken away from them, either temporarily or for good.

'Anyway, I must get on.' Elsa sighed heavily again to emphasise how many important tasks she had waiting for her and what immense pressure she was under. But Freyja, who knew the director's role from personal experience, was unimpressed by her martyred tone. The job had to be done conscientiously, like any other. It wasn't as if many people were just sitting around, twiddling their thumbs at work. 'I'm absolutely swamped,' Elsa said in a long-suffering voice. She gave Freyja a 'we're all in this together' smile, received an insincere one in return, and took herself off.

Once she was alone, Freyja found herself thinking that maybe she should take the plunge and apply for that police liaison job after all. Elsa was perfectly OK as a boss. She was a decent director of the Children's House, certainly no worse than Freyja had been. In fact, there was nothing in her manner or behaviour to justify the irritation she inspired in Freyja. If she were being honest, Freyja knew that it was because she missed being director herself, though she was perfectly aware she'd never get the job back. Did she really intend to continue coming in here year in, year out, still aggrieved that she had messed up? No. That would be a very bad idea. Far better to go and work at the police station and let Erla get on her nerves instead.

Freyja looked round her little office. Although she had done nothing to make it cosy, she felt at home here, as she did in the Children's House generally. Perhaps she wasn't that ready to jump ship after all. She sighed.

Her phone was lying silent on the desk. She picked it up to check she hadn't forgotten to unmute it after Tristan's abortive interview. But the sound was on. Neither Huldar nor anyone else had rung, texted or emailed. Clearly, there was no news.

Freyja decided to pass the time by reading what they had on Tristan's mother. Her appearance had suggested she was an addict, so there must be reports on her fitness as a parent. Since Freyja had access to Tristan's records, presumably she ought to be able to access his mother's too. The USB stick hadn't contained any specific information about the parents; their circumstances had only been mentioned when relevant to the reports on the children.

The mother's name was Berglind Sigvaldadóttir. It didn't take Freyja long to track down her records. She'd had Tristan young, when she was just sixteen. By then she'd already started doing drugs but had managed to come off them during her pregnancy, apart from cannabis, which she freely admitted to having smoked several times. A bit like other pregnant mothers admitting that they allowed themselves a sip of champagne on New Year's Eve.

The boy had apparently been a healthy and robust baby, in spite of all his mother's joints.

But parental responsibilities had proved tough for Berglind. Not only was she very young, but her drug habit had arrested her development. As a result she had been more than usually reliant on her own mother, who was also single; certainly more than was appropriate when it came to forming a connection with her son. Thanks to this security net, Berglind had gradually slid back into her old ways. During Tristan's first year she had vanished for the odd night or two; by the time he was four she was going missing for a week at a time, and by the time he was ten she had been known to disappear for a month or more. But Tristan's grandmother was always there to come to the rescue – right up until the day she died, when Tristan was eleven. It was then that things had taken a turn for the worse because there was no longer anybody to cover up for Berglind.

At first, left alone with her son, with no one there to bail them out, Berglind had got a grip on herself and showed a genuine willingness to clean up her act. She'd started turning up to interviews with social workers, and had done repeated stints in rehab. This may have been partly due to the fact that she had been on hard drugs for more than ten years by that point and the gloss had long since worn off the lifestyle; her fellow users were starting to lose their teeth, and the drugs no longer gave her the same buzz. She was growing tired.

However, as Berglind learnt the hard way, it was one thing to go to rehab, another to stay clean after you got out. The longest she managed to stay off drugs was six months. According to all the expert opinions recorded in her files, she loved Tristan and wanted to succeed as a parent. But the experts also agreed that her ability to do so was not consistent with her desire, and even when she was clean she had trouble meeting her son's basic needs. It was almost as if their roles had been reversed: the boy looked after her, rather than vice versa.

The authorities had decided to take the boy into temporary care for twelve months to give Berglind the opportunity to get her life back on track. It was her last chance. If she didn't pull herself together, children's services would start exploring permanent solutions for her son.

This was the point at which Tristan had ended up in Bergur's care. He was supposed to be at the home for three months while waiting for a temporary foster home to be found. But although he was a good, well-behaved boy with no drug issues, this had proved surprisingly difficult. The upshot was that Tristan had spent the entire twelve months with Bergur. His mother, initially taking seriously the threat of his permanent removal, had quit drugs, started attending AA meetings and got a part-time job through an organisation that helped people who had been out of work for long periods. Berglind's last employment before that had been a summer job in the city parks department when she was fourteen. Freyja assumed, from her limited knowledge of the drugs scene, that since then, Berglind had probably earned cash in hand from time to time – on her back. But of course that sort of thing was unlikely to show up on someone's CV.

Six months after Tristan had been removed from his mother, Berglind had gone spectacularly off the rails. She had started turning up for visits doped out of her skull, trying to act sober. She missed interviews and didn't answer her phone when attempts were made to contact her. But around the time a permanent care order was looming, she had managed to pull herself together again, and the temporary solution was extended. The decision about permanent removal of her son had been postponed for another twelve months. There was still hope.

Tristan, then thirteen, was sent to another temporary home. There he had met Rósa who was twelve and had only recently found herself in the clutches of the system. They spent four months together before Rósa was removed into foster care, from which she had subsequently absconded. Tristan, on the other hand, remained at the home until mould was discovered on the premises, after which he was moved and spent the last three months of his second year in care with Bergur.

In the end, Berglind had managed to quit the drugs again and Tristan, then just fourteen, had been allowed to go back to live with her. But that wasn't the end of the story. There had followed periods of differing lengths when his mother had lapsed, then gone into rehab, and he had again been placed in temporary care, more often than not with Bergur.

His last spell in care had been when he was sixteen. His mother had slipped up, but pulled herself out of the gutter unbelievably fast and had been allowed to have her boy home again. Since then they had struggled on, though the social workers were under the impression that Tristan covered up for her when she went off the rails. Still, he would soon be eighteen, after which he would no longer be the responsibility of children's services. There were more than enough younger children who required their care; children for whom there might still be hope.

From the reports Freyja had read, it was evident that Tristan and his mother had an unhealthily co-dependent relationship. Berglind had never properly grown up, and after her mother died, the job of caring for her had fallen to her eleven-year-old son. That couldn't be good for either of them. He was overly attached to her and she was over-reliant on him. In view of this, it wasn't impossible that he might resort to unorthodox methods of protecting her, just as parents are capable of doing when their children are in trouble.

If Bergur had taken advantage of Tristan's mother's vulnerability, the boy might well have hit on this method of exacting revenge; telling lies about him and persuading his friend Rósa to back him up. The idea might have seemed clever at first but circumstances had conspired to change that.

Freyja closed the files, let go of the mouse and checked her phone again. Nothing. She sighed. There was no chance of an interview with Tristan today, at least not one that she could attend. She had to collect Saga from nursery school in less than an hour.

She was dying to know what was happening. Had the police got hold of Tristan or his legal adviser? Had they announced that he wouldn't be coming back, either today or tomorrow? If so, the boy would have to be summoned before a judge.

Freyja couldn't resist the temptation any longer. She had to know what was going on. She selected Huldar's number, but the longer it rang the more awkward she felt. Wasn't he going to pick up? That would be mortifying.

Just as she was expecting to be transferred to his voicemail, Huldar finally answered. 'Hi. Sorry. I left my phone in my coat pocket. It was lucky I heard it at all.'

'Is there any news?'

'Yes, finally. We've just got hold of the lawyer. They're coming in tomorrow. At one. Keep the day free.'

'What about Bergur? Are they going to let him go?'

'No, not as things stand.'

'I've just heard something. There may be nothing in it but I thought you should know.' She repeated Bergur's sister's suspicions regarding the mothers of the kids in Bergur's care. A short silence followed, after which Huldar said he would bear it in mind. He added that he couldn't quite see how it was relevant, even if it were true. Freyja didn't bother to explain her theory. She wanted to assess the boy's credibility for herself. If, by the end of tomorrow's interview, she still believed her theory was plausible, she would share it with Huldar. No doubt he had plenty of other things to think about at the moment, without having to listen to her speculating about the case.

'Hey. There's one thing.' Huldar sounded oddly elated.

'What?'

'There's something I need to show you. Trust me, you won't want to miss it.'

'OK.' Freyja didn't know if he expected her to come down

to the station or if he was planning to email her. 'If I'm going to come in, it'll have to be quick because I've got to collect Saga. For the last time for now. After tomorrow I'll be free to attend interviews twenty-four seven.'

'Look, I'm flat out here at the moment but I'll drop by your place this evening. I'll bring burgers.' Huldar had many good qualities but his taste in food wasn't one of them. 'I'm hanging up now, before you can say no. See you later.'

Freyja realised that he had gone.

Chapter 31

Freyja placed Huldar's phone carefully on the kitchen table. The photo of the doll filled the screen, in shocking contrast to the mundane mess of fast-food packaging and leftovers. 'So the doll did exist and hadn't been thrown in the bin? Rósa wasn't talking nonsense.'

'Looks like it. There's absolutely zero chance it's a coincidence. A doll that's been at the bottom of the sea, exactly like she said. It has to be the same one.'

'But what was Brynjólfur doing with it? Does this mean there could be some truth in what Rósa claimed about her mother being murdered? Could Brynjólfur have been the killer?'

Huldar reached for the phone and returned it to his pocket. 'Who knows? We may never get an answer to that. Everyone connected to the incident is dead. All we know is that his ex-wife says she gave him permission to put some more stuff in storage several years ago and she believes the doll must have been part of it. The storage company has confirmed her story. The wife phoned and told them to let Binni have access to the unit. That was late the same day that Rósa's mother was found dead. The following day he went to the storage place and picked up the keys, then returned them. Since then, no one else has asked for them until last Sunday when his ex-wife cleared out the unit. So the doll was put there by Binni. I don't know how the hell we're supposed to find out any more. We've hit a dead end.'

'God, that's frustrating.' Two frown lines appeared between Freyja's eyebrows. Huldar thought how well they suited her, along with the informal hoodie and grubby jeans she was wearing. Her feet were bare in her open-toed slippers, her toenails painted pink. Usually she went around dressed like a law student on her way to a job interview. Looking at her now, he felt a sudden impulse to invite her camping with him, but this wasn't the moment.

'Is there really no way to get to the bottom of it?'

'Probably not.' Huldar knew what she was thinking. It was hard to accept that some riddles would never be solved. The human race had centuries' worth of unsolved mysteries to puzzle over, and, in the great scheme of things, this one was unlikely to be remembered for long. The story of Rósa's mother's death wasn't dramatic enough to survive. If her nose had been missing or a stranger's arm had been found in her bathtub, the story would have had a chance. Especially if the origin of the body part had never been discovered. Realising that his mind was wandering, Huldar picked up again from where he had left off: 'Perhaps it really was an accident. The thing that makes me think Brynjólfur can't have done anything to Rósa's mother is the doll itself. Would you kill a woman, steal the doll, then hang on to it? Usually people try to get rid of evidence that could connect them to a crime.'

'No. I wouldn't. But then it's highly unlikely I'd kill someone over a doll, let alone over a horrible specimen like that.' Freyja shivered.

'I can't believe the doll was the motive. I'm guessing it was an accident: the woman slipped and fell, and the doll ended up in Brynjólfur's possession by some perfectly natural set of circumstances – if anything about that doll can be considered natural.'

At this point Saga bashed Huldar on the leg with a cuddly toy that was probably supposed to be a dinosaur. She had barely touched her burger and insisted on getting down from her high chair. Since then she had been amusing herself by throwing the dinosaur for Molly to fetch. Her reach was so short, however, that the dog hardly needed to move from her place. It was fortunate the toy was soft, given the violence with which the little girl was now beating it against Huldar's leg. He got the message and lifted her onto his lap, only to regret it when she shoved the dinosaur in his face, all soggy from Molly's slobbery chops.

'Does anyone know what's happening tomorrow? About Tristan, I mean?' Freyja ate a chip that must be cold by now. 'Will he continue to be interviewed as a witness or will his status be changed to suspect?'

'Haven't a clue. It's not my decision.' Huldar pinched Saga's nose. 'The meeting to discuss it was still going on when I left the office. I just kept my head down so I wouldn't get sucked in there. I'll find out tomorrow morning, which is good enough for me.'

He had plenty of other things to keep him busy, though he couldn't discuss the business of the bones with Freyja. Lína had hit the jackpot when Erla sent her out to investigate the rubbish-filled ditch in an attempt to get rid of her. It now appeared all but certain that Lína's antisocial campers were the people whose remains had turned up on the seabed. The shoe in the ditch matched the other shoe that had been found on the end of the skeletal leg, and that was just the beginning.

Lína had beaten both Interpol and the British police to it when it came to identifying the owners of the bones, though, in defence of these institutions, the information from the DNA analysis had only reached them on Saturday and they had probably still been at the stage of registering the case. But still, Lína was a hero.

A name found on a debit card in the inside pocket of one of the coats had turned out to be on the Interpol list of missing people. And a second name had been linked to the same disappearance, which involved a young British couple called Leonard Vale and Abby Endler, who had last been seen in Spain. The police were now trying to discover how and when they had travelled to Iceland, since they didn't appear to be on any airline passenger list or to have arrived with the Norröna ferry. Lists of passengers and crews had been requested for a two-week period either side of the couple's disappearance in Spain, but their names were nowhere to be found. Still, it wasn't impossible that they would turn up on closer investigation, since there were nearly a hundred flights to Keflavík Airport every day, and not all the twenty-four airlines serving the route had delivered their lists yet. Moreover, one of the companies had gone bust, which meant that their passenger lists might never materialise. It would be sod's law if the names of the unlucky Brits had been on them.

Further information had been obtained from a phone call to Interpol. According to a member of the international police, who knew something about the case, the young couple hadn't mentioned any plans to travel to Iceland, which was why it hadn't occurred to anyone to search for them there.

Their families and friends said they'd been intending to go to Spain for two weeks but had vanished without trace from their hotel halfway through their holiday. The Spanish authorities had concentrated on looking for them in Spain, as there had been no indication that they had bought air or train tickets out of the country, or had access to a car. An examination of the couple's invoices revealed that they had paid for the flights to Spain and the hotel themselves, and the bookings had been in their names.

They had taken all their luggage with them when they abandoned their hotel, leaving their room empty. They hadn't spoken to reception and none of the other guests remembered hearing them discussing their plans or seeing them leave.

The couple's credit card had been over the limit, and they hadn't used it for two days before vanishing from the hotel or at any point after that. The debit card found in the coat pocket hadn't been used either, and the account it belonged to turned out to be empty.

The couple's last posts on social media dated from the morning of their disappearance and had been made via the hotel's wi-fi connection. According to the Interpol representative, the posts had offered no clues to their fate. Abby had posted a photo of the two of them smiling under an umbrella beside a swimming pool, with the caption: *It's not where you go, it's who you travel with*. Leonard had posted a photo of a small waste-paper bin overflowing with empty beer bottles, with the message: *Save water – drink beer*. The bin was the same type as those found in the hotel rooms, but the couple's room had been cleaned by the time their disappearance was reported. No one remembered whether the beer bottles had been in the bin when the cleaners had come round.

In other words, the couple's electronic trail had provided no answers, and no witnesses had come forward with information about their disappearance. Nor had Leonard and Abby's phones been picked up by any network.

The Interpol representative did add one fact that he thought might explain why the couple had gone missing. A sizeable heap of opioid pills had been found in a litter bin in the hotel grounds when it was emptied the day after the couple vanished. The discovery was reported to the local police who had subsequently made the connection when the couple were reported missing. The stash had consisted of around 1,200 loose pills, mainly 80 mg OxyContin. Interpol believed the two events were linked. The young couple must have got themselves into a situation that was out of their depth. The theory was that they had agreed to act as drugs mules and carry the pills back to Britain but that they had got cold feet, ditched the drugs and made a run for it. To cover their tracks, they had probably hitched a lift, paid for bus tickets in cash or got a lift somewhere with a fishing boat. To another city or even another country.

The alternative was that the smugglers had caught up with them.

The hotel employee who had spotted the pills had kept them to hand over to the police but thrown away the rest of the rubbish. Unfortunately, this meant that the bag or packaging the pills had been tipped out of was not available for fingerprinting. No prints had been found on the pills themselves, apart from those of the observant hotel employee. The upshot was that the police had no evidence to confirm their theory and their investigation had soon reached an impasse.

The young couple's names had been added to the missing-persons' lists held by Interpol and the British police, and the file had soon been closed and shelved. The inquiry might have remained open if family or friends had alerted people to the couple's disappearance via social media and kept the case in the public eye, but this hadn't happened. The couple seemed to have had relatively few friends and not much of a support network at home. Now, however, the dust would be blown off their files.

Huldar was longing to tell Freyja about Abby and Leonard. He couldn't stop thinking about them, as if the mystery of how they had ended up at the bottom of the sea off Iceland had hooked its claws into him and wouldn't let go. The young couple's fate wasn't only gut-wrenchingly sad, it was also hard to get one's head around. He didn't for a second imagine that Freyja would be able to suggest a solution to a problem that had left Interpol scratching their heads. He just wanted to talk about the couple to alleviate the sickening feelings of incomprehension, anger and sadness that their demise was churning up inside him. His thoughts kept returning to the photo he had seen of the two young Brits, smiling and happy, seemingly without a care in the world. The contrast was so stark when juxtaposed with the harrowing images of the skeletal remains fished up from the sea, as if his brain was intent on presenting him with the worst before-and-after photo comparison imaginable.

'I really feel for Tristan.' Freyja picked up another cold chip, changed her mind and put it back. She didn't seem to notice how distracted he was. 'It's not easy growing up with a mother who's an addict. Or a father, for that matter. Did you see the woman? She looked terrible.'

Huldar ducked as Saga swung the dinosaur at his face. 'I've seen worse. But that doesn't alter the fact that the poor kid didn't exactly win at life's lottery. I hope his mum'll be able to turn over a new leaf, but, let's face it, that's pretty optimistic. I gather she's addicted to opioids and that more than ninety per cent of opioid addicts lapse after treatment. More than half of them in the first week.' It was a relief to focus on Tristan, rather than the deceased British couple. Although the kid had it bad, his circumstances were a whole lot better than theirs.

Freyja looked despondent. 'She's been to rehab several times. She managed to stay clean for a while but then slipped up again. If there's a ninety per cent failure rate, we'll just have to hope she's among the ten per cent.'

Huldar gave her a reassuring smile as he engaged in a tug-of-war with Saga over the dinosaur, while thinking privately that if he'd been offered a bet on the woman's chances of beating her addiction, he wouldn't have taken it. On the other hand, he would have emptied his bank account if asked to bet on Saga's chances of becoming a future Cross-Fit champion. She was unbelievably strong for her size. He let go of the soggy dinosaur so suddenly that the little girl nearly toppled backwards off his lap. 'Whoa!' Glancing up, he saw that Freyja didn't look unduly disturbed. Yet another point in her favour. His sisters always behaved as if their children were made of china when he was messing about with them. They would hover around him, squawking like a flock of Arctic terns, ready to grab their sons in case Huldar tossed them up in the air or dropped them on the floor. It was a wonder his horde of nephews hadn't grown up to be total mummy's boys.

'Have you made any progress with finding out how Rósa knew about Bergur before she was placed at his home?' Freyja held out a chip to Molly who swallowed it without chewing, then readied herself for the next.

'No. There's been absolutely no time to look into that. We're still trying to find out where the girl was hiding prior to her death. Hopefully things will become clearer once we know that.' When Huldar had slipped out of the office to fetch the burgers and take them round to Freyja's, Gudlaugur had still been at his desk, waiting for the list of Rósa's mother's former colleagues to come through. It appeared that the HR records of the office she had worked for had got into a bit of a mess when they'd merged with another agency. But the information was being collected. Once the list had been sent over, the police would be able to use the men's ID numbers to establish which of them now lived in the Seljahverfi area. In Huldar's opinion this was a waste of time. He was convinced the man they were after was Fridrik Reynisson, the owner of the fishing boat, but he supposed it wouldn't hurt to make sure that there weren't other candidates as well. There hadn't been time to interview Fridrik today anyway, since Erla wanted to be present but had been too tied up.

Freyja put an elbow on the table and rested her chin in her hand. 'Tell me something. Do you enjoy working for the police?'

'Enjoy it?' Huldar thought for a moment. 'It's rewarding. It can be tough, but I'm OK with that. Anyway, someone has to do it, so why not me?' From Freyja's expression, he realised he wasn't doing a very good job of selling the profession. He had no idea why she should be wondering about his job satisfaction but took it as a sign that he was gradually getting into her good books. He could have sworn she was looking at him differently these days. She no longer rolled her eyes when he appeared and she had twice let him in bearing burgers. He was fairly sure that hunger wasn't the only reason. Based on his long experience of getting women into bed, Huldar reckoned Freyja was showing distinct signs of being receptive to his advances. But although his instinct was seldom wrong in these matters, he didn't dare push his luck. She was as prickly as a porcupine and he risked being on the sharp end of her spines if he got it wrong. It was better to proceed with extreme caution.

Then there was the child on his lap. Even a master of the bedroom arts like him couldn't see how he was supposed to seduce Freyja with Saga in the picture. Still, according to Freyja, the little girl would be going back to her father tomorrow and after that his way would be clear.

'Why are you smiling?' Freyja was dangling the last chip over Molly's gaping jaws.

'Oh, sorry, my mind was wandering.'

Freyja dropped the chip and Molly's jaws snapped shut. 'Anyway. If someone was offered a job with the police, would you recommend that he or she take it?'

'Him, yes. Her, I don't know. It's harder for women. At the moment, anyway. Why don't you ask Lína? She could give you a better answer than me if it's a woman you're asking for.' It didn't occur to Huldar to suggest talking to Erla. The less contact she and Freyja had, the better. 'Who are you talking about, by the way?'

Freyja dropped her gaze and got to her feet. 'Oh, no one you know.'

Huldar doubted that. He had developed an instinct for

when people were telling the truth and when they were lying. This was a half-truth, at best. But he didn't press her. He didn't want to risk annoying her and sacrificing his newfound popularity for someone who had nothing to do with him. He just hoped she wasn't asking on behalf of her brother, Baldur. He had no chance of getting a job with the police, with a criminal record like his. Though, on reflection, maybe the police should relax their criteria, because Baldur and his associates must have an unrivalled inside knowledge of the underworld that would come in extremely handy, particularly now. 'One question, Freyja: do you think Baldur might have heard of Brynjólfur and maybe even know who he was selling drugs for? I don't believe for a minute that he was capable of importing them and organising the distribution himself.'

'Baldur? He's never been involved in dealing. He's working as a guide these days.' Freyja broke off, apparently regretting having said this much. 'Well, he's recently got a job as a tourist guide.'

'In spite of that, I'm sure he knows more about the market than many people do.' Huldar chose his words carefully, wary of the prickles that had risen a little at the question about her brother. 'Not because he's in the business himself.'

'Yes, maybe.' Freyja sounded hesitant. 'I do need to ring him, actually.'

'It would be brilliant if you could ask him. The Drug Squad's completely stumped.' Huldar's eyes dropped to Saga's dark head. Her hair looked different from how he'd remembered it; it was standing out in a halo of static. He stroked it flat but it sprang up again. 'But maybe it's not a good idea to discuss it while . . . you know who . . . is listening.' He jerked his chin at the fuzzy little head.

'I can go into the other room.' Freyja ran a hand over her own hair and Huldar now noticed that it was full of electricity too, though not as bad as Saga's. He wondered if there was something in the air of the flat but when he touched his own head, his hair felt normal. Realising it probably wouldn't be a good idea to comment on it, he lowered his hand and waited for Freyja to come to a decision about whether to call Baldur. Finally, she made up her mind and took the phone into the bedroom hallway, leaving Huldar alone with Saga and Molly.

He could hear the sound of her voice but, to his relief, couldn't make out the words. While he was waiting, he and Saga took it in turn to throw the dinosaur for Molly to fetch. The results were very different but Saga seemed oblivious to the fact and clapped enthusiastically every time she managed to throw the soft toy beyond her own toes, but never clapped for Huldar, even when he lobbed it to the other end of the flat.

After yet another long throw by Huldar, the dinosaur landed by the door to the room Freyja had said the owner was using for storage. Molly bounded after it but instead of snatching it up in her jaws and bringing it back, she stopped by the door, flattened her ears and growled.

'What's in there, Saga?' Huldar pointed to the door. Just like last time, Freyja had kept darting glances in that direction while they were eating. But whenever he himself happened to look over there, she had made some remark at random, in a rather high, strained voice, as if to distract him.

'Ssssss. Ssssssss.' Saga opened her eyes wide in an exaggerated expression of fear.

Was she trying to say, 'Shhh'? Why did they have to be quiet? Surely there couldn't be someone in there? Huldar dismissed the idea as absurd but remained perplexed. He was still groping for a possible explanation when Freyja returned. 'What did he say?' he asked.

Freyja blew out a breath. She was still holding the phone. 'Right. So, according to Baldur, Brynjólfur didn't start dealing until recently.'

'How does he know that? Is he sure?'

'I have no idea how he knows. All I know is what he told me. If you need more details, you'll have to ring him yourself, though I'm pretty sure he'll hang up on you. I had to prise every word out of him. He doesn't like leaking information to the police and I had a nightmare trying to talk him into it. Eventually, he spilled the beans, but only after I'd told him Brynjólfur was dead, so he wouldn't be getting him into trouble by telling us what he knew.'

'Sorry. Go on.'

'Anyway. Apparently, Brynjólfur recently popped up as a dealer. He'd been a user for years and a heavy drinker too, but he'd never sold so much as a gram of weed. Baldur doesn't know who he was selling for and said that a lot of people had been wondering about that. A man like Brynjólfur wasn't exactly a reliable person to entrust your stock to. He only sold opioids, not dope or cocaine or MDMA or amphetamines. Only prescription drugs.'

'So Baldur had no idea who could have supplied him with the drugs?'

'Nope, none. I asked him specifically about that – if it could have been a doctor, for example – but all he'd heard was a rumour about the drugs coming from Spain.'

'That figures.' Huldar was bursting with questions but he didn't want to risk wearing out her patience.

'He also said that whoever was behind the business must have been a complete amateur if he was using someone like Brynjólfur to circulate the stuff for him. In fact, Baldur was pretty gobsmacked by the idea.'

'Was he acquainted with Brynjólfur then?'

'No. Not personally. But he immediately knew who I was talking about, and that Brynjólfur lived in the container colony on Grandi. Apparently, the man used to go back and forth between the Hladgerdarkot treatment centre and the refuge at Kumbaravogur, and possibly hung out at the halfway house in Vídines as well. Baldur insisted that he couldn't have been dealing much at any of these places as they're all in the arse end of nowhere. His words, not mine. Actually, he was surprised that Binni had managed to get himself moved, because apparently people are fighting over the small amount of accommodation that's available in the city. It's understandable, when you think about it, because homeless people and addicts rarely have cars, so it's no fun for them living out in the sticks. But that's how social services get them out of sight – they sweep them under the welfare carpet, so to speak.'

'Can I interrupt a minute?' Huldar didn't want to lose the focus on what Baldur had said and it sounded as if the conversation was veering off track into a debate about the ills of society. He was afraid she might forget something her brother had told her if she got distracted. When Freyja nodded, Huldar went on: 'Had Baldur heard any rumours about who could have killed Brynjólfur?'

'No. Nothing. He was up in the highlands with a group of tourists when the murder took place – he's still there, actually. But he was sure it must have been the person who supplied him with the drugs. Committed in a fit of rage, probably, because he'd discovered that Brynjólfur had stolen the pills for his own use. Or spent all the money. Baldur couldn't imagine why anyone would have wanted to get rid of him otherwise. Except maybe rival dealers.'

'That's not impossible.'

'Then he added that murders don't always have a motive.' Freyja fell silent and folded her arms.

Huldar wasn't about to disagree with this. 'It's not uncommon for drunk people to get into fights that end in disaster. Over some trivial nonsense that they wouldn't even have thought worth raising their voice over when they were sober.'

'Ssssss. Ssssss.' Saga tugged at Huldar's trouser leg and pointed to the door of the mysterious storeroom.

Freyja clapped her hands. 'Coffee! Who wants coffee?'

Huldar accepted a cup. While Freyja was making it with an unnecessary amount of clatter, he couldn't stop wondering what was behind the closed door.

As if he didn't have enough mysteries to deal with just now.

Chapter 32

Tuesday

Erla surveyed the group in the meeting room. There were more people present at today's briefing than there had been for weeks, as those officers still in the country had been recalled from their summer holidays. Naturally, the mood was despondent, given the gravity of the situation, but the sourest faces of all belonged to those who had been prematurely dragged back to work. The only times their scowls disappeared were when they were replaced by looks of bemused incomprehension. Huldar was glad he'd been involved from the start or he would be looking as bewildered as they were: skeletal remains and a doll on the seabed, a murdered teenager, a murdered homeless man, drug dealing, and the shock retraction of a sexual abuse allegation.

A simultaneous meeting was taking place in the Sexual Offences Unit, where the mood was probably even more disconsolate. There they were discussing the latest twist in the abuse case and considering their next steps, including how to handle Tristan during his interview that afternoon. Freyja was due to attend that meeting. Hopefully she would be able to advise them as they must be at their wits' end.

Erla looked at the projector screen, then back at her team: 'As you can see, we've got a lot of ground to cover. Regarding the skeletal remains, I want us to prioritise finding out how and when the British couple travelled to Iceland. They didn't swim here and since there are no transactions on their accounts to show the purchase of tickets with a plane or a ship, we're left with only two alternatives: either someone else bought the tickets for them or they were given a free lift on a boat. If we can find the answer to that, we'll probably be able to nail the person who put them at the bottom of the sea. The tent that turned up on the south coast proves they camped here, and although that doesn't rule out the possibility that they later fell overboard during a boat trip, it's also plausible that they were pushed, whether alive or dead. Bear in mind the blood-stains on the tent that are currently being analysed. From the amount of blood, they're unlikely to have cut themselves on a tin opener.' The large photo that now flashed up on screen, showing the dark stains on the inside of the tent, removed any doubt where that was concerned.

Lína stuck her thin arm straight up in the air and started waving it back and forth when Erla pretended not to notice. The Sexual Offences Unit hadn't requested her return after she'd finished going through Binni's boxes, but Erla hadn't complained as she was only too grateful for an extra pair of hands at a time like this, especially when it was Lína who had got the case moving. This didn't make Erla feel any more kindly towards her, however. 'What?' she snapped, her voice as frigid as if she had breathed out the word in dry ice.

'Are there any signs of stab wounds on the bones?' Lína lowered her hand.

'If you'd let me continue, I was just getting to that.' Erla clicked on the next slide, which was a composite of several from the first and second bone finds. Erla explained that only one of the bones had shown signs of knife damage. This was the ulna – one of the forearm bones – from the female. Once the bones had been cleaned, another cut had been revealed, similar to the one they had already observed. The conclusion of the expert who had examined them was that the incisions had been made by a sharp knife, probably with quite a short blade. In his opinion, the injuries would be consistent with the subject raising her arms in self-defence. Erla then added that they would not have been the cause of death. Fatal stab wounds were usually made to the front or back of the torso or neck, but unfortunately no bones from these parts of the body had been recovered from the seabed.

This was followed by a grisly description of how the limbs and head tended to break away from the torso, which would then float up to the surface due to the accumulation of gas caused by bacterial action during decomposition. The torsos were thus assumed to have drifted further out to sea where birds would have pecked at them until the gas was released, after which they would have sunk again. There was no point searching for them at this point, since the sea was vast and there was no way of guessing where the torsos would have ended up.

'To recap, the urgent priority now is to find the person who enabled them to travel to Iceland. Frustratingly, the couple had no known connection to this country, so it won't be easy. But we do know that the person who rented the bikes they were using had paid for them anonymously, in cash. There was no name on the booking either. Apparently, an inexperienced member of staff let himself be tricked into accepting just the booking number. He was sacked when the bicycles weren't returned. We're going to bring him in and see if we can create an identikit of the person who paid for them. Hopefully that'll happen today or tomorrow. He'll also be asked to confirm that the British couple were the people who turned up with the printout of the booking to pick up the bikes. We're sourcing photos of them and other people for comparison, to do it by the book. But the first step, as I said before, is to find out how the hell they got to Iceland. With any luck it was by plane, because in that case it should be relatively easy to trace how the tickets were paid for.'

'Could they have been smuggling drugs?' The questioner didn't bother to raise his arm. He was an old hand who still couldn't get used to the idea of taking orders from a woman and dealt with the situation by behaving at times like a naughty school kid. To make matters worse, he was one of those who had been brought back early from their holidays, which had put him in an even nastier mood than usual.

Erla's eyes rested on him with an expression of distaste, as if she'd spotted a rotten lettuce leaf at the bottom of her fridge. 'If I could speak without constantly being interrupted, we'd get through this a lot quicker. I was just coming to that.' Erla looked back at the others and carried on: 'According to the Spanish police, there's evidence to suggest the couple were acting as drugs mules – mules who changed their minds and ditched the dope. But there's no indication that they had ever been linked to drugs before. This would have made them ideal for the job, of course. As for their motive – we know they were skint. So the answer to your question is, yes, they may well have been smuggling drugs. We can't be sure they threw the whole lot away, though it's hard to see why they should only have offloaded part of the consignment. Unless they didn't have room for all of it.'

Erla paused a moment, then returned to the agenda: 'We need to find out who supplied Brynjólfur with the drugs he's rumoured to have been selling. So far we haven't been able to dig up any other obvious motive for his murder, though it's possible that it could have been a sense-less attack by someone under the influence of alcohol or drugs. His neighbour has been released from custody as it seems unlikely he was involved, and Brynjólfur's family also appears to be in the clear. Who knows? Perhaps the person who killed Brynjólfur is also the one who killed the British couple. After all, a knife was involved in both murders.'

Erla changed the slide and a huge picture of the doll flashed up on the screen. 'Turning now to the most serious case we're dealing with, we've got CCTV footage from Smáralind and the bus that confirm the main points of Tristan's story. He and Rósa first appear in the shopping centre at ten to seven; they buy themselves burgers, then go to a film that started at eight and finished at quarter past ten. They can be seen wandering unhurriedly around, then leaving the building, and are next caught on camera at eleven minutes past eleven as they climb aboard the number twenty-four bus. They sit down, talk a bit, then Rósa starts fiddling in the pockets of her coat. She gets up and jumps out at the stop on Dalvegur, calling something to Tristan on her way out. We know nothing about her movements from then until her body was discovered at half past nine on Saturday morning. The time of death is estimated at just after midnight.'

Again Erla fell silent, but this time only to reach for a glass of water and take a long drink. The room was so quiet that they could all hear her swallow. She resumed: 'We've received a list of former colleagues of Rósa's mother, Dísa. It appears that only one of them is registered as living in Seljahverfi. His name's Fridrik Reynisson and he's the man who took the mother and daughter out on his boat five years ago when they caught the doll in the net. Later that night Dísa died and the doll vanished, only to turn up again, all these years later, in Brynjólfur's storage unit.'

Lína's hand shot up again. Erla, realising the young woman would go on waving it until she got her attention, nodded irritably.

'If you believe that Rósa was hiding at his place, why not search it?' Lína squared her shoulders and added: 'If you do, I'd like to offer my services.'

Erla rolled her eyes. 'When and if we conduct a search of the premises, you will not be involved. May I remind you that you're only a summer temp.'

The old chauvinist emitted a bark of laughter. Erla shot him a dirty look before turning back to Lína, who protested: 'But I've been involved in a search before. When I was here on work experience, remember?'

Erla pretended not to hear this. 'I'll see what I can do, Lína. It would certainly be useful for you to build up a range of experience.'

Huldar smiled privately. Erla would do anything to avoid pleasing the old git, even if it meant doing Lína a favour, however much that must stick in her throat.

'OK, first things first,' Erla said. 'We'll start by talking to Fridrik Reynisson. There may not be any need for a search warrant, if he decides to cooperate. We should also bear in mind the possibility that Tristan was wrong or that he invented the detail about the mother's colleague, or that Rósa lied to him. Let's just hope we get more out of the boy when we interview him later. It's possible he's been sitting on information that he's been unwilling to share with us up to now. But there are other urgent tasks too. There are no CCTV cameras showing the traffic along the road past Lake Hafravatn, so we'll have to examine the footage from the nearest ones. It'll be a hell of a job to piece them together, but, on the plus side, the post-mortem shows that Rósa was dumped in the lake in the early hours, when there's little traffic. With any luck, we'll soon be able to identify a suspicious vehicle and then at least we'll know what make of car we're looking for. That should make our job easier.'

Erla waited to give her team a chance to ask questions but no one said a word: they had all seen how she dealt with those who did. So she carried on reviewing those lines of inquiry where the investigation was making progress and others where they were at a standstill. She outlined the tenuous connections between the three cases and also their link to a fourth – the abuse case currently being investigated by the Sexual Offences Unit, stressing that they couldn't make any assumptions at this stage. Everyone was to focus on the task assigned to them and not waste any time on trying to work out the bigger picture.

After handing out the assignments, Erla brought the meeting to a close. Gudlaugur was given the job of checking whether there had been any known links between Rósa and Bergur before she was placed at his home. Lína was to examine the British couple's social media activity in the hope of finding some connection to Iceland or an Icelander. Huldar got off scot-free as he was to join Erla for the interview of Tristan.

Huldar caught the looks his colleagues sent him when his name wasn't called. Clearly they had put two and two together and made five. They reckoned they knew why he'd got off so lightly. No doubt the rumour mill would start up, insinuating that he and Erla were seeing each other again – as if their one-night stand had ever constituted 'seeing each other'.

Just wait until Erla's pregnancy started to show. Then the whispers and gossiping would go into overdrive. His colleagues were as capable as his sisters of reading things into situations where there was nothing to know.

But such worries would have to wait.

The meeting room emptied as Erla turned off the computer and projector. Huldar waited to walk out with her, not giving a damn that it would provide even more material for idle tongues. He knew the battle was already lost. Yet in spite of himself, he spoke with a little more emphasis than usual, making sure his voice carried, when he asked if she wanted him to prepare for the coming interview with Tristan.

Erla puffed out her cheeks, then exhaled. 'Let me think . . . I'll let you know.' She went into her office and shut the door, leaving Huldar standing there with nothing to do.

He soon got bored of sitting at his desk, awaiting orders from Erla that didn't come. He went out twice for a smoke and fetched himself three coffees. He googled everything he could think of about Fridrik Reynisson, who was suspected of having sheltered Rósa, but it didn't get him far. The man seemed to have passed almost invisibly through life: his name cropped up a few times in old track records from the Athletics Association; he turned up in two pictures taken at meetings of the Association of Small-boat Owners, and there was the odd mention of him in connection with the Marine Research Institute where he now worked. Very few results came up connecting him to the Transport Authority, where he had previously been employed at the same time as Rósa's mother, Dísa. His name appeared under his mother's death notice, along with the names of his brother and father, and also in the family details parts of her obituaries. The day he was forty, he earned a mention in the *Morgunbladid* newspaper as one of those celebrating landmark birthdays, and once he had been interviewed in a vox pop: No, he wouldn't be going to the World Cup.

A search of the Police Information System drew a blank. The man had never fallen foul of the law. He was a respectable citizen who kept a low profile and got on with his life without causing any ripples. All of which begged the question: what the hell had a character like that been thinking when he decided to shelter a runaway teen? The answer wasn't to be found online, that much was sure.

There was no point discussing it with Gudlaugur, who was absorbed in his own assignment. So far he hadn't let out any victory cries, so presumably he wasn't getting anywhere yet. The same applied to the rest of the team; every single person had their nose pressed to their computer screen but no one had come up with anything significant. Not even Lína.

Huldar went over to her and sat on the edge of her desk. 'How's it going?'

'Good.' Lína smiled. Even in a nuclear war, he reckoned she would be one of the few to maintain her innate optimism. She would hold her head high as her fellow citizens crumpled around her, staring hopefully at the horizon, even as she counted the mushroom clouds. 'I just don't know how far back in time I should go. They've both been on social media for nearly ten years. And to make matters worse, they were on all the sites. Not equally active on all of them, but still.'

'My advice would be to concentrate on the latest posts. Work backwards. I doubt their school days will have any relevance to the inquiry.'

Lína pushed herself away from the desk. 'It's a weird assignment. I'm looking at photo after photo of young people who are dead. Smiling faces one day, dead the next. They look as if they were so happy.'

Huldar folded his arms across his chest, wondering if he should state the obvious: 'You know social media isn't a window into people's real lives, Lína. You're not exactly peering through the keyhole. This is more like watching a play that you might call: "My Life as I Wish It Was All the Time".'

'I do know that, Huldar.' Lína shot him a glare that could have been borrowed from Erla's arsenal. 'But it's still very sad.'

He was quick to agree. All the cases they were dealing with were sad: Rósa, the young couple, Brynjólfur. Their fates were all pretty tragic. Tristan's too.

'Can I see?' He got off her desk and came to stand beside her. 'It would be helpful to be able to picture something other than bones when we're discussing these people. I've only seen the one photo of them.'

Lína rolled her chair back to the desk and reached for her mouse. 'Do you want to see Instagram or Facebook? They don't have any selfies on Twitter.'

Huldar shrugged. He knew little about social media. 'You decide.'

'OK.' Lína opened a picture that showed the young couple in swimming costumes, seated on a plastic sun lounger. They were leaning together. The man had his arm around the woman and they were smiling brightly for the camera. It was a selfie; her bare arm could be seen stretching out of the frame. In the background was a basic-looking swimming pool and a scattering of other hotel guests, either on the side or in the water. At first sight, the couple appeared as happy and carefree as you'd expect holidaymakers to be. But on closer inspection you could see that their smiles looked forced; the young woman's face was scarlet, although they were sitting under an umbrella, and the young man's forehead was beaded with sweat. Clearly they were sweltering.

'Is that her last picture?' Huldar thought the caption underneath the photo matched the final entry they had been told about.

'Yes. Taken in Spain, just before they vanished.'

'Are there any other photos from there?'

'Yes. She posted a lot. He mostly put up pictures of shelves of bottles in the hotel bar or the beer cooler. Not selfies of them, like she did. Neither of them posted photos of food, which I interpret as meaning they didn't eat anything that would look good in a picture. Maybe only cheap junk food like burgers.'

'I'm sure you're right,' Huldar agreed. 'They were broke.' The hotel and its garden looked to him like pretty basic budget accommodation. He nodded at the screen. 'Any more pics of them?'

Lína ran through the young woman's photos from the Spain trip. One after the other they filled the screen, all more or less identical: Abby and Leonard on the side of the pool, Abby and Leonard on the balcony, Abby and Leonard in the evening in streets packed tight with restaurants and bars. That was the only picture in which their smiles appeared genuine and there wasn't a drop of sweat to be seen on either of them.

Yet another photo of the swimming pool area appeared on screen. Abby was alone in the foreground, her sunglasses sliding down her sweaty nose. The caption just said: 'Hot.' Perhaps it was supposed to have a double meaning.

The picture was so large that the people in the background were clearly visible. Huldar immediately spotted Leonard. He was sitting on a high stool at a small swimming-pool bar, which was no more than a counter really, with a straw roof. On the bar in front of him was a tall beer glass, half full – or half empty, depending on your attitude to alcohol. Behind Leonard was a man with a beer-gut, holding his wallet in the air, no doubt placing an order for the same.

'That's the first picture she took in Spain. Apart from one at the airport. Do you want to see that, or his pics?'

'No. That's fine. Thanks, Lína.'

Out of the corner of his eye, Huldar saw Freyja appear with Hafthór from Sexual Offences. So the meeting must be over, though Hafthór's expression suggested it hadn't achieved much. If Tristan withdrew his allegation, their case was as good as dead for want of corroborating evidence. No meeting could change that fact.

'Ready for action?' Huldar managed to scoot over and catch up with Freyja and Hafthór just as they reached the door to Erla's office. He tagged along with them, telling himself it was to make sure that Erla didn't start any funny business with Freyja in Hafthór's presence. It wouldn't do Erla's reputation any good. Nor would it help if they caught her with her head in the waste-paper bin, throwing her guts up. He darted a glance through the glass wall and was reassured to see her face looking its normal colour.

'Yes and no,' Hafthór said soberly. 'We'll see. We're trying to prepare ourselves for the fallout. It's all we can do. After what happened last time, there's no telling how this interview's going to end. Is Erla in?'

Hafthór turned to the door, knocked lightly and went in, with Huldar and Freyja on his heels. Huldar caught a glimpse of the papers Hafthór was carrying. On top was a document with a photo attached to it with a paperclip. It was of a middle-aged man with fleshy cheeks and high temples; clearly a mugshot taken after he had been arrested, fingerprinted and booked in. Huldar recognised the background and the man's bemused expression of shocked disbelief. Photos taken following an arrest were never what you'd call Instagram material.

Erla opened her mouth to speak but Huldar got in first. 'Who's that in the picture?'

Hafthór turned the sheaf of papers over, frowning at Huldar in surprise. 'That's the suspect. Bergur.'

'Bergur?' Huldar held out his hand and asked if he could get a better look at the photo. As he studied it, he could feel the others staring at him as if he was crazy. Why should it matter what Bergur looked like?

Huldar handed back the papers. 'I may be mistaken but I could have sworn this man's in one of the photos taken in Spain by Abby, the young British woman whose bones we found in the sea.' Seeing Erla's open mouth, he added hastily: 'I'd better double check.'

Chapter 33

There was a constant bustle of activity at the police station. People seemed too restless to stay long in one place, whether they were supposed to be sitting at their computers or had just returned with new information, after being sent out on a variety of missions. Freyja concentrated on not getting under anyone's feet. She had completed her allotted task but no one had bothered to give her another.

Ever since Huldar had identified Bergur in the British couple's holiday snaps, the subdued atmosphere had lifted. The detectives straightened up, their faces brightening as if the sun had suddenly broken through the clouds and shone in through the office windows. At last a shadowy link had been established between two of the cases; there was a connection between the bones on the seabed and the care-home case. Its precise nature remained obscure, however. As did the question of whether the murders of Rósa and Binni were part of the same story, though it was at least clear that Bergur couldn't have been the killer. He had the best possible alibi since he had been in custody when they were committed.

When it came to Bergur's dealings with the British couple, however, they were on firmer ground. Almost everyone agreed that he was the overweight man with the wallet in the photo from Leonard and Abby's Spanish holiday. After examining his Facebook page, the police discovered that he hadn't posted anything during the period in question. That was unusual, as he was generally very active on the site. His posts were mostly innocuous; he never referred to politics or other topical issues, so anecdotes from a swimming pool in Spain would have fitted right in with his usual content. That left two possibilities: one, the man hadn't had an internet connection or, two, he hadn't wanted to draw attention to his trip. The police were working on the latter assumption.

Freyja's job had been to find out from children's services whether Bergur had been on holiday at the time and to talk to his closest colleagues in case he'd mentioned the trip to them. In turned out that he had gone on leave for ten days but he hadn't spoken about his holiday to anyone afterwards. A few said they'd asked where he'd been as he'd come back looking unusually tanned, but he'd just said something vague about having gone out of town. Next, Freyja had spoken to Elsa and asked her to check with her cousin, who was Bergur's sister's best friend. It had only taken half an hour to get an answer. Elsa had rung her cousin who had rung Bergur's sister, and then the round of phone calls had come back to Freyja. Yes, Bergur had gone to Spain in May. His sister had asked why they wanted to know. Freyja said she wasn't at liberty to say and rang off. Her reply was now no doubt winging its way back to the sister.

After this, the Sexual Offences Unit had examined Bergur's credit-card statements and found activity consistent with the purchase of a trip to Spain and transactions in shops and restaurants as well as cashpoint withdrawals in the country. Analysis of emails on the man's laptop, which had already been confiscated in connection with the abuse case, revealed an air ticket and a booking at the British couple's hotel. On the other hand, there was no evidence that he had paid for the couple's tickets to Iceland. It remained unclear how they had travelled to the country, and what the nature of their relationship with Bergur had been.

It was a quarter to one. Freyja scanned the office for Huldar. Tristan would be arriving any minute and she was afraid they would forget to alert her when they entered the meeting room. But she couldn't see Huldar anywhere – or the other two, for that matter. Perhaps she had better hurry along to the room anyway, so she wouldn't be the idiot who turned up late. It was vital to her that it should start on time; she would die of stress if it dragged on past four o'clock. Baldur was due into town at two and he was supposed to collect Saga from her nursery school, but he couldn't always be relied on. Freyja wouldn't be able to relax until she knew he'd kept his word, and the last thing she wanted was to be distracted by watching her phone during the questioning. She sent Baldur a text and received an immediate reply that everything was cool; he might be a bit late but she needn't worry. She instantly regretted sending the message.

When she got to the meeting room she found it locked and no one around. There were two chairs in the corridor outside but she didn't want to sit down for fear of looking like a patient outside a doctor's waiting room. They were the same kind of padded armchairs as the one that had been used to jazz up the interview room for the care-home inquiry. She hoped they weren't now planning to redecorate the meeting room with the chairs, the Gorbachev–Reagan picture and the wilting pot plant.

In the event, the first people to turn up were not Erla and her team but Tristan, his mother and his legal adviser, Magnús. None of them appeared to be looking forward to what was to come, but the boy's mother was in by far the worst state. Her complexion was as grey and sickly as it had been last time and she avoided eye contact when Freyja shook hands. Hers felt as limp as an empty rubber glove. The lawyer obviously had the least emotional investment in the case: he was detached and calm, and soon stepped aside to deal with phone calls while he was waiting.

That left the three of them standing there in agonised awkwardness. Tristan's gaze flickered around the featureless corridor in search of something to fix on. His mother sank down on one of the chairs, keeping her eyes lowered. Freyja had to bite back the urge to ask the haggard woman if she was OK. In the end, she decided to offer them a drink. The mother mumbled, 'No thanks,' and Tristan shook his head. He sat down beside his mother and began gnawing at his cuticles. His mother shot out an arm without looking up and pulled his hand gently away from his mouth. He desisted.

'Where is everyone? I want to get this over with.' Tristan glanced agitatedly up and down the corridor.

'I'm sure they'll be here any minute.' Freyja checked the clock and saw that there were still five minutes until the interview was due to begin. If Erla and her team were to turn up now, there was every chance it would start punctually. But there was still no sign of them. Instead, Bjarni Einarsson, Bergur's lawyer, now appeared, carrying a battered briefcase that was so heavy that he was listing slightly to one side. He came up and greeted them curtly: 'Hello.' His tone was cold, leaving them in no doubt that he wasn't pleased to see any of them.

He shifted the briefcase in front of him so he could support its weight with both hands, then turned to Tristan with a chilly expression: 'So, Tristan, have you made up your mind? Are you going to persist with these false allegations against my client?'

Tristan didn't grace this with an answer. Instead, he looked round at his own lawyer, Magnús, who was standing with his back to them, absorbed in a phone call. Then, his cheeks flushed, Tristan dropped his gaze. Surprisingly it was his mother who raised her head, her timidity forgotten, and snapped: 'Who the fuck are you?' She must have seen the man storm out of Tristan's last interview, but presumably he hadn't paused to introduce himself.

Freyja intervened to prevent the row that was brewing. She addressed the lawyer, Bjarni: 'If your presence is a cause of distress to Tristan, you can be sent out of the room. So I'd watch it, if I were you.'

The lawyer muttered huffily that she had misunderstood him. Tristan's mother was directing a baleful glare in his direction. Her pallid skin and the black circles under her eyes lent her scowl a peculiar venom. The lawyer was quick to avert his gaze. Luckily, the awkward situation was defused when Erla, Hafthór, Huldar and Gudlaugur swept into the corridor with the IT man on their heels. Tristan's mother dropped her eyes to the floor again and Bergur's lawyer's manner instantly became as smooth as butter. Magnús, the boy's legal adviser, finally ended his phone call and joined the group.

It transpired that Tristan's status hadn't changed: he was still to be interviewed as a witness. The decision had been taken in-house. This meant his lawyer had to wait in the corridor and Freyja guessed he had taken his phone out again the moment the door shut behind them. He and Tristan's mother were unlikely to have much to say to each other. It would be hard to imagine two more different people: Magnús in his expensive pressed suit and polished brogues, organised, his life under meticulous control; Berglind in her threadbare anorak and grubby trainers, her life in tatters.

Tristan was as neatly presented as he had been the previous day. He gave off a powerful whiff of some strongly scented washing powder that would no doubt become oppressive if the interview dragged on, especially when combined with the powerful reek of aftershave from Bergur's lawyer. Freyja took care to sit as far from him as she could and just hoped the others weren't having a similar reaction to the smell of her nit shampoo. She caught Huldar's eye as she sat down. He gave her a wink and she smiled. It was good to know there was at least one friendly face in the group, which was more than poor Tristan could hope to find.

Erla and Hafthór took it in turns to grill the boy. It felt like an unequal table-tennis match, with two players against one, but they soon realised this and switched tactics.

The questions were more or less the same as last time. Most were about Rósa. It was clear to everyone as the barrage of questions started to get repetitive that they were avoiding the subject of Bergur; they were planning to postpone that for as long as possible.

Tristan answered everything in more or less the same words as the previous time. He spoke clearly and looked his interrogators in the eye. When Erla finally brought up something new, his demeanour didn't alter.

'We have reason to believe Rósa had heard of or knew

Bergur before she was placed with him and before you two first met. Do you know anything about that?'

Bergur's lawyer woke up on hearing his client's name. He had been on the verge of dropping off – or suffocating on the noxious fumes of his own aftershave.

'Yes. We met at a different home like I told you. I'd stayed at Bergur's before but she hadn't. She'd heard of him, though.'

'Did you two become friends straight away?'

'Yes.'

'Would you say you quickly became close, confiding in each other about private matters?'

'Yes, I would.'

'Did she confide in you about how she knew Bergur or where she'd heard of him?'

'Yes, she did.'

Erla, who had been prepared for a flat denial, couldn't hide her astonishment. Recovering quickly, she went on: 'Could you share that story with us?'

'Someone told Rósa that Bergur had killed her mother.'

Bjarni, Bergur's lawyer, jumped to his feet and banged the table so hard it echoed. 'What in God's name is going on? I'm not sitting here and listening to this. My client has had to suffer enough thanks to this boy's defamatory lies. Surely there's a limit to how much of this rubbish we should have to put up with? It's outrageous that this boy should bring false allegations, then recant, only to bring new, even worse ones now. He's citing the word of a deceased witness who never made any such claim while she was alive.'

Erla cut him off, in a voice that sounded as if acid was dripping from every word. 'Sit down and shut up or get out.'

'I demand that you record my objection.'

Pointedly ignoring him, Erla turned her attention back to Tristan. After a moment, Bjarni sat down again with a disgruntled air, obviously afraid of losing his seat at the table.

'You were saying, Tristan . . .'

'Rósa wanted a chance to see him. To find out what he was like. No one would listen to her, so she wanted to find some proof that would make people believe her. Make the police believe her.'

'Who told her that Bergur was responsible for her mother's death?'

'Binni. The guy on Grandi. He was at her mother's funeral. He came up behind her afterwards and whispered that he was sorry. He said it was all the doll's fault – it should have stayed at the bottom of the sea. Her mother would still be alive if it wasn't for the doll. Then he mentioned Bergur and told Rósa to keep away him. He said Bergur had killed her mother by accident to get hold of the doll and that it wouldn't be a good idea for her to end up at his home. It would be best if she stayed out of trouble so she never had to go into care. But at that point someone noticed that Binni was bothering Rósa and came and chucked him out. He was drunk.'

Erla and Huldar exchanged glances. Huldar gave a faint nod and took over the questioning. He knew the story of Rósa's obsession better than anyone else at the table, bar Freyja. 'Tristan. I've looked at the files from the time when Rósa went to the police with her suspicion that her mother had been murdered. She never mentioned Brynjólfur – Binni, that is. Or Bergur either. Your story isn't consistent with what she said then.'

'She didn't know Binni's name. No one would give it to her. They just said he was some drunk who shouldn't have been allowed in. Rósa thought that if she admitted a drunk had told her, the police would say she shouldn't take any notice of him – that drunks talk nonsense. But Rósa knew what drunks are like. Her grandmother drinks. The fact is, when they're drunk, people often tell the truth about things that they refuse to discuss when they're sober.'

'How did Rósa find out that the man was Binni, if no one would tell her who he was at the funeral or afterwards? Did she learn it from someone else later?'

'No. Her grandparents refused to discuss it. Perhaps because her grandmother's an alky too. I don't know. But two years ago, when a girl who'd been at the home with us for a while committed suicide, we went to the funeral and the party afterwards.'

'The reception,' Gudlaugur blurted out, earning himself a filthy look from Erla.

'Whatever. Anyway, there was a sort of visitors' book there that we were supposed to sign. Then Rósa remembered that there'd been a book like that at her mother's funeral, so she decided to ask her grandmother if she could have it. She found a signature in it that looked like it had been written by someone who was drunk. And it was him. But it was hard to find him because he'd signed it "Binni Briefcase", instead of putting his patronymic.'

'It can't have been easy to track him down with only that information to go on. Especially since he spent most of his time on the streets. I don't suppose she looked him up on the internet?' Huldar's voice was matter of fact, devoid of any sarcasm.

'I helped her. I asked Mum and it turned out she knew who he was.' The boy went red. He took a deep breath, then continued: 'Mum had heard that Binni had just moved out of town to some treatment centre in the countryside, but she said he wouldn't last long there. He'd be back on the street before you knew it. So Rósa used to go downtown regularly to look for him. She never had any luck, though; not until some homeless guy told her Binni'd just moved to Grandi. That's when she found him. About a year ago. She started going round to see him in the hope of getting the whole story but it didn't work. He was too out of it most of the time, and when he wasn't, he wouldn't admit to knowing anything.'

'Did she find out why Bergur should have wanted the doll?'

'No, I don't think so. Not as far as I know. But she did hear something else.'

'What?' The word was forming on everyone's lips as Huldar said it.

'Bergur killed her father as well. Binni did tell her that much. That was supposedly an accident too. They had a fight while they were fishing. Bergur pushed her dad over and he drowned.'

Bergur's lawyer reacted to this with outrage. 'Stop right there!' he bellowed.

'Sit down and shut up or get out.' Huldar said, echoing Erla's words and seemingly getting just as much of a kick out of saying them.

'Tell me, Tristan, did Brynjólfur ever tell Rósa where the doll was or how he came to have it in his possession?'

'No. She never said anything about that. She'd have told me.'

Huldar inhaled deeply, then let out his breath in a sigh. 'Why on earth didn't you two come to us? An investigation into the kind of crimes you're describing is best dealt with by the police, not by kids. That's what we do all day long – investigate crimes. What were you and Rósa thinking? How were you planning to get justice?'

'There wasn't any plan. We hadn't got that far. You lot had the chance to investigate but you screwed up. Rósa didn't want to talk to you again. She might have changed her mind if she'd had any proper proof that would have forced you to do something. But she died before she could get hold of it.' Tristan broke off and clamped his lips shut for a moment. 'I'd promised. I'd promised not to say a word.'

Huldar and Erla shared another look. Erla shook her head slightly but before Huldar could work out what she meant, Tristan coughed and started speaking again: 'There's something I want to say.'

'Go ahead.' Huldar sat back and gave him the floor.

'I'm going to stick by my decision to withdraw what I said about the abuse. Not because it didn't happen. It's just that I know there's no point. He won't be charged because my word won't be enough. The judge will believe him. So I withdraw my accusation.'

Hafthór leant forwards. 'A crime has been reported to us and it's our duty to investigate it, regardless of what you say now. Whether the prosecutor will decide to pursue the charges is another matter.'

'Can I say something else?' Tristan asked.

'Please do.' Hafthór waved a hand at him.

'Bergur used the addicts he met through his job to distribute drugs – pills, like Oxy.'

A peculiar rattling noise exploded from the lawyer's throat but he didn't say anything. Freyja got the impression he had relaxed a little after this latest revelation. No doubt he thought that the more excessive Tristan's accusations were, the better it would be for his client. It would be simpler to sweep all Tristan's claims off the table if the boy overreached himself.

If so, Tristan's next words must have cheered him up still further, because it seemed the boy hadn't finished. 'And he killed the people whose bodies were found in the sea. They were supposed to bring a load of pills to Iceland but they threw them away. So he murdered them and dumped their bodies in the sea. Not alone, though. With help from somebody else.'

The lawyer's patience was at an end, so presumably he didn't think the string of far-fetched allegations was doing Bergur any good after all. Leaping to his feet, he demanded the interview be suspended. This time no one ordered him to sit down and shut up.

Chapter 34

Tuesday

'According to the Police Information System, Bergur wasn't at the river at the time of the accident.' Huldar laid a printout of the incident report on Erla's desk. 'I'd have noticed his name, anyway, when I looked at this the other day. On the other hand, Brynjólfur was there and so was a passer-by who witnessed the incident and confirmed that it was an accident. Perhaps we should get hold of him?'

Erla skimmed the text. 'Oh, shit. It happened nearly ten years ago. As if the witness would have anything to add to his previous statement. I think we'll have to face the fact that either Tristan swallowed too much of Rósa's bullshit or he invented the story himself.'

'What for? Why would he do that?'

'Don't ask me. Maybe he hates Bergur. Kids in care don't always have much time for the people who are supposed to be looking after them. Perhaps the guy was useless. That doesn't necessarily make him a serial killer, though. I'm actually starting to think it might have been a weird coincidence that he was at the same hotel in Spain as the British couple.'

'No. I don't believe that for a minute.' The thought had crossed Huldar's mind after he'd listened to the stream of accusations Tristan had come out with, but although he had his doubts about the boy's claims, he was absolutely sure Bergur was linked to the British couple – and not just because he had been standing beside Leonard at the bar. 'Tristan had no way of knowing there was a picture showing Leonard and Bergur together, so his claim about the link can't have been a shot in the dark, can it? There's been no official disclosure to say that the bones belonged to a young British couple, or that they travelled here from Spain. I just don't buy the idea that he made up a story that by a million-to-one chance fits the actual events.'

Erla didn't respond, which meant she agreed with him: she never could back down gracefully. Instead, she changed the subject. 'I've just received a summary of the passenger lists from May. They've all come in, apart from the ones from the company that's gone bust. The British couple are nowhere to be seen on them. But the guy who went through them made a list of all the passengers who missed their flights out of Iceland. Some of the airlines also sent information about passengers who took a later flight. That leaves only five no-shows, out of which there's only one couple travelling together.'

'OK . . . and?'

'And nothing. The names belong to two Icelanders who live in Spain. They're back in Spain now, according to Facebook. They must have flown back with a different airline after they missed their flight.'

'Can I see?'

'Sure.' Erla indicated the folder on her desk. 'The summary is at the front. All the passenger lists are at the back. The lettering's so tiny you need a magnifying glass to read it. But for God's sake don't bother. You won't find any more than the guy who compiled the summary.'

Huldar had no plans to do so. It wasn't long until the next interview. which was bound to be much less dramatic than Tristan's. No lawyer had expressed any interest in attending and there was little likelihood of their having to suspend it halfway through. Both Erla and Hafthór had agreed that it would be better to investigate Tristan's wild allegations before continuing the interview with him.

Yet, even though he hadn't attracted a crowd like Tristan, the next person due to be questioned was an important witness. He was Fridrik Reynisson, former colleague of Rósa's mother and owner of the boat that had fished up the doll which Forensics were now examining. They had succeeded in uncovering the necklace, which had turned out to have a small metal pendant on it, engraved with the letter A. They hadn't yet discovered where the doll was made or sold, but this was of secondary importance. The plug underneath the doll had proved to be an integral part of its design, which Forensics thought was probably for emptying water out of it if a child put it in a bath or swimming pool. Given how often the subject of drugs had come up in connection with the cases they were investigating, Huldar had wondered if the doll could have been filled with pills and used for smuggling. Perhaps they had still been inside when it was fished out of the sea, which would explain why someone might have been so desperate to retrieve it. Erla had been thinking along similar lines.

'Lína, you couldn't have a look at these people for me, could you?' Huldar put the folder on her desk, placing his finger on the name of the Icelandic couple. 'I'm wondering if it's possible that the British couple used their tickets to travel to Iceland. It's probably a long shot but who knows? You're so clever, if there's anything there, you'll find it.'

Lína didn't smile or thank him for the praise, just took it as her due. She read the names and got straight down to work. 'When do you need the information?'

'I'm going into an interview. I'll drop by afterwards. We'll see what progress you've made by then.'

Fridrik Reynisson proved as nondescript as his online profile had suggested. He was a quiet man in his early forties, clean shaven, with neat, curly hair. He gave the impression of having woken up that morning expecting nothing but another average day at work. He spoke in a low voice as he answered their questions, as if from a desire to be self-effacing, though he could hardly hope to escape notice in the small interview room where he had the starring role. He was deeply shocked when Erla told him at the outset that he was being interviewed as a suspect in the inquiry into Rósa's murder. He went pale and his eyes bulged, showing their whites. He swallowed audibly.

'We have reason to believe you sheltered Rósa Thrastardóttir during the week between her disappearance from her foster home in Reykjavík and last Friday.' Erla's eyes bored into Fridrik's as he shifted uncomfortably in his chair. 'Is that correct?'

Fridrik drew over the glass of water he had been offered, raised it slowly to his lips and took a sip. His hand was trembling so badly that the water slopped around in the glass as he put it down again. 'Erm. Could I ask a question before I answer that?'

'Go ahead.'

'Would it be breaking the law if I had?'

'Yes, possibly. You risk being found to have contravened

article 193 of the criminal code. I'll read it for you.' Erla picked up a printout and read: '"Any person who deprives parents or other proper persons of authority over or custody of a child who is a minor, or who assists in the deprivation of such authority or custody, shall be subject to fines or imprisonment for up to sixteen years or life."' Erla put the printout down again. 'As Rósa was a minor and in the custody of the Reykjavík Child Protection Agency, the act of sheltering her while she was absconding comes under this definition.'

She went on relentlessly: 'If it transpires that you had sexual intercourse with her before she was fifteen, or seduced her after she'd reached that age, we're talking about punishment within the more severe end of this framework, although you would avoid a fine.'

Huldar smiled grimly to himself. The post-mortem had revealed that Rósa was still a virgin and showed no sign of damage to her anus. But there was no need to tell the man that.

Huldar watched as the remaining colour drained from Fridrik's face. The man slid his trembling hands under the table. Although he didn't know it, he could in fact save himself the worry about serving a life sentence. Rósa wasn't the only minor who had absconded from the custody of children's services. In most cases the kids concerned were addicts who turned to far more insalubrious characters than Fridrik for help. Up to now it had proved almost impossible for the police to get permission to forcibly remove children in such circumstances. It was only recently that they had succeeded in prosecuting certain dodgy individuals for violating the provision.

Erla had no intention of pursuing this course against

Fridrik. All she wanted was to establish where Rósa had been staying and who had killed her. Fridrik was a possible candidate, if it turned out that he had provided the girl with a roof over her head, but Huldar had to admit to himself that he found the man a very unlikely suspect.

Erla twisted the knife in the wound: 'And if you turn out to be responsible for her death, you can expect a prison sentence of sixteen years. Minimum. More likely eighteen. If, on the other hand, you turn out not to be implicated in Rósa's murder or to have sexually assaulted her, a reduced penalty may be considered if you freely volunteer the information and provide an honest account of what happened. This could even result in the charges being dropped altogether.'

Fridrik needed a few moments to take all this in. His hands were fidgeting under the table and he kept gulping. In the end, he pulled himself together and started talking in a shaky voice: 'I want to make it absolutely clear that I had nothing to do with Rósa's murder. Nothing. And I never laid a finger on her or had the slightest sexual interest in her. Never. All I did was feel sorry for her and let her stay with me when she was having a tough time. If I hadn't done that, she'd only have gone somewhere else, and she might have fallen victim to exactly the kind of thing you were describing – been sexually abused, I mean. I'm very sorry if I caused concern to the people who were responsible for her, but I did notify the authorities that she was safe.'

'So it was you who sent the letters to the Child Protection Agency?'

'Yes.' Fridrik bowed his head, as shamefaced as a schoolboy. 'I didn't want to send an email or make a phone call because they would have been too easy to trace back to me.'

'Was it always you she stayed with, for all these years, whenever she ran away?'

Fridrik nodded and Erla prompted him to answer aloud for the recording. 'Yes, I think so.' The man rubbed a hand over his forehead, then took another sip of water. 'She first came to see me about a year after Dísa – her mother – died. She wanted me to go to the police with her to tell them about the doll we fished up from the sea. She had some crazy idea about her mother being killed because of the doll. She said no one would believe her but they'd believe me. I told her the police had already called me to ask about the doll. It wouldn't change anything if I told them again. I also told her that the detective I'd talked to had thanked me for my information but said they saw no reason to take any further action. The case was closed and the fact the doll had really existed didn't change anything. Her mother had probably thrown it in the dustbin. I tried to get Rósa to agree that this was the likely explanation but it was no good. She was obsessed with it.'

'Were you in a relationship with her mother before she died? Closer than just work colleagues, I mean?' Erla raised her eyes from her notes. 'Were you a couple?'

'No. We weren't a couple. We were just friends.' Fridrik flushed.

'So you knew Rósa slightly before her mother died?'

'I'd met her several times. She used to come to work with her mother occasionally when the schools were on holiday. Then we took that boat trip. So you could say I knew her, but not well.'

'What were you thinking of to let her stay with you, when you knew children's services were looking for her?'

Fridrik coughed. 'I can't really explain. It began with her

visiting me – the first time was the one I just described. After that she took to dropping in from time to time. She used to come alone on the bus. I couldn't help feeling sorry for her. She was an orphan and just, well . . . just so alone. She had nobody else in the world and I could hardly push her away.' Fridrik fell silent, took a deep breath, then continued. 'The first time she stayed, she arrived late in the evening, so I gave in and let her sleep in the spare room. She begged me not to call the police to come and take her away, saying all she wanted was to spend one night in a proper home. She left straight away the following morning, as she had promised, and it didn't occur to me that this would become a regular thing. The spare room gradually became hers. It just happened. Perhaps I let it because we got on so well together; we went out on the boat and watched films on TV. She used to lie on the sofa and read. Sometimes I cooked for her. Sometimes she cooked for me. I anticipated that once she was eighteen and independent, she would move in properly. But . . . then what happened, happened and now nothing will ever come of it.'

Neither Erla nor Huldar said anything. To Huldar, it was clear that Fridrik had been lonely and welcomed Rósa's visits. But as the man seemed pretty normal, he must have experienced some inner tension between his pleasure in her company and his guilty conscience over sheltering a runaway teen. No doubt he had found some way of justifying it to himself, as people so often did.

'It didn't cross your mind to make an official application to foster her?'

Fridrik gave a dry, humourless laugh. 'Huh, right. Because a request like that would have gone through like a shot, wouldn't it? A single man adopting a teenage girl? No, the thought didn't enter my head. I couldn't exactly tell them that Rósa had already been staying with me and was happy at my house, could I?'

Evidently, Fridrik had considered the possibility.

Erla brought the conversation back to the point. 'Rósa was murdered. You knew her well. Are you aware of anyone who would have wanted to harm her?'

'No. God, no. No one.'

'Did she tell you where she was going that evening?'

'Yes. She was going to meet her friend, Tristan. I've never met him myself. She didn't tell me what they were planning to do but she mentioned coming home early. She had her own key, so she could come and go as she pleased.'

Huldar and Erla exchanged glances. No key had been found on Rósa's body.

Leaving this aside for now, Erla prompted him: 'And after that? Was she going to meet someone else?'

'No. She was planning to come home. Home to my place. But she didn't show up. I thought she must have gone back to the foster home. She used to do that sometimes, without telling me.'

Erla nodded. 'I see. What about you? Where were you?'

'I was at a barbecue. A party. At my brother's place. I went there at half past seven, which was a bit more than half an hour after she'd left to meet Tristan. When I got home, she wasn't there.'

'Can your brother confirm that you were at his party?'

'Yes, of course. So can the other guests.' Fridrik looked unaccountably embarrassed, then added: 'Well, the ones who noticed me, that is. I didn't stay long. I was home by nine.'

'Rósa died at around midnight. You say you were at home. Can anyone confirm that?'

'No. No one. But I *was* at home. I didn't go out again after that.'

Next, Erla asked if he had been drinking that evening and Fridrik replied that he had been driving. Then she repeated some of her earlier questions and received the same answers. Like most people who had sat in the chair before him, Fridrik grew increasingly irritated by the repetitions. When he'd had enough, he presented them with a new piece of information. 'Someone broke into my house on Sunday evening. I didn't report it, because nothing was stolen. All they did was trash Rósa's room. I don't think they took anything but I can't be sure. She didn't leave many belongings in there, or any cash.'

Erla's next questions were concerned with the break-in, but elicited nothing of any use. Since Fridrik was adamant that no one knew Rósa had taken refuge with him, he couldn't explain why someone would have broken in purely to search through her stuff. All he could think of was that her murderer must have forced her to reveal where she had been hiding. But Huldar was troubled to hear that a window had been broken to gain entry because it meant that whoever had taken the key out of Rósa's pocket was unlikely to have been the murderer. Otherwise surely he'd have entered by the front door?

After they had milked every last drop out of the burglary, Erla went back to her original line of questioning, before deciding that they'd got as far as they were going to for now. They'd been hoping for something more substantial that would bring them a step closer to the solution, but they remained totally in the dark.

Before the interview ended, Fridrik agreed to go home with a police escort who would take Rósa's belongings away and check her room for fingerprints. He didn't protest about having his own prints taken or providing a saliva sample for his DNA profile. Lastly, he told Huldar his brother's name, so he could confirm that Fridrik had been at the barbecue.

Huldar managed to note it down without betraying his astonishment.

'Look at this. The independent witness into Rósa's father's death was called Fjalar – Fjalar Reynisson.' Huldar jabbed a finger at Erla's screen so hard that it dimpled and the letters in the man's name were momentarily distorted.

Erla frowned thoughtfully. 'Yes. I see that. I *can* read. But what do you want me to do about it? Iceland's a small country. We can't go after him on that basis alone.' Putting on a different voice, she said: 'Fjalar, we need to talk to you about a fatal accident you witnessed, because your brother knew the victim's daughter.' She broke off and looked Huldar in the eye. 'We'd be a laughing stock.'

'But . . .'

'No buts. Try and dig up more info if you're so sure this Fjalar has something to hide. You don't even have a theory about what he's supposed to have done. Killed Rósa? Broken into his brother's place while simultaneously hosting a barbecue? He had a house full of guests the night Rósa died, remember?'

Huldar pushed himself off Erla's desk where he had been leaning his hands while bending over her computer screen. He ran his fingers through his hair, trying to imagine how

Fridrik's brother could be mixed up in the case. But it was no good. He was all out of ideas. 'OK. I'll do that.'

After closing Erla's door behind him, Huldar walked over to Lína's desk. She must be used to going through other people's social media accounts by now. Perhaps she could find out something useful about Fjalar Reynisson.

'Lína.'

She looked up and smiled. 'I've checked it out for you. That Icelandic couple look a bit dodgy to me. As far as I can work out, they're serious addicts. They're both on the Police Information System for possession. For repeated offences, in fact. They supposedly flew to Iceland in May and didn't turn up for their flight back, yet if their Facebook pages are anything to go by, they were actually at home in Spain all the time.'

Huldar tried to appear interested in this news. He would have been pleased to hear it before he got hold of Fjalar's name, as it represented a major step forward in the investigation into the fate of the British couple. This was almost certainly the explanation for how they had got to Iceland – using tickets bought in the names of two young Icelandic addicts, who would now have to be questioned. 'Great, Lína. That's brilliant.' He smiled as enthusiastically as he could. 'Listen, I've got another job for you.'

'But—'

'It shouldn't take long. I just want you to have a look at this man for me. Check if he seems suspicious at all. I did a search for him on the information system but he hasn't committed an offence since losing his licence twenty years ago for drink-driving. But maybe you could find something interesting on his social media sites, since you're such an expert.'

'OK. What's his name?'

'Fjalar. Fjalar Reynisson.'

Lína glared at him. 'Fjalar Reynisson? Are you joking?'

'No.'

'That was what I was about to tell you when you interrupted me. Look.' She handed him the folder of passenger lists that had been lying open on her desk, then pointed to an entry she had marked with yellow highlighter. 'It's awfully small, but see? The tickets used by the British couple were bought with a credit card belonging to a man with that name.'

Lína withdrew her finger and raised her eyes to meet Huldar's. 'Fjalar. Fjalar Reynisson.'

Chapter 35

The smart kitchen looked like a bomb site. The sink was full of pots and pans, and all the work surfaces were covered in empty packaging, spices and utensils that Freyja had used while cooking. Unfortunately, the results hadn't lived up to expectations, and couldn't justify the Herculean cleaning task she was left with. She had to face facts: she was no masterchef.

'Very good.' Huldar put down his knife and fork with apparent satisfaction. His plate was spotless, so it seemed he actually meant it. Then again, coming from a man who mainly lived on burgers, this praise wasn't worth much.

At least the red wine was good. Freyja reached for the bottle and topped up their glasses. She had been planning to offer him coffee and shop-bought cheesecake for dessert but had decided not to bother. The food was lying like lead in her stomach, leaving no room for anything else.

'Right. Now you have to tell me everything, like you promised.' Freyja leant back in her chair. She had been dying of curiosity all week to hear what had been going on behind the scenes in the Rósa case, having been forced to content herself with what she'd read on the news sites. Her role had been abruptly terminated, with the explanation that no more young

415

people were to be interviewed for now. The inquiry into the care-home abuse case had been put on hold while an investigation was being carried out into its putative connection to the murders.

Freyja had swallowed her pride and tried several times to get hold of Huldar on the phone. The last she had heard, on Tuesday afternoon, was that Bergur had met the British couple in Spain, the boat owner Fridrik had admitted to sheltering Rósa, and his brother, Fjalar, was apparently mixed up in the affair as well. But an awful lot had happened since then.

When she'd tried Huldar on Wednesday and Thursday, he either hadn't answered his phone or had excused himself on the grounds that he was busy and would ring her back later. He had finally done so at lunchtime on Friday, with a deal: he would tell her everything if she invited him to supper. She had accepted, and now here they were.

Huldar was looking well: the progress they were making in the investigation clearly agreed with him. He had also made an effort with his appearance: he was freshly shaven and his hair was neatly combed. What's more, he got into her good books by immediately asking after Saga and Molly. She was pleased that he showed an interest in her little niece's wellbeing and told him that Saga and the dog were staying with Baldur; they were fine and didn't miss her at all. They were too busy spending the fortune Baldur had received in tips from his tour group. He seemed to have decided to blow it all on ice-cream, children's amusements and bones for Molly, which was a far better use for it than many other things he was known for spending his money on. He had collected Saga ten minutes late the day he'd got back to town, which, in Baldur's world, was equivalent to arriving fifteen minutes early. He had called shortly afterwards to ask what on earth had happened to his daughter's hair. Freyja had feigned ignorance, sparing him the nit saga and keeping her fingers crossed that her blitzkrieg against the lice had had the desired effect.

'We believe Rósa's murder has been solved. And the mystery of the bones, too. In the end it turned out they were both part of the same case.'

Freyja prompted him to continue, reminding him that her duty of confidentiality was still in force. According to the news, a suspect had been arrested for Rósa's murder but the police weren't releasing any details. After all her efforts in the kitchen, Freyja felt she deserved to be told who it was.

'Rósa's murderer was Fjalar Reynisson, the brother of the man who originally fished the doll out of the sea. Fjalar's a businessman who rents out summer houses and campervans to tourists here in Iceland, and a holiday apartment in Spain to Icelanders.'

'What?'

'It's a long story.'

'I've got all the time in the world.'

Huldar smiled at this, then went on: 'Fjalar was a very ordinary guy with a small business based around these assets. When it didn't bring him the big bucks he'd been hoping for, he started importing drugs from Spain. He got the idea when some people he'd rented his apartment to were caught by customs trying to bring opioids into Iceland. Bergur won't be released from custody any time soon either, because he's believed to have assisted with the distribution of the drugs.

We haven't worked out all the details yet but the bigger picture is more or less clear.'

'How did the police find out?'

'We tracked down the air tickets the young British couple had used to get here. They had been purchased in the names of an Icelandic couple who live in Spain. When we spoke to them, they turned out to be very eager to cooperate. Or, rather, they were once they'd been threatened with extradition . . . But the upshot is that they agreed to work with us. That's when the ball really started rolling.'

'How? How would an Icelandic couple living in Spain know what had been going on?'

'They're not exactly pensioners who retired there for a life in the sun. They're drug addicts who'd found a local doctor who was relaxed about writing them prescriptions for opioids. The amount he prescribed for them is unbelievable. The pills were then imported to Iceland, often by the couple themselves. But back in the spring they relapsed and after that they weren't in a fit state to do any smuggling. Customs would never have let them into Iceland without taking them aside for a thorough inspection, it was that bad. That left Fjalar with a problem, since the market was crying out for the stuff and supplies were running low.'

'So what happened? Did Bergur go out there to find someone to act as a mule?'

'No, not exactly. Fjalar went apeshit and sent Bergur over to talk sense into the Icelanders when it became obvious what had happened. He was supposed to force them to clean up their act, and, if that didn't work, to bring the drugs home himself. Since Bergur had originally been responsible for recruiting the couple, Fjalar saw it as his problem. Bergur also took care of recruiting dealers at this end, by virtue of his position as manager of a home where a lot of young addicts were placed. In other words, he used those poor kids to distribute the drugs, and from time to time drafted in members of their families as well, if they were addicts too. The young man in Spain was actually on the list of witnesses who Sexual Offences wanted to talk to, because he'd been a resident at Bergur's home.'

'Christ!'

'Yup. You can expect to attend more witness interviews next week, because now we'll have to question all the kids again. This time we need to ask them all whether they sold dope – or were approached about selling dope – for Bergur. I reckon he knew which ones would be receptive, so I'm hoping it was the exception rather than the rule that the kids got mixed up in it. He's unlikely to have bothered trying to recruit the ones who were clean. But the kids who did drugs would have had useful connections.'

'There's one thing I don't understand. It sounds as if Bergur was a lot more active than Fjalar in the business. What on earth can have induced him to take on all the dirty work? And what exactly did Fjalar do?'

'Bergur was under Fjalar's thumb. You see, Fjalar had something on him that he used to blackmail him into working for him. Meanwhile, Fjalar's role was just to look after the finances. Oh, and to allow the Icelandic couple to live in his Spanish apartment. Before that a young addict had lived there, another member of Bergur's drug mule academy. And before him, another kid in the same boat.'

Huldar paused for a sip of wine. He sucked it through his teeth, making a bit of a face. When Freyja asked if he'd prefer a beer, he accepted eagerly. Once he had the glass in front of him, he took a long draught, then carried on with his story.

'But Bergur only had to visit the couple in Spain once that spring to realise that they wouldn't be getting on a plane any time soon. Since he had no intention of smuggling the drugs himself, he saw his opportunity when he got talking to a young Brit at his hotel. The guy was joking that he and his girlfriend should have booked a trip to Iceland instead because they were dying of heatstroke in Spain. When Bergur offered him the tickets, he jumped at the chance. Bergur claims the man was aware that the tent he gave them contained a bag of illegal drugs, but of course we only have his word for that. It's possible the young Brit accepted the tent without having a clue what he was getting himself into. Information from the Spanish police suggests that the guy ditched the pills before flying to Iceland, so presumably he did know about them but got cold feet. If he'd come across the dope by chance, he's more likely to have called the police and reported it.'

'Why were they killed? Because they'd thrown away the drugs?'

'Yes. Probably. And maybe to make sure they didn't talk.'

'What was the original plan?'

'Bergur says the British guy was supposed to hand over the dope at the campsite in Laugardalur, the day after the couple arrived in Iceland. Not the same day, because Bergur wanted to keep an eye out in case there were any signs of a police operation in the area. He didn't see anything, so he assumed they hadn't been rumbled and the coast was clear. But the Brits weren't at the campsite. Bergur claims he told Fjalar and that Fjalar went mental. He hunted the couple down and killed them both in a fit of rage when the young man couldn't hand over the dope.'

'Hunted them down? Weren't they in a tent? How did he find them?'

'Bergur had fixed a tiny GPS transmitter to the tent so he could keep track of the couple as they came through customs. If they spent a suspiciously long time at the airport or the tent went from there to the police station, he would know to keep away from Laugardalur. But, in the event, he'd chickened out of using it for fear that if the police confiscated the tent, they'd find the transmitter and might be able to trace the person who was monitoring it. But Fjalar forced him to activate the transmitter when he couldn't find the couple, and discovered that they were in Sudurland, near Hveragerdi. Fjalar waited until dusk, then went after them. He caught Leonard outside the tent, the girl inside.'

The lead weight in Freyja's stomach grew even heavier at the thought of the poor young tourists being slaughtered like that. She gulped down some wine but it didn't help. 'I don't need to hear the details.'

'No. I can understand that. Anyway, there was no sign of the transmitter when the tent was found. Bergur claims he removed it when he disposed of the camping gear in the ditch. Fjalar had taken the bodies away with him the night he killed them but left all their belongings behind. They'd been camping just off the Ring Road, at the foot of a mountain not far from Hveragerdi. Bergur went and removed all trace of them, afraid the crime would be discovered and the camping gear traced to him. I can't say he did a very good job of it. But he claims he panicked.'

'How did the bodies end up in the sea?'

'Fjalar took them out in the boat that same night. He weighted the bodies down with rocks and threw them overboard. He chose the brothers' favourite fishing spot in case anyone wondered what he was doing out there in the middle of the night. If anyone asked, he could claim he'd gone out fishing because he couldn't sleep. He was careful to sail the same course as he usually did, in case anyone spotted the boat on the radar. And the bodies sank straight down, right in the spot where the doll had once been lying.'

Freyja let out the breath she'd been holding in. The red wine was starting to have an effect and she had to focus hard to follow the thread.

'What did Fjalar have on Bergur that could possibly be worse than all this?'

'Well, for starters Fjalar witnessed the fight Bergur had with Rósa's father, Thröstur, that led to Thröstur drowning.'

'What?'

'Yes, you heard right. Rósa's father and Brynjólfur – that's Binni Briefcase – and Bergur were all salmon fishing in the Brunná river in Öxarfjördur, where Fjalar happened to be fishing as well. The three men were sharing two rods; Fjalar had a third. They didn't know each other. When the friends arrived, Fjalar was already there, and Binni and Bergur got into conversation with him. They were drinking and invited him to join them. While this was going on, Thröstur was sitting in the car.'

'In the car?'

'I'll explain why in a minute. Anyway, Binni soon left Bergur and Fjalar and went back to the car to try and persuade Thröstur to change into his angling gear and join them in the river. He was partly successful. Thröstur changed his clothes and put on his waders. But instead of fishing, he went over to Bergur and pulled him away from Fjalar to settle an argument they'd been having. They started quarrelling and it ended with Bergur knocking Thröstur into the water, where he drowned. It can't have helped that the three friends had been drinking in the car on the way there and were all half-cut.'

'The driver too?'

'Yep. Bergur, too, who was driving. That's why he got scared when Thröstur drowned. He was terrified of being charged with manslaughter. Brynjólfur was pissed as usual, but Fjalar still had his head screwed on and took control of the situation. He sent Bergur back to town, while he and Brynjólfur pretended they had been the only people there to witness the accident. Thröstur had slipped and fallen while crossing the river, and drowned as a result. They didn't have to change many details of what had actually happened and the story sounded perfectly plausible. Bergur got away with it, but if he'd known how much it was going to cost him, I bet he'd rather have faced charges. Fjalar saw his chance; he'd been fantasising about importing opioids from Spain but was hampered by having no contacts on the home market – until he met Bergur, who had told him what he did for a living.'

'What about Brynjólfur? Why did he go along with it?'

'Because Bergur and Thröstur hadn't been quarrelling over nothing. They were in deep shit and couldn't agree on what to do about it. The thing is, Bergur had run over a child on their way to the river. A six-year-old girl, who had died. Thröstur wanted to ring the police; Bergur didn't. Perhaps

Rósa's father wanted to do the right thing because he had a daughter the same age. Or because the little girl had died in his arms after the accident.' Huldar let out a long breath. 'Remember the accident I told you about? The one the Húsavík police were busy with when the drowning was reported? It was that accident.'

'Yes, but you didn't say anything about a hit-and-run.' Freyja felt sick to the stomach. 'And why the hell don't I remember this? A hit-and-run resulting in a child's death? Surely I'd remember that, even if it was ten years ago? Wasn't it in the news?'

'Yes. It was. It happened in the north-east, on the road between Húsavík and Kópasker. Remember the map of traffic fatalities? Ironically, this was one of the accidents I mentioned to you when you asked me what the map showed. But the men engineered it to look quite different. The little girl was called Adalheidur. Her father had left her sitting in their car at the side of the road after it broke down. He was going to walk to Húsavík for help and told her to wait for him. His phone battery was dead.'

'Oh yes! I do remember that. But wasn't she run over by her father's car? That's how it was reported, if I recall correctly – that the girl had got in the front seat, fiddled with the controls and accidentally released the gears. Then she got out for a pee or something and the car ran over her?'

'Yes, that's how it appeared. But it seems the truth was different. The girl apparently saw them coming, got out and tried to wave them down. Why, no one knows, unless it was to ask them to turn round and drive her to find her father. They spotted her too late, but Bergur stopped and started to reverse towards the car she was standing beside. They were in a big pick-up, the kind with a camper shell on the back, so he couldn't see that she'd started running towards them. He reversed over her. The wheel ran over her head.'

Huldar took another mouthful of beer but didn't seem to enjoy it this time, perhaps because he had a bad taste in his mouth.

'They put her in their car, intending to call for an ambulance and drive to meet it. But she died in Thröstur's arms in the back seat before they could even close the doors, and they lost their heads. Bergur snatched the phone away from Brynjólfur before he could make the call, saying there was no way he was going to prison. He was drink-driving and it would make no difference that it had been an accident. He'd be sentenced and would probably have to do time. Rósa's father was in shock. He froze and didn't protest; just sat there in the car while Brynjólfur and Bergur laid the girl on the ground behind the broken-down vehicle, took it out of gear and positioned it so it ran over her head – it actually stopped on top of her. She was lying there dead when her father came back accompanied by a mechanic. It never crossed anyone's mind that the girl hadn't caused the accident herself by fiddling with the gears.'

Huldar took a long swig of beer. 'It wasn't until the men reached the river that they realised the doll the girl had been clutching had been left on the floor of the pick-up. She hadn't let go of it until her grip slackened when she died. Thröstur was in such a state that he had just sat there, unable to speak, with the doll at his feet.'

'Oh my God.' Freyja wanted to knock back the rest of the wine in her glass to make listening to the story more bearable but she resisted the temptation and made do with a sip. She was torn between longing to know what had happened and dreading hearing about the grisly details.

Huldar carried on when it became clear that she had nothing else to say. 'Of course, Bergur and Binni weren't particularly pleased to see a stranger on the riverbank but they thought he might find it suspicious if they reversed down the track. So they got out, determined to behave as if nothing had happened. Thröstur couldn't do it, though, and when Binni tried to coax him into copying their nonchalance, the whole thing ended like I told you – with Thröstur dying.'

'How can people behave like that? Like those three?'

'Not everyone would be capable of it. Look at Thröstur, for example. He couldn't do it.'

'The doll you mentioned, was it the one that was fished out of the sea?'

'Yes. The girl's parents say it is. The doll was still wearing the necklace their daughter had put on it, though its clothes had rotted away. At the time, the father hadn't thought about the doll's disappearance. When he reached the scene of the accident, he had too much else on his mind, understandably. It was only when the mother wanted to put the doll in the coffin with their daughter that he went back and searched along the side of the road. That was several days after the accident. When he couldn't find the doll, he assumed someone must have seen it and taken it away with them, not realising why it was lying there. What else was he supposed to think?'

'Why's Bergur confessing to all this now?'

'Oh, he's not. We got the story from Fjalar. They're competing to put the blame on each other and Fjalar probably wants to make sure that Bergur comes out of it as badly as him. Otherwise there's a risk Bergur will get the lighter sentence. Apparently Fjalar got the story from Brynjólfur, who was forced to accept a lift to town with him as Bergur had left in the pick-up. Fjalar had noticed that Brynjólfur was acting suspiciously, hiding something in a bag, and he saw that it contained Thröstur's blood-stained clothes – the ones he'd changed out of when he put on his fishing gear. Binni admitted the whole thing when Fjalar put pressure on him. Fjalar had witnessed Bergur's quarrel with Thröstur, so he knew something was up. He demanded to know what was going on and refused to lie for Bergur unless he told him everything. So Brynjólfur apparently decided to confide in him. Or maybe he was too drunk to lie convincingly. After they got back to town, Fjalar offered to dispose of the doll for them. He took it out to sea with him the next time he went and threw it overboard in the brothers' favourite fishing spot. Brynjólfur held on to the blood-stained clothes; that came to light when we spoke to his ex-wife again. She'd found them in the storage unit with Binni's things but hadn't handed them over to us. When she heard the story I just told you, she admitted that she'd found them. She was probably afraid that if she didn't, we'd get a search warrant for her flat, and she'd be found guilty of concealing a crime. The blood on the clothes will be analysed to confirm that it belonged to Adalheidur, though I assume that's pretty much a given.'

Freyja topped up her glass again, then rose and fetched another beer for Huldar. He must need one. 'Didn't the police find it odd that Binni didn't have a car of his own? How did he say he and Thröstur had got there in the first place?'

'The police who attended the scene don't appear to have

noticed, or else their minds were on the fatal accident that had happened nearby. It wasn't the Húsavík force – they were busy dealing with the little girl's death. Maybe Binni claimed they'd come by bus or hitched a lift, and nobody bothered to make a note of it in the report. Like I said, the officers would probably have been more preoccupied with the other, even more tragic accident.'

'And the doll?'

'It vanished for five years, until Frikki caught it in his net in the exact same place Fjalar had chucked it overboard. Rósa's mother put a photo of it on Facebook, where Bergur happened to spot it. Some mutual friend of his and Rósa's mother had shared the post. In a panic Bergur rang Fjalar, who claims he ordered him to go and get it and delete the woman's Facebook status before the little girl's parents stumbled on it. What happened next is unclear.'

'Oh?' Freyja watched Huldar stick a finger under the aluminium ring on his beer can and pull it up. Then he filled his glass until the froth was in danger of overflowing down the sides.

'Bergur says he paid one of his former charges to do it. The boy in question is dead, so we'll probably never know if the theft of the doll was connected to Rósa's mother's death. Or how the doll ended up in Brynjólfur's possession. At that time he was hanging around with drug addicts and alcoholics of all ages, so it's possible he bumped into the person who stole the doll, recognised it and was allowed to have it. You never know, he may have intended to come clean about the little girl one day. He'd kept Thröstur's blood-stained clothes, after all. The doll and the clothes would have been guaranteed to make people sit up and listen.'

'And Brynjólfur's murder? Who was responsible for that?'

'We still don't know. Fjalar flatly denies having anything to do with it and Bergur's definitely innocent because he was in custody at the time. We're fairly sure Fjalar must be guilty. Bergur claims that Fjalar insisted they add Binni to the sales team when he thought Bergur's kids weren't doing a good enough job. It's not unlikely that Binni made big inroads into the goods himself and that Fjalar decided to get rid of him. Bergur managed to get a consignment to Iceland this summer, to replace the one that had been lost in the spring, but Fjalar had still taken a big hit on the previous deal, both in outlay and in terms of lost sales revenue. So it stands to reason he wouldn't have been happy about any further losses. We're going over CCTV footage from the business premises on Grandi in the hope that Fjalar's car will turn up somewhere. Of course, it's possible he arrived on foot, in which case he could have approached the containers unseen, but I'm not worried about that. We'll find a way of proving it.'

Freyja drank some more wine. She needed Dutch courage to listen to the next bit. 'What about Rósa?'

Huldar evidently felt the same. He took a long swig of beer before embarking on the tale. 'That's an ugly story. Establishing what happened there was the hardest of all. But this morning Fjalar finally cracked after realising that he's not going to get away with it. We found biological traces from Rósa at his house. And in the boot of his car.'

'In the boot?'

'Yes. He took her body up to Lake Hafravatn. Hid it in the boot of his car.'

'But who killed her and why? She can't have been mixed

up in the drug business, can she? Unless . . . Did Bergur use her to deal for him?' Freyja considered herself a peace-loving person, so it was uncomfortable to experience such a powerful desire to push Bergur off a cliff. A desire that had been growing stronger every time Huldar opened his mouth.

'No. She wasn't involved. She ran into Fjalar by pure bad luck. She lost her key in Smáralind and seems to have thought she was locked out. We know this because the key turned up in lost property at the shopping centre. Anyway, Rósa decided to go and wait for Fridrik outside his brother's house in Hjallahverfi. That's why she jumped out of the bus on Dalvegur. Apparently Frikki never stayed long at his brother's parties but she couldn't have known that he'd already left by nine. Presumably she didn't realise he'd driven there either, since he was going to a party where the drink would be flowing. But in the end she got bored of hanging around, so she decided to knock on the door and ask to speak to Frikki. We don't know why she did that when the police had advertised that she was missing and her face was all over the internet. Perhaps she assumed she could get away with it because she seemed able to go wherever she wanted without anyone noticing her, as if it was enough to change her clothes and comb her hair into a different style.'

'You mean Fjalar killed her in the hall with a house full of party guests?'

'Not quite. But not far off. He went to the door and unfortunately for Rósa he recognised her straight away, in spite of the changed clothes and hairstyle. He said he'd taken a good look at the missing-person notice because Bergur had warned him back in the spring that Binni had half a mind to tell

Thröstur's daughter everything about how her parents died. He'd already told her something but couldn't remember exactly what he'd said. Fjalar recognised the danger she represented. And Binni too.'

'So what did he do?'

'He says he got a bad shock. His immediate thought was that Binni must have blabbed before he died and that she had come to have it out with him. He hadn't a clue about her connection to his brother because Fridrik had kept very quiet about it, understandably enough. Fjalar didn't want his guests seeing her so he grabbed her by the arm, dragged her into the garage with him and closed the door behind them. He said she didn't scream or struggle. Maybe she was paralysed with shock. We'll never know. The guests didn't notice anything as they were all outside in the garden, enjoying the rare spell of good weather.'

'Did he kill her in the garage?'

'Yes. First he shook her and tried to force her to tell him what Binni had said. At first she didn't seem to know what was happening, then it slowly dawned on her that he must have had something to do with her parents' deaths. He says it was a terrible mistake, because by the time he eventually realised that she had no idea who he was, it was too late. He'd betrayed himself. He was left with no choice but to get rid of her. But first he'd managed to force her to tell him why she'd knocked on his door, and that's how he learnt that she'd been staying with Frikki. At that point she still believed he was going to let her go. But instead he throttled her.' Huldar took another mouthful of beer. 'He put her body in the boot of his car which was in the garage, waited until his last guest had left, then drove up to Hafravatn and dumped her body in the lake. He didn't dare go out on the fishing boat for fear the police would make the connection between the discovery of the bones and Rósa's death.'

'What a disgusting monster. What kind of man would do something like that?' Freyja shuddered. She wanted to get in the shower and wash herself, as if she had been tainted by what she'd heard. But since there was no chance of that with Huldar there, she would have to rinse her insides instead. She took another big gulp of wine.

'This is the man who invited his brother to supper on Sunday evening to make sure he was out while one of his addict lackeys broke in to Frikki's place and searched Rósa's belongings for a diary, notes or a computer – for anywhere she might have written down what she knew. He didn't find anything, though, because there was nothing to find. Rósa kept the little she knew in her head.'

'What about the bodies in the sea? How did she know about those?'

'Bergur thinks she must have been eavesdropping and heard Fjalar telling him about it. He'd come by the care home to speak to Bergur the day after he'd dumped the British couple in the sea. Rósa and the other kids were supposed to be at school, but after Fjalar had left, Bergur realised that she had come home sick after her first class. He said she hadn't behaved at all strangely when he discovered that she was in her room, but that she was a good actor. The only explanation he could come up with was that she must have been listening at his office door, then made herself scarce before he opened it. He didn't think she could have seen Fjalar, though, because he was wearing a baseball cap with his hood over it.'

Huldar seemed to have finished. Freyja was relieved but then couldn't stop herself from asking two questions that were tormenting her: 'What about Rósa and the evening Binni was murdered? Did she turn up on CCTV?'

'No. There was no sign of her, though she could have approached on foot without being caught on camera. We'll never know.'

'And Tristan? I got the feeling he was lying when he said he'd been at home that evening.'

'No. He was telling the truth. His mother confirmed his alibi and although she is not the most reliable witness we have nothing concrete that contradicts her statement. Neither Rósa nor Tristan seem to have been anywhere near Grandi that evening. The girl the half-blind neighbour saw had probably just come by in search of drugs. She must have left in a hurry after seeing all the blood, leaving footprints as she went.' Huldar grimaced. 'It was a horrific sight.'

After this description and the conversation that had preceded it, there was no question of tucking into the cheesecake. The blood-red cherry sauce covering it would have had unfortunate associations in the circumstances.

'Would you like a coffee?'

'No, thanks. I'm happy with beer.'

Freyja smiled. She didn't want coffee either.

A second bottle of red stood open on the coffee table, empty beer cans surrounding it like pawns defending a queen in some booze-based game of chess. Which Freyja was losing. She was feeling drunk, a lot drunker than she'd have liked, especially as it was 11 p.m. At midnight her thirty-day stint of celibacy would officially be over and beside her sat Huldar

Jónas, a man who was always up for it. Usually this was a source of extreme irritation to her but now it seemed a positive advantage. Her woozy brain registered the inconsistency but chose to regard it in the same light as . . . as people who do card tricks. Normally you don't want them at your parties but they're great when you need a children's entertainer. In other words, flaws can be virtues, in the right circumstances.

'Do you know any card tricks?' Her voice slurred as she tried to enunciate this, but Huldar understood.

'Me? No. Do you want to see a card trick?'

'No.' No, she was after something quite different.

When Freyja awoke it was to a headache that she had expected to avert by forking out for a more expensive bottle than usual. Snatches of memory from the night before started hitting her like shrapnel. Some were hazy, others all too clear.

She raised her head with extreme caution from the pillow. Her tongue was furry and she felt a desperate need to crawl to the bathroom, put her mouth under the tap and turn it on full. Only when she had achieved a sitting position did she manage to turn her head to see the other half of the room. Realising there was no one there, she couldn't help laughing, though the pain in her head throbbed in accompaniment. How could she ever have dreamt that Huldar would change? But then her eye fell on the note lying on the bedside table and she reached for it with all the speed of a geriatric sloth. It came as a surprise to her that she could even read. The message confirmed what she had long known: that she could never keep a secret when she'd been drinking.

*Had to go to work. I dare you to apply for the police liaison
job. Will be in touch and come by later. With burgers. And a
hamster for the snake. Yours, Jónas.*

Freyja put the note down and laid her aching head back
on the pillow. Although her physical state left much to be
desired, she felt good. And with the feeling of contentment
came boldness. She would apply for the job. Why not? A
change could only make things better.

She closed her no doubt bloodshot eyes and smiled. Good
things lay ahead. She was sure of it.

Chapter 36

September

The choppy sea did its best to upset Berglind but failed. She was aware of the cramps in her tender stomach and the dull ache in her head, but that was nothing. She wanted to screech at the waves, how dare they think she couldn't handle a bit of seasickness? Compared to withdrawal symptoms, this kind of discomfort was no worse than mild period pain.

She was freezing but she couldn't wrap her coat any more tightly around herself because the lifebelt was in the way. It was the only one on board and Tristan had insisted she wear it. He could swim; she couldn't. Frikki, the boat owner, had become terribly embarrassed when she put it on, and started apologising for the fact it was so dirty. Berglind wanted to tell him not to worry, she'd seen worse, but she stopped herself. She had an idea that Tristan wouldn't want to be reminded of her past at that moment. He deserved to be allowed to forget it, even if it was only for a few hours.

Despite the raw cold, the afternoon was turning out to be a success. So far nothing had gone wrong. She hadn't said anything stupid to Frikki, and Tristan appeared to be enjoying the fishing, even though they had caught very little. He kept inviting her to join in, but she preferred to stay out of the way and watch.

Frikki turned from the gunwale and looked at her doubt-fully. He was constantly apologising, apparently worried that she was bored. 'I wish I'd ordered better weather,' he said.

She smiled with her lips pressed together, as she did when she wanted to hide the state of her teeth, but didn't say anything, wishing he would just concentrate on his fishing.

They had met him at the funeral of Tristan's friend, Rósa. Apart from the teenagers filling the rows at the back – Rósa's school friends, presumably – there were very few mourners in the church. Just an elderly couple and a smattering of people Berglind took to be relatives. There was also a handful of social workers who had got to know the girl while she was in care, but since they were attending the funeral during working hours, on full pay, Berglind didn't feel they counted. Then there were some cops she recognised from when she had accompanied Tristan to the police station for his inter-views. They were in plain clothes but she recognised them anyway. No one can be an addict for twenty years without being able to spot a cop at a hundred metres.

And then there was Fridrik.

She had immediately noticed that he seemed as eager to skulk in the background as she was. He had hung his head and lowered his eyes when the police appeared, and gone out of his way to avoid the family members after the service. Perhaps that was why he had got talking to her and Tristan on the steps of the church. All three of them felt like outsiders among the weeping teenagers and sombre adults who came out following the coffin. As the brother of the murderer, Fridrik was even more unwelcome than Berglind. She wasn't used to having anyone below her in the pecking order – not in the company of sober types, anyway. As a result, when he'd asked if her son was Tristan, instead of simply nodding she had introduced herself and asked who he was.

Afterwards she had withdrawn a little to let Fridrik and Tristan talk. The man was keen to tell her son how well Rósa had spoken of him and how important his friendship had been to her. Tristan had replied in monosyllables, unable to return the favour. Since her son had tearfully poured out the whole story of his friendship with Rósa, Berglind knew that the girl had never said a word to him about Fridrik, either good or bad.

Tristan had opened up to Berglind about a number of things, including the fact that the man he had accused of abusing him had never done anything of the kind. What he had done was sell drugs. And he had killed both Rósa's parents. Berglind had stiffened on hearing this but she hadn't said anything, just let him go on with his tale.

Tristan told her that Rósa had overheard the man talking to some mate of his about dealing and also about two drugs mules whose bodies he'd dumped in the sea. Tristan had wanted to go to the police but Rósa had told him there was no point. She knew because she'd tried before.

There was nothing Tristan hated more than drug dealers, as Berglind knew only too well. He blamed them for the state she was in, not without some justification. Without drugs, there was no question that her life would have turned out differently. Because of his corrosive hatred, Tristan had refused to accept that they could do nothing. Instead, he had come up with the idea that they should accuse the man of sexually abusing him. The man wouldn't escape unscathed from an accusation of that kind, whether or not Tristan and Rósa were believed in court.

They had put their plan into action. Tristan had gone to the police with his complaint. Rósa was supposed to back up his story later by swearing that she'd witnessed the man assaulting him. The kids knew their names wouldn't be made public unless they chose to come forward, so they had nothing to lose. But when time dragged by and his complaint wasn't acted on, Tristan had got in touch with a newspaper and given an interview, on condition that it was anonymous. After that, things had finally started moving and seemed to be going exactly according to plan. Rósa was supposed to run away, then later reappear and support his claims. That way, the kids had thought there was less of a risk it would look like collusion. They would probably have got away with it too.

But Rósa's murder had changed everything. Tristan hadn't felt capable of carrying on without her. Not only had he lost his best friend but he had found himself alone, facing the police and an army of lawyers.

Berglind had stroked her weeping son's hair and told him to withdraw his accusation. He was to say that he'd heard cases like that never ended in prosecution and that he couldn't face having to rake up all the bad memories for nothing. The police would try to make him change his mind but he would just have to stick to his guns. He had frequently shown her that he could do that. She had phoned a lawyer who had often helped her out when she was in trouble, and persuaded him to take on Tristan's case for next to no fee.

Tristan leant away from the side of the boat, looked round and smiled at her. She smiled back. His face was free of the worries that habitually clouded it whenever he looked at her. Usually, when she met his big blue eyes, they were overshadowed by an anxious frown, but now his whole face was glowing with happiness.

It was a good day and she was pleased with herself for having accepted Fridrik's offer of a boat trip, once he'd eventually managed to stammer it out. She didn't know what had prompted it but guessed he wanted to do something, however small, to help compensate Tristan for the loss of his friend. After all, it was Fridrik's brother who had murdered Rósa. Fridrik had told them that he would probably have to sell the boat as neither he nor his father or uncle could afford to buy his brother out. And he assumed his brother would lose everything now that he was facing a long prison sentence: apparently all his assets were encumbered by sky-high debts. But Fridrik intended to go out fishing as often as he could until the day came when the boat had to be sold. If she and Tristan wanted to come along, they'd be more than welcome. Tristan had immediately said yes, but Berglind had hesitated, then given in, as it was easier than objecting. Throughout her life, she had almost invariably chosen the path of least resistance.

As Berglind watched the horizon, mesmerised, her mind emptied and her thoughts evaporated. That was dangerous. Because, sure enough, the intense craving kicked in. The feeling was miserably familiar, triggering a tired old train of thought about needing just one more hit; that one hit would be enough. Just one more and after that she was prepared to be clean for the rest of her life. But she knew that wasn't true: if she fell now, she would sink to the bottom.

'If you'd like a coffee, I brought a thermos along. I don't suppose it's very good, though, and I forgot to bring any milk, but it'll probably warm you up.' She snapped out of her thoughts to see that Fridrik was holding a medium-sized fish; she had no idea what kind. He gestured towards his backpack with the fish still in his hand. His expression was one of concern and she was willing to bet that he thought she was too physically fragile to cope with the buffeting wind. But looks could be deceptive and in truth she was anything but fragile. Her body possessed a wiry strength, driven by her craving, that few would have believed just from looking at her. It was one of the very few perks of being an addict.

'Oh. No, thanks.' Berglind was grateful for the big hood she had pulled up over her head. She found any attention from strangers uncomfortable, especially when it involved pity, but the hood provided her with a little shelter. She would have given anything to be invisible.

Fridrik grew embarrassed and seemed on the verge of saying something, but thought better of it. He dropped the fish into a battered tub on deck and turned his attention back to his line.

Berglind recalled all the good advice and rules she had picked up during her countless spells in rehab. How did it go again? Yes: she mustn't ignore the craving when it hit her but acknowledge it and ride it out. Yeah, sure. None of the advice offered a magic cure, but magic was what she really needed. She wasn't strong enough to overcome her addiction in a face-off between her and the drugs. The times she had managed to stay clean had been for Tristan's sake. For him and no one else. If she'd been alone, she wouldn't have given a damn about what happened to her. She had already done so much damage to herself that it could never be undone. The best she could hope for was to patch up her life suffi-ciently to satisfy the requirements of children's services. But even that involved a lot of work on Tristan's part. He cleaned the flat, bought food to fill the fridge and aired the place whenever the social worker was due round. She herself got too wound up for days beforehand to be of any use.

Just one more hit. One more chance to float away from this situation and forget all the things she had done wrong over the years.

Forget the past. What she wouldn't give for a memory eraser. Without memories, it would be easier to turn her back on the bewitching lure of being high.

She would begin by erasing the memory of that evening five years ago. The evening when she had let herself be talked into helping out one of her junkie mates who had been paid to do a break-in. He was supposed to climb through a window, delete a post on the occupant's Facebook page and steal a doll that was probably in the bathtub. He'd told her that if she helped, he would split the money between them. He knew where he could get his hands on some Contalgin and, if they hurried, they could be mainlining it within the hour. He could have saved himself the bother of nagging her; of claiming that he couldn't fit through the open window they found round the back of the flat; of saying that she would have to climb in for him, even though he was skinnier than she was.

He could have saved himself the bother, because the lure of the Contalgin was so strong that she didn't raise any objections but went ahead and squeezed her way in, knocking over a pile of empty drinks cans hidden behind the curtains. She had frozen with fear but there had been no sound from inside the flat and no one seemed to have heard. Perhaps the place was empty. She had jumped down to the floor and gone straight over to the laptop that had been left open on the coffee table. It wasn't locked and it had taken her no time to open Facebook and delete the status, which was a photo of a hideous doll sitting in a bathtub.

Next job.

Berglind had tiptoed into the hall leading to the bedrooms. One door was wide open and inside she saw the footboard of a double bed. The parquet creaked under her feet and she bit her lower lip, unsure what to do next. Flee through the window or keep going? The thought of the needle and the rapturous bliss as she injected the drug into her vein removed all doubt.

She had crept to the door of what she guessed was the bathroom and opened it warily, only to find herself face to face with a terrified woman. They hadn't exchanged a word and neither had screamed. The woman had taken a step backwards, tripped over her pyjama bottoms, which were round her ankles, and lost her balance. Her head had hit the edge of the bath hard. Although Berglind's hearing had been damaged by all the blows she'd received over the years, she couldn't help hearing the sickening crack of the woman's skull.

She had clasped a hand over her mouth as she stared at the woman twitching on the floor. Blood had leaked out, quickly forming a pool around her head. Then the woman had stopped moving and her eyes had closed, while her mouth hung slackly open.

Without pausing to think, Berglind had entered the bathroom, taking care not to tread in the blood or touch the woman as she reached for the doll. Then she had hurried back to the window, thrown out the doll and closed it. After that, she had left by the door of the flat, out into the corridor, then out of the building.

There had been no one waiting in the garden. Her mate had vanished, taking with him the meagre amount that had been paid in advance. Although the full payment was much more, what he already had in his pocket would be enough for one fix. The allure of an immediate high had simply been too tempting. Nothing new there.

She had picked the doll up from the grass in the hope that she could use it to force him into telling her who requested the break in so she could collect the money, then made off. She'd headed straight round to see a dealer who was sometimes kind enough to give her drugs against a promise to pay later. She had to take something urgently to wipe out the memory of the woman on the bathroom floor.

It was an accident. It was an accident. It was an accident. She had kept repeating the words in her head. When she passed a man on his way home from a night stroll he had stared at her strangely and she'd realised that she was muttering it aloud.

The dealer was having a party and some girls let her in. They were much younger than she was and had pulled disgusted faces when they saw the horrible doll. One of the guests, an old addict and drunk that she knew, came over and asked where she'd got it. She'd pushed him away and walked off, but when he'd called after her that he was prepared to swap her a Contalgin tab for the doll, she'd turned round. The deal was completed rapidly, without a word, and she'd taken herself into a corner, pulled the gear from her pocket and swiftly departed into a state of oblivion where she hadn't been responsible for the death of an unknown woman.

'Mum!' It was Tristan's turn to wave a fish in her face. It

was considerably bigger than Fridrik's and its metallic scales glistened.

She smiled at him, hoping she wouldn't have to cook it. She'd never cooked a fish, let alone gutted one. Perhaps she should try. It would please Tristan and she owed him that much at least. He was usually the one who threw something on the table and tried to coax her into eating.

Berglind made up her mind to do it. Cook the fish. Shape up. Beat her addiction. Stop dwelling on the past. Both the distant past and more recent events. Start a new life and do her best to be a good mother to Tristan. He would soon be a young man and then she would be alone. She had to be able to hold out until then. Take it one day at a time.

She hoped fate would grant her this one favour. Up to now, it hadn't exactly treated her kindly. But perhaps that was unfair. After all, fate had recently spared her the horror of Tristan finding out that it was she who had killed his best friend's mother. A fact she had been totally unaware of until recently. A fact she would give anything to forget.

One evening she had given up the struggle, slipped out and taken a bus into town where she had visited two dealers, neither of whom would give her an advance. But one had tipped her off about a new guy out on Grandi who she might be able to coax into giving her a hit, so she had headed over there in search of a container unit with a purple door. She had walked behind the Marina hotel, hugging the shore to avoid bumping into all the people coming and going from the restaurants in the area, then made her way down Fiskislód to the container colony. One of the residents had called out to her, asking if she was there to see Binni. When she said yes, he'd asked if she'd buy a Coke for him. She'd refused and he'd gone back inside, swearing about stupid girls. It was years since anyone had called her a girl.

Berglind had knocked on the purple door and heard a voice say, 'Come in.' There on the sofa sat a familiar-looking bloke with a dirty pillowcase and a tea towel wrapped around one leg. It was the man who had swapped a Contalgin tab for the doll all those years ago. The coincidence hadn't surprised her. Iceland was small and the world of Icelandic addicts even smaller.

She'd introduced herself and come out with her request. The man hadn't commented on whether he was prepared to advance her something. Instead, he'd started going on about the bloody doll. She'd stared, hypnotised, at the drugs on the table in front of him, only half listening to his ramblings. Right up until he mentioned Rósa's name. Then she'd torn her eyes away from the pills and started paying attention. It hadn't been easy to follow as he was completely off his head, but she'd got the gist. The man wanted to come clean before he croaked. He said it wouldn't be long and Berglind reckoned he was right.

She'd been too shocked to protest about what he'd said next. The man was going to tell the police everything so the girl, Rósa, would know what had happened to her mother and father. The girl dropped in on him regularly in the hope that he would tell her the story and it wouldn't be fair on her if he took it with him to the grave. He regarded Berglind's visit as a sign from above that he should hurry up and get on with it. Berglind had given the doll to him all those years ago and that was the proof he would need to make them believe him. After this, he had come out with a string of incoherent stuff about a little girl on the road and her poor parents who deserved to hear the truth as well. Berglind had had no idea what he was on about.

When he'd finished, he'd looked Berglind in the eye and said he was going to turn her in too. She had stolen the doll and been responsible for Rósa's mother's death. There was no point doing things by halves when you were having your final reckoning with God. It was all or nothing.

Berglind had begged him not to mix her up in it, telling him she had a fatherless son who would be left without a mother too if she went to jail.

At that the man had looked up, smiled mockingly and said: 'Wouldn't he be better off without you?'

At that moment two thoughts had crystallised in Berglind's head. One: she had to get her hands on some of the pills on the table. Two: this man had to go. Tristan mustn't find out that she had killed his best friend's mother. It just mustn't happen. Berglind had taken out the knife she used to crush pills, gone round behind the sofa, jerked the man's head back and drawn the blade right across his throat. Then she had watched as he clutched at the wound, emitting a rattling noise as he tried to stem the geyser of blood. A few seconds later he had fallen silent and his arms had dropped to his sides. She had gone back round the sofa and grabbed a handful of OxyContin, leaving the rest behind.

She'd hurried away, pausing only to take the longed-for dose in the first alleyway she'd come to.

When she'd woken up the next day, she'd found her coat pocket empty. Tristan had flushed the pills down the toilet, leaving her racked with withdrawal symptoms and the memory of what she had done. She didn't know which was worse.

'Right. That's probably enough for today.' Fridrik was looking at the sky. 'The weather's supposed to turn.'

Tristan made a half-hearted protest but Fridrik was firm. They helped each other tidy away the tackle, then Fridrik went into the small wheelhouse and turned the boat for home. Tristan came over to his mother and she put her arms round him, resting her head on his shoulder. He was taller than she was now and she hadn't even noticed.

Berglind felt hot tears welling up in the corners of her eyes. This was no good – she had to deal with it. What had been done couldn't be undone. She couldn't go back in time and act differently, and erasing her memory wasn't an option. But there was nothing to be gained from dwelling on things that had gone badly, even disastrously wrong. No amount of wishing would ever undo the past.

She had to make a new beginning, starting now. Here and now. Throw the past overboard, let it sink to the bottom and never look back.

Berglind gazed towards land, in the direction they were heading. At the houses, apartment blocks and the city's small handful of high-rises. From here you couldn't see the seedy little dens, the dark alleyways where she had spent much of her existence. It was as if they had been blotted out. She took it as a message from above. When she climbed ashore, she would begin a new life. A life among decent people – in the sun, not in the shadows – built on the ruins of the old one. For Tristan's sake.

For the first time in ages, Berglind felt good. She recognised the feeling as optimism – something she hadn't experienced in a long time. She switched off her thoughts and simply enjoyed standing there with her son at her side. But the instant she let down her guard, her addiction raised its ugly head.

Just one more time.
To celebrate her new life.
Just one more time.
To bid farewell to the old one.

The doll sat on a steel tray in the Forensics department, surrounded by broken barnacles and dried-up white worms. Its arms and legs were still encrusted to some extent in this repulsive armour. One arm was stretched out towards the young technician who had been called in to work on a Saturday.

He avoided looking at it as much as possible. Not because he was afraid but because it wasn't a pleasant sight. He had the absurd feeling that the doll wanted him to get the cleaning over with. That it was reaching out to twitch at the back of his white coat and ask him this one favour: to restore it to its original appearance. The intention was to return the doll to the parents of the little girl it had once belonged to, but this wasn't going to happen any time soon. The doll was important evidence in a murder trial and there was no way they were going to dig up the girl's grave to retrieve it if it was required in court.

He looked away. Not because he was afraid. He just didn't like the matted hair, the rows of holes in the scalp, the black eyehole and the single eye that seemed to follow him around the lab.

The computer beeped to alert him to an email. He opened the message and read the brief communication from his boss. He could go home; apparently the job wasn't that urgent after all.

The suspect in the case had had an accident in the Litla-

Hraun Prison. He had slipped in the shower and banged his head on the toilet bowl. They were operating but it was touch and go, and if he didn't make it, the trial wouldn't go ahead. Since the police already had his confession, there was no point wasting precious overtime trying to make an already thorough case for prosecution watertight. The email said that on Monday the technician would be re-assigned to helping the team who were working on consolidating the case against the other defendant, Fjalar Reynisson.

The young man shrugged. He was neither relieved nor disappointed at getting off early. He switched off the computer and tidied up. He labelled the samples from Bergur Alvarsson, which would presumably now just go into storage. Because he was still fairly new in Forensics, he didn't know what happened to evidence in circumstances like these.

As he turned off the light on his way out, he could have sworn he saw the doll smile.